"To[...] [...]ce and
hur[...] [...]plexi-
ties [...] [...]us."
—*[...]Reviews*

"Action packed and fast paced, this was a fabulous read."
—*Fresh Fiction*

"*Con & Conjure* is a great addition to a wonderful series, and I'm looking forward to *All Spell Breaks Loose* and whatever else [Shearin writes] with high anticipation." —*Dear Author*

Bewitched & Betrayed

"Once again, Ms. Shearin has given her readers a book that you don't want to put down. With Raine, the adventures never end."
—*Night Owl Reviews*

"*Bewitched & Betrayed* might just be the best in the series so far! . . . an amazingly exciting fourth installment that really tugs at the heartstrings." —*Ink and Paper*

"If you're new to Shearin's work and you enjoy fantasy interspersed with an enticing romance, a little bit of humor, and a whole lot of grade-A action, this is the series for you."
—*Lurv a la Mode*

The Trouble with Demons

"The book reads more like an urban fantasy with pirates and sharp wit and humor. I found the mix quite refreshing. Lisa Shearin's fun, action-packed writing style gives this world life and vibrancy." —*Fresh Fiction*

continued . . .

"Lisa Shearin represents that much-needed voice in fantasy that combines practiced craft and a wicked sense of humor."
—*Bitten by Books*

"The brisk pace and increasingly complex character development propel the story on a roller-coaster ride through demons, goblins, elves, and mages while maintaining a satisfying level of romantic attention . . . that will leave readers chomping at the bit for more."
—*Monsters and Critics*

"This book has the action starting as soon as you start the story, and it keeps going right to the end . . . All of the characters are interesting, from the naked demon queen to the Guardians guarding Raine. All have a purpose, and it comes across with clarity and detail."
—*Night Owl Reviews*

Armed & Magical

"Fresh, original, and fall-out-of-your-chair funny, Lisa Shearin's *Armed & Magical* combines deft characterization, snarky dialogue, and nonstop action—plus a yummy hint of romance—to create one of the best reads of the year. This book is a bona fide winner, the series a keeper, and Shearin a definite star on the rise."
—Linnea Sinclair, author of *Rebels and Lovers*

"An exciting, catch-me-if-you-can, lightning-fast-paced tale of magic and evil filled with goblins, elves, mages, and a hint of love interest that will leave fantasy readers anxiously awaiting Raine's next adventure."
—*Monsters and Critics*

"The kind of book you hope to find when you go to the bookstore. It takes you away to a world of danger, magic, and adventure, and it does so with dazzling wit and clever humor. It's gritty, funny, and sexy—a wonderful addition to the urban fantasy genre. I absolutely loved it. From now on Lisa Shearin is on my auto-buy list!"
—Ilona Andrews, *New York Times* bestselling author of *Fate's Edge*

Magic Lost, Trouble Found

Ace Books by Lisa Shearin

MAGIC LOST, TROUBLE FOUND
ARMED & MAGICAL
THE TROUBLE WITH DEMONS
BEWITCHED & BETRAYED
CON & CONJURE
ALL SPELL BREAKS LOOSE

All Spell
Breaks Loose

Lisa Shearin

ACE BOOKS, NEW YORK

THE BERKLEY PUBLISHING GROUP
Published by the Penguin Group
Penguin Group (USA) Inc.
375 Hudson Street, New York, New York 10014, USA

Penguin Group (Canada), 90 Eglinton Avenue East, Suite 700, Toronto, Ontario M4P 2Y3, Canada
(a division of Pearson Penguin Canada Inc.) • Penguin Books Ltd., 80 Strand, London WC2R 0RL,
England • Penguin Group Ireland, 25 St. Stephen's Green, Dublin 2, Ireland (a division of Penguin
Books Ltd.) • Penguin Group (Australia), 250 Camberwell Road, Camberwell, Victoria 3124, Australia
(a division of Pearson Australia Group Pty. Ltd.) • Penguin Books India Pvt. Ltd., 11 Community
Centre, Panchsheel Park, New Delhi—110 017, India • Penguin Group (NZ), 67 Apollo Drive,
Rosedale, Auckland 0632, New Zealand (a division of Pearson New Zealand Ltd.) • Penguin Books
(South Africa) (Pty.) Ltd., 24 Sturdee Avenue, Rosebank, Johannesburg 2196, South Africa

Penguin Books Ltd., Registered Offices: 80 Strand, London WC2R 0RL, England

This is a work of fiction. Names, characters, places, and incidents either are the product of the author's
imagination or are used fictitiously, and any resemblance to actual persons, living or dead, business
establishments, events, or locales is entirely coincidental. The publisher does not have any control over
and does not assume any responsibility for author or third-party websites or their content.

ALL SPELL BREAKS LOOSE

An Ace Book / published by arrangement with the author

PUBLISHING HISTORY
Ace mass-market edition / June 2012

Copyright © 2012 by Lisa Shearin.
Map by Lisa Shearin and Shari Lambert.
Cover art by Aleta Rafton.
Cover design by Judith Lagerman.

ISBN: 978-1-937007-71-3

ACE
Ace Books are published by The Berkley Publishing Group,
a division of Penguin Group (USA) Inc.,
375 Hudson Street, New York, New York 10014.
ACE and the "A" design are trademarks of Penguin Group (USA) Inc.

PRINTED IN THE UNITED STATES OF AMERICA

10 9 8 7 6 5 4 3 2 1

In loving memory of my grandmother Mary Gladys Shearin. Your love of life, devotion to family, and delight in the written word was an inspiration to me and to all who had the honor and privilege of knowing you. You will always live in our hearts and be cherished in our memories.

Acknowledgments

To Derek, my husband. A man of infinite patience and endless encouragement. Your love and support make everything possible.

To Kristin Nelson, my agent. I can write secure in the knowledge that the business end of my career is in the best possible hands. Thank you for that and the editorial tough love. I'm becoming a better writer because of you.

To Anne Sowards, my editor. Your sharp eyes never miss a thing, and your gracious words always soften the blow. It's a joy and a privilege to craft Raine's adventures with you.

To Katie Lovett, an awesome fan and the winner of my Name That Book contest with the absolutely price-less and perfect title: *All Spell Breaks Loose*.

And, as always, to my fans. Thank you for allowing me to share my stories with you. You're the best.

Chapter 1

I was going to Hell and had no clue what to pack.

Regor was the goblin capital, home to my friend Tam and thousands of other goblins. Their home. My Hell.

I'm Raine Benares. An elven seeker whose job used to be finding lost things and missing people, usually in nice, safe places like prisons and war zones. Now, thanks to a run-in with a soul-sucking rock looking for someone to call home, the entire world was about to turn into a war zone, and yours truly was the epicenter.

Yesterday the world-ending stone known as the Saghred had been stolen. I called it several other names not repeatable in public. The thing had attached itself to me and magnified my magic; and even now that it was thousands of miles away, we were still bonded. The goblin who had ordered it stolen needed me dead to break that bond and transfer control of the rock and all of its power to himself. To stand a snowball's chance in Hell (excuse me, Tam's home) of destroying the rock, I needed to stay very much alive.

Hence my dilemma—save the world or die a slow and painful death. Though I couldn't exactly call my situation a dilemma. A dilemma implied you had a choice. If it was up to me, somebody else could save the world; I'd just rather keep breathing. However, if I managed by some major miracle to do both, I wanted to be properly dressed for it. Head-to-toe steel surrounded by a platoon of Conclave Guardians should do the trick. Some people would call that paranoid; I called it barely adequate accessorizing.

But I wouldn't have a platoon, and head-to-toe steel would make running away more of a challenge than I was up for. I was armored, both leather and steel, enough for protection, but without impeding any sudden need to retreat. Less than a dozen of us would be sneaking into Regor, stealing the Saghred, destroying it in a way that would hopefully not do the same to me, and getting back to Mid with the same pieces and parts that we left with.

A handful of us against the might of the goblin king, the goblin army, and probably some absurdly huge demons who owed them all favors. Oh yeah, and one soul-hungry rock.

And how could I forget an all-powerful, fledgling goblin demigod by the name of Sarad Nukpana?

Survival would take a miracle.

Especially since I didn't have a lick of magic to my name.

The Saghred had stolen my magic, then the goblins had stolen the stone.

It sucked to be me right now.

I was going to where my worst enemy was and I had no magic. Well, that wasn't exactly true. I had a spark, and if I held it against a wick long enough, I might just be able to light a candle. Sarad Nukpana was constructing, and about to open, a Gate big enough for an army to go through, a hundred goblins at a time—and doing every last bit of it with magic. He could teleport an army, and right now I'd work up a sweat lighting a candle. We'd love to be able to destroy the Saghred *and* the Gate, but our first priority was the rock.

The plan was simple—or simply suicide. Nukpana had the Saghred, but we still had the Scythe of Nen. Literally eons ago, the demon king had it forged so he could cut into the Saghred like an oyster and slurp up the souls inside. In theory, the Saghred could be destroyed if it was first emptied of souls. It was a logical solution, but this was a soul-snatching rock that had kept itself intact through the ages by making its own logic and luck. And it wasn't exactly a solution, or even a good idea, to let the souls out. Most of them hadn't been nice people to begin with; in fact, a lot of them could give Sarad Nukpana competition in the evil megalomaniac department.

While some would want nothing more than to float off to their great reward, others—powerful and evil others—would infest and possess the first bodies they could take. That presented two problems. One, they could possess us; the problem there being obvious. Two, they could possess any Khrynsani in the immediate vicinity of the high altar. That would be Sarad Nukpana and his craziest and most powerful black mage allies. Evil plus evil equals extremely undesirable.

The world had enough problems without *that* happening.

Unfortunately, even if Sarad Nukpana gave us a clear path to the Saghred, we still needed the help of one goblin in Regor to keep those souls from infesting and possessing— Kesyn Badru, Tam's first magic teacher, the man who tried to prevent Tam from running down magic's dark path to do the things an entirely-too-powerful young mage had no business doing. Tam had been more like his teenage son, Talon, than he'd care to admit, and had successfully destroyed anything resembling a relationship with his teacher. For all we knew, when we found him, Kesyn Badru might try to turn Tam into something squishy on sight or simply kill him. From what I'd heard about Tam's youthful indiscretions, I really wouldn't blame Kesyn Badru in the least.

The way things were stacking up, Sarad Nukpana might be easier to deal with.

Kesyn Badru was an expert on Reapers. Reapers basically worked for Death, gathering wayward souls and taking them to where they needed to go next. When we opened the Saghred, we needed plenty of Reapers standing by for the cleanup of any souls who refused to move along nicely.

Bottom line: slicing into the Saghred with the Scythe of Nen and letting the souls inside go free could make it possible for us to destroy the stone.

Or not.

And since I was bound to the Saghred, the Reapers we needed to collect the souls might collect me, too.

Or not.

Yesterday Sarad Nukpana's thief had forced our hand. We had no choice but to try to do all of the above. And if it let me—or Mychael, if I wasn't alive to do it myself—smash the thing into a million pieces, it would be worth it. Simply stealing the Saghred back was no longer an option. Sarad Nukpana had to be stopped, and whatever I had to do would be worth it.

If I died, I would have died to save millions from torment, slavery, or death at Sarad Nukpana's hands. I'd been telling myself all night that it'd be a good and noble death.

I'd never been more terrified in my life. I was almost sick with it.

There were easier and certainly less painful ways to commit suicide. The only upside to this whole thing was that we'd be leaving for Regor within the hour. That didn't leave much time for me to imagine all the ways Sarad Nukpana, the Saghred, or the Reapers could kill me. The less time I had to ponder any of those, the better.

Leaving here within the hour, and arriving in Regor seconds after that.

I despised mirror magic, but I had to admit that it was a damned efficient way to get from one place to another.

To tell you the truth, I was scared to death of it. Partly because I didn't understand how the finer points of the art worked. Stepping into one mirror and instantly walking out of another one hundreds or even thousands of miles away sure as hell wasn't a parlor trick—and mirror mages knew it. Superior to everyone else was how the best of them saw themselves; though most felt that simple worship would suffice. I'd never met a humble mirror mage.

I did a last check of the pack I was taking with me. More weapons than anything else, small and easily concealed. What couldn't be hidden was already strapped to me. I wasn't taking much by way of clothes—one change of everything in case what I was wearing picked up a couple of unsightly bloodstains or sword slashes. It'd been my experience that running for your life was best done while carrying as little extraneous weight as possible.

I slung my small pack over my shoulder and opened the door.

Standing there, hand raised to knock, was one of the last people I expected.

Piaras Rivalin.

He was a tall young elf, with big brown eyes and dark brown curls that would have made him look perfectly at home painted on the ceiling of some fancy chapel. To the pair of Guardians posted outside my door, Piaras was an eighteen-year-old cadet in their order. To me he was the little brother I'd never had, but always wanted.

I'd known Piaras since he was twelve. The self-possessed young man standing in front of me had grown up fast over too short a period of time. No one had given him a choice, either. For the two of us, the past three months had been one deal-with-it-or-die moment right after another. Piaras had faced and fought things that would have sent most kids his age scrambling under their beds. To make it even worse, he was in nearly as much danger from Sarad Nukpana as I was. The bastard knew how much I loved Piaras; knew it and wouldn't hesitate to use him to get to me.

Piaras's dream had been to become a Guardian, and here

he was in the uniform and armor of a cadet. In my opinion, he should have been on one of the ships trying to evacuate the other students from the island before the goblins invaded.

I stared up at him. "Come to see me off before you get your butt on an evac ship?"

"Yes and no."

"'Yes' you're getting on that ship, and 'no' you're not here to see me off, right?"

"Reverse them."

"Dammit, Piaras. I—"

"Paladin Eiliesor gave us all the choice. I chose to stay."

"You should be on a ship."

"I'm needed here."

From most kids his age, those words would come off sounding stubborn. From Piaras, it was steadfast and decisive. I knew I wouldn't be able to change his mind, but if he wasn't going to be stubborn, I would.

I lowered my voice. "And *I* need you alive. While I'm in Regor I need to know you're safe."

"Raine, I've already reported for duty—"

"Then un-report." The vehemence in my voice surprised even me.

"You're not un-reporting." There was no accusation in his voice; he was simply stating a fact.

"Regor is the last place I want to go, but I don't have a choice. You do."

"You have a choice," Piaras said. "You're going because you couldn't live with yourself if you didn't go. You know you can help, so that's what you're going to do. Same with me. What I'd really like is to hide under my bed in the barracks, close my eyes, and have every last bit of this crap go away. But that's not going to happen, so here I am."

I glared at him. "You know you're too young to be this smart, don't you?"

Piaras flashed a smile that was probably making the coeds swoon. "It's a burden I bear."

"I'm sure I don't want to know, but where are they sending you?"

"Here."

I blinked. "What?"

"Sir Vegard ordered me to take his place as your bodyguard—"

As my bodyguard, Vegard Rolfgar had been shot, tortured, and attacked by demons; damned near dying from all of the above. He'd wanted to go with us to Regor, but Mychael had made him acting paladin instead and put him in charge of the evacuation.

With a life of their own, my fists went to my hips. "You are *not* going to Regor. I don't care who—"

Piaras grinned and held up a hand. "Vegard wants me to see you safely to the mirror room and then report back to him." He stopped and half winced, the sudden embarrassment in his big eyes making him look like that awkward twelve-year-old again. "He ordered me to do one other thing."

I narrowed my eyes. "And what is that?" Vegard was about to get more trouble from me than he'd have from any invading goblin army.

Piaras stepped forward. "Uh . . . he told me to give you this."

Piaras hugged me. Hard. My feet left the floor somewhere in the process. I should've been grateful that Vegard had Piaras stand in for him; a hug like that from Vegard probably would've cracked a couple of my ribs. When Piaras showed no signs of letting go, I suddenly realized that hug wasn't just from Vegard. I wrapped my arms around Piaras's neck; my face buried against his shoulder and fiercely returned his hug. If I didn't make it back, this could be the last time I'd ever see him. My eyes swam with sudden tears.

Piaras started to put me down.

"No, no. Wait." I sniffed and tried for a smile. "I have something for . . . Vegard, too. Give him this." I grabbed both sides of Piaras's head and planted a big kiss on his forehead, and then hugged him again. That wasn't just for Vegard, either.

The Guardians behind us snickered.

Piaras blushed to the tips of his pointed ears. "I'll just tell him about it, if you don't mind." He picked up my pack where I'd dropped it to hug him. "I'll get this."

"Thank you." I'd be carrying it myself soon enough, and who knew for how long, so I'd take help now while I could get it.

Every Guardian we passed on our way to the mirror room had somewhere to go and was moving fast. Either that or they were already there and standing guard. To a man, they had one thing in common—the same grim and determined expression. I didn't know what was behind some of the doors being guarded, but I almost felt sorry for anyone who tried to find out.

I had to move just as fast to keep up with Piaras's long strides. "After seeing me to the mirror room, what next?"

"Pardon?"

"Your orders. What are they?"

"Once you're all safely through, I guard that mirror until you come back."

"Guard?"

"If anyone tries to get into the mirror room who doesn't belong, they'll be taking a long nap and waking up in a small cell."

Piaras could do it; I had no doubt—and neither did any of the hundred or so Guardians he'd accidently put to sleep after he'd been here only a few days. Piaras was a spellsinger, probably the best of his generation. His voice was a deep, rich baritone—and a weapon. As far as magical skills went, spellsinging wasn't all that rare, but Piaras's level of skill was. Rare, powerful, and deadly.

I had a thought I didn't like, but it was a possibility, a very unpleasant one.

"What if someone comes back through our mirror besides us?"

Piaras gave me a grim smile that he should have been too young to have. "We're equal opportunity sleep-inducers."

"We?"

"Maestro Cayle will be standing guard with me."

I experienced a short, but oh-so-welcome, moment of relief. I hadn't had many of those lately so I enjoyed it while I could. Maestro Ronan Cayle was the best spellsinger there was. If anyone's ass needed kicking—mage, mundane, or demon—Ronan was the man to serve it up. He was also Piaras's spellsinging teacher. If Piaras wouldn't leave the island on an evac ship, knowing that Ronan would be with him was a comfort I'd gladly take.

"Is Talon staying, too?"

Piaras blew out his breath. "Oh yeah."

"I understand he and Tam had quite the throwdown about that."

"Heard by half the citadel."

Talon Nathrach was Tam's son. As former chief mage and magical enforcer to the goblin royal House of Mal'Salin, Tam was part of the team going to Regor. Talon's mother had been an elf, which made Talon a half-breed, an abomination to both old-blood elves and goblins. The goblin court in Regor was packed to the walls with old-blood goblin aristocrats. From what I'd heard, they'd kill Talon on sight.

Talon becoming a Guardian cadet was Tam's effort to teach his impulsive son responsibility, respect, and, above all, control. I told Tam he shouldn't hold his breath.

"You can't exactly blame Talon," I said. "He just found his father, and now that father is leaving." I left the "and maybe never coming back" unsaid. Piaras knew it as well as I did.

"Paladin Eiliesor ordered Talon to report to Sir Vegard for duty."

I winced. "Bet that didn't go over well."

"No, it didn't." Piaras grinned. "Though walking back to the barracks last night with Talon tripled my knowledge of Goblin profanity."

Just before the stairs that led down to the citadel's lower levels, we passed several openings in the outer walls that looked over the harbor. I stopped, and Piaras and our two Guardian escorts did the same. It was a long way down to the harbor, but I knew crowds of people when I saw them. Students and townspeople—there had to be hundreds of them—being put on any ship in Mid's harbor that could raise canvas, and get them off of the island. Hopefully to safety. There were merchant ships, Guardian warships, and five pirate ships belonging to my cousin and uncle—Phaelan and Ryn Benares. Father and son, who, between the two of them, were responsible for the vast majority of the high-seas crime in the seven kingdoms. Phaelan had brought me and Piaras to the Isle of Mid on the *Fortune*. Uncle Ryn had arrived later with his flagship the *Red Hawk* and three of his best fighting vessels to do what a father and uncle did best—protect the people he loved. Commodore Ryn Benares, the most feared pirate in the seven kingdoms, was a big softie. No one outside the family knew that, and to preserve the cooperation and resulting profitability that the Benares name instilled in every ship to cross our path, we kept that information to ourselves.

Uncle Ryn had originally come to Mid to protect me and Phaelan. But now the students of the Conclave college were in the worst kind of danger. Sarad Nukpana needed sacrifices to keep his transport Gate stable and working—magically talented sacrifices. The kids attending the Conclave college were the best of the best; they'd be the top mages of the next generation. Nukpana saw them as fuel for his invasions.

Uncle Ryn wasn't concerned that heading up the student evacuation would damage his fearsome reputation. He'd told me that he didn't give a shit what anyone thought, though he could always claim that the Conclave paid him to do it, which they hadn't. Uncle Ryn was helping out from the good of his own big heart.

The students were being evacuated youngest to oldest. Getting every student off the island would take time, time that the Isle of Mid may or may not have. The students least able to defend themselves—magically or otherwise—were being shipped out first. Due to the need to transport as many students as quickly as possible, each student was being limited to only one small bag, large enough for a change of clothes and a few personal items. Everything else would be left behind. The hope was that they would be able to return soon.

That depended on us, whether we succeeded in destroying the Saghred.

Or even lived long enough to try.

For a place that was the center of the survival chances for the known world, the mirror room was amazingly non-chaotic. I wasn't complaining. Considering that we were headed into the goblin capital, which was essentially under siege from within, massing an army for invasion, and in possession of a stone of cataclysmic power bonded to yours truly—I'd take all the peace and quiet I could get.

The mirror room itself was plain, but not the contents. I counted twenty mirrors, each taller than a tall man and at least twice as wide. They were mounted on massive wooden frames. Some were simple; others were ornate. All had runes or spells carved into the frames. At least a half dozen of the mirrors were mounted to the stone walls and were as wide as they were tall. The only reason I could see for having something that big would be to get as many fighting men from here to there as quickly as possible. And the room was big enough to do it. A hundred paces long and half that wide.

As much as I disliked and distrusted mirrors, I had that

feeling multiplied by a hundred for the elven mage standing in front of one of the smaller mirrors, hands extended toward the swirling surface, consumed with concentration.

Carnades Silvanus. Formerly second in command of the Conclave after the archmage himself. The former golden boy of the Conclave and the Seat of Twelve. Now the most famous jailbird on the island. He'd been caught with his fingers in the treason pie, and his signature on the documents funding the traitors' and terrorists' fun and games. Then there was also the small matter of the attempted assassination of a goblin prince. Carnades had been stripped of his title and position in the Conclave and on the Seat of Twelve. The elven government had frozen all of his assets. I'd been directly responsible for Carnades getting caught doing all of the above; as a result, he hated me with a passion bordering on obsession. He was also the one man who could get us to Regor in time to stop Sarad Nukpana's rampage of world domination—and back again after we got the job done.

Oh yeah, I had warm and fuzzy feelings about that arrangement.

"I don't like it," Piaras said.

I didn't have to ask what *it* was. I wasn't the only one Carnades Silvanus had been gunning for since we'd arrived on Mid.

"Carandes is the best mirror mage there is," I told him. "Plus, he's the man with the mirror in Regor. If we had another choice, we'd take it, but we don't."

Piaras scowled. "You have to trust him."

"Trust has nothing to do with it. This is about necessity, pure and simple."

"Necessity might be pure, but Carnades sure isn't."

Truer words had never been spoken. "That's why we'll be keeping magic-sapping manacles on him as much as possible."

"He's not wearing them now."

"Yeah, gives me the creeps, too." I kept my voice level,

which was a nifty contrast to my galloping heart rate. That was the first thing I'd noticed when we'd walked through the door. Normally, a sight like that wouldn't freeze me in my tracks like a mouse in a room with a sadistic cat, but being without magic was not my normal. If Carnades found out and managed to get me alone, all that would be left after the spell he'd sling at me would be a greasy spot on the floor. Piaras didn't know, and I wasn't about to tell him. If he knew, he'd worry. A lot. Staying on the island in the face of a goblin invasion was enough; Piaras needed to focus on saving his own hide, not worrying about mine any more than he already was.

Carnades's elegantly long-fingered hands were extended toward the mirror before him, his posture one of extreme concentration on his work. I muffled a snort. Carnades was looking at the mirror, but his concentration was more than likely aimed at how to screw us over, either before, during, or after we stepped through his mirror into a cave outside of Regor.

"Carnades can't tap his magic while wearing those manacles, and he needs his magic to get us through the mirror," I told Piaras. I shrugged. "Or obliterate us all, jump through the mirror, and run like hell." My tone was joking, but I wouldn't be surprised if the bastard tried it.

"I think those gentlemen will have something to say about that," said an amused voice from behind us. "As will I."

As Guardian commander and paladin, Mychael Eiliesor was as ready as he could be to step through that mirror and into Regor. His usual armor was sleek, formfitting dark steel. What he wore now was still sleek, but matte black, and definitely not Guardian-issue. The two of us were going to stand out enough by being elves; Mychael didn't want to announce that he was a Guardian, too. Of course, our goal was not to be seen at all. I didn't let my mind dwell on how unlikely *that* was to go as planned.

Instead I let my mind dwell on, and my eyes enjoy, the scenery that was Mychael.

He must have felt me watching him.

Mychael looked down at me, his eyes darkening, his smile holding a hint of danger—the fun kind. "We don't have time for that," he teased.

"Time for what?" I asked, all innocence.

"Everything you're thinking."

Piaras cleared his throat. We were keeping our voices down, and he wasn't standing right next to us, but there was nothing wrong with the kid's ears. After all, he was an elf.

"Sir, do you want me to see what's keeping Maestro Cayle?" he asked.

Mychael smiled. "Ronan knows where we are, Cadet Rivalin. As you were."

The tips of Piaras's ears flushed pink. "Yes, sir."

Four Guardians were standing around Carnades—hands glowing with magic at the ready, weapons doing the same—just waiting for the elf mage to so much as breathe wrong.

I shifted uneasily. "They do look rather eager to cut loose on Carnades, don't they?"

"Ready and all too willing," Mychael assured me, the sparkle in his sea blue eyes saying he'd like to get to Carnades first.

A big part of Carnades's evil-master-plan-gone-wrong had been to either disband the Guardians, or use them as his personal enforcers once he'd seized the archmagus's throne. Mychael had been the man standing in his way. Carnades's plan had Mychael standing before an executioner.

"They're not the only ones," boomed a voice from the doorway.

Archmage Justinius Valerian entered the room and crossed over to us in a sweep of formal robes that had to weigh as much as the old man's lean and grizzled body.

I looked him up and down. "Aren't you a little over-dressed for an invasion?"

"I need to stand out, girl. There's hundreds of panicked old coots running around this island in mage robes. I don't want any of them to doubt who I am and how far I will kick the asses of any of them if they don't do as I say. Immediately. I've told the lot of them to leave their egos at home, not to give me any lip, and we all just might live through this."

Justinius had called an emergency meeting of the Conclave of Sorcerers early this morning to warn them of our situation and to tell them that Vegard would be acting paladin until he said otherwise. The Conclave was the governing body for every magic user in the seven kingdoms. In my opinion the only thing worse than a bunch of arrogant mages was a bunch of arrogant bureaucratic mages.

"How'd they take the announcement about Vegard?" Mychael asked.

"Exactly the way I expected them to. Started asking a bunch of questions that had nothing to do with the security of this island and the safety of our students, and everything to do with politics."

"And they wanted to know where I was going," Mychael said.

"And why. The less people who know about this mission, the better chance of success."

"And survival," I added.

"That, too. I didn't take questions; just gave them all something to do. Any who have the strength and skill to take out a goblin black mage or a major-class demon and aren't squeamish about doing it are now under Vegard's command. The rest of them would just be in the way, so I ordered them home to pack a bag, same size as the students. They'll be evacuated only after the last student is gone."

"You're Archmage Popularity right now."

Justinius shrugged. "It'll keep them off the streets and out of my hair." He glanced at Carnades and lowered his voice. "Is he giving you any trouble?"

"He's not an eager member of this team," Mychael told him, "but he's doing his job."

Carnades's job was to get us through the mirror to Regor—and safely back again. The last part was the carrot Justinius was dangling in front of the elf mage. If we all made it back safely, he wouldn't be executed for his crimes, regardless of the result of his trial. The length of his prison term would be up to the Conclave or elven justice systems. Both were still arguing over who would get to try him first. But Justinius could, and did, offer Carnades a deal—if we lived, so would he. He might be behind bars for the rest of his life, but unless he had an "unfortunate accident" while in prison, at least he'd have a life.

"I trust Carnades about as far as one of my spindly legs could drop-kick him," Justinius was saying under his breath.

The old man's rangy frame might not be able to wrinkle Carnades's robes, but Justinius Valerian was the strongest mage in the seven kingdoms. Period. Using his magic, he could kick Carnades to the far side of the farthest continent. I was grateful that he'd come to see us off. Even better, the old guy wasn't alone. Being the archmage meant he didn't go anywhere without his six huge Guardian bodyguards.

Carnades lowered his hands and took a deep breath that shook as he exhaled. Whatever he'd just done, it'd taken a bit out of him. Just as long as he had enough juice left over to get us to Regor. Mychael walked over and took Carnades's magic-sapping manacles from one of his Guardians, but made no move to put them back on the elf mage. The other Guardians closed ranks around Carnades. I assumed it was too close to the time to leave to put them on again, so they were just going to go with close-quarters guarding.

"Is the crate through?" Mychael asked Carnades.

"It will be in the cave waiting for us when we arrive." The air coming off a glacier was warmer than Carnades's voice. Nope, we definitely weren't turning our backs on him.

"Crate?" I quietly asked Mychael.

"With food, water, blankets, medical supplies."

If we got ambushed by half the goblin army, there wouldn't be enough of us left to bandage.

"In case one of us gets a bad hangnail?"

Mychael managed a grim smile. "Something like that—"

Sirens wailed, lightglobes set into the walls flashed blue, and Piaras and I damned near jumped out of our skins.

Oh hell.

Sounded like Sarad Nukpana got tired of waiting.

Chapter 2

The thing about all hell breaking loose is that unless it breaks loose right in front of you, you have no idea what to do.

While my brain dashed between run, fight, dive to the floor, or just stand there and shake, my hands took the more practical approach and got hold of some pointy steel. Other than Carnades, there were no bad guys to stab at the moment, but that could change. No sense being unprepared.

Meantime, the alarms continued to shriek like freaking banshees.

And the rest of our team wasn't here.

Dammit to hell.

"What *is* that?" I shouted over the din.

"Call to arms." Mychael ran to the door. "Allek?" he shouted down the hall.

"Attacks in the city, sir!" came the response. "We're on it!"

Mychael spat something under his breath and extended his hand, palm up. A clear globe instantly appeared above his hand with an image of Vegard, from the shoulders up, visible inside.

"Report," Mychael ordered.

"Breaches in the city." Vegard had to shout to be heard over some din of his own. "The four outer districts. I've dispatched response teams."

"Reinforcements are on the way," Mychael told him.

"Sons of bitches are coming through as far from the citadel as possible," Justinius said. "By the time our boys get there, they'll have come, taken what they came for, and gone."

I didn't have to ask the old man where they'd have come and gone from. Mirrors and/or small Gates. Or what they'd come to take—any student or mage they could get their hands on and drag back with them. Until his monster Gate was ready, Sarad Nukpana was starting his fun and games with mirrors and smaller Gates.

"Are they Khrynsani?" Mychael was asking Vegard.

"Negative. Regular army, a lot of them."

Mychael swore. Justinius swore. I broke out in a cold sweat.

Sarad Nukpana and the goblin king had started the invasion—or were about to—and more than half of our team wasn't in the mirror room yet.

In addition to Tam, there was Imala Kalis, director of the goblin secret service; Prince Chigaru Mal'Salin; two of his bodyguards; and my father, Eamaliel Anguis. Imala had been secretly helping to organize and equip the goblin Resistance while seemingly loyal to the goblin king. Prince Chigaru was the choice of Tam and Imala—and the saner members of the goblin nobility—to displace and replace his brother, the king. My father, Eamaliel Anguis, was the previous Saghred bond servant and, thanks to prolonged contact with the rock, was now 934 years old. His soul's present home was in the body of a twenty-year-old Guardian. He'd led the original team that had taken the Saghred from another insane goblin king about nine hundred years ago, so he had firsthand experience with the crap we'd be stepping into when we stepped through that mirror.

Good people to have with us. Now, if they'd just get their asses down here, we could go.

"Sir, they're not engaging," Vegard was saying. "At least not fully. Hit-and-run tactics. It's like they just want to be seen."

Mychael scowled. "Draw our men out."

Out, as in away from the citadel.

Justinius answered my unspoken thought. "The citadel's on lockdown; no one's getting in."

"Unless they're getting in the same way as the rest of them," Mychael growled. "And the same way we're getting out."

Mirrors.

Oh no.

That didn't have to mean here in the mirror room. There were other mirrors in the citadel. Last month, we'd come through one to escape the demon queen. It led from the bowels of the old citadel on the other side of the island to the containment rooms here. Down here.

With us.

Even the best-kept secrets were seldom completely kept secrets. It'd been my experience that the bigger the risk, the bigger the chance that secret had sprung a leak. If Sarad Nukpana knew we were coming to Regor through a mirror in the citadel, then he probably knew our exit mirror was in that cave; which meant that goblins could be waiting for us on the other side to escort us to the front of Nukpana's Saghred sacrifice line, starting with me.

If so, the only thing the bastard had to do was sit back and wait. He had what we wanted. He had the Saghred. He also had hundreds of hostages, nobles who supported Chigaru over his brother the king. All he had to do was wait on us to arrive to start the party.

The only way we'd know any of that for sure would be to step through the mirror.

"We need to go!" Carnades screamed over the sirens. "Now!"

For once, and probably for the only time, I agreed with him, but that didn't mean I had to like it or what it meant. We did need to go, but going now would mean me, Mychael, and Carnades alone in Regor. Oh yeah, the elf mirror mage would like that. Kill us (or at least try), then run for his miserable life. He'd have to keep running, but he'd be free—until he pissed off another entire race and got himself dead. I had news for him—we weren't going anywhere without the rest of our team. Tam, Imala, and Chigaru were goblins who knew Regor like the backs of their hands. After 934 years attached to the Saghred, Dad knew every trick that rock could pull to keep itself in one piece.

And even though Tam's teacher hadn't spoken to Tam in years, Tam was our best chance of finding him once we were in Regor. After that, it'd be up to Mychael. He was known throughout the seven kingdoms as the Paladin of the Conclave Guardians, and had the respect that came with the job. However, Mychael's powers of persuasion wouldn't do us a damned bit of good if he didn't have anyone to persuade.

A sudden creepy-crawly sensation ran down my back that had nothing to do with goblins running amok in the city or Carnades within spell-slinging distance behind me. Power was building; power that wasn't from Guardians with a collective case of magical jitters and nothing to smite. Even with no magic myself, I sensed it.

It was dark. Ugly.

And it was here.

A deep throb came from the far corner of the room, from a mirror mounted on the wall, framed in dark, rune-carved wood. Hands encased in armor tipped with bright steel claws ripped through the canvas covering. Goblins came through, armed with blades and crossbows. They were between us and the door; we were between them and Carnades's mirror.

Like I said, ugly.

Nine Khrynsani, two of them mages. That was as accurate a count as I could get or cared to get as I scurried to the left to give myself room to fight. I left the power packers to Mychael and Justinius. I had a sword in each hand and balanced on the balls of my feet, ready to move in whatever direction the closest goblin picked. More Khrynsani poured through the mirror like a black-armored wave, and Piaras's voice rang out from behind me, a commanding baritone aimed at the Khrynsani. I recognized the quickly cascading notes and words as a spellsong I'd heard Mychael use before. The goblins should have dropped in their tracks.

They kept coming.

With some kind of dark plugs in their ears.

Oh crap.

They'd known spellsingers would be guarding the mirror room.

We'd been betrayed from the inside out. Now our enemies were in here with us and deaf as doornails to any spellsong Piaras or Mychael could throw at them.

"Where's Tam?" Piaras shouted. I wasn't the only one who knew we needed to get through that mirror while we still could.

I parried a lunge that came entirely too close to finding its mark. "Good damned question."

Piaras had a sword in one hand, a long parrying dagger in the other, and was putting both to good use. His opponents lately had had a fatal tendency to underestimate him because of his young age and brown eyes. Anyone who looked that innocent couldn't have the nerve or instinct to kill. They soon found themselves wrong on all counts, not to mention dead. Piaras wasn't a killer, but two months ago, his mind had been briefly taken over by Sarad Nukpana. The goblin's link with Piaras and his ultimately unsuccessful attempt to control his mind had left the kid with the goblin's masterful skill with a sword, among other deadly talents. Nukpana knew only too well how to kill, and as a result, so did Piaras.

Two Khrynsani found that out the hard way.

Seconds later, an explosion blew the door off its hinges as well as disintegrated a goodly chunk of the stone wall around it. Several Khrynsani who'd had the misfortune to be standing too close went flying.

Tamnais Nathrach was reckless, his magic powerful, and danger was just another way to have a good time. The man also knew how to make a damned fine entrance. Tam had weapons anywhere he could strap them. He was going home and was amply prepared for a less-than-warm reception. Tam followed up the concussion spell he'd used to destroy the door with his armored fists.

Behind Tam came Imala, Prince Chigaru, and his two bodyguards. Since we'd be stepping through a mirror to Regor, they were all armed and armored for trouble. That was good, because we had plenty of trouble right here, no walking through a mirror needed.

Carnades Silvanus was now somewhere behind me. He was even more likely to kill me than the goblins were. Fry me where I stood, then claim that one of the goblins had done it, or that his shot went wide and it was a horrible accident. With all the heavy firepower flying around, accidents weren't just possible, they were likely, and I was the first person one was likely to happen to. In an enclosed space, spells were just as likely to hit your own people as taking out the people you were actually aiming at.

I barely managed to avoid being brained by the pommel of a thrown knife. I had no clue who had done the throwing. Right now, my biggest challenge was finding space to fight without killing, or being killed by, my own people.

Technically, Carnades was one of my own people. That thought was just scary enough to make me risk a quick glance behind me. The mirror mage had his hands full, literally and figuratively, as one Khrynsani had jumped him and another was about to join the fray. I'd never thought of Carnades as the brawling type, but I'd learned never to underestimate survival instinct. He had nothing left to lose except his life, and everything to gain by taking ours and leaving the goblins with the blame.

Carnades's hands were around a goblin soldier's throat, his hands flaring with silver light. The Khrynsani let out a shriek you wouldn't have thought could come from a grown man. The screams stopped and Carnades tossed him aside, the dead goblin's throat a smoking ruin of blackened flesh.

Mychael wrenched the helmet off of a dead goblin and hurled it at the mirror they'd come through. Just a normal throw probably would have done the trick, but Mychael didn't want to risk anything except a direct hit. There was magic behind that helmet missile, and it hit, turning the mirror's reflective surface into a spiderweb of shattered glass. Nothing else would be coming through that.

Stopping the flow of goblins was good, but taking their escape hatch away had the undesirable effect of turning homicidal Khrynsani into homicidal and desperate Khrynsani.

But the remaining Khrynsani were outnumbered and they knew it.

Or they should have.

Anyone in their situation looking halfway happy was, in my opinion, all the way suicidal. If that was the case, these boys were about to get their wish.

One of them grinned until his fangs showed.

Mychael swore, seconded by Tam.

I didn't need to sense what they did. I could see it.

A clawed hand, a massive hand, punched through the mirror right next to Carnades's. The hand was attached to and followed by a scaled arm corded with thick muscle. Nothing that big should have been able to move that fast, but apparently no one had ever told that to it—whatever it was. There wasn't any need to shatter the mirror it was coming through; the monster did that all by itself, squeezing its hunched shoulders and horned head through the glass, snapping and reducing the frame to splinters. That it had destroyed its own escape hatch didn't seem to bother it at all. In fact, judging from its dingy, yellow eyes and a mouthful of smiling fangs to match, it looked downright happy about where he was.

Happy and hungry.

Piaras launched into a litany of curses in Goblin. Someone had been around Talon too long. Then I saw what Piaras had seen. Spellsongs wouldn't do any good on this thing, either. It didn't have plugs in its ears.

It didn't have any ears.

Though I was betting it'd bleed. Problem was getting close enough to stick it with something sharp without having it do the same to us, namely with the hooked claws attached to the fingers that were dragging the ground.

"Down!" Justinius roared.

The old man didn't have to yell twice. I hit the floor, with Piaras a split second behind me. At that moment, Justinius Valerian, archmage of the Conclave of Sorcerers and the most badass spellslinger there was, opened up on the monster. It was beautiful—in a seriously gory way. Justinius's hands glowed incandescent white as he hit the monster with a fireball hard enough to embed the thing into the bedrock on the other side of the room.

At least that was what should have happened.

The fireball punched a hole the size of a shield through the monster's midsection, but instead of the monster's insides spilling onto the outside, suspiciously shaped blobs plopped wetly onto the floor.

Suspiciously shaped like the monster they'd fallen out of. Oh hell.

Then Mychael was there, pushing me and Piaras toward Carnades's mirror, away from the monster population explosion taking place before our eyes. Tam's spells and Imala's steel were trying to keep up, but some of the little buggers were getting past them.

Suddenly things seemed to slow down to the point that

we had all the time in the world to get through that mirror. I knew it hadn't, and I knew we didn't; it was just my mind's way of giving me a little more time to figure out how to survive the next few seconds.

"Go!"

Justinius Valerian roared that command and gathered his power for another strike. He probably had more power than anyone or anything in this room combined, but he couldn't keep up that kind of attack for much longer. He knew it, and he didn't care. What he cared about was getting us through that mirror to Regor.

"I'm not leaving you!" Mychael shouted at the old man.

"The hell you're not!"

He was right. We had to go. The attacks in the city, the mirrors, the Khrynsani, and the monsters—they were all here in Mid to keep us from getting to Regor. Either we made it and got that rock out of Sarad Nukpana's hands—or no one was going to make it.

Carnades was opening the mirror.

I got a throwing knife in my hand. If Carnades made a run for it without us, he wasn't going to be alive when he got to the other side.

"Fall back!" Mychael shouted.

I told myself that Justinius and the remaining Guardians could handle this. Reinforcements would come charging through what was left of that door any second. I didn't believe that and probably neither did the old man, but he was doing it anyway. He'd sacrifice himself if necessary to ensure that we got to Regor.

"I can't hold it!" Carnades screamed.

We had to go. Now. Piaras was going with us. We had no choice and neither did he. The Khrynsani had earplugs, and the monsters didn't have any ears. Piaras had Sarad Nukpana's sword fighting skills, but he didn't have the battlemagic skills to survive this. Though I didn't know what would be worse: to stay here with the goblins and the rapidly growing mini-monsters, or dive through that mirror to possibly be ambushed by Sarad Nukpana and his sadistic Khrynsani.

Both sucked. Both were unavoidable. Choose one or the other; there wasn't a third option.

Prince Chigaru's two bodyguards put themselves between the prince and the Khrynsani. One guard took a crossbow bolt to the chest that'd been meant for Chigaru.

The other was poised to plunge a dagger into his prince.

I drew breath to scream a warning. I needn't have bothered.

Imala saw the bodyguard move.

She moved faster.

The goblin never knew what hit him, and died staring at his prince, dagger still raised to strike, confusion in his dying eyes.

"Jabari? *No!*" Chigaru screamed in disbelief and denial.

Betrayal was contagious as hell today.

Another bolt came out of nowhere.

Carnades spun to face it as if he had eyes in the back of his head. A nimbus of glittering frost formed in front of this hand, deflecting the bolt and sending it slamming into the chest of the goblin who'd fired it.

The shooter wasn't aiming at Carnades.

He was aiming at the mirror. Our mirror.

More Khrynsani crossbows were raised, all with one target—a mirror they were hell-bent on shattering.

Mychael stood back-to-back with Carnades, shielding the elf mage while he worked frantically to stabilize the mirror.

Tam shoved Imala and Chigaru through the mirror, and all but threw Piaras toward it.

Mychael didn't turn and look; he knew I was still there. *"Go!"* he screamed.

Tam's hands gripping my shoulder made sure that this time, I'd do as told.

I dived into darkness.

Chapter 3

I landed flat on my face, and spent the next few seconds spitting out dirt.

My hands were out in front of me with gravel embedded in my palms. My knee had rammed itself into something painfully solid. My other leg was pinned under some kind of weight. Basically I was folded up and smushed. After my eyes had finished tearing up, I started to blink them open, then realized with a rush of panic that they *were* open.

Dark. Pitch-dark. Hand-in-front-of-your-face, no-can-see dark. Not to mention cold and wet. Water drizzled like a light rain from somewhere in the darkness behind us.

I tried to make a lightglobe and got a pitiful spark. No amount of effort would get it any bigger or brighter.

The weight on my leg moved. Instinctively, I kicked.

"Ow!"

Piaras.

"Sorry. Where are you?"

"Right where you kicked," came his pained retort.

A blue lightglobe flared to life, and hovered briefly above Mychael's open palm before he released it to hover by his right shoulder, and he peered into the dark as best as he could see with elven eyes.

"Tam?" he called in a low whisper.

"Clear as far as I can tell," Tam said quietly from somewhere ahead in the dark.

No Khrynsani. But for how long?

Mychael's lightglobe showed me that I'd somehow managed to slam my shoulder *and* knee into the corner of what I assumed was our supply crate. No wonder I hurt.

Mychael, Tam, and Imala were on their feet; the rest of us had landed on other body parts, none of them particularly dignified. I grunted as I got to my feet and rotated my shoulder. Not dislocated, no breaks.

"My lucky day," I muttered.

Piaras looked around him. "Yeah, lucky."

I didn't want Piaras to be here, though it was better to be here and alive, than in that mirror room and probably dead. But the last place he needed to be was in the same city as Sarad Nukpana. The glance I shot at Mychael said all of that and then some. After me, Piaras was next on Sarad Nukpana's slow-and-agonizing-revenge list. Mychael knew all of that as well as I did.

"Welcome to the team, Cadet Rivalin," he said.

Carnades muttered something that I couldn't quite make out, but Mychael heard it clearly enough.

The rocks I'd landed on were softer than Mychael's expression. "He's here and a member of this team—a qualified member."

Out of the corner of my eye, I caught the glint of the magic-sapping manacles that Mychael held loosely in one hand behind his back. My heart went into double-time beating. Carnades wasn't cuffed. Dammit, dam—

Tam took a quick step toward Carnades from the side. For a split second, Carnades's attention was on Tam—not on Mychael, who closed the distance and snapped the manacles on the distracted elf mage.

Mychael stepped back. "Thanks, Tam."

"Don't mention it."

Carnades's glare, at them both, was pure murder.

Piaras laid his hand flat on the damp cave wall. "This is Regor?" he whispered to no one in particular.

My knee popped and I winced. "A cave a few miles outside of it."

"Damn," he whispered in awe.

I agreed with the word, not the sentiment. There was nothing awe-inspiring about being within a few miles—or even closer—of Sarad Nukpana. Terror-stricken was about right. I didn't think any of that had sunk in for Piaras. Yet.

Tam had conjured a lightglobe of his own and sent its glow back toward the mirror. Carnades's eyes followed the light to get a look at his mirror. The elf mage's face suddenly contorted with rage.

"Fuck!" he roared. The echo in the cave ensured that we all got to hear the word at least five times.

"Silence!" Imala hissed.

Tam spat a choice word of his own, drew one of his swords, and vanished back into the dark of the cave. If anyone was waiting to ambush, beat the crap out of, and dump us at Sarad Nukpana's feet, Carnades had just done a damned fine job of announcing our arrival.

I looked back at the mirror and bit back my own verbal contribution.

The tip of a crossbow bolt protruded from the mirror's surface. The mirror itself was cracked, broken, worthless. Cracks radiated out from the bolt like a spider's web. Carnades's word choice confirmed loud and clear that we had no way home.

Instead of punching through the mirror, that bolt could have just as easily punched through any one of us. When Carnades had slammed that mirror shut behind us, the bolt had been trapped like a fly in amber. There was definitely a cracked mirror here and most likely a destroyed mirror there. Neither one could get us out.

Tam, Imala, and Chigaru were home. The rest of us were trapped in Hell.

I didn't know about everyone else, but my morale had just hit an all-time low.

Chigaru was speaking in low hissing tones with Imala. Without his bodyguards—or at least the one who hadn't tried to kill him—the goblin prince no doubt felt as naked as the day he was born. He'd been on the run from his brother for years, and every second of that time he'd been surrounded by guards and armed courtiers. Now he was within ten or so miles of his brother and his army—without any guards. I sympathized and could have told the prince that I knew exactly how he felt. I was in a similar predicament without my magic. Since Carnades didn't know that, I kept my mouth shut.

"Jabari would never betray me," Prince Chigaru was saying. "It was chaotic; he must have—"

"It was no mistake, Your Highness," Imala told him firmly.

"I don't believe it. I can't."

"Well, obviously you're wrong," Carnades snapped.

Chigaru growled and lunged for the elf mage. Fortunately, Tam got the prince by the arm as soon as he saw Carnades open his mouth to speak. A wise man, Tam. At this rate, Carnades would be lucky to make it out of the cave alive.

"Are there any unbroken mirrors nearby?" I asked anyone who might know.

"In the city," Imala replied.

Tam released the prince's arm, but kept his eye on him. "There are dozens . . . in the palace."

Lovely.

"Say we destroy the Saghred and find a nice, big, intact

mirror." I was looking at Carnades. "Could you get us home with one of those?"

"Of course."

"Details of how you can accomplish that would be nice."

"There are four blanks in the citadel mirror room," Carnades said. "I have one in my home, and another in my Conclave office."

"Blanks?"

"A mirror that is not linked to a specific destination." Carnades's words dripped with contempt, presumably at my ignorance.

I ignored it and him. I could always punch Carnades later. In fact, that image was going to be my happy thought for the entire trip.

Mychael shot a warning glance at Carnades. "The four blanks in the mirror room were against the opposite wall from ours," Mychael explained. "Their surfaces were flat, no ripples, no reflections of the people in the room. They could be our way back."

Mychael left "if they weren't destroyed" unsaid. My low morale appreciated that.

"We would need to locate either a blank or active mirror in Regor," he continued. "Carnades would redirect it to one of the blanks on Mid."

"How long does that take?" Piaras asked.

"About half an hour for most mirror mages," Mychael replied.

"I could do it in fifteen," Carnades said disdainfully.

A jerk, but a talented one. "That could be fatally slow if we've got half the goblin army on our collective ass," I noted. "Do you think you could speed it up?"

"That is as quick as *anyone* could link two mirrors," Carnades hissed. "I have just as much motivation to escape Regor as you do."

That statement couldn't be more true. Sarad Nukpana hated Carnades as much as he did me. So hopefully there'd be plenty of potential getaway mirrors to choose from—and Carnades would be plenty motivated to break his own speed record when we found one of them.

I knew I couldn't see past our meager lights into the rest of the cave, but that didn't stop me from trying. "Why isn't there a welcoming committee here? Not that I mind Nukpana being rude, but I do have a vested interest in why."

"And I have a vested interest in air," said a muffled and all-too-familiar voice—from *inside* the crate. "Could someone let me out?"

Never think that a situation couldn't get any worse.

Our crate contained something besides supplies.

It had Talon stowed away inside.

It probably should've taken a crowbar to get into that crate, but Tam ripped into it just fine with his bare hands—probably so he could wrap them around Talon's neck. From the look on Tam's face, the kid would have been better off staying in the box, air or no air. Once Talon got a look at his father's face for himself, I think the kid agreed with me.

Talon was even more scrunched up in the crate than I had been when I slammed into it. He'd wedged himself into one corner, his knees tight against his chest, head bent forward, hands clutching what looked like a small ham. My stomach rumbled.

Tam was virtually shaking with suppressed rage, and for once, Talon did the smart thing and kept his mouth shut.

"Cadet Nathrach," Mychael said. "What a completely unpleasant and *unauthorized* surprise."

Talon looked from his dad to his commander. "I can explain."

"I seriously doubt that." Tam reached in, grabbed his son by the front of his uniform, and, with a hard twist and pull, popped Talon free from the supplies, leaving a roughly Talon-shaped indentation in a stack of blankets. But Talon, being Talon, the moment he was out he started talking. Bad idea. It was like the kid couldn't help himself.

"I didn't take any supplies out to make room for me."

I didn't think Tam heard one word the kid said.

Discipline—either of the self or the plain variety—wasn't a big part of Talon's thinking. He'd been on his own for much of his young life, and had used his magic any way he had to in order to survive. Talon was nearly as talented a spellsinger as Piaras, so the kid had some nifty tricks up those gray uniform sleeves, and he didn't think twice about whipping any of them out. That there were consequences to his actions, especially to others, was just beginning to occur to him. If he ran into a problem, he had a trick to fix it. Magic wasn't the cure-all solution to everything. Tam was trying to teach his son that. Regor was no place for Talon to continue his education.

The kid was the proverbial loose cannon. Powerful but unfocused, the majority of his magic remained uncharted waters—deep uncharted waters. That description applied to Piaras, too.

And both of them were stuck here with us.

"If we survive this," Tam growled, "we're going to have a long and *very* meaningful talk."

"I'll look forward to it, sir."

"No, you won't. I can't change that you're here, but I can and *will* change your future attitude about reckless behavior. Do I make myself clear?"

Talon glanced at Tam's unyielding face and gulped audibly. "Completely, sir."

Mychael broke the silence. "Tam, you're familiar with this cave; you'll lead us out. Cadets Rivalin and Nathrach, our bad luck is your good. Three of our team members didn't make it through the mirror. There's a backpack for each of you. Let's stock up and move out."

Just because there weren't any Khrynsani here to meet us didn't mean they weren't on the way. We got our gear quickly and quietly.

"Elves, get behind a goblin," Tam ordered.

Carnades stiffened. "What?"

Tam spoke as if explaining the obvious, which he was. "Goblins can see in the dark; elves can't. We can't have any light, and we can't make any sound."

Carnades struggled to get his pack over his shoulder. "Why not put Raine at the front? She can just obliterate anyone who comes at us."

I'd had enough of Carnades, and we hadn't been in Regor for more than five minutes. "And announce ourselves to every Khrynsani within a hundred miles," I said. "Great plan."

"I merely suggest putting our most effective weapon out front," he said smoothly. "The goblins know what Raine is capable of. In my opinion, we would remain unmolested."

I hated to admit it, but I agreed with him. If I'd had all of my power there for the calling, I'd want to be out front, and screw the consequences. I'd blast my way into Regor. Anything to get this over with as quickly as possible. But I didn't have my power, and even if I did, I couldn't use it for exactly the reason I told Carnades. Big magic would attract big attention of the goblin army kind. There was safety in sneaking.

"If I start a fight, they're going to finish it," I told Carnades. "Are you looking to get 'finished'?"

Imala slung a pack over her shoulders, settled it on her back, and began tightening the straps. "Sarad knows we're here, but if we get our asses moving, and if Raine keeps her magic to herself, he may remain ignorant of our exact location." She shot a meaningful look at Carnades. "Silence—both of voice or magic—is the best way to ensure that Sarad remains that way."

What a polite way to tell Carnades to keep his mouth shut. Court goblins did have a way with words.

We lined up and left the back of the cave. There were more than a thousand miles between Mid and Regor. It had been late morning in Mid, so the sun had probably just risen here.

Though you wouldn't know it from where we were. Caves were absurdly dark.

Tam was leading. The rest of us followed behind, more or less in a goblin-elf order, our footfalls muffled. Not bad for shell-shocked elves in the pitch dark. Though as my eyes adjusted as much as they could, I saw that the cave wasn't completely dark. Faint green phosphorescence clung to the damp walls from what I guessed was a fungus of some sort. The light let me at least make out Prince Chigaru's shoulders in front of me.

Shoulders that suddenly stopped.

The sharp whistle of an incoming crossbow bolt announced we weren't alone anymore.

I dived to the right, toward the cave wall. There was no room for swords, not to mention it was still too freaking dark. I drew one dagger in case someone tried to bring death up close and personal, but I kept it by my side. It'd suck to stab one of my own team; well, except for Carnades.

Mychael and Tam were out front. I couldn't see them, but I could hear them. Imala had enough magic to shield Chigaru, who had none. Carnades had probably crawled into a crack in the wall with his hands over his head. Either that or a Khrynsani had tacked him to the wall on the first volley.

The twang of bowstrings was abruptly replaced by steel-on-steel combat.

The goblins were happy to continue trying to kill us in the dark. Mychael's shout of a two-word spell killed their happy real quick.

Light, blazing like the sun at high noon, lit the cave. Happy turned to pained shouts and hisses. Tam, Imala, and Chigaru didn't like it, but each had shielded their eyes with one hand and kept weapons moving in the other.

Amazing thing about survival instinct—when your body realizes it's in deep and stinky stuff, your eyes find a way to see just a little better than they ordinarily could; your hearing is just a little sharper; your reflexes faster.

I didn't see the Khrynsani's lunge at my left side; I felt the air displaced by his movement, and slashed my long dagger across the back of his wrist. With a pained hiss, the goblin jerked his sword back only to instantly close distance with his dagger, giving me a slice of my own. I detected a flash of fang-filled grin right before he stepped in for what he thought was the kill. The Khrynsani froze for a fraction of a second, but it was long enough for me to bury my blade between his ribs.

The last expression on his face wasn't just terror; it was recognition. The goblin saw me and knew who I was, and for those two blinks, he'd been scared pissless. The way my day had been going, it was nice to be appreciated, even if it was for a power I didn't have anymore, or at least not right now, when I could really use it.

Two Khrynsani were moving on Tam, and Mychael's sudden sunlight didn't stop their forward momentum. I couldn't throw a knife that far, and even if I could, I'd probably just hit them in the head with the pommel.

Rocks were much easier.

We were in a cave, so rocks were plentiful. No one was charging me, so I scooped up a fist-sized rock, and chucked it hard at the head of the Khrynsani closest to Tam. It took him in the temple, and he went down like the rock that'd hit him.

Unfortunately, some of the Khrynsani had been a little faster than their brothers in adjusting to the light, and I became the center of a lot of unwanted attention.

They recognized me, too.

Damn.

Judging from the number of Khrynsani readying spells and mouthing incantations, Sarad Nukpana had told them that I was to be the guest of honor. Flattered, I did not feel.

All the rocks in that cave weren't going to save my bacon.

But a volley of bolts to the Khrynsani's backs did.

I didn't know how many Khrynsani were in that cave,

but the newcomers had put a dead-on-target bolt in each and every one.

They were hooded and cloaked, but I caught a glimpse here and there of gray skin. Goblins. The Khrynsani were dead, but the newcomers had reloaded and held their crossbows at the ready.

At us.

One goblin stepped out in front of the others. Tall and rangy from what I could tell. He stared straight at Tam, then turned his hooded face toward me.

"Nice throwing arm," he said.

I flexed my hand around the rock I still held. "I stay in practice. You never know who you're going to meet." I tossed a rock casually in one hand, and spoke without taking my eyes off the goblin. "Tam, he seems to know you. Who have we just met?"

"My brother," Tam said, his eyes never leaving the robed figure.

I damned near dropped the rock on my foot. "Your *what*?"

"His brother, Mistress Benares." The goblin raised his crossbow and leveled it at Tam. "Welcome home."

Chapter 4

Brother?

I had questions tumbling all over themselves to get out. Like why hadn't Tam told me he had a brother, to how did that brother know we were going to be here, and the biggie—what the hell was he doing aiming a crossbow at Tam?

Phaelan had been on the receiving end of some less-than-warm receptions by a few of his siblings before, but none had gone as far as contemplating murder (at least not openly), which looked like exactly what Tam's brother was doing. He'd seen Tam, identified Tam as his brother, and still had the business end of a crossbow aimed at him. Though with growing up together anywhere near the goblin court, who knew what kind of brotherly resentments this guy had? Just our luck it'd be the seething, bottled-up variety.

The rock in my hand had this guy's name on it—whatever it was—if he brought that bow up to his shoulder. When it came to talking sense into his brother, I hoped Tam knew what he was doing.

Tam held up a hand to stop any of us who might be thinking what I was thinking, namely bounce a rock or spell off this guy's hooded head. Tam's other hand dropped to where he kept his favorite throwing dagger. That confirmed there wasn't going to be a hug of brotherly welcome in the immediate future. Other than that, Tam didn't move; I thought it prudent to follow his lead. None of the goblins were moving, either. Their weapons weren't aimed at us, but they weren't lowered, either, though the same was true for us. Distrust was just as contagious as betrayal today.

There were ten goblins that I could see, with a couple probably standing watch outside the cave mouth. They were armed and armored in a mismatched kind of way. Their armor wasn't bad and their weapons were slightly better, but it all looked like they'd used what they'd found or taken. Uncle Ryn's and Phaelan's crews operated the same way. But these people weren't pirates. Some of them had the look of experienced fighters; the others held themselves and their weapons like staging an ambush was relatively new to them. They outnumbered us, though surprise had been their only advantage, but it had worked well enough. The cave floor littered with dead Khrynsani was proof of that.

However, at least six of them were mages. Good ones. Without my magic, I couldn't sense their power, but I didn't need to sense it when I could see it with my own two eyes. Experienced mages often left a hazy shimmer behind for a few moments after they'd worked some form of magic, whether defensive wards or offensive spells. Mychael and Tam could take this group on, and probably take them out, but their level of battlemagic combined with enclosed spaces would have fatally unintended results. Carnades's possible contribution didn't even enter into the picture. If the spells started flying, the only side Carnades would be on was his own.

Tam's brother reached up with the hand not holding the crossbow and pushed back his hood. Oh yeah, he was Tam's brother, no doubt of that. He wore his black hair long, and, like his brother's, it was tightly bound down his back in a goblin battle braid. He looked slightly younger, and his features were a little sharper than Tam's, but they'd be no less swoon inducing to the general female population.

Tam was utterly, preternaturally still. "What are you—"

"Doing here?" his brother finished. "It looks like we're pulling your ass out of a very large fire." The goblin paused, his expression card-shark blank. "Or did we interrupt a business meeting?"

"Business?" Tam hissed. He gave a sharp kick to the Khrynsani corpse at his feet that had died by his hand. I had to wonder if Tam would've preferred it if his boot had connected with his brother instead. "How dare you imply that—"

The goblin shrugged. "Well, you might not be who you say you are."

"What?"

"You might not be who—"

"I heard what you said," Tam snapped.

Talon was standing right behind me. I heard him draw breath to make his own contribution, and I reached back and pinched the hell out of whatever skin I could latch onto. Talon squeaked, but then he did exactly what I'd intended—kept that mouth of his shut and didn't give his dad any more trouble than he might already have.

I didn't know the circumstances behind this tit for tat, but I'd seen Phaelan and his brothers engage in it often enough that I knew where it was going. Phaelan and one brother or the other usually ended up on the ground in a messy wrestling match. Tam and his brother were both heavily armed, and Tam was heavily magicked. This would just be messy.

Anyone who ambushed and killed Khrynsani waiting to ambush and kill us might not be our friends, but I couldn't see them being our enemies. Just about the last thing I thought we'd be doing was standing in a damp cave with dead Khrynsani while Tam and his brother engaged in some kind of alpha male sibling rivalry.

Tam's brother shrugged. "You were recently possessed by Sarad Nukpana. You let Raine Benares over there kill you rather than stay that way." He made a sound that was somewhere between a snort and a laugh without the humor. "You getting yourself possessed by someone else wouldn't be the strangest thing I've seen this week. And a possessed man certainly wouldn't hesitate to kill a few of his lackeys to make a disguise more believable." He paused meaningfully. "I need proof that you're my brother."

Just proof? That didn't sound like a man about to kill his brother out of rage or vengeance. Maybe Tam hadn't pissed him off after all. That'd be a pleasant surprise. I bit the inside of my cheek to keep from smiling. Crossbows pointed at us or not, this could be good.

"Which would be more convincing?" Tam drawled. "To regale your friends here with how when you were fourteen, you fell face-first out of Countess Na'Ghal's boudoir window into a pile of horse manure with her enraged husband in pursuit, or your eighteenth birthday when you treated yourself to a pair of ripe Caesolian—"

"I believe you," his brother said quickly, lowering the crossbow.

Tam smiled, and it was genuine. "Are you quite certain? It would be no trouble. I assure you I recall both events in exacting detail—or dozens of similar . . . shall we say, unfortunate moments from your past." Tam nudged the body at his feet with the tip of his boot. "Though we shouldn't stand around until reinforcements arrive for this pack of jackals, so I could just cut to the good parts."

"I said I believe you." Tam's brother rested the butt of his crossbow against his hip, bolt pointing at the cave's roof. He turned and glanced over his right shoulder. "What do you think?"

"I believe him," said an amused voice from the shadows

near the cave entrance. "However, it would be prudent to be absolutely certain that he's telling the truth. Perhaps Tam should share that birthday story. After all, the truth is in the details." Another goblin stepped into what light there was, his body glowing from a faint red protection spell. A good one. The spell winked out.

"Jash Masloc," Tam said, grinning until his fangs showed.

"Good to see you, Tam." The mage turned to the others. "Stand down, ladies and gentlemen. Our guests may not be nice, but they are friends." The mage bowed gallantly from the waist. "Prince Chigaru, Director Kalis—welcome home, such that it is. Your Highness, this wasn't the welcome you should have received."

"But it was the one we expected, Count Masloc," Chigaru said.

"Sarad has a twisted sense of propriety," Imala noted. "How did you know we were coming?"

"Thankfully, we still have spies close to King Sathrik who can still get messages out." Jash Masloc smiled. "Even under siege, the goblin court is still the court. Secrets are merely gossip that hasn't been spread yet. There's more than one chamber in these caves. We didn't know which one held your mirror—and neither did these poor bastards—until Magus Silvanus announced your less-than-happy arrival."

I resisted the urge to shoot Carnades a dirty look—or better yet, tell Tam's brother to just shoot him. "Our exit mirror got busted," I said.

"That would explain the . . . outburst."

Not more than ten seconds on the other side of the mirror, and Carnades had come close to getting us slaughtered—or worse, captured, tortured, and then slaughtered. Having Carnades Silvanus in our immediate vicinity was going to get us killed before we even got into the city. But if the looks our new goblin friends were giving him were any indication, Carnades would be on his best behavior. He might not know the goblins in the cave with us, but they certainly either knew or had heard of him. Or maybe Carnades just reeked of bigot.

Tam walked quickly toward his brother.

His brother held up a placating hand. "I knew you were telling the truth. I didn't doubt it for a minute."

"Yes, you did. At the very least, you doubted my motives."

Tam's brother slung the crossbow's strap across one shoulder just as Tam caught him up in a bear hug.

"Of course, I doubted your motives," he said with a big grin, returning the hug. "You're a Nathrach, aren't you?"

Tam made quick introductions. His brother was Nathair, or Nath to his friends. When Tam had finished introducing everyone else, he turned to Talon.

Oh boy.

More than a few of the Resistance fighters had the fine features of pure-blooded goblins, or the "old families" as I'd heard Tam call those like them. I wasn't sure telling Nath and his heavily armed playmates that he was an uncle of a half-breed was such a good idea.

Talon knew that as well as I did. The kid sucked in a double lungful of air and held it.

"And this is Talon Nathrach." Tam smiled and gestured Talon over to him. "My son."

Talon came forward. Cautiously. Probably one of the first times in his impulsive little life that he'd ever done anything with caution.

Nath did a few seconds of stunned blinking and staring. "A nephew," he finally managed. "I'm an uncle."

"That's usually the way it works," Tam agreed.

Stunned gave way to a broad grin. "You're definitely a Nathrach. You're damned near as good-looking as I am."

Talon got a big welcome-to-the-family hug, and I got some dust in my eyes. Yeah, it was dust.

If any of the goblins with Nath had a problem with Talon, they hid it well. They wanted Sathrik off the throne, but had been part of the goblin court until they'd had to go into hiding. These men and women had plenty of practice hiding things other than themselves; contempt for a half-breed would be a snap. I'd be keeping an eye on Talon. Though my eyes would have plenty of company from Tam, Mychael, and Piaras. The kid would be safe, or someone would be sorry.

"All these reunions are nice," I said, "but shouldn't we be getting the hell out of here?" I indicated the body at my feet. "It's been our unfortunate experience that where there's one pack of Khrynsani, there's another sniffing around nearby."

"You heard the lady," Nath said. He knelt and began to pilfer the body of the Khrynsani closest to him. "Let's get what we can and get out."

The Khrynsani should be grateful that we killed them. If Sarad Nukpana had found out that they'd let us escape, they would have all gotten a fast promotion—right to the front of the Saghred sacrifice line. With Nukpana, I couldn't imagine failure meaning anything except death. Which meant any patrol that came after them would be intensely motivated not to fail.

"This patrol is to report in every hour," Jash Masloc said. "Their last check-in was about ten minutes before they heard Magus Silvanus, so work fast."

I didn't need to be told twice. I knelt to see if the dead Khrynsani at my feet had any gifts to offer a less-than-optimally armed elf. Nath and his people were doing a fast and efficient job of not leaving any weapons lying on the ground. Sarad Nukpana made sure his men had only the best. What a guy. As a result of his largesse, now we had the best.

As I moved up to the goblin's upper torso, a glint of reflected light caught my attention. A chain lay against his neck, and from where his head lay at an angle, a marble-sized pendant had rolled to rest in the hollow of his throat.

No way in hell I was touching that.

"Mychael," I said. "You better look at this."

"What is it?"

"Something I'm not touching for all the tea in Nebia."

He looked and he didn't get any closer. Nice to know that my instincts were still working, even if my magic wasn't.

"What is it?" I asked.

"A spy orb." Mychael called to the goblin mage. "Jash?"

"The leader of every Khrynsani patrol is supplied with them," he said. "They pulsate when they get close to strong magic," he explained to me. "It's how they found our mages in the capital. Only the most powerful can tamp down their magic enough to be non-detectable. The iron ore in the walls of this cave is shielding us now. Sarad Nukpana issued spy orbs for you, Mistress Benares. There are hundreds of various sizes concealed around the city. He knew you'd come, and he wanted to know when and where you entered the city when you did." Jash Masloc's dark eyes narrowed. "The Saghred must have gifted you with extreme stealth; I sense absolutely no magic from you. Nor do you have discernable shields."

I gave him a smile that hopefully didn't look like the wince I felt. "The rock didn't live this long without knowing the value of silence. Not to mention, the less between me and my targets, the better."

I knew I wasn't going to be setting off any kind of magical alarm inside this cave or out; and even though Tam trusted this Count Masloc guy, I didn't want him knowing that. Tam didn't speak up, so I took that to mean he agreed with me.

The spy orb suddenly flashed with a white light, and I couldn't get my eyes closed fast enough. In addition to spots, I now saw three of everything. Great.

"Shit!" Mychael spat.

"Out!" Jash Masloc yelled to his people, not bothering with quiet. "Go, go, *go!*"

Mychael grabbed the pendant's chain with his gloved hand and snapped it from around the corpse's neck, careful not to touch the pendant. He dropped it on the cave floor and slammed the heel of his boot down on the crystal, leaving nothing but dust.

Welcome to Regor.

Chapter 5

I hated tunnels. Always had, always would. At least I would if we got out of this one alive.

We were getting into Regor the same way Nath and his Resistance buddies had gotten out. We'd go under the city walls. Unfortunately, under meant underground.

I'd noticed that since the Saghred had latched onto me like a love-starved leech, I'd spent entirely too much time underground. Smuggling tunnels, sewage tunnels, dungeons, catacombs, and even your run-of-the-mill spooky basement, which had turned out to be demon infested. Thanks to the Saghred, I'd taken the scenic tour of them all. Though also thanks to the Saghred, I'd managed to survive all of the above. Maybe spending so much time underground because of the Saghred was some kind of twisted preparation for what was shaping up to be the mother of all subterranean excursions.

I swore to myself that if I got out of this alive, anywhere the sun didn't shine, I didn't go. No exceptions.

The only sky we'd seen was in the short dash from the cave with Carnades's mirror to the cave we were now in. It had been a beautiful sunny day. Though the goblins around me had seen the bright blue sky as neither beautiful nor comforting—at least not comfortable. Goblins liked the dark. A lot. I guess somebody had to.

Caves were basically hollowed-out rock. In my opinion, a tunnel of hollowed-out dirt was just a grave waiting to collapse. It wasn't a matter of if it would happen; it was when. The second time a troop of mounted horsemen thundered by overhead and clots of dirt fell from what passed for a ceiling, I thought that moment had arrived. While being squashed under tons of dirt would take care of all of our problems; it wasn't the solution I was still hoping for.

Us alive. Sarad Nukpana dead. The Saghred reduced to dust, like the dirt presently covering my hair.

"Are we there yet?" Talon asked.

I muffled a snort.

"When we're there, we'll stop walking," Nath told him.

If someone had given Nath and Talon a more-than-passing glance, they would have thought the two goblins were brothers. I estimated that Nath was about ten years older than Talon, which made me seriously question the wisdom of putting Nath in charge of a retrieval mission. Maybe that was why Jash Masloc was his shadow. The goblin mage gave the impression of steady calm, and that Tam respected him said even more. I knew for a fact it didn't take much to send Talon flying off the handle. I hoped Nath had more of a grip on his impulses than his nephew did.

I had to hand it to everyone—for a crowd of people, they moved almost without a sound. Other than his one question, even Talon was keeping his mouth shut. The kid was probably scared to death. He'd never been to Regor, and he certainly had never been surrounded by this many pure-blooded goblins. And if traveling with heavily armed goblin Resistance fighters bothered Piaras, you'd never know it.

The Guardian cadet uniforms and armor were helping both of them. There weren't any goblin Guardians, so perhaps the Resistance thought Talon must have been especially kick-ass in the magic and military departments to be recruited. Out of the corner of my eye, I saw two of the female Resistance fighters giving Talon the once-over. I knew that look. Heck, I'd given that look. These ladies weren't evaluating Talon's military prowess. Good thing the kid didn't notice those glances, or we'd never get him to shut up.

"Where are Mother and Father?" Tam asked his brother. "Are they safe?"

Nath hesitated, then he and Jash Masloc exchanged a tense glance.

"Where are they?" Tam's voice promised pain to whoever had made his parents not safe.

"Mother's fine," Nath told him. "If being in charge of the Resistance means that you're fine. For every one of our people the Khrynsani take, Mother and her agents kill two—or more if they can get them."

"Impressive," Imala murmured.

"If we had another couple of months, Mother could probably empty the Khrynsani temple."

I spoke. "Tam, a woman who's in charge of the Resistance and picks off Khrynsani doesn't exactly sound like a stay-at-home mom."

"Before she met our father, Mother was one of the finest mortekal in Rheskilia."

"Mortekal?"

"Loosely translated as 'noble taker of life' or 'righteous executioner.'"

"A mortekal doesn't kill for money," Imala explained. "They kill because it needs to be done. Though a mortekal will accept payment for expenses and any extenuating circumstances surrounding the target."

"There was a serial killer in the northern provinces that neither the local law enforcement nor the garrison there could stop," Nath said. "The people took up a collection and hired Mother. She had the bastard's head on a pike in a week."

"I'll bet you two never had a problem with bullies growing up."

"None," Tam said. He reached out and grabbed Nath by the shoulder. "You haven't answered my question. Where's Father?"

Nath's voice stayed steady. "There was an ambush. Our latest intelligence has him imprisoned in the temple dungeons."

"Sarad Nukpana is mine." Tam's words were low and calm and chilling as hell.

"You're welcome to him, but it was Sandrina Ghalfari who did the taking."

That name sounded familiar.

"Sarad's mother," Imala told me.

"That thing has a mother?" I blurted.

"Now she has joint command with Sarad," Jash said. "His injuries prohibit him from assuming all of his duties. Plus, the scope of their plan is too large to be handled by one person alone. It seems Sarad trusts Sandrina enough to share power with her."

"Such a nice son," I muttered. "Until she turns her back."

"Or until he turns his," Tam said. "Sarad is merely insane. Sandrina is evil."

"She'd give the demon queen a run for her money?"

Tam nodded once. "Sandrina Ghalfari poisoned and murdered my wife. She did the same to her husband to secure his title and fortune. Now she has taken my father. Her life is mine."

The tunnel began a gradual upward slope and the ground beneath our feet from packed dirt to solid rock. I was relieved to see the walls and ceiling do the same thing.

When Jash Masloc stopped, we all did.

My hand crept toward my sword hilt as I peered into the dark beyond the torches' light. Nothing but a lot of dark, but that didn't mean there wasn't anything inside.

"We're coming up on the base of the city walls," Jash said. "Sarad Nukpana has sensors anchored to the top every fifty feet."

"To sense what?" Talon asked.

"Magic," Jash said. "And yes, they can sense all the way down here, so push your magic down as far as it will go."

I hoped Talon knew how to tamp. Surely, Tam had taught him how, but had the kid been listening when he did? We were about to find out the hard way.

Back when the tunnel walls were still dirt, Jash had told us the plan. If we passed under the walls and into the city without incident of the ambush kind, we'd be splitting up. It was the best plan I'd heard all day.

In my opinion, sneaking was an activity best done solo. If others had to tag along, there shouldn't be more than a handful sharing the shadows with you. Any more than that and you'd be tempting fate, luck, and any anything else you'd care to name. That we'd made it this far undetected was a towering testament to goblin stealth and elven desperation. Once we were inside the city, we'd be moving even faster than we had been. That was something else I was all for. Movement kept sitting ducks from becoming dead ducks.

Jash signaled us to stay put and walked forward on nearly silent footfalls. The flame of his torch illuminated a ragged opening only the height and width of an average man.

The city wall of Regor. Home of Sarad Nukpana, the Khrynsani, and the Saghred—all of whom wanted me dead and gone, and the more painful they could make my death, the better. To make the experience even more enjoyable, it appeared that we'd have to go through the opening in that wall single file. Alone.

Great.

Hopefully no one's magic would hiccup when they passed through. I felt more than a few nervous glances on me. I had news for them; my magic wasn't what they needed to worry about. Sarad Nukpana had been close enough to me on numerous occasions to have set those sensors to *me*, not just to my magic. If that was the case, we were all screwed. It wasn't like I could tamp down myself.

"I'll go through first," Jash told us. "Nath, you follow. That'll test the sensors against mage and mundane."

Imala spoke. "If you weren't detected when you went through the first time—"

"The first time, Sarad knew Raine Benares wasn't with us," Jash reminded her. "Thanks to the spy orb that Khrynsani captain was wearing, Sarad may now know differently. If he knows she's here, he's had ample time to have the sensors recalibrated."

To me. Or to anyone who had the bad luck to be with me.

"Sorry about that," I said.

"We're not," Nath chimed in. "We live for flipping off Death."

"If those sensors could be set for me, then I should be the last one through." I kept my voice down for the obvious reasons, but spoke loud enough that the goblins heard me. They'd probably volunteered for this duty, but it never hurt to make nice with the locals. Nothing said nice like giving your new allies a head start on running for their lives if I set off those sensors.

A few of the Resistance fighters graciously inclined their heads in my general direction; a couple more gave me what might have passed for smiles under better circumstances.

All of us had our magic locked down tight. Well, all of us except for me. My magic was probably on vacation on a sunny beach somewhere, toying with the idea of never coming home.

"I'll wait as well," Mychael said.

Piaras stepped forward. "Me, too."

I shot him a look that summed up what I thought of that idea.

Piaras wasn't backing down. "I'm a Guardian cadet and our sworn duty is to guard and protect the Saghred and prevent it from being wielded by those who would use that power to destroy."

It sounded like he was quoting out of the Guardian handbook or something. Heck, if there was one, he'd probably already memorized the thing.

A mischievous grin flitted across his mouth. "Just doing my sworn duty."

"You've been talking to Vegard too much."

"My conversations with Sir Vegard have been highly educational."

"I'll bet."

Talon slid up beside Mychael, speaking in a whisper out of only one side of his mouth. Impressive. "Is guarding Raine a required Guardian cadet activity?"

Mychael fought a smile. "No, Cadet Nathrach. It's not."

Talon's shoulders sagged in relief. "Oh, good." He glanced at me. "Don't take it the wrong way, but you're dangerous to be around."

"I've noticed that. I don't want to be around me, either."

Tam clapped a hand on his son's shoulder. "You're going through with me."

"With?"

"To make sure that magic of yours doesn't spring an ill-timed leak."

Jash and Nath squeezed through the crack in the city wall without incident. The other goblins followed, including Prince Chigaru and Imala.

Chigaru didn't have any magic. Odd how the family who had ruled the goblins for the past two thousand years didn't have a spark of magic to their names. A few could sling a respectable spell in a pinch, but for the most part, they were all nulls. Which said a hell of a lot about their other skills—like terrifying their subjects. There had been coup attempts down through the centuries, but if one Mal'Salin went down, there was always another waiting in the wings.

If our lives suddenly decided to turn ideal, Sathrik and Sarad Nukpana both would choke on a chicken bone, preferably at the same time, emptying the big chair and the space behind it for Chigaru and Tam.

Carnades was next to go through the opening.

The elf mage had slithered his way to one step away from being archmagus. Carnades was patient, waiting for the chance to make his move, be it in politics or getting his chains around my neck. He went through without a peep. Those magic-sapping manacles were downright handy.

Tam and Talon went through together, with both of Tam's hands on Talon's shoulders. If the kid didn't like it, he kept his opinion to himself. He knew what was waiting inside those walls. Staying on Mid and reporting to Vegard during a goblin invasion probably looked like sweet duty right about now. Mychael kept a hand on Piaras's shoulder. He knew Piaras's abilities, and that the kid could squelch his own magic, but now wasn't the time to take chances. We'd be taking plenty of those later.

It was my turn.

I could swear I felt the air pressure drop as everyone took a deep breath and held it. Mychael and Tam remained on the other side of the opening, the torchlight showing me their expressionless faces. They knew as well as I did that Sarad Nukpana could have had something other than magic being picked up by those sensors. Magic was the only thing they could help me cover up, so taking the next couple of steps without setting off alarms throughout the city was all up to me.

I tried to empty my mind, which shouldn't have been that much of a challenge, and went with the breath-holding thing, too. As I stepped through, my heart decided to skip a couple of beats. That part wasn't my idea, but I wasn't opposed to the sensors picking up a dead person if they noticed anything at all.

Nothing.

At least nothing I could hear. Everyone else was looking up and around like they expected Khrynsani to drop through the ceiling or jump through the walls. Neither happened, and my heart started beating double time again. I told myself it was just making up for stopping for a second there, not that I was scared out of my wits.

Jash motioned for us to follow him. There were three directions open to us. Two appeared to go to the right and left of the opening, running against the city walls. We'd followed Jash into the one that went straight—and apparently deeper into the city. The rest of the Resistance fighters split into two groups and disappeared down the two tunnels running along the city walls.

Nath drew close to Tam and Mychael. I was close enough to hear him. "The others will make their way to our other hideouts."

Tam exchanged a look with Mychael. "And we're going where?" he asked.

Nath gave his brother a genuine, warm smile. "Home."

I could see why a race that wasn't that fond of sunlight would have tunnels running under their city. Though if they got us from here to wherever and whatever Nath referred to as home, I had no problem with them. The problem I did have, had everything to do with the tunnels' condition. The floor was completely smooth with no loose paving stones or chipped walls to trip on. The tunnel looked well maintained and well . . . used. A lot. And it stood to reason that they were maintained by city workers, which was part of the government, all of which was King Sathrik Mal'Salin. To my overactive and paranoid imagination, every new curve and turn in the tunnel was a Khrynsani ambush waiting to happen.

Piaras was staying every bit as close to me as Vegard always had. I didn't want Vegard to be here, but at the same time I missed my big Guardian bodyguard. My shadow was definitely feeling lonely without Vegard's solid and reassuring presence to keep it company. I didn't want to think about what he was going through right now. From my bodyguard to acting paladin on Justinius's proclamation, and then, on top of that, dealing with a probable dress rehearsal for a goblin invasion. Was Vegard's biggest problem invading goblins or pigheaded Conclave mages questioning his authority? Had the goblin soldiers stopped streaming through mirrors and mini-Gates once we'd dived through Carnades's mirror? Or had they seen an opportunity and taken it?

Along with any students and mages they could get their hands on.

Mychael's knights were good; they were the best, but outnumbered was outnumbered, and with attacks coming from all over the city—

"They're going to be fine," Piaras said quietly.

I gave him a sidelong glance. "So now you can read minds, too?"

"No, I'm just worrying about the same things."

"Is Katelyn evacuating with the other students?"

Piaras nodded once. "I put her on Phaelan's ship myself. She didn't want to go, and neither did a lot of the other girls."

Katelyn was Katelyn Valerian, Piaras's girlfriend—and Justinius Valerian's granddaughter. I'd met some of Katelyn's friends. Those girls could sling spells faster and fight better than half of the Guardians' cadets. Ever since their inception when the Isle of Mid was founded over a millennia ago, the Guardians had been an all-boys club. Since coming to the Conclave college, Katelyn had been a thorn in her granddaddy's side about changing the rules to let girls compete for places in the Guardians' cadet corps. If I made it back to Mid in one piece, I'd be having a chat with Justinius on those girls' behalf. They deserved the chance.

Piaras was smiling. "And I told Phaelan if he didn't keep his hands off Katelyn, I'd fix it so he'd turn into a sea slug at every high tide."

"You don't know how to do that."

"Phaelan doesn't know that."

"He bought it?"

Piaras flashed a grin. "Hook, line, and sinker."

Priceless. I'd loved to have seen Phaelan's face.

If my cousin so much as looked at the girl wrong, he'd better hope Piaras got to him first. Justinius actually could turn him into a sea slug.

"He's too quiet," Piaras murmured.

I didn't have to be a mind reader to know he wasn't talking about Phaelan.

Carnades hadn't uttered a word since we'd left the cave. Surrounded as he'd been the entire time by armed goblins who knew how to use what they carried, even Carnades must have realized the smartest thing he could do was to keep his mouth shut. I didn't know if being manacled and surrounded by armed goblins was his worst nightmare, but it had to rank up near the top, though you'd never know it to look at him.

Carnades saw me looking at him. His eyes glittered, then reverted back to studied neutrality. If the elf mage was shaking in his designer boots, he'd decided he was the only one who was going to know about it.

Piaras was right. A quiet enemy was a bad enemy. Quiet tended to mean plotting, and eventually one way or another, plots bore fruit. I knew that Carnades Silvanus was hoping to harvest an entire orchard.

A piece of dark peeled away from the shadows just ahead.

I sucked in a breath and held it like it was my last. Considering what blocked the passageway ahead, it just might be.

A Magh'Sceadu.

It was tall, almost hobgoblin in shape—if hobgoblins were made of black ink. They were blink-of-an-eye fast, with bodies warm and pulsing, like living quicksand. Any part of you that a Magh'Sceadu pulled inside its body stayed there. I'd seen one of them just flow right over a Khrynsani black mage trying to contain it. One glide, one gulp, one gone mage. Magic attracted them and magic fed them, and mages were meals. The more magic you threw at them to defend yourself, the tastier a morsel you became. Khrynsani black mages created Magh'Sceadu to absorb and store magic. They then harvested the power for other purposes.

Like fueling the creation of a giant Gate.

Or feeding a certain starving rock.

Piaras and I had once faced six Magh'Sceadu in an abandoned section of Mermeia appropriately named The Ruins. The only reason we'd survived had been the Saghred. It'd used me as a conduit to force-feed all six more power than they could hold.

I didn't have the Saghred now.

"That's new," Nath commented, without moving anything, including his lips.

"And that's why there aren't any guards down here," Mychael murmured.

I swallowed hard. "Maybe it ate them."

"Why is it just standing there?" Piaras asked.

Talon's eyes bulged in disbelief. "Why are *we*?"

Tam slowly maneuvered toward the front. "It's not attacking, so it's probably full."

My stomach did a slow roll. "Full?"

"Though if we ran, it would chase us down," Imala said. "Do you have sentries in these tunnels?" she asked Jash.

"Not in this section."

"It's standing there as a beacon to other Magh'Sceadu," Tam said. "I can feel it."

"Ringing the dinner bell?" I asked.

"Jash, is there a way around that thing?" Mychael asked. "A quick way?"

As if by some silent signal, the Magh'Sceadu turned and flowed quickly down a side tunnel.

As a second one rose up right behind Talon.

The only thing between Talon and that Magh'Sceadu was about ten feet of space.

And me.

Talon just stood there, frozen in terror and disbelief. The sound that tore its way out of his throat tried to be a shriek, but the kid choked on it.

It moved. I didn't have time to.

The Magh'Sceadu passed me by, ignored me completely.

I didn't have magic. Talon did.

And now everyone knew that I didn't.

Including Carnades.

Piaras's dark eyes met mine for a split second. He'd seen me not use magic in the mirror room or in the cave against the Khrynsani, and that the sensors in the city walls set for the Saghred hadn't detected a thing when I'd passed through.

There'd been nothing to detect.

Piaras knew.

Disbelief and terror flashed across his face and hardened into determination. I couldn't save Talon, so Piaras would. He wouldn't fare any better than Talon. He knew that, but he was going to try anyway.

I wanted to scream in frustration, but I couldn't even get the thing's attention. To the Magh'Sceadu, I might as well not even exist.

It shot straight at Talon.

Chapter 6

Talon knew defensive magic, but none of it was going to work.

Everything slowed down to the speed that meant it was all over except the cleanup. Talon's lips formed the first word of a shielding spell. All it'd do for the Magh'Sceadu was coat Talon in a magical powdered sugar topping.

And I couldn't do a damned thing to stop him from being dragged inside of a nightmare.

I'd seen it before on the streets of Mermeia. I'd been trying to locate a missing elderly street magician. I'd found him through a seeker link, but a Magh'Sceadu had found him first. The old man had tried to fight back, his fists sinking into the Magh'Sceadu's towering mass like black quicksand. The rest of him followed. The thing hadn't taken him quickly. No one had been on that dark street corner that night. As the Magh'Sceadu had wrapped itself around the old man's head, I could hear his muffled screams coming from inside.

I wouldn't let that happen to Talon.

Tam lunged forward and threw Talon behind him, thrusting his hands palms out toward the Magh'Sceadu.

The thing stopped.

Tam and his power didn't.

Black magic was about as close to the Saghred as mortals could get. However, the power of the strongest black mage was a grain of sand on the beach compared to what the fully fed Saghred could do, though the penalty for using that magic was the same. You used it, and it used you. The payback wasn't immediate, but the magic would get what it wanted. Like borrowing money from loan sharks—when it came time to pay, you could run, but you couldn't hide. They'd get back what they loaned you, with interest, and they'd be perfectly happy taking it out of your hide.

Black magic would gleefully carve it out of your soul.

Tam got the power boost now. He knew he'd pay later.

A dark shimmer, like morning mist rising off a harbor, formed around Tam's extended hands. The Magh'Sceadu shifted uneasily. At least that was the way it looked to me. The air in the tunnel grew heavy, pressing down on us. Tam wasn't immune to his own spell; his shoulders bowed under the strain of increasing its power. The tunnel got darker, even darker than it already was. Shadows spread like oil outward from Tam's hands to coat the floor, walls, and ceiling. I shook with sudden cold, as if the darkness suffocated not only the light, but what little warmth the air held. Normally when a mage of Tam's strength gathered their power, the air around them was charged with it, crackling with the intensity of magic about to be unleashed.

This was different. This was wrong.

Anti-magic.

I couldn't imagine anything else that would work on a Magh'Sceadu.

Emptiness spread from Tam's fingers, radiated from his body. In the sphere of his spell, in the spreading shadows was a void, an emptiness where magic was not, where life did not exist. Death was an absence of life; this was an absence of everything.

The Magh'Sceadu recoiled.

I wanted to.

"Run!" Tam's voice was tight with the strain of holding the spell.

An oily, glistening fog spread up the tunnel walls, flowing with increasing speed toward the Magh'Sceadu. It lapped hungrily at the edge of the creature's feet, base, whatever, sending it skittering backward a good ten feet. It stopped there, hovering.

It was too late to run.

From the tunnel where the first Magh'Sceadu had gone, more shadows separated from the dark. More Magh'Sceadu. Coming for us.

They charged. A roar of wordless fury ripped itself from Tam's throat, taking with it every last bit of endurance, strength, and power that he possessed, channeling it through his body and slamming it into the oncoming Magh'Sceadu. The darkness of Tam's black magic swallowed them in a wave. Magh'Sceadu didn't have voices, but that didn't stop them from screaming from inside that darkness, screaming like their countless victims had screamed. I didn't hear it; I felt it. Their screams climbed to a fevered, panicked pitch that vibrated in my bones.

Then silence. Nothing moved in the shifting darkness where the Magh'Sceadu and Tam had been.

Imala shoved Carnades aside. "Tam!"

Tam staggered out of the dark. He managed one step toward Imala before he collapsed.

The darkness of Tam's spell dissipated enough to see where the Magh'Sceadu had been.

Gone.

It'd taken the Saghred for me to destroy six Magh'Sceadu in The Ruins. Tam had taken out four by himself.

I didn't know how he'd done it, and right now it didn't

matter. Getting out of here did. Black magic made just as much noise as, if not more than, the regular variety. Sarad Nukpana and his Khrynsani minions would be listening for any and all of it. Worse, Nukpana knew that Tam was a dark mage.

The residue from the spell clung to Tam, spreading up his arms and over his chest. Tam was finished with the spell, but the spell wasn't finished with Tam. It had consumed four Magh'Sceadu, and it wanted more.

Talon darted around Piaras to get to his father. Piaras made a grab and missed. Nath didn't.

"It's not safe," Nath said through clenched teeth. He was finding out the hard way that Talon was stronger than he looked. It took both arms and all of his weight to hold Talon back.

"Safe?" Talon snarled. "He wouldn't hurt—"

"He wouldn't hurt you; his magic would," Nath said.

Jash and Mychael had sprinted down the tunnel toward Tam, stopping just out of arm's reach.

I saw why.

Tam was smeared with the gelatinous residue of his own black magic. He'd put everything he had into destroying those Magh'Sceadu. The monsters were gone, but the spell was still here. Tam collapsed before he could contain it, and the spell turned on him. If Mychael couldn't stop it from spreading, the spell would consume Tam as it had the Magh'Sceadu.

With a word and gesture, Mychael's hands glowed blindingly white, like twin suns. The spell covering Tam recoiled. Mychael quickly knelt and laid his hands on Tam's shoulders. With a sizzling hiss, the gel scuttled away from his glowing hands. Mychael's incantation came quickly, the words sharp, the tone commanding. He wasn't asking that black magic goop to leave; he was ordering it. The spell wasn't going without a fight, but it was going.

Everyone's attention was on Mychael and Tam.

Except one.

The only warning I got was the scuff of boots.

Carnades's shoulder rammed into my ribs, expelling what air I had, and we both went down. He landed on top of me, clawing at my neck with his fingers, desperate to get his hands around my throat.

"Filthy, lying bitch!" he spat.

This wasn't a straight-up fight. Neither one of us could use magic. Yeah, he was bigger than me, but those chains were just going to keep him from frying me and my throat like he had that Khrynsani in the mirror room. He could choke me the old-fashioned way just fine.

Carnades Silvanus had been directly or indirectly responsible for every attack and near fatality that either myself or the people I loved had endured since this whole crapfest started. Now Tam had almost died and worse to protect all of us—including Carnades.

I'd kept my temper and fists to myself.

No more.

I wanted to scream every murderous thought I'd ever had about Carnades Silvanus. But I didn't need words; my knees and fists and feet did it all for me. My torso was pinned under him, but my legs weren't. I couldn't ram my knee into his nuts, but all other options were wide open. I twisted hard toward Carnades, and pounded my right knee up into the base of his ribs. Once. Twice. Hard and harder. It felt good.

Carnades grunted with each blow, and his weight shifted off me for a fraction of a second. It was an opening, and I took it. I snarled and twisted again, landing a left hook to the side of Carnades's head. I was aiming for his temple, but hit closer to his eye. I wasn't picky. Any punch that landed on Carnades felt good.

A leather-armored forearm wrapped around Carnades's throat in a choke hold, jerking the elf mage off of me in one smooth move.

Piaras.

Oddly, Carnades wasn't trying to get his hands up high enough to dislodge Piaras's arm, and I caught a quick glimpse as to why.

He had a knife.

One of mine that had been tucked into my belt.

Piaras saw and acted. He snapped Carnades's wrist up and away from his body. The mage screamed. Piaras didn't break Carnades's wrist; that was up to Carnades. He could either drop the knife or kiss his wrist good-bye. I could have kicked that knife out of Carnades's hand, but Piaras had the situation well in hand. He had nearly as much reason to hate Carnades as I did, and I wasn't going to deny him some much-earned payback. The pressure of Piaras's arm locked around Carnades's throat was turning the elf mage's face a lovely shade of blue.

Carnades cut his losses and dropped the knife. Piaras dropped Carnades—on his face. His boot lodged firmly in the elf mage's back would keep him from getting any more bright ideas.

The entire fight happened too fast for anyone to jump in, though everyone knew I'd wanted that fight for a long time and that I didn't want any help.

Nath started toward me. I held out a hand, stopping him. "I'm fine, take care of Tam."

Nath glanced at Carnades's face. The elf mage had the beginnings of a beauty of a black eye.

"Nice," he said.

I panted and gave him a winded smile. "I take pride and joy in my work."

Mychael was on his feet, supporting a mostly conscious and all intact Tam. Mychael gave Piaras a quick nod of approval. Piaras tried not to smile. That wouldn't have been Guardianly.

Carnades spit out a mouthful of dirt, and if looks could have killed, we all would've dropped dead.

"Nath, where we're going, is there a place secure enough for our prisoner?" Mychael asked.

I didn't miss Carnades's change in status, and neither did anyone else.

Nath smiled wide enough to show his fangs. "Oh, yeah."

Raine doesn't have any magic. Oh hell.

It had to be what everyone was thinking, but no one was saying. We didn't have time to dawdle for questions.

Tam's anti-magic not only destroyed the Magh'Sceadu; according to Jash, it also wiped our trail clean. Unfortunately, the sudden absence of four Magh'Sceadu wouldn't go unnoticed.

That would tell whoever was monitoring that particular Magh'Sceadu pack that the hunters had become the prey. That would most definitely get the Khrynsani's attention. Not to mention the flare of magic that had gone up courtesy of Mychael. None of it could have been avoided. Though at least for the moment, there was no sign of pursuit.

Nath set a fast pace and we more than kept up. With Tam still trying to literally get his legs back underneath him, and Mychael and Jash all but carrying him, Imala took it on herself to keep Carnades motivated to keep moving. By the time we took our second and all-too-brief break, Tam was walking on his own and hadn't wanted to stop, but Mychael insisted. If he hadn't, I would have. Tam was leaning against the tunnel wall, the stone at his back barely keeping him upright. His head was back and he was panting.

Imala started toward him, but Tam waved her away.

"I'm fine," he managed.

"Bullshit."

"Don't . . . touch."

His skin would still be crawling from the spell's contact; the last thing he wanted was anyone touching him, especially anyone he cared about.

"If you fall flat on your face, may I touch you then?" Imala's voice dripped with sarcasm.

Tam gave her a weary smile. "Please do."

Regor's sewers were like the sewers in every other city I'd ever been in. I'd ended up in pretty much all of them, and they all looked the same: brick or rough-hewn stone usually covering dirt. Sometimes you got lucky and a ledge had been built on one side for maintenance workers to keep them from having to go wading. The maintenance workers in this section of Regor weren't lucky. No ledges. On the upside, there also wasn't anything to wade through. The stone pavers beneath our feet were stone dry.

"At least it's not wet," I noted. "And relatively rat free."

"This section isn't used much anymore," Nath replied. "The walls aren't in the best shape."

"Yeah, I've been trying to ignore that."

"A new system has been built either parallel or above these. The rats don't have much to eat down here, so they stick to the new system."

"So do the Khrynsani," Jash added.

"Vermin with vermin," Prince Chigaru muttered. "How appropriate."

The tunnel sloped gradually upward. I saw light up ahead, streaming down through a barred grate on the street above. Nath held up his hand. We stopped.

Tam's brother crept forward in complete silence. There was street debris hanging down from the opening. We must have been just beneath street level.

Nath turned and gestured to Tam, who moved soundlessly to stand beside his brother. He stood there looking out; Nath was watching him. A slow smile creased Tam's lips, though it was sad and bitter. Never taking his eyes from his brother's face, Nath gestured the rest of us forward. I had to stand on tiptoe, but I saw what Tam was seeing.

It was a street, residential, from the look of it, palatial from the grandeur of the houses along it. But it was one house in particular that had Tam's attention. Talon came quietly to stand beside me. He didn't need to stand on tiptoe.

In Mermeia, the only things comparable were palazzos along the Grand Duke's Canal. I knew that being the goblin queen's chief mage would have its perks, but dang.

Tam's house was four stories, constructed of pale stone and marble that still gleamed even after who knew how much neglect. An ornate black wrought-iron fence surrounded the property, with a gate opening onto a circular gravel carriage drive and front garden. Overgrown now, it still showed signs of having been elegant once.

"It's beautiful, Tam," I said quietly.

A ghost of a smile played across Tam's lips. "Yes, it is."

What wasn't so beautiful was the boarded-up windows, broken shutters, and a sign nailed to the front doors that I couldn't quite make out.

"What does it say?" I asked.

"Tamnais Nathrach, traitor to his king and his people," Nath said.

"What's the small print?"

Nath waved a dismissing hand. "Property of the king, trespass under pain of torture, death, dismemberment, etcetera, etcetera."

"And that's where the Resistance is holed up?" I asked. "Uh, isn't that a little obvious?"

"The Khrynsani have searched it more than once," Jash said. "And they continue to keep it under occasional surveillance, which is why we're never seen on the surface. Sometimes the best place to hide is the most obvious."

Nath flashed a huge grin. "We could hardly call ourselves the Resistance if we didn't spit in the king's eye every chance we get."

Words had been painted on the boards covering the windows. I could see those just fine. "Murderer" and "traitor" were some of the nicer things written about Tam on his own home. The others made my blood boil.

Tam was completely unruffled—at least on the outside.

"Khrynsani penmanship?" Mychael asked.

"Unfortunately not," Imala said. "The king has organized our youth into a feeder organization for the Khrynsani. You join or your loyalty and that of your entire family is suspect. Sathrik sees it as a way to get new blood from the old families. Young minds, easily influenced. Young men and women who are held up by Sathrik as the models of our next generation. The king honors them, promises them power, and fans the flames of hate and bigotry—then handsomely rewards those who act on his poisonous ideology."

All signs of playful humor were gone from Nath's eyes. "More than a few of them have turned in their own parents as traitors to the crown."

"And people think I'm trouble," Talon muttered.

The tunnel to Tam's house was guaranteed not to attract attention. Why disguise a doorway with magic when muck worked even better? The door looked like the rock around it; no seams indicated that anyone had ever thought of cutting a door through there. Then there was the icing on the disguise cake. Slimy and smelly icing. Icing no one would want to get near, never mind touch, at least not with bare hands. And to ensure that the slime and fungus growth didn't stand out, an entire section of the tunnel, both walls and ceiling, had been seeded with the furry fungus, gradually fading as it got closer to where the sun shone faintly from a grate in the street overhead.

The door opened into a wine cellar. Though there wasn't any wine here anymore; I guess that just made it a cellar.

Tam looked around, bemused. "Been drinking much, Nath?"

"On the king's orders, Sarad Nukpana confiscated all of

it when you left," Nath said. "As well as anything else he liked. The house has been pretty much stripped."

Tam didn't say anything, but I could see the additional items added to the tally of what Tam planned to take out of Sarad Nukpana's hide.

Racks lined the stone walls and ran in rows everywhere else. They were all empty. One rack had been made to hold casks. Likewise empty, except for a few smashed ones on the floor. The cellar was lit by small torches. Looked like we were expected. There were fine crystal lightglobes suspended from the ceiling, but they were dark. I guess even small light magic could attract Khrynsani patrols.

The torchlight was barely bright enough to reach the floor, but it was enough to see that the floor was covered with broken dark glass. Wine bottles. Someone had tried to clear a path to the stairs on the far side of the cellar, plies of glass shards mounded on either side of a path of exposed flagstones.

An elderly goblin stood motionless at the end of one of the racks. His clothes were dark and formal, and looked like a uniform of sorts. They had been carefully mended, and were as neat and proper as they could be, but they had clearly seen better days.

The old goblin stood straight and dignified.

Tears stood in Tam's eyes. "Barrett."

The butler indicated the wooden tray he held holding a single bottle. "The king appropriated the silver and the crystal, and either took or destroyed all of the wine. However, I managed to hide a case of your favorite port. I didn't think you would be inconvenienced by partaking from the bottle." He bowed slightly from the waist. "Welcome home, Your Grace."

Tam crossed the floor to Barrett in three strides, taking the port in one hand, and wrapping his other arm around the old butler's thin shoulders, pulling him into a hug.

Barrett's voice was muffled against Tam's chest. "Sir, this is unseemly."

"Yes, it is," Tam agreed, his voice thick with emotion, hugging him harder.

A voice came from the shadowed stairs.

"Will I get such a warm greeting?" said a low, feminine voice from the shadows. She stepped forward, the torchlight illuminating a silken sheet of hair so black that it had blue highlights. Her dark eyes shone with a sharp wit and keen intelligence. The goblin woman held herself with exaggerated dignity, as if she was uncertain of the reception she was going to receive—or undecided on what reception she was going to give.

Tam released Barrett, but other than that, he didn't move.

"Mother," he said quietly.

Chapter 7

"*I am glad you are home.*"

"Are you?"

"I am." Her half smile came tinged with sadness. "Though if I were not, could you blame me?"

Tam didn't hesitate. "No."

No one said anything for one long and very awkward minute. At least. Anything I could have said wouldn't even have put a knick in the tension in that air, so I kept my mouth shut. And yes, it is possible.

I didn't need any kind of link with Tam or to be a mind reader to hear the words between the words. Tam had hinted over the years at the damage done to his family when he embraced black magic, and again when he'd been forced to flee Regor after his wife's murder.

Wordlessly, Tam gave the bottle of port back to Barrett and walked slowly toward his mother, stopping just out of arm's reach. Wise man.

"I have shamed my family, my family name, and the

ancestors who gave it to me," Tam said. "I do not expect nor deserve forgiveness for my choices and actions. I have come home to offer my service, my devotion, and my life if need be. I only ask that you would do me the honor of accepting it."

Lady Deidre Nathrach took one step toward her son and, for a few silent moments, did nothing. Then she gently put her hands on either side of Tam's face, drew his forehead down to her lips, and kissed him softly. With a trembling sigh, she touched her forehead to his.

Tam's breath shuddered.

I sniffed. A couple of others sniffed from the shadows.

Tam's arms remained by his side, and he bowed his head farther.

Deidre Nathrach's hands dropped from Tam's head to his shoulders, wrapping her arms around her son in a fierce embrace. With a soft cry, Tam returned the embrace, lifting his mother's feet off of the floor.

"Candle smoke," Nath said, noticing my sniff. "There's no accounting for cheap wax."

I dabbed at my eyes. "So that's what it is."

Deidre released Tam, but their heads remained close, whispers between a mother and son that no one else needed to hear.

When they parted, Tam introduced Mychael, Piaras, and me. No doubt, Lady Nathrach knew Imala and Prince Chigaru.

Once again, he stopped when he got to Talon.

Talon was standing in the shadows, as close to the door we'd come in as possible. Tam glanced at him and winked. The kid didn't move. If he hadn't still been standing upright with his eyes open, I'd have said he'd quit breathing. Tam seemed confident of his mother's reaction to a half-breed grandson. Talon was only going to believe it when he heard and saw it.

"Remember when I was eighteen and went to Brenir for the summer?" Tam asked his mother.

"How could I forget?" Deidre said. "A few of your more memorable antics nearly caused an inter-kingdom incident."

"That's not all," Tam said.

Terrified or not, Talon's sense of drama wouldn't let him pass up an entrance line like that. "He got an unexpected souvenir."

Talon's bravado ended there. Oh, he still stood straight and tall, his trademark devil-may-care expression on his face, but the truth was that Talon did care. Nath had accepted him readily enough, but Lady Deidre Nathrach was a woman whose opinion and regard Tam clearly cherished. Tam had accepted Talon, risking his reputation, high social standing, and even his life to protect him.

Talon was terrified of losing all of it.

Terrified that if Deidre Nathrach rejected him, Tam might be forced to do the same. I knew it was ridiculous, but what was running through Talon's mind right now had nothing to do with logic and everything to do with keeping his knees from knocking together.

Tam's mother didn't move. "Come closer," she told Talon.

Talon did. Reluctantly. He'd been standing in the shadows. Between him and his new grandmother was light, not a lot of it, but enough. Deidre noted Talon's light skin and his aquamarine eyes. He inclined his head to her and clearly thought about leaving it there. But he took a breath, raised his head, and unflinchingly met his grandmother's sharp eyes.

She spoke to Tam, but her eyes stayed on Talon. "Is he impulsive, stubborn, arrogant, and believes himself irresistible to women and impervious to death?"

Whoa, that sounded familiar. I bit my bottom lip to stop a grin.

Tam suddenly looked like a schoolboy who'd been caught doing all of the above. "Yes, ma'am."

"And how much trouble does he either create for himself or attract on a daily basis?"

"All of it."

Deidre looked at Talon, her lips curling slowly into a crooked smile. "If that is the case, you are most definitely your father's son." She turned to Tam and smiled until her fangs showed. "Payback is indeed hell, isn't it?" she all but purred.

Tam sighed. "You don't know the half of it."

"I'm quite certain that I will be finding out."

Tam gave his son "the look." "You won't find out because there will be nothing to see since Talon will be on uncharacteristically *perfect* behavior. Do I make myself clear?"

"Perfectly," Talon replied without hesitation.

The kid's eyes had a twinkle that didn't bode well for any promises, stated or implied. Tam had merely asked Talon if he'd understood him. The kid understood just fine; it didn't mean he was going to do it.

It wasn't like Tam to not cover all contingencies. Seeing his mom again after a couple of years must have rattled his cage. Though anything Talon promised not to do was going to get done anyway if the situation presented itself. Tam should have simply saved his breath.

Besides, Talon keeping his nose clean would signal the end of the world as we knew it.

Unless Sarad Nukpana and the Saghred beat him to it.

Imala and Tam were greeted with smiles and handshakes. Prince Chigaru was welcomed with respectful bows.

I felt about as wanted as something that came in the house on the bottom of someone's boots.

It wasn't disgust exactly, more like they saw me as something useful, but something that no one wanted to be anywhere near. Kind of like a having a rat problem and being forced to get a really big snake.

"Ain't it grand to feel wanted," I muttered.

"Pay them no mind, Raine," Imala said. "It's your power

that frightens them. You've become quite legendary, you know."

I snorted. "If only they did know."

"And they can't," Imala whispered back while smiling reassuringly to an older gentleman who looked ill at ease in his armor. He had a single long dagger tucked into his belt. Probably the only weapon they trusted him to have. Others looked much the same: all armed, all scared, but all determined to topple their king.

It was a mass suicide waiting to happen.

They were probably hoping that I'd go first.

Deidre Nathrach ushered us into what she and Tam called the dining room. I would have called it a banquet hall, albeit a banquet hall that'd had a rough time of it recently: shredded wallpaper; most of the gilt trim hacked off; and holes either punched, kicked, cut, or chopped into the walls.

However, the dining room had the benefit of being in the back of the house. The windows were boarded up from the outside and the curtains were drawn on the inside. We could light candles, but couldn't have a fire in the fireplace and risk smoke from the chimney giving us away. The table was intact. I guess it'd been too big for Sarad Nukpana to get it out the door, and he decided not to have it chopped to bits. The thing was big enough to seat at least two dozen people. The Khrynsani had left enough chairs so that we all could sit down. My feet and back had never been so grateful. Our supply packs were necessary, and they weren't particularly heavy—for the first couple of miles. After that, I'd started wondering how much I actually needed food and weapons.

"Tell me what happened to Father," Tam asked his mother.

"He had taken a team to intercept a shipment of weapons going from the harbor to the Gate construction site. Your father knew we needed those weapons." Force of will kept any emotion from her face. "They were ambushed."

I remembered the old goblin with the one dagger. Perhaps it was all they'd had to give him.

Imala scowled. "Betrayed."

Deidre nodded once. "The Khrynsani were waiting for them. Four were killed; the other four captured. Cyran was among those captured."

"Do you have proof that he's still alive?" Tam asked.

"One of our lookouts witnessed the attack. They saw Cyran loaded into a prison wagon. He'd been wounded, but not fatally."

Tam shifted uneasily. "I take it he knows where all the cells are based."

"Yes," she said tightly.

That one word said a lot. It implied another word. Torture.

"We'll be in another location before tomorrow night," she added.

As the leader of the Resistance, Cyran Nathrach would know where their bases of operation were, their plans, the names and cover identities of their agents. Everything. He would definitely know about this house. Tam's father would probably be more valuable to Sarad Nukpana alive than dead, but with Nukpana, "alive" covered a lot of ground. It didn't matter how strong you thought you were; everyone had a breaking point. And if anyone could torture you to that point quickly, it'd be Sarad Nukpana. Deidre was Cyran's wife, but now she had to be a practical leader.

"When was he taken?" Tam asked.

"Two nights ago."

Damn.

Tam's expression darkened. "Nath said he's in the temple dungeons—and that Sandrina Ghalfari was with those who ambushed him."

"She was. Word we have received said that it was she who knew where our people were going to be that night. Sandrina was always a bright girl. A narcissistic, conniving, overdressed and underbred murderess, but bright."

If those weren't catfighting words, I didn't know what were.

"Sarad and Sandrina have been locking away anyone capable of opposing him," Deidre continued, "either directly or by their influence. Our most powerful mages and best military minds are locked in those temple dungeons." Growing anger made her voice sharper. "We had a team trained and ready to destroy that Gate Sarad's building outside the city. They were captured the same night as Cyran. Every last one of them are in those dungeons."

"Do you have someone on the inside?" Imala asked.

Deidre shook her head. "Not among the dungeon guards."

"I have two agents who—"

"Dalit and Airan?"

"Yes."

"They're already working with us," Deidre said. "Airan has told me which of our people are in the general dungeon population, but the high-ranking prisoners are being kept apart from the others. That is all he was able to find out."

"I know where those cells are," Imala said.

"So do some of our most gifted people, both mage and mundane," Deidre countered. "They can't get anywhere near them."

Tam's smile was chilling. "They didn't spend five years at the queen's side and live to tell about it."

"What does that have to do with—"

"Hiding and hearing, Mother. I know several passageways around the palace *and* the temple. Many a night I stood between the walls listening to my enemies—both court and Khrynsani—plot my death. I'm alive, most of them are not."

"I also know of several ways into the temple," Imala said.

"How many guards are around the Saghred?" Mychael asked.

"I can answer that one, Paladin," Jash Masloc said. "Fifty guards around the clock since it arrived. However, those are just the ones in the temple and within sight of the altar. Unfortunately for anyone's long-term health and survival, those fifty Khrynsani weren't taking their eyes off of the Saghred. Though I believe the Khrynsani refer to it as worship."

Those boys definitely weren't going to like what we wanted to do to their newest deity. Stabbing and shattering weren't going to go over well at all. I didn't harbor any illusions that yelling, "Hey, look! Something shiny!" would get them all to look the other way while we got destructive on their precious.

Mychael told her the plan—Kesyn Badru, the Reapers, the rock, and us. When he finished, the room was silent again, this time with shock and a healthy heaping of disbelief.

Deidre glanced at Tam, a trace of amusement in her eyes. "I must say, my darling boy, that you and your friends are taking our family's reputation of adventurousness to the point of insanity."

"Someone has to take the big chances."

Deidre closed her eyes and let out a resigned sigh. Then she opened her eyes and regarded Mychael. "Paladin Eiliesor—"

"Mychael, please."

Deidre smiled slightly. "Mychael. Isn't there any way to avoid unleashing Armageddon? Sarad seems to have already taken care of that. Wouldn't your plan be unnecessarily redundant?"

"If there was any other way, we would do it," he assured her.

"And Tamnais, you believe that Kesyn Badru, the teacher you publically turned your back on and whose career you unwittingly ruined, will help you summon these Reapers."

"He always hated Sarad, and the feeling was more than mutual," Tam said. "A chance to ruin Sarad's dream of world domination? Kesyn would never forgive me if I *didn't* let him have a piece of that."

Jash spoke. "Mistress Benares, I take it that you will be using your unique skill set to clear a way to the altar once we're in the temple?"

Tam raised a brow. *"We?"*

"Of course, 'we.' I'd never forgive you, either, if you didn't let me have a piece of Sarad Nukpana." Jash looked at me, waiting for his answer.

I looked back at Jash.

Silence.

"Is there something I should know?" While Jash's question was directed at those of us who'd come from Mid, his eyes were on me.

Just because no one had said anything about the Magh'Sceadu ignoring me and making a beeline for Talon didn't mean they didn't know what that implied. My ribs and I had no doubt that Carnades knew. Yes, if any of us used magic we'd essentially be sending up a flare for Sarad Nukpana and his Khrynsani to locate us. But if there was no way out, no way to survive other than using magic, these goblins were counting on me being able to lay waste to whatever or whoever was about to do the same to us, namely fifty worshiping Khrynsani. The only thing I could lay waste to right now was a good dinner. The Resistance needed to know—at least the people in this room should. Mychael and I'd agreed that if we had to admit to anything, we'd say that my magic had become unreliable after my last encounter with the Saghred. That was the understatement of the millennium. While not entirely the truth, it wasn't a lie. My magic could come back at any time. We didn't think it was going to, but we didn't know that for sure.

I glanced at Mychael and received a quick nod in return.

Oh, boy. Here we go.

I took a deep breath and dived in. "While vaporizing Sarad Nukpana and his boys would be the quickest—and undeniably the most satisfying—way to get to the rock, it's not exactly a realistic part of our plan right now."

No one said a word. Tam took a big swig of Barrett's rescued port straight from the bottle.

I wished I had some.

I hit the highlights of what had happened in the elven embassy dungeons, and how the Saghred had consumed an elven mage through me; and while the rock was at it, it'd given my magic a figurative kick in the teeth. However, I was still left with all of the fun of being linked to the thing.

Lady Deidre Nathrach was stunned. I suspected it was an emotion she didn't have much experience with. "You don't have any magic?"

I shrugged. "It comes and goes, ma'am." I decided partial truth would go down better than the full variety. I didn't think the spark I was occasionally able to muster counted as a resurgence of my magic, but it was better than admitting I was potentially a permanent mundane in a room full of goblins, one of whom—namely Prince Chigaru—didn't like me all that much to begin with. I'd rather keep the possibility open that if he messed with me, there wouldn't be anything left of him to mess with anyone else ever again.

Prince Chigaru had been sitting quietly through all this, his fingers steepled in front of his face. "When was the last time you had your magic?" he asked quietly.

I'd had the answer to that one ready to go. "Yesterday on Mid." I didn't mention that magic was a miniscule spark on the tip of my finger.

"Your magic vanishing, do you know before it happens?"

"No advance warning, if that's what you mean."

"It is." The prince turned to Imala. "Did you know about this?"

"I did."

"And you did not tell me." No direct accusation, just hard eyes. Mal'Salins didn't like being given bad news.

"It had no bearing on our mission. We had to come here regardless. We're taking many risks; this is merely one more, and Raine is bearing the brunt of it."

I had to hand it to Imala—if lying had been a profession, she could have made a fine living doing it.

"Besides," she continued coolly. "How do you think Raine feels?"

"What Raine feels is not—"

"Highness," Imala reprimanded.

"It must concern her greatly." The prince's verbal turnabout was quick enough to give him whiplash.

Turnabout notwithstanding, Chigaru was still unhappy, which likely was a cover for fear. It was my experience that creatures with fangs tended to react badly to fear, so I wasn't going to show any of my own.

I offered a nonchalant shrug. "I'm adapting."

Tam stepped in. "Right now, we need to find Kesyn Badru."

"Good luck," Jash said. "No one knows where he is."

"Is there a chance he was captured?"

Deidre shook her head. "We'd know by now. None of our people in the palace or temple have heard of him being brought in."

Jash gave a short laugh. "Impressive as hell considering Sarad's been pulling out all the stops to find him."

"What did he do?" I asked.

"Kesyn Badru was also Sarad's teacher."

I blinked at Tam. "He taught *both* of you?"

Deidre's lips twitched in a smile. "Some men attract more than their share of bad luck."

I jerked my head toward Talon. "Worse than this one?"

"Infinitely."

Jash spoke. "Mistress Benares, excuse my bluntness, but if you don't have any magic, then why are you here?"

"I really don't have a good answer to that—at least not a sane one. Me getting myself bonded to the Saghred started this whole mess, so I'm here to do everything I can to end it." I tried a smile, but it probably came off looking as scared as I felt. "You guys aren't the only ones who live for flipping off Death."

Chapter 8

Our meeting was over, and Mychael and Tam were speaking in hushed tones with Jash Masloc in the wide hallway outside the dining room. A young goblin, entirely too small for the sword he wore, stood quietly behind Jash waiting for them to finish. He held a folded stack of what appeared to be clothing.

Imala strode down the hall toward us, carrying a small stack of handbills.

She handed them to me. "Confirmation that Sathrik and Sarad know we're here, and have for at least long enough to get these produced and distributed throughout the city."

Piaras stepped up and looked at them over my shoulder.

Wanted posters.

Crap in a bucket.

I flipped through them.

Me, Mychael, Tam, Imala, but not Chigaru. Interesting.

"Why isn't the prince included?" I asked.

"Sathrik's exile of Chigaru is considered a private, family matter," Imala replied. "To the people, Sathrik has gone out of his way to convey that he is 'greatly saddened and disappointed' by his brother's betrayal and abandonment of their people."

"*Abandoned?* I take it that's Mal'Salin-speak for forced to run and hide for years or be captured, imprisoned, and killed in a dark dungeon."

"Essentially, yes," she drawled. "You're getting good at this."

"It's never been one of my goals, though it's nice to know I'm good at something right now." I flipped through the posters, noting the amount of the reward on each one. "I guess we ought to be flattered. Sathrik's not being stingy for any of us. There's nothing less than a fortune on any of our heads."

The last two posters were of Piaras and Talon.

"So much for if Sarad Nukpana knows we tagged along." Piaras tried for a chuckle and it actually almost sounded like one. "My first wanted poster, and a respectable amount, too. Phaelan would be proud."

I wasn't proud. I was petrified. Nukpana knew Piaras was here. He wanted to get his sacrificial daggers into Piaras almost as badly as he wanted to do the same to me. He'd almost succeeded that night on an altar in The Ruins. The only way I'd been able to save him was by tricking Nukpana into touching the Saghred with his bloody hand. He'd never fall for anything like that again.

Piaras knew what that wanted poster meant, too. He'd been the one chained helpless to that altar, gagged so even his spellsinger's voice couldn't save him.

"Sathrik's putting his money where his mouth is," Tam said from behind me. "He wants us off the street and in a cell. Fast."

"He's afraid of us," Imala said. "The last thing he wants is a morale boost for the Resistance."

Mychael stood silently next to Imala. Jash was still talking to the young goblin, hopefully out of earshot.

"Carnades is locked down tight, right?" I asked him.

"Oh yes."

"What if he starts talking about, you know . . . Raine not having any magic?" Piaras asked. "Will anyone believe him?"

Tam smiled. "Carnades can talk all he wants to. No one will be able to hear him. I made sure that cell is and remains soundproof."

I blinked. "You've got a prison cell in your basement?"

"I didn't build the house. I simply make use of existing facilities."

Imala looked at Mychael. "Carnades Silvanus has violated the terms of his parole. I realize this prisoner is under your authority, but he's now on goblin soil. I am well within my rights—"

"To execute him," Mychael finished. "Yes, you would be well within your rights."

If Carnades had somehow managed to kill me, Sarad Nukpana could have immediately taken the Saghred's power and we'd all be worse than dead. We couldn't rely on Carnades in any situation, but his attack on me had been the final proof.

"The prince wants him dead," Imala said. "Now. I informed him that while we are now home, that you, Raine, and Piaras are not. So while Silvanus remains useful, I am concerned that the risk now may outweigh any possible usefulness later."

"We've got to find Kesyn Badru," Mychael said. "Forgive me for asking, Imala, but are the two guarding him among your best?"

"They are."

"Then that will have to do. Carnades isn't going anywhere. Kesyn Badru may have already."

Piaras cleared his throat. "Sir, you said I'm a member of the team. I want to help."

Mychael and Tam exchanged a glance.

"What is it?" I asked.

"Thank you for volunteering, Piaras," Mychael said. "We have to go out into the city and I need for you to stay here."

"But, sir, you—"

"I'm not finished, Cadet."

"Sorry, sir."

"You are to guard Prince Chigaru."

"Isn't Director Kalis—"

"Going to find Kesyn," Imala said.

"I've been away for almost two years," Tam said. "The city has changed a lot since then. We'll need Imala with us." He paused. "Piaras, I would consider it the greatest of personal favors if you would also keep Talon out of trouble while we're gone."

"No favor needed, sir. I've kind of assigned myself that duty anyway."

"And a fine job you've been doing."

"If you say so."

Tam wasn't being sarcastic and Piaras knew it. The times that he'd tried to keep Talon from running headfirst into danger, Piaras had ended up neck deep in it himself. However, they were both still here, and a large part of the credit for that went to Piaras.

I snorted. "Guarding Talon is almost as dangerous as guarding me. You've gone from apothecary's apprentice to bodyguard for the next goblin king in three short months. Impressive."

Piaras swallowed. "No pressure."

"Just do your best," Tam said. "That's all I or anyone else could ask."

"That much I can do."

"I'm going to give Talon the same duty of guarding the prince," Mychael told Piaras. "One, it'll keep him occupied. Two, perhaps the two of them will actually stay together and make it easier for you."

"Hopefully."

"Just try to keep both of them from doing anything stupid."

"Put them to sleep if you have to," Imala said. "You have my permission and blessing."

"And if you're found here and have to clear out," Mychael

continued, "do what you can to keep them together . . . and well, as safe as you can."

Piaras's eyes had gotten progressively larger with each word. I couldn't resist giving him a big slap on the back.

"No pressure on your first mission, huh? We get to find a mage who doesn't want to be found while playing hide-and-seek with Khrynsani patrols. It sounds almost tame in comparison."

Piaras looked at Mychael in mute appeal. Mychael was immune.

"I'm afraid that's an order, Cadet Rivalin. There's no way we're taking those two with us, and for everyone's safety and well-being, we can't leave them here under their own supervision."

Nath walked up and overheard. "You didn't assign Mother to him? Damn, I was hoping for some backup."

Tam smiled. "She too much for you?"

"And for you, too. Always has been. Speaking of too much to handle, you started the ball rolling that ruined Kesyn Badru's career. If he spots you first, you might just find him quicker than you want to."

Jash walked toward us carrying a stack of something dark. "Paladin, here are the clothes you requested."

Mychael jerked his head at Piaras. "They're for him."

"Change out of my uniform, sir?"

"If you have to step foot outside of this house, what you're wearing will get you killed. You'll attract less danger to yourself and others if you get out of that uniform. A Guardian isn't the uniform he wears, but the actions he takes."

Piaras looked down at the pile of miscellaneous dark clothing topped by a quilted leather arming jacket with steel plates glinting dully on the underside. It wouldn't keep out a bolt, but a crappy shot would probably be deflected. It would serve him well against most small-arms attacks. I'd prefer it if Piaras were encased in head-to-toe armor or, best of all, if he weren't here at all, but this would have to do.

Talon appeared from around the corner. He'd changed out of his uniform, too. Talon wearing dark clothes in less-than-optimal condition made him look like a young high-wayman who'd been too long between a good score—dashing, yet disreputable.

Talon picked distastefully at the frayed fabric. "I had to do the same thing." He shrugged. "I've worn worse." He brushed at mud that looked like it'd been on there a long time, and wasn't coming off anytime soon. "Once."

"It's called blending in," I told them both. "Sometimes being the center of attention only gets you killed first."

"Then I'll suffer the indignity," Talon said.

"I thought you might."

"One more thing, Cadets." Mychael handed each of them a gorget. The steel collars were high enough to protect their throats with a bib of overlapping armored scales to keep a blade from going up underneath it.

Talon took the gorget, but held it with as few fingers as necessary. "And I would want to wear this because . . . ?"

"Because the preferred way to kill a spellsinger is with a bolt through the throat," Tam told him.

Talon's eyes got a little wide. "Got anything bigger? Even tackier, perhaps?"

"Where was the last place your teacher lived?" I asked Tam.

"The oldest section of the city, near the south wall."

"One of my people told me that the Khrynsani have searched it before," Imala said, "and still have it under surveillance."

"We've also eliminated the next two most likely places Kesyn would be," Tam said. "Jash says one burnt to the ground six months ago, the other is being used by the Khrynsani as a base of operations in the outer city."

"Which leaves us with . . . ?" I prompted.

"One of the last places any of us want to go."

Chapter 9

Sneaking was best done at night.

But when the people you needed to avoid were goblins, broad daylight was the way to go.

It wasn't like we were strolling down the middle of the street, but I still felt as naked as the day I was born. Though I had to admit there was something strangely liberating about doing my sneaking and death dodging on a sunny afternoon. It almost made me forget there was a humongous price on my head.

Almost.

Sarad Nukpana and his allies were in control of the city. Goblins weren't fond of direct sunlight, so they stayed inside if at all possible. That simply meant we weren't likely to see as many goblins on the streets, and any goblin out and about would be cloaked and hooded. Worked for us. Mychael and I could hide pale skin, ears, and eyes that were a color other than black. We were cowled, cloaked, and cautious.

Where Imala was leading us, we saw more rats than

goblins. In fact, we didn't see anyone—but that didn't mean no one was seeing us. Since it was the middle of the day, empty streets and shuttered shops shouldn't be all that unusual. But too many of the shops I'd caught glimpses of through the alleys we'd passed weren't just shuttered; they were closed, and looked like they had been that way for a while.

Imala noticed me noticing.

"The people are afraid," she said. "My agents have told me that Sathrik no longer limits his arrests to magic users."

I frowned. "I imagine the Saghred will take plain old souls when it can't get the magic-flavored kind."

Imala nodded. "Sathrik knows that the people of this city are more than capable of rising up against him. Those who are able and willing are helping us."

"With the rest hiding behind locked doors until this is all over with."

"The majority of goblins are peace loving. All we want is to live our lives and raise our families."

"So where does the goblin national pastime of spying and intrigue fit into that?"

Imala smiled. "Between the living and raising parts."

It didn't look like this had always been the bad part of town. Though with Sarad Nukpana in charge, the entire city now shared that distinction. The town houses along the length of street we were on now looked for the most part as if they'd been abandoned, discarded for something new and trendy.

Kind of like what Tam had done to Kesyn Badru all those years ago.

And Tam felt responsible, at least to a point. Like many mage-wannabe teenagers, Tam had thought he wasn't being taught fast enough. Pretty much without fail, teenagers were confident that they knew everything; they underestimated their limitations and overestimated their abilities.

Magic wasn't only about casting spells and building wards; it was knowing when to do it—or, most important, when not to do it and why. That meant acknowledging your shortcomings, your weaknesses, and taking responsibility for the consequences of your actions—things a lot of egocentric, magically talented teenagers weren't keen on doing.

Sarad Nukpana and Tam had both been Kesyn Badru's students. Nukpana had chosen the dark path; Tam had rejected it—eventually. Now we were going to find Kesyn Badru and ask the guy to save civilization as we knew it by helping us.

By helping Tam.

Tam had reasoned that his former teacher would be hiding where no one would come looking for him—and he meant no one, not even Sarad Nukpana.

There was a house that was considered cursed, possessed, haunted, you name it; this place had it. And since the people doing the considering were goblins; that said a lot in my opinion. Before we'd left his house, Tam had given us the quick and dirty details on this place. People either went in and were never seen again, or they felt the sudden need to kill the friend who'd gone in with them. Down through the years, a few families had been stupid or suicidal enough to actually buy the place and move in. They ultimately came out in either coffins or straitjackets—and others had never come out at all. But the icing on the cake was when Tam told us that as a boy even Sarad Nukpana had been scared of the place. What scared you as a kid tended to stick. So if Kesyn Badru wanted to be left alone—and he did—there was no place he'd rather be.

Yeah, I saw this ending well. Kind of like Carnades being responsible for getting us safely home. Look how that had turned out.

We approached the house from the back, using a narrow side street that was little more than an alley running between the dark granite wall surrounding the house and separating it from the one next door. Roots had grown up underneath the walls and street cobbles, making walking a challenge; and the dead leaves crunching underfoot made doing it quietly impossible.

I'd noticed that more than a few of the more affluent goblin homes had sharpened iron spikes along the tops of their walls. They might have been meant as a deterrent to thieves; or, heck, considering that these were goblin homes, they may have been meant to be decorative for all I knew.

This house's wall didn't have spikes. It had vines. Vines whose sole purpose appeared to be growing thorns the length of my fingers with the sharpness of my favorite stiletto. They weren't decorative, at least not to me, but they were most definitely a deterrent. It told me one thing loud and clear—this house and Kesyn Badru did not want visitors. I wondered if he'd take into consideration that we didn't want to be visitors. If we'd had any choice at all, we wouldn't be lurking outside of the gates of his newly adopted home.

Above the wall and the thorns loomed a hedge. Beyond that I could just make out the house's roofline with the rain gutters ending at the eaves of the house in honest-to-God gargoyles that looked like some sort of goat demons. The place had "evil villain hideout" written all over it. It made me wonder what Sarad Nukpana's house looked like.

Unlike some of the other formerly fine homes we'd passed, there were no broken windows. Though with the overgrown bushes, I couldn't see the downstairs windows, so neither could any wandering pack of Sathrik's Khrynsani youth looking for some twisted fun. There wasn't any shattered glass on the second and third floors, either. One of the king's punks could have easily chucked a rock or ten that high. Either no one had the guts to try, or the house tossed rocks back at their throwers. Judging by the creepy-crawlies presently working their way up to my neck, either one was possible.

"So, based on your hunch, we're going into a house that makes people kill their friends."

Tam gave me a smile that looked more than a tad nervous. "Told you Regor was exciting." The smile vanished. "Kesyn doesn't consider me his friend; and I don't want to find out what this place would make him do to a brat who helped ruin his life. So be glad you're not me."

I glanced at one of the goat demons again. "I've been glad I'm not you for quite some time."

A rusted iron fence surrounded the grounds. By "grounds" I meant property. The place was so overgrown that I had no clue what the actual grounds looked like. A broken stone pathway led to what I assumed was the front door. I assumed because I couldn't see it for all the under- and overgrowth. Once we got close enough, I saw that one of the front doors sported the same sign as Tam's house—no trespassing by order of the king, resulting in death, dismemberment, etcetera. I wondered if the house had eaten the poor sot who had to nail the sign to the door.

The other door was opening slowly, complete with creepy creaking.

Normally, an open door would be a welcoming thing, but the knot in my gut found it even less welcoming than Sathrik's death and dismemberment sign.

Tam started forward. Imala got a hand on his arm, stopping him.

"We're dealing with a pissed-off mage who has who knows what lurking in those bushes. Plus, he hates you. And you propose to walk right up to a conveniently open door—"

"Which I don't think the wind opened," Mychael added. "Mainly because there isn't any wind."

"Psycho houses don't need wind," I muttered.

Mychael held a loaded crossbow pistol by his side, the tip of the small but lethal bolt bright with magic. I hadn't even seen him draw it.

"Think it's an invitation from a Khrynsani patrol?" he asked.

Tam's gaze grew distant. "I don't sense any."

"And I don't smell any," Imala added. "Would Kesyn Badru know if you were here?"

Tam tensed. "He always did."

My body decided to have itself a good shiver. "Well, that leaves either psycho house and/or psycho goblin."

Mychael's sharp eyes were fixed somewhere beyond that open door. "Okay, Tam. He was your teacher. How do you want to play it?"

"I'm going in. Alone."

"No one goes anywhere without backup."

"Then I go first."

Imala drew a curved short sword. "No one's going to deny you that."

I indicated the sword. "What are you—"

"In case we're not Kesyn's only guests today."

I kept my eye on the street. If a Khrynsani patrol appeared at the gate, we'd have three possible exits and none of them were appealing: charge into a pissed-off mage's hideout, hack our way through the undergrowth to hopefully escape, or hack our way through the Khrynsani patrol and hopefully survive.

Something scuttled and rustled its way through the undergrowth to our left, and I caught a glimpse of a pair of eyes that were way too yellow to belong to anything with friendly intentions. The rustling quickly scurried around behind us.

Imala's eyes suddenly went huge. I looked where she was looking.

Uh-oh.

I couldn't see the gate. It was probably still there, but I couldn't see it through the hedge that had moved—yes, moved—across the path. Our exit had just been completely blocked by plants, plants with roots that should've kept them from doing things like that.

Imala tapped Tam on the shoulder. He turned and saw.

"Kesyn ever do *that* before?" she asked.

"Son of a bitch."

"I'll take that as a maybe."

Mychael cautiously started toward the door. "Looks like we're being encouraged to come in."

We went inside.

The only light was from the open door, spilling a single beam of sunlight onto the black-and-white-tiled marble floor. Though neglect had turned that into black and dingy yellow. Above our heads was a massive wrought-iron chandelier, beyond that only featureless murk. Tam and Imala could see in the dark just fine. Neither of them went for additional weapons, so I assumed nothing carnivorous or merely homicidal was charging out of the dark at us.

In response, the door slammed shut behind us.

And locked.

Instantly my hand was on my sword hilt. I didn't draw it, but I wanted to. I really, really wanted to. But before the lights had gone out, the only people close enough to stab were friends. Hopefully they still thought I was a friend, not someone they suddenly decided needed murdering.

"Easy," Tam said, making no attempt to keep his voice down. Maybe he was talking to me; maybe to a mage whose door slamming might be about to escalate into deadly spell slinging.

Or a vindictive house.

"Easy," he repeated.

I'd take it easy, but I wasn't taking my hand off of my sword.

The lights slowly came up. Pinpricks of flame like tiny eyes grew into candlelight. Either Kesyn Badru or the house was being polite to a pair of night-vision-impaired elves, or he and/or it wanted to get a good look at our last expressions before he/it killed us.

Tam's home had been stripped clean. This house was badly in need of cleaning. It was all too obviously untouched, either by Kesyn, Khrynsani, or a housekeeper. The marble floor in the entry wasn't the only thing that looked like it hadn't been cleaned since Chigaru's mom was on the throne. A long hallway extended into spooky darkness on our right. The furnishings appeared to be nice enough, but it was difficult to tell for sure since everything was covered in sheets of cobwebs, moving as if with a life of their own in the disturbance of air when the door had slammed shut. I hoped we wouldn't be meeting the spiders that had made those.

"My nerves don't need this," I muttered.

"Well, that locked door will keep anyone from coming at us from behind," Imala noted.

"I'm more concerned about what'll come at us from the front."

"Sir," Tam called.

Silence.

Mychael shimmered slightly with a protection spell; Tam likewise shielded. Their combined wards reached back and around, enfolding me and Imala in their protection.

Imala gave an exasperated sigh, stopping just short of an eye roll.

"It's a big house, Tam," Mychael said. "If he'd barricaded himself anywhere, where would it be?"

Tam took a deep breath, closed his eyes, and I assumed tried to sense Kesyn Badru.

I began to sense the house.

I didn't hear any sound other than our own breathing, and nothing moved except for the shifting cobwebs. Yet I had a growing awareness of a presence, a solitary entity, not the haunting of spirits or demons that I'd expected. I'd never been able to detect anything like this before, even when I'd had my magic. Maybe the absence of magic enabled me to perceive other things, other levels of existence. Who knew? I certainly didn't. And the how and why didn't matter; finding Kesyn Badru and living long enough to get out with our sanity intact did. However, my awareness of this thing could be knowledge; and an opponent you knew was an opponent you stood a better chance of surviving.

The entity didn't live—or whatever—in the house; it *was* the house. Not merely the stones and wood, this thing had been here before the house had been built, buried for literal ages, deep in the bedrock below the foundation. When the house was built, its foundation bit into the bedrock containing the entity. Over the years it had become a part of the house itself, indistinguishable from the timber and granite. The closest my mind could comprehend was that the house's wooden frame had become the entity's skeleton; the granite walls its outer shell.

It was ageless, crouched and waiting.

And it was hungry.

Like certain predators, the entity knew how to attract its preferred prey. People with volatile emotions, unbalanced minds, violent tendencies—the entity called to them when they passed close enough to the land and later the house built on the land that it had taken for its own. It called to them and eventually claimed them—as well as those who its seduced ones had brought with them—friends, lovers, family, children. It fed on the violent emotions of its chosen prey, and the terror of their victims.

Fed and was content.

The entity wasn't content now.

It hadn't called to us, and we sure as hell didn't want to be here. Which meant that none of us were certifiable, which was good to know. But just because none of us were nuts now didn't mean the entity didn't have the ability to make us that way, and the thing had locked the door so it could give it its best shot. It wasn't like we didn't have anything for the entity to work with. We all had violent tendencies aplenty. This thing hadn't survived and thrived for however long as it had by starving. When it hungered, it would feed, one way or another.

Exactly like the Saghred.

I hadn't fed the Saghred—at least not of my own free will. And I wasn't feeding this thing, either.

"Raine?" A voice called my name from far away.

I snapped out of my thoughts to Mychael's hands on my shoulders, shaking me.

I looked up into a pair of concerned and wary blue eyes: concerned for me, wary of what might be in my mind with me.

"Think happy thoughts," I told him.

His fingers tightened on my shoulders. "What?"

"This thing feeds on the other kind." I gave them the quick and dirty version of what I thought the house was and what it wanted.

Tam glared down the long hallway that suddenly seemed to have gotten longer. "Then let's get what *we* want and get out."

I'd like nothing more. Though other than Tam's process of elimination with Kesyn Badru's possible hideouts, we had no guarantee that the old man was even here. And if he was, had the house turned him into its pet loony—a magical heavyweight loony who believed he had every reason to strike Tam dead and anyone else in his immediate vicinity?

The entity didn't wait for the old man to put in an appearance.

It literally unleashed Hell.

Creatures out of a psycho's nightmare charged us from all sides, including overhead and underfoot. The floor buckled and tilted, sending us sliding toward the gaping maul of what looked like a giant rat with a mouthful of serrated fangs. Tentacles tipped with hooks shot up through the floor. I didn't have magic, but I had steel, and I put what I had to good use. Tam shouted two words of incantation, stopping Imala's slide into the rat's mouth as if she'd slammed into an invisible wall. The borderline panic in her eyes screamed how Imala felt about really big rats and somehow the entity had known it. Apparently the insight I had into it worked both ways. The entity knew what scared me, what scared each one of us. Since none of us were crazy, at least not to the point of making us a decent meal, the thing went with violence and terror. Either one would make us tastier to it, so the entity set about forcing us to strike at it, scare the crap out of us or, best of all, both.

My worst fears didn't take a genius to figure out. I wasn't what anyone would call complex, so my opinions, emotions, and fears all lived together close to the surface. The entity scooped them up like dice on a table. The Saghred, Sarad Nukpana, torture, dagger through the heart, eternity inside the rock—all were there for the knowing and exploiting.

Apparently Mychael, Tam, and Imala were better at hiding any fears they had, as evidenced by the increasing fury with which the entity attacked with anything in its arsenal.

Hornets the size of giant bats threw themselves by the dozens against Tam and Mychael's shields in sacrificial waves, their bodies bursting into flames on contact, making room for the next attack. The shields were holding, for now. But Mychael and Tam couldn't hold it for long. We'd all fought for our lives multiple times since breakfast, and Tam had taken out four Magh'Sceadu that had nearly eaten—

Four Magh'Sceadu appeared as if on cue.

Dammit.

"Sorry!" I yelled while trying to unthink them. It didn't work and wouldn't work, at least not with bat-hornets igniting inches from my face.

"Shut up!" The bellow seemed to come from everywhere at once. Neat trick. A master spellsinger's trick.

I froze; so did the others. Even the Magh'Sceadu looked around.

"Idiots! Get in here!"

Mychael and Tam's so-called impenetrable shield was ripped from top to bottom, opening it into the long hallway that wasn't dark anymore—and wasn't a hallway. A tunnel of blue light extended from the shield to what had been a blank wall. A small section was open and filled with an enraged old goblin, aged somewhere between sixty and roadkill.

Kesyn Badru, I assumed.

Tam hesitated, torn between possible death by the entity and equally likely death by his pissed-off teacher. That Tam was afraid of him—and that he'd ripped our shield like a piece of wet paper—told me Kesyn Badru was seriously badass. That was all I needed to know. I ran down the tunnel toward him. I'd take badass over bat-hornets anytime.

When I got within sniffing distance, I knew what the old man had been doing to pass the time while hiding out in a possessed house. Coming from a family of pirates, I knew what a crew coming back from shore leave smelled like. My nose told me loud and clear that Kesyn Badru had been on shore leave a long time.

Once the four of us were inside, he slammed the section of wall closed and rasped out some wicked-sounding words. The opening vanished, leaving us in a single room that had been sealed—walls, floor, and ceiling—with a thick, gelatinous coating. Ick. It must have been some kind of solid ward. Fortunately, the coating on the floor had hardened. However, since we were in here, and the entity and its playmates were out there, being in a room coated in ick was perfectly fine with me.

Kesyn Badru glared at us with some seriously bloodshot eyes. "What the hell are you trying to do, bring the roof down on my head?" He didn't pause for an answer; he just turned those bloodshot eyes on me. "You're that Benares girl, aren't you?" His eyes darted up and down, taking me in, inside and out. He snorted. "That's all you've got? I'm not impressed."

I just stood there and blinked. "Uh . . ."

Badru turned on Tam. "And thank you once again for fucking up my life," he snarled, "or what you left me of it. What are you going to do next, boy? Stomp my balls?"

The room shook like a toy building block some evil kid was trying to break in half.

That didn't even slow Badru down. "The best damned hiding place in the whole city, and you screwed it up."

Mychael put himself between the goblin mage and Tam. "Magus Badru, we need your help."

Something hit the other side of the wall next to me like a giant fist.

"What do you call what I just gave you?" Badru snapped. "And who the hell are you anyway?"

"Paladin Mychael Eiliesor of the Conclave Guardians," he responded in formal, flawless Goblin.

"Conclave, eh?" The goblin chuckled, a dry rasp that sounded like he hadn't used his voice for anything other than yelling in a long time. "Those old bastards send you here to save their wrinkly asses?"

"We came to destroy the Saghred." Mychael dropped the formality and went with angry paladin. Mychael had had it. We all had.

That got the goblin mage's attention.

"That's a fancy way to kill yourselves. I prefer staying drunk—and alive."

Something hit the ward over our heads with enough force that fist-sized gobs of ward goop fell from the ceiling. I barely avoided getting splatted with the stuff.

Badru didn't so much as bat an eye. His full attention had landed on Tam like a slab of granite. "Well, what do *you* want?" He actually didn't snap or snarl. "You come home after two years with the head lady of the secret service, the

Conclave's paladin, and that unfortunate elf girl who had the piss-poor luck to be in the wrong place at the wrong time with the wrong rock." He crossed his arms over his chest, smiling now, though some might say he looked more like a wolf that'd spotted its next meal. "What is it, boy?"

Tam told him everything. Why we were here, what we had to do, and when we had to get it done.

And how we needed his help to do all of the above.

"So, you need me to be your Reaper wrangler," Badru said. "If I'm all you've got, you're scraping the bottom of a bone-dry barrel. Am I your last hope, too?" he asked Tam. "Or are you just slumming and playing tour guide for your friends?"

Tam drew himself up and I half expected to hear something Talonesque come out of his mouth. He surprised me. "Sir, you're our *only* hope."

Tam had been eating an awful lot of humble pie since we'd arrived. It looked like he was developing a taste for it. Swallowing your pride might choke you the first time you had to do it; but apparently the next one went down a little easier.

"You were disgraced and banished because you refused to step back from what you stood for," Tam continued. "You refused to teach rich, young thugs a level of magic they had neither the morals nor restraint to learn." He paused. "I was foremost among them."

The old goblin's eyes glittered. "You think so?"

"I know so. I've turned from the dark path."

"Yeah, I've heard people talking. Talk isn't necessarily the truth."

"I have renounced black magic."

Kesyn Badru's sharp black eyes looked like they were boring through to Tam's soul. "Not entirely, you haven't."

Tam shifted uneasily. "When there is a great need, when no other magic would—"

"Save lives," Mychael said. "Sometimes it is necessary to do what is distasteful for a greater good."

Badru studied Tam, all signs of drunkenness gone. "And you think you've grown enough sense to tell the difference?"

"I'm trying, sir." Another slice of humble pie. "Knowing the right thing to do isn't always easy."

"There's more to why we need your help," I told the mage. Best just to come right out with it. "My magic is gone."

"Yeah. So?"

"And . . . I don't have any magic."

"That's obvious. Don't worry, I don't think anyone inside these rotten city walls would have a clue."

That was more than a little disconcerting. "How can you tell?"

"I don't smell any magic coming off of you."

"You mean sense?"

"I say what I mean. Smell. Others may sense, but I smell. Don't let it worry you, little missy. It's a gift—or a curse—depending on how you look at it. I can see people for who and what they really are." He looked at Tam appraisingly. "So, while there's no cure for stupid, you at least seem to have found a treatment."

"Thank you, sir. I think."

A chorus of disembodied howls, screams, and roars shook the room around us.

Kesyn Badru walked to the nearest wall, pressed his hands up past his wrists into the goop, and started murmuring. I couldn't hear what he was saying, but the wall began glowing with the same blue light of the tunnel he'd created for us to escape through.

The howling, screaming, and roaring stopped. Instantly and completely.

"The beastie thinks we've vanished." He scowled at the lot of us. "Though with the four of you here raising a ruckus, we only have less than an hour before it cranks up again."

I shifted uneasily. "It senses and feeds on emotions, doesn't it?"

Badru nodded. "No emotion and no violence equals no problem. Staying drunk helps."

Finally, an activity I could agree with.

Imala looked at the faintly glowing walls. "How do we get out?"

Badru shrugged. "With what you have planned, I don't want to get out."

"*We* do."

"Then I imagine leaving this room, then running like hell, would be as good a plan as any."

Tam moved close enough to his former teacher that Badru could have punched him in several sensitive areas. "Sir, we can't do this without you." He hesitated, the smooth muscles working in his jaw. "Please help us."

Amazingly enough, Kesyn Badru seemed to be actually considering it, though he took his sweet time doing it. "I'll be honest with you," he eventually said. "I'm sitting the fence on that whole 'saving the world' thing the lot of you are bent on doing. From what I've seen lately, there's not much out there that deserves saving. Now, destroying this rock that's become Sarad Nukpana's reason for living—I'll have to admit that has a certain appeal. Not because it'll save anyone; because it'll annoy the hell out of Sarad."

"Actually, sir, I'm planning to kill Sarad," Tam told him.

"Destroy his reason for living, *then* kill him. Even better." Badru pondered this while he absently scratched at something under his robe. "I'd be risking my life a couple dozen times before we get to the fun part." He scowled. "*If* we get to the fun part. There's not enough money to pay me to take this job." The old goblin mage stopped and smiled, showing two missing teeth and a chipped fang. "But anything that ends with publically humiliating and killing Sarad Nukpana? Hell, I'll do that for free."

Chapter 10

Kesyn Badru clapped his hands once and rubbed them together glee-fully. "So, who you going to murder?" he asked me.

I blinked. "Murder?"

He gave me a flat look. "I've been drunk; I've never been hard of hearing." Badru jerked his head in Tam's general direction. "When the boy was telling me the who, what, when, where, and why the hell of you all being here, he said that you have to wet that demon blade of yours with some-one's blood before it'll cut into the Saghred. So, who's the unlucky winner?"

I didn't have to think about that one. "Whoever tries to keep me from getting to the rock."

"Well, at least that part shouldn't be a problem. You'll have plenty of Khrynsani trying to get at you who need stabbing. When the time comes, don't be shy about it. Punc-ture as many as you can; you want to make sure that blade is as wet as it needs to be." Badru turned to Mychael. "Mind me asking who you're taking with you to bust your way into that temple?"

"The four of us, yourself, possibly a few others."

Badru raised one shaggy brow. "A few. Possibly."

"Better for stealth." Mychael flashed a smile. "Because we're not busting in."

The old goblin looked at us like we were all a fistful of arrows short of a quiver. "Uh-huh. I'm assuming you know that if this stealth of yours doesn't work, you're Saghred chow. And note that I said, 'You're Saghred chow.' After everything I've been through, I've never once considered suicide." He shot a pointed glance at Tam. "Homicide, I've thought about on many occasions, but never suicide, and I'm not about to start now. So unless you've got bigger guns than I know of, the chances of you getting that rock without getting dead are next to none, and you'll be taking that chance without me."

"Don't count us out that easily, sir," Mychael said. "I've spent the better part of my professional career perfecting glamours and veils. I've studied Sarad Nukpana for years. I know his voice, mannerisms, how he moves—"

The old goblin simply gaped at Mychael. "You're going to glamour as that cretinous worm and just saunter up to the altar."

Mychael grinned. "I imagine Sarad Nukpana won't be challenged by anyone if he wants to commune with the Saghred. He would always have guards or a mage escort with him; and conveniently, Khrynsani have a fondness for hooded robes. There should be no problem acquiring robes for temporary use."

"Paladin, in my long life, I've only said this to one other man—your balls drag the ground."

"Thank you."

"Either that or you're stark raving nuts."

"The next few hours will tell. Glamouring as Sarad is

but one plan. Coming back alive from any mission means being flexible. Stay flexible. Stay alive."

"Admit it, sir," Tam said. "You have to appreciate the irony. Sarad used a thief glamouring as Mychael to steal the Saghred. I'd love to see Mychael glamoured as Sarad to destroy it."

"That still doesn't answer my question," Badru said. "I don't care what parts any of you have dragging the ground. No answer from you, no help from me. How are you getting in?"

"We're not walking in the front doors, sir, if that's what you're worried about," Tam said. "Imala knows a passage that was created during the last renovation. I have a tunnel that was built during the original construction."

Badru's eyes narrowed. "Do you know if either one's been compromised?"

Imala answered that one. "As of last month, neither one was known to anyone other than Tam and myself."

"A lot of bad can happen in a month."

Amen to that.

Badru smiled slyly. "I know a way in that you wouldn't need to worry about any Khrynsani guards at all."

Now Tam and Imala looked at the old mage like *he* was crazy. Mychael and I shared a blank stare.

"Is this an idea you'd like to share with us elves, too?" Mychael asked.

"There's a cave about a mile from the harbor," Badru told us. "It's set into the cliffs just above sea level. The cave opens into tunnels which lead up into the temple."

I glanced from Tam to Imala. "That sounds nice enough, but I take it there's a reason why we don't want to go that way."

Tam answered me. "There are usually several reasons living in those caves at any given time."

"Sea dragons," Imala clarified.

That did it. Kesyn Badru had spent too much time in a possessed house.

I'd seen a full-grown sea dragon before just off the coast of Stiren. Lucky for us, it must have just eaten, and wasn't interested in either Phaelan's ship or crew. The only difference between sea dragons and Khrynsani was the way they'd kill us. Personally, I'd rather be stabbed than eaten. Sea dragons didn't care if you were dead before they started eating you.

"In addition to guarding the sea cave entrance, the Khrynsani use the dragons for garbage disposal," Badru told us. "Corpses of sacrifices, prisoners who outlive their usefulness, Khrynsani whose loyalties become questionable." He hesitated. "The one unfortunate part is that the tunnels end near the temple dungeons, which I'd really rather not visit."

At the mention of the temple dungeons, Tam's eyes lit up, and suddenly Kesyn Badru wasn't the craziest person in the room anymore. I knew exactly what he was thinking, and I wasn't any happier about that idea than I was with playing hide-and-seek with hungry sea dragons.

"Tam, we can't risk—" I began.

"Our most powerful mages and top military minds—all imprisoned by Sarad because they refused to bow to him." Tam looked at Mychael. "We'd have an army that's on *our* side."

"And your father."

"Yes, and my father. It won't make up for everything I've done, but it'd be a start."

"I like even odds," Mychael said. "But if evening the odds risks the mission, it's not worth the attempt."

I bit my bottom lip. "Though . . ."

"Not you, too?"

I raised both of my hands defensively. "Hey, just trying to do that 'stay flexible, stay alive' thing you were talking about. As little as we need something else to do while under

Sarad Nukpana's nose, this might be just the thing we need to buy us some time. Sometimes chaos is a good thing. A bunch of vindictive battle-hardened mages and warriors loose in the temple on the eve of Sarad Nukpana's greatest triumph. Yes, Nukpana will have to leave guards around the Saghred, but he'll have no other choice than to send the rest of them to stop that prison break."

Tam spoke. "Mychael, with their help, we might just be able to destroy the Saghred *and* Sarad's Gate. Mother said the team that's trained and ready to destroy that Gate are in those dungeons. At the very least, we'd be giving these men and women the dignity of dying while fighting instead of waiting to be slaughtered like animals. To me, that's a chance worth taking."

Mychael frowned. "I know they won't take orders from me, and you didn't exactly leave a clean record when you had to get out of town."

"Imala, would they listen to you?" I asked. "Or would they think you were still working for Sathrik?"

"Shit," she swore mildly.

"Yeah, that's what I thought."

Part of why Imala Kalis had been able to gather so much inside information on King Sathrik's plans was that, technically, she still worked for the guy. For goblins, maintaining dual alliances came as naturally as breathing. But this wasn't a game for the men and woman Sarad Nukpana had imprisoned in those dungeons, and Imala telling them she was one of the good guys might not go over well.

"Think you could convince them that you wouldn't set them free just to turn around and set them up?" I asked.

"They would listen to you," Tam said quietly.

I blinked. "Me? You know I'm an elf, and I think that's going to be fairly obvious to them, too."

"You're also the Saghred's bond servant."

Imala nodded. "Our people know who you are, and that includes what you look like."

"But I don't have any magic."

"It doesn't matter," Tam said. "They know what you've done to thwart Sarad Nukpana, and they know that he wants—and needs—you dead. You're here to destroy the Saghred. Mychael is the paladin of the Conclave Guardians, the keepers of the Saghred for the past thousand years." He flashed a grin. "The two of you have the hero credentials; we'll just be there as your trusty sidekicks."

I snorted. "Yeah, right."

"That we're trusty or sidekicks?"

I gave him a crooked smile. "Either one."

"I haven't spent all of my time in this house," Badru said. "I've been out, and there are some people I still trust to talk to. From what I've heard, Sarad's keeping those prisoners healthy and well fed. Apparently that rock doesn't like weak food. I'm sure those boys and girls would like nothing better than to pay Sarad back with interest for fattening them up for the slaughter."

"Okay," Mychael began. "I'm not saying we're going to do this thing, but how many cells are there and how do they open?"

"A dozen cells on two levels," Tam said. "All but a few of them open with the same key. The chief guard and his senior officers each have one."

"How many officers?"

"Usually four."

"Think we can get our hands on one?" Mychael shot Tam a meaningful look. "Quietly?"

Tam's grin was slow and borderline evil. In that moment, he looked entirely too much like Talon. "He'll never know what happened."

Kesyn Badru's instructions for getting out of the house were simple: run like hell and don't look back. Throughout my professional career, I'd successfully used that strategy many times. I was glad to be able to say that it worked this time, too.

It was full dark once we got outside. The streets would be busier, and the odds for getting stopped and/or captured would be greater. We were still cloaked and hooded, and Kesyn Badru was sporting a battered, wide-brim hat. Since we were headed for the harbor, then the sea cave, the most direct route would have us going under a place I'd heard a lot about, and had absolutely no desire to visit.

Execution Square.

It had another fancy-sounding name, but over the centuries, it'd been used to make public examples of anyone unlucky or stupid enough to piss off a Mal'Salin monarch. If we managed to get Chigaru on the throne and he started pulling that all-powerful crap, he'd be getting another visit from yours truly. Only I'd have the family fleet backing me up. Phaelan and Uncle Ryn would happily blast his butt off of that throne. If I risked my life to help put someone on a throne, they damned sure better behave when they got there.

To get to Execution Square, Badru led us through parts of the city where you hoped you were carrying more steel than the thugs waiting around the corner, in the next doorway, and down the alley you just passed. Between the five of us, we must have been packing enough, because no one jumped us. While it didn't exactly give me the warm fuzzies, it did lessen the white-knuckled death grip I had on my dagger.

Badru stopped at a narrow stair that ran against the side of a building. The stairs went down to somewhere. The first four I could see; the rest disappeared into the dark.

He readjusted the brim of his hat. "There's twenty steps with a door at the bottom," he said. "We'll make some light once we get inside. Watch your step."

A storage room led to the sewers, which led to a cobweb-filled tunnel. Before we'd left the house, Badru had filled a small knapsack with odds and ends he said would come in handy. He'd given us each a ball not much larger than a die, an invention of his. You shook it and the liquid inside made almost as much light as a lightglobe. Plenty of light, no heat, and, best of all, no magic. If you needed to put it out quickly, you just stuck it in your pocket.

Fire of any kind would have been bad walking through cobwebs. But the nice thing about them being here was that it meant no one else had been. I briefly wondered if Magh'Sceadu could flow through cobwebs. We moved fast and in complete silence. We had a destination and we wanted to get there as quickly as possible.

I estimated we'd been walking for nearly an hour, when Kesyn Badru stopped and we did likewise. I couldn't see much in the dim light, but I could hear plenty. Voices, footsteps, a lot of both—and all coming from directly over our heads. Quick glances darted between Badru, Tam, and Imala. Though this time, I didn't need anyone to tell me that something was happening in Execution Square and crowds were gathering to watch. I didn't see any way that this could be good.

Tam and Imala extinguished their lights and ran in absolute silence down the dark tunnel toward the square. While we waited, Badru fished around inside his knapsack and pulled out a square of cheese. I'd thought the old goblin's breath had smelled bad enough from drinking, but that stink couldn't begin to compare with that cheese. I was more than grateful when Tam and Imala came back soon after.

"Sathrik's about to give a speech from the palace balcony," Tam said.

Mychael blew out his breath. "We might need to hear this, but at the same time, I don't want to waste the opportunity of having everyone's attention focused on the king."

"Sathrik's usually good at getting to the point quickly," Imala said. "An orator he's not."

"Where's the closest and safest place to listen?" Mychael asked.

Imala started back into the dark. "Follow me."

The voices got louder and more numerous, and I tried my best not to think about hundreds, maybe thousands, of goblins standing just a few feet above our heads. Imala glided silently to a storm grate set in the roof of the tunnel. Light from torches or lightglobes in the square above flickered down to the dirt floor. She stood just beyond their glow, perfectly still, listening. Elven eyes were no match for goblin night vision, but our ears were just as good. So what she heard, we all heard.

"The outer perimeter is secure, sir," said a voice from above.

"And the streets beyond?"

"Closely watched."

"Good. Assume your post, Captain."

Palace guards or Khrynsani. Either wasn't good if we were found, but we weren't going to be found. We were here to listen and leave. As far as I was concerned, we couldn't get to the leaving part soon enough.

Imala turned toward Tam and flicked her index finger under her nose.

"Khrynsani," Tam barely whispered.

I raised a questioning brow.

Tam's grin flashed in the shadows. "Imala's always claimed she can smell the stench. The incense they burn in the temple could choke a horse."

I gave Imala a smile of my own as my pulse sped up at the thought of Khrynsani directly above me.

Imala motioned us forward. Another ten minutes or so passed as the sound of the crowd in the square above grew even louder. Usually in a crowd gathering to hear a speech, there were snide comments and jokes about the dignitary about to speak, laughter and idle chatter. I didn't hear any of those things.

"How many?" I mouthed silently to Tam, pointing up.

He bent his head to my ear. "The square can hold five thousand."

My heart suddenly tried to flip in my chest. I tried taking a deep breath, then another. There wasn't enough air. I broke out in a cold sweat and my breath came shallow and fast.

Sarad Nukpana.

He was here.

He was up there now, on the balcony that couldn't be more than twenty feet away. The goblin was gazing out over the crowd, looking, searching for us.

For me.

I didn't need to see him to know. I could feel him.

I curled my nails into my palms and clenched my fists until my fingers ached. I could do this. I *would* do this. I wouldn't be terrified into paralysis simply by the bastard's presence. He could only do this to me if I let him.

I wasn't going to let him.

Mychael was looking down at me, concern in his eyes.

"Nukpana's here," I mouthed.

We should go. Now. Sarad Nukpana wasn't in the temple. And if he was here, out in public, he had brought enough Khrynsani mages and guards with him for protection. More protection for him meant less protection for the Saghred. We weren't going to get a better chance at the rock.

Mychael's jaw clenched, and I could virtually hear his thoughts—consisting almost entirely of four-letter words. He agreed with me.

The crowd above us fell silent.

I seriously doubted Sathrik was going to announce the details of his dark, evil, and insane plan to his people, but you never knew. Sometimes you got lucky and insane included stupid.

It didn't take Sathrik long to get to the topics he really wanted to rub everyone's collective nose in. "You all know that Princess Mirabai has granted me the honor of her hand in marriage. She wanted me to inform you, our loyal subjects, that she is eager to assume the duties and responsibilities of being your queen. Please join us in celebrating our marriage tomorrow night in our most revered temple."

Good thing Prince Chigaru wasn't here to get that happy news. He'd have clawed his way through the grate above our heads in a frothing rage to get his hands around his brother's throat. Princess Mirabai and Chigaru had been engaged; that is, before he was forced to run for his life. Looked like Sathrik was intent on taking everything Chigaru had left—beginning with his woman and ending with his life. Though the whole setup smelled like something Sarad Nukpana would have cooked up to lure Chigaru out into the open.

"The fear that has gripped our kingdom and especially our capital is all but over," Sathrik continued. "Four nights ago, our police led a raid on a known terrorist headquarters and captured many high-level operatives. We interrogated them to discover the location of the last few terrorist cells. Our efforts have been fruitful, and tonight we will begin cleansing our city of their poisonous influence before our wedding day, so that our nuptials may truly be the celebration it should be."

I felt sick to my stomach.

Tam's house. The Resistance fighters. Piaras, Talon, and Chigaru.

"Adding to our joy, the Saghred, the ancient heart of our people, has been returned to us," Sathrik continued. "Our brave Khrynsani brethren, led by my dear friend Sarad Nukpana, have risked much, and some have made the ultimate sacrifice and have given their lives so that the heart-stone of our people could be returned to us. The power of the goblin people will grow, and all shall know our strength." Sathrik paused, long enough to let the silence turn to tension. "And those who have betrayed our kingdom and its people shall pay dearly for their treason. Your new queen and I will celebrate the joy of our union with all of our loyal goblin subjects. Immediately following our union in royal matrimony, the Saghred's full power shall be reborn and realized with the souls of those who have betrayed us—all of us."

Sathrik continued speaking while Tam had moved to stand farther down the tunnel, where there was another grate. He was staring up, utterly frozen, his eyes wide with fury—and fear. Imala was by his side, her hand on his arm. Kesyn Badru was two steps behind them. All were looking up at who- or whatever was just beyond that grate. Mychael quickly closed the distance between them. When he saw what they did, the word he mouthed left no doubt that we had a problem. Correction. Another problem.

I went and looked and agreed. No one had to tell me who the man was on the left side of the balcony, positioned so everyone could see him. As an example, a warning in chains.

Tam's father.

It was as if I were looking at Tam twenty years from now.

Cyran Nathrach stood tall and proud, wearing his shackles like badges of honor. He looked straight ahead, refusing to acknowledge the presence of his captors on the balcony with him. He knew why they had brought him here, to serve as an example, a deterrent. His defiant posture said loud and clear that he served no one, bowed his head to no man.

Tam hadn't moved a muscle, but his pulse was pounding in his throat. I knew what he wanted. Tam wanted to rip that grate off, cut his way through the Khrynsani guards ringing the balcony, and do the same to anyone who made the fatal mistake of getting between him and his father.

Sarad Nukpana was standing behind Cyran Nathrach and Sathrik Mal'Salin, but close enough to Tam's father to be seen by most of the crowd as claiming Tam's father as his personal captive, displaying him to the crowd. To the Resistance.

To Tam.

Sarad Nukpana had changed even in the two days since

I'd last seen him, when he'd tried to drag me along with the Saghred through that Gate he'd torn into a basement in Mid. Only weeks ago, Sarad Nukpana had been a bodiless specter, newly escaped from the Saghred. His rotten soul had ultimately ended up in the just-dead corpse of his uncle, Janos Ghalfari.

Now Sarad Nukpana looked like himself.

He'd briefly had access to the Saghred's power, and in just those few hours of contact had absorbed enough magic to restore his face and body. His hair was again a youthful blue-black shimmer. His face unlined and beautiful. And his hands bore only white scars where the Gate's magic had essentially cooked them inside the steel gauntlets he had worn. Hands he was obsessed with getting on me.

Sarad Nukpana had taken the Saghred, but he hadn't taken me. If he had, there was no doubt in my mind that I'd be standing beside Cyran Nathrach, in magic-sapping manacles, on display to the goblin people. Next to the Saghred, I'd be Nukpana's most prized trophy. He'd display me and then he would sacrifice me, exactly as he would be doing to Tam's father.

In an instant, I saw me standing beside him, looking out at the thousands of goblins gathered in Execution Square, chained, my body unable to move, but my eyes spotting Mychael and Tam through the grate, so close, yet far enough that they couldn't come any closer, helpless to do anything. But I knew better—they wouldn't be helpless; they would do whatever they had to do to free us, even if it meant their capture and death.

Sarad Nukpana knew this.

Tam wouldn't stand by and do nothing while his father was tortured and killed. He would rescue him, and as Tam's friends, we wouldn't let him risk his life alone.

Sarad Nukpana knew. All he had to do was wait.

That wouldn't stop Tam. Sarad Nukpana knew that, too.

Sathrik continued speaking. "Earlier this evening I

named Lord Chancellor Sarad Nukpana as my heir until such time as my new bride and I celebrate the birth of our first child. He has been my friend and steadfast ally during this difficult time in my rule when some of my subjects, your fellow citizens, blasphemed against you, me, and the kingdom we all revere. The stability of the throne and your safety and prosperity are—"

"The king isn't shielded," Mychael said in the barest whisper.

Tam's head snapped toward Sarad Nukpana. The goblin black mage's lips were curled in a half smile and he had moved a few steps closer to Cyran—and away from the king. The people in the crowd probably thought his smile was polite attention to his king's speech, and his movement away from Sathrik as deferring to the king's presence.

"—our only concern," Sathrik continued. "Like myself, Lord Chancellor Nukpana has sworn to uphold and protect the sanctity of the goblin throne and . . ." Sathrik gestured to where Sarad Nukpana was supposed to be standing. The king froze as annoyance, confusion, then wide-eyed realization and terror passed in a wave over his face.

Sarad Nukpana's smile broadened, and he regally inclined his head.

For all to see, he was acknowledging his lord and king's compliment.

He had removed Sathrik's shields, and had just given someone a clear shot at the king.

The assassin took it.

A bolt took King Sathrik Mal'Salin square in the chest and passed completely through, exiting his back and slamming up to the fletching in a royal guard standing directly behind his king.

His dead king.

A second bolt caught Sarad Nukpana in the upper chest, spinning him to the ground.

"Mortekal!" more than one voice shouted.

Deidre?

Oh, unholy hell.

"No!" Cyran Nathrach screamed, as guards quickly surrounded and dragged him off the balcony.

Tam's head snapped around as if he could somehow see through the crowd to his mother's killing perch.

"Protect the king! Protect the king!" Khrynsani guards surrounded Sarad Nukpana, lifted him from the ground, shielding his body with their own.

Deidre's bolt was sticking out of his shoulder.

He wasn't dead. The bastard was still alive.

"That monster has more lives than a cat!" Imala snarled.

Tam turned and started to run toward the last turn we'd taken to get under the square, the place where he could get to the street—and his mother. Mychael grabbed his arm and almost got his own ripped off in the process. There was some deadly serious wrestling, but Mychael got Tam pinned, their faces inches apart.

"Not now!" Mychael growled. "Everything your parents did will have been for nothing! Is that what you want?"

Tam's fangs were bared and his eyes were blazing. One sharp twist of his head and he could rip out Mychael's throat. They both knew it. Mychael could have moved out of range without releasing his grip on Tam. He didn't. Instead he relaxed his hold.

"Tam, we strike when we can win." Mychael's voice was low and intense. "We will win; we *will* get them back. I swear it."

Though until that time, Sarad Nukpana was the goblin king. He'd always been the one pulling Sathrik's strings. Now it was official.

The king is dead. Long live the king.

Like hell.

Chapter 11

Sarad Nukpana was the goblin king.

Sathrik Mal'Salin's assassination had reduced our archvillain population by one. Sarad Nukpana had taken a crossbow bolt in the shoulder. That would slow a normal person down for a couple of days. Unfortunately for the population of the seven kingdoms, Nukpana wasn't normal. I wasn't even sure if he even qualified as a person anymore. Regardless, he had to slow down long enough to get that bolt dug out of his shoulder. Then maybe he might even spend an additional hour going through the motions of mourning his king.

We had no way of knowing for sure if the mortekal everyone was screaming about was Deidre. But Cyran's scream told us that he'd seen his wife—and probably had seen her either captured or killed. As to why Deidre went for Sathrik first . . . it might have been as simple as take the target you know you can hit. Sarad Nukpana had made it easy for her. That didn't explain how she'd been able to stick a bolt in

Nukpana, or how he knew of her plans. All of that didn't matter, at least not now.

Sathrik Mal'Salin hadn't needed to tell us his evil master plan. By setting him up for an assassin's bolt, Sarad Nukpana had told the world his intentions. He not only wanted to wipe out the Resistance, but the entire Mal'Salin dynasty. My mind reeled at the implications. With Sathrik dead, Nukpana would step in and take the king's place with his mother, Sandrina Ghalfari, ruling and terrorizing at his side, ousting the Mal'Salins and creating a new ruling family dynasty. The Resistance would take the blame for the assassination. Sarad Nukpana would claim it was their fault the kingdom was in chaos on the eve of their triumph that was a thousand years in the making. The Resistance would be hunted down to the last man, woman, and child.

Execution Square was chaos, but right now, chaos was good.

The assassination had caused a virtual stampede, and no one paid any attention to anyone or anything other than themselves and getting the hell away from the square. We were going away from it as fast as our legs and need for concealment allowed. Tam knew ways through the city where we could pass unseen or at least the risk would be less.

We had to get to the temple, and we had to get there fast. Unfortunately, with Sathrik's Resistance roundup being carried out in the city, Tam's house was no longer safe. There might still be a chance that the Khrynsani hadn't raided it yet. We had to warn them—and get Piaras, Talon, and Chigaru out of there. We would take them with us as far as the tunnels immediately beneath the temple. We'd go after the Saghred, and they would be safe until we returned.

If we returned.

We smelled the smoke from two blocks away.

The Resistance had worked to make Tam's house look deserted.

It was definitely empty now.

Deidre may or may not have escaped after assassinating Sathrik; no one could have escaped this. Windows were knocked out, smoke as if from a recently extinguished or burnt-out fire was still smoldering.

The air stank of smoke—and magic.

Even without mine, I could sense that people had been fighting for their lives here and using every spell and blade in their arsenals. Fought and lost.

Tam and I lunged forward; Mychael and Kesyn Badru each grabbed an arm.

"You going off half-cocked isn't going to help you or your boy get to the end of this night alive," Badru told Tam. The old goblin took a flask out of a hidden pocket in his robes. "Let a professional stagger in there first."

He pulled his hat down so that the brim hid at least half of his face, and then proceeded to stumble out of the bushes, muttering to himself and weaving his way down the edge of the street, occasionally stepping in the gutter and barely regaining his balance and blistering the air blue with a few choice—and highly creative—words, his voice again dropping to a drunken mutter.

He stopped and stood swaying in front of a royal edict tacked to a streetlamp post outside of Tam's gates. We'd all seen and read it. It warned of imprisonment for defying the military curfew and defacing the signs they were written on.

Badru belched noisily and fumbled around inside his robes again.

This time he didn't pull out a flask.

The old goblin proceeded to take a piss on the sign.

I think we all needed that. Defy authority and boost morale at the same time. It just went to show that wisdom didn't always involve book learning. That was one gifted old man. It also proved that whoever had destroyed Tam's house wasn't there anymore. I'd never heard of a soldier who could have resisted taking the shot when a drunken citizen was taking a piss on a sign that basically ordered him not to piss on that sign.

The old goblin had established without a doubt that the coast was clear.

Not wanting to tempt Fate any more than we already had, we still kept to the shadows. Yeah, it was night, but anyone who might be watching was a goblin, and we weren't in a mood to take chances.

Badru was coughing and waving his hand in front of his face. Dammit. I didn't consider smoke from whatever fire was burning might keep us out. Though smoke or no smoke, I was going—

"Not smoke, girl," Badru said. "Well, not entirely."

"Navinem," Tam spat.

"What?" Smelled like burnt tar to me.

"A drug."

"It's almost dissipated, but I wouldn't suggest we go running in there yet." Badru gestured to me and Mychael. "Though these two might benefit from a snoot full."

I took an experimental sniff. "Of what?"

"The elven military occasionally uses navinem for some of their elite troops," Mychael said, looking up at the second-floor windows. They looked empty and he knew that, but staying among the living meant staying on your toes. "Makes them feel impervious. It's a powder, and can be swallowed, but when you want to use it on large numbers of goblins, heating it turns it into a gas."

"Why would someone shoot Tam's house full of 'elf ego boost'?"

"Because it doesn't boost goblins," Imala said. "Exactly the opposite. Panic, terror, whatever you fear the most is what you'll see with just some of the hallucinations; the rest are worse."

Meaning Sarad Nukpana could have had the house surrounded, gassed, and could then stroll in and herd everyone inside out.

Everyone except the elves.

The only two elves in that house were Piaras—and Carnades Silvanus.

I felt the growl building in the back of my throat. I didn't have magic, but I had knives. If Carnades had hurt Piaras, no spell, incantation, or curse would keep me from killing him.

"Tam and I will lead," Mychael was saying. "We'll do a room-to-room search. Quick, methodical, and safe."

"Not safe for any Khrynsani bastards still inside," I said.

Or an elven mirror mage.

Mychael's smile was more like a baring of teeth. "No, not for them." He turned to Tam. "Do you want me to go in first and see if it's dissipated enough for—"

Tam answered by taking the lead.

The inside of the house hadn't been in the best shape before; now it was completely demolished. It was apparent that magic had been used, the dark and nasty kind. Entire sections of walls were scorched black.

A flash of something pale appeared on the edge of my vision. I damned near jumped out of my boots and had a dagger quivering in each hand.

It was an outline of a man against a burnt section of wall. No blood, just a perfect outline of where the man was—and now wasn't. The outline was too tall to be either Piaras or Talon.

"What the hell did that?" I breathed.

"He was Khrynsani," Tam said. "Wearing full battle armor." He indicated the broad reverse shadow showing the head. "Complete with helmet, probably equipped to filter out the navinem."

Imala kicked at a mostly melted sword. It had been a broad, curved blade, about four feet long—until someone or something had turned it to melted steel in his hand. The outline of the man and sword was burned into the wall.

The sword was basically slag. The Khrynsani holding it had been vaporized.

"Any of your agents powerful enough to do something like that?" I asked Imala quietly.

"None that were here."

Mychael's hands glowed with restrained blue fire as he stepped forward to peer down the dark main hallway. "Carnades is."

My second-worst enemy could be lurking in the shadows, watching us, tanked on elf ego boost. That was one ego—and power—that didn't need boosting. If Carnades did that to a Khrynsani, what would he have done to Piaras?

What had been a massive iron chandelier in the ballroom ceiling was now a twisted pile of metal and shattered crystal on the ballroom floor. The ceiling where it had been now sported a hole almost as broad as the chandelier itself. There were people-sized holes in the walls, with some going all the way through into the next room. Others were body-shaped imprints in the plaster.

However, there were no bodies or people in sight.

A chunk of the chandelier shifted—and groaned.

Weapons came out, wards went up, and that moaning lump was immediately surrounded.

An arm fumbled its way clear of the rubble as a familiar head full of tousled brown curls emerged.

Piaras.

I reached him first. No one stood a chance of getting there before I did. He was pinned under four chandelier arms. He should have been crushed, but by some miracle he wasn't.

"Ow." Piaras blinked his eyes open and winced.

I tried to lift one of the iron arms; it didn't budge. "Don't try to move."

Piaras snorted.

Snorted?

"Like I could," he said.

Mychael and Tam lifted up one corner of the chandelier while Imala and I carefully dragged Piaras out.

"What happened, Cadet?" Mychael demanded.

"Ow."

"Yes, I understand that part. Now what happened?"

"The son of a bitch dropped a chandelier on me." Piaras shook his head to clear the broken crystal in his hair. "Oooh, bad idea."

"Who?"

"Carnades." Piaras gazed blearily around as Mychael and I helped him to his feet. His eyes found Tam and gave an apologetic grin. He indicated the nearby holes in the walls. "Sorry about the mess, sir."

Tam blinked. "*You* did those?"

In response, Piaras gave him a lopsided grin. "Me and the son of a bitch."

Mychael got a small chair that I swear was the only unbroken piece of furniture in the room and guided Piaras onto it.

"Thank you, sir," Piaras said gratefully. "Carnades sold us out. Somebody had to pay him back." He grinned again. "I'm somebody." He nodded proudly toward the biggest hole in the wall. "And I did something."

Mychael ignored everything that implied. "Where's Carnades?"

"I don't know, sir. The chandelier must have knocked me out."

When it should have squashed and killed him.

Navinem.

"Piaras, look at me," I said.

He did and I looked at his eyes. Piaras's eyes were normally large and dark brown, but now his irises had opened to the maximum, but even direct light from Mychael's lightglobe didn't bother him.

Hell, it didn't look like anything bothered him.

"Are you hurt?" Mychael asked.

Piaras quickly stood to show how completely non-injured he was. He smiled like a mischievous little boy. "Ready for more duty, sir. That was fun."

Fun?

"I can see that." Mychael gazed around. "Now, how did you end up throwing Carnades through a wall?"

Piaras told him, and I got angrier with every word.

Deidre had at least two traitors in her nest. With goblins' love of intrigue and complex alliances, it'd have been a wonder if all of her people had been loyal to someone and something besides themselves and their purses. Unfortunately for us, one of Deidre's traitors was one of Carnades's guards. Ever the braggart, while Carnades had been hurling slabs of wall at Piaras, Carnades had told him that in exchange for his freedom, he'd told his guard that the all-powerful Raine Benares had been reduced to a magical null.

My stomach roiled at the news.

The Khrynsani had hacked their way through a few strategically placed boarded-up windows and thrown what were basically navinem grenades into the house. More Khrynsani followed with more grenades. The drug-laden smoke spread, leaving panic and then immobilizing despair in its wake. The masked Khrynsani barely broke a sweat rounding up the goblins of the Resistance.

"Talon and Nath? Where are my son and brother?" Tam's face was stone, but his eyes promised murder.

"I didn't see Nath," Piaras said, "but Talon set fire to a pair of Khrynsani dragging Prince Chigaru out."

Mychael and I exchanged a stunned glance. "Would that have been in the front hall?" I asked carefully.

"That's the place. When Talon told them to drop the prince, they laughed at him." Piaras gave a low whistle and shook his head. "That was a really big mistake. Then there was shouting, screaming, and a flash of bright light. Then I couldn't watch anymore; Carnades was throwing chunks of wall at me."

"It seems Talon is a little more elf than he appears," Mychael noted.

"And a lot more talented," I murmured.

"Since he's only half-goblin," Imala said, "the drug would also remove his inhibitions."

Tam almost smiled. "Talon didn't have any of those to begin with. Right now, I'm grateful for it."

"Piaras, do you know where Talon and the prince went?" Imala asked. "Did they escape?"

"Sorry, ma'am. I was . . . occupied."

Kesyn Badru sat in the chair Piaras had vacated and took a hit off of his flask. "So we've got your boy running around looking for trouble—"

"Nothing new there," Imala said.

"And he may or may not have Prince Chigaru with him." Badru turned to Mychael. "You think we need to search the house for this Carnades person?"

"To be on the safe side, yes," Mychael said.

Piaras kicked at the chandelier. "If he was still here, wouldn't he have made sure this thing had finished me off? And if it hadn't, wouldn't he have taken care of business himself?" He gave a half shrug. "I mean, it stands to reason."

"Yes, Cadet, it stands to reason." Mychael put a finger to his lips. I knew that gesture; he was keeping himself from smiling.

Apparently I wasn't the only one who found Piaras's casual attitude about his own near death most un-Piaras-like. But unlike me, Mychael and even Tam found Piaras's newfound badassness amusing.

Men.

Mychael saw my disapproving glance, but it only made him have to fight harder against that grin. "We'll check the house just to be sure," he told Piaras.

Piaras nodded in approval. "That would be prudent, sir. Should I check the basement or upstairs?"

"What you should do is sit down."

Piaras opened his mouth to protest.

"That would be an order, Cadet Rivalin. If I know Carnades Silvanus, and I do, you'll have other opportunities to settle your score."

With a happy smile, Piaras plopped down on the floor, sitting cross-legged. "I'll look forward to it, sir."

"I'm sure you will," Mychael muttered.

I followed Mychael out into the hall.

"How long will that navinem stuff last?" I asked.

"Depends on how much he inhaled. If he was exposed from the time the attack started until they left, it could be another whole day."

I gave a low whistle. "That would be good."

"That would be very good."

"Though we can't have him blasting his way into the temple."

"No need to worry. Once we're on the move, he'll be all business."

"The things Piaras did to Carnades," I began uneasily. "He's never done anything like that before. You said navinem makes elves feel impervious; you didn't say anything about sprouting new talents." That twist was way too close to what the Saghred had done to me for my comfort.

"Piaras is still young, just coming into this power," Mychael explained. "One of the things navinem does for you is makes you willing to try things you've never done before. That or simply react on instinct—which is probably what happened with Piaras."

"So Piaras and Carnades entertained themselves throwing each other through walls."

"Looked that way."

"If this stuff made Piaras feel all kick-ass, it did the same to Carnades."

Mychael nodded, his blue eyes sparkling. "That's precisely why I'm so impressed."

"But Carnades is one of the most powerful mages—"

"In the top five percent."

"That makes Piaras—"

"A diamond that won't be in the rough for much longer."

Chapter 12

So far, so good. No Carnades.

Piaras was disappointed. Me? Not so much. Today had been one fight or disaster after another, and I, for one, didn't want any more excitement, at least for the next hour.

Mychael and Tam had finished searching the house. Tam had run upstairs to make a quick raid on a weapons stash he had hidden in the walls of his bedroom. Mychael was talking in low tones with Piaras, and Imala was down the hall pulling weapons out of her supply pack. Kesyn Badru was standing with me keeping an eye and ear on the front door, on guard for any additional Khrynsani visitors.

Carnades had told one of Sarad Nukpana's spies that I didn't have a spark of magic to my name. If that spy had gotten away . . . and made it back to his boss . . .

I dropped my forehead into the palm of my hand and groaned.

"Headache, girl?" Badru asked.

"Yes, sir, and his name's Sarad Nukpana."

The old goblin laughed. "I've had that headache for years. And since we're probably on our way to get killed together, you might as well call me Kesyn."

I nodded, then winced at the movement. Great. Now I was getting a real headache. "Though at least I'm still in one piece, and I'm not in one of Nukpana's cells—unlike Tam's father." I shot a quick glance upstairs. Tam was still in his room, but I lowered my voice anyway. "I feel like I know him pretty well, but I've only known him for two years. You taught him."

Kesyn held up a hand. "I tried."

"He's a good man," I insisted.

The goblin mage glanced at the upstairs landing and sighed. "Yes, he is. I don't want to lose him again."

"Well, demigod or not, Nukpana's not the man I'd put my money on in *that* fight. He's got Tam's father, and maybe his mother and brother, so when those two get—"

"That's what scares me, girl."

"I hope it doesn't come to that, either. But if Tam can catch him flat-footed—"

Kesyn smiled sadly and shook his head. "That's not what I mean. To fight black magic, Tam will use black magic. He's already admitted to using it once since he got here."

"On Magh'Sceadu that were about to eat his son."

The goblin mage responded with silence. "You say you know him," he eventually said.

"I do."

"You know about his use of black magic in the past."

I didn't move. "Some."

"This is the most dangerous time in Tam's rehabilitation, though he believes he's already completed it. Some of the people he loves most in this world might lose their lives if he doesn't do something about it."

I clenched my fists. "If I still had what the Saghred had given me, *I'd* do something about it. But I can't, and Tam knows it."

Kesyn nodded. "Cursed rocks aren't the only way to get power. There are demons who would gladly give Tam what he needs to fight Sarad. Right now. Calling them is quick and easy. The vermin make it easy to call, hard to say no—and impossible to pay them back. Tam wants this; he wants to kill Sarad Nukpana. He will kill and he will enjoy it. Black magic is intoxicating. Demons make it even more so. And they like keeping their mortals alive and owing them plenty."

"Their souls?"

"Worse. Favors. Favors are demon currency. And if you don't play, you pay. Tam can call a demon and make a deal, but if he backs out on it or even *tries* to back out, the demon will drag Tam to Hell for his personal amusement—for eternity."

"Tam doesn't have to fight Sarad Nukpana."

"What do you think the chances are that he'll even try to avoid that confrontation?"

I took a deep breath and blew it out. "Icicles in Hell kind of chances."

"Exactly. The sacrifices begin tomorrow night; the time for subtlety is gone." Kesyn slid down the wall to sit on the debris-covered floor, pulled out that chunk of stinky cheese again, and took a bite. "I've never questioned Tam's strength or his skill. He has both in spades; more than any student I've ever taught. With Cyran imprisoned, and the rest of his family missing, Tam's rage and desperation will only add fuel to the fire. Black magic feeds off of equally dark emotions. The goblin court is a natural and fertile breeding ground."

"If you start playing the game to survive, soon the game is playing you."

Kesyn nodded. "And you don't mind it, either. Being adept at the game keeps you alive. The better you are at the game, the more political power you gain. For the magically gifted ones, the growth in that area is exponential.

Unfortunately in our royal court, it's also unavoidable. Once in the court, it is nearly impossible to leave."

"So I heard. But Tam left for two years."

"And now he's back again." Kesyn wearily rolled his neck, the bones cracking. I felt the sudden urge to do the same.

"Power is seductive, Raine. But I imagine you know all about that now."

I'd used the Saghred to kill nine firemages just a few weeks ago. Yes, I was killing people who had been hired to and were bent on slaughtering every living being in that hotel. I'd killed those firemages, using the Saghred's power to consume them in their own fire. I'd told myself that they deserved to die. If I hadn't killed them, they would have killed hundreds. Mychael had tried to reassure me, comparing what I had done to what he did in battle. I agreed with him; it had to be done.

But Mychael hadn't killed enemies on a battlefield with near-giddy joy.

I had.

It was the Saghred. The rock was behind that sick joy. I would never enjoy causing death.

Or would I?

That question was what had kept me from falling asleep easily at night since then. That was what woke me up in the still, quiet hours, lying in my bed, heart racing. Mychael had been sleeping by my side, but that hadn't helped. I felt tainted, wondering what I would be like if I never rid myself of the Saghred. How long would it take until I became like those firemages? I'd seen their faces; they had reveled in their destructive power.

So had I.

Those firemages had been elves; their targets had been goblins, Chigaru's court-in-exile. Many elves—too many elves—would have seen those firemages as patriots, loyal to their kingdom and race, cutting the head off the Mal'Salin serpent before it could grow. I was seen as a traitor by those same people for stopping and killing those they saw as fighting to preserve the elven race.

No doubt many of the goblins who had heard Sathrik's speech agreed with his recognition of Sarad Nukpana and his Khrynsani as heroes. They had fought, killed, and died to bring the Saghred back to the goblin people. They were merely good soldiers serving their king and people.

Over nine hundred years ago, the Saghred had been theirs. My father taking the stone and putting it in Guardian custody had made him, in the eyes of those same goblin people, a common thief. The goblins who backed Sarad Nukpana could just as easily find themselves chained to the temple altar; but for now, he was a hero. And now he was also their king.

It was all about perception.

For everyone, whether elf or goblin, it was all in the perception, pure and simple. Though my actions hadn't been pure, and my reasoning was far from simple.

I had killed.

And I would do it again.

It had been the right thing to do, for what I believed to be the right reasons. That I'd enjoyed the act of killing was the Saghred's doing. I wasn't like that.

I would never be like that.

Tam would never be like that.

Kesyn Badru had been closely watching my face the entire time. "Almost any action can be justified," he said quietly.

"We all do it."

The old goblin nodded once. "Every last one of us—good or evil."

I didn't have to worry about using the Saghred again. I didn't have a choice; the rock had taken that away from me, too.

Maybe that was a good thing. The best thing.

Or the thing that was going to get us all killed.

I raised my eyes to the top of the staircase. Tam was still upstairs.

"I still feel like myself," I said in a small voice. "I don't feel like the Saghred ripped a hole inside of me and dragged my magic out kicking and screaming. Yeah, the Saghred consumed that elven mage through me. I felt it when he died, his soul pulled out of his body, through mine, and into the rock. But I didn't feel any part of me leave. I'd had a decent amount of magic to begin with, and over the past few months, the Saghred had been giving me more power nearly every day. Something that big doesn't vanish without a trace." I glanced down at the goblin mage. "Does it?"

"Have you asked yourself why the Saghred took your magic?"

"Just constantly. I assumed it was being a spiteful rock."

"The Saghred is a simple thing. When it hungers, it feeds. But critical to you right now—it protects itself. You didn't feed the Saghred, so it took that elven mage. And from what you've told me, your magic vanished about the same time that shape-shifting goblin thief stole the Saghred for Sarad Nukpana." Kesyn stretched his legs out in front of him with a sigh. "It's simple—the rock got a better offer. And to prevent you from interfering, the rock bound your magic. The Saghred didn't take your magic and leave you with just a spark. It bound and gagged your magic, and a spark was all that could get out."

"But Nukpana put sensors around the city. Magic sets them off. I didn't."

Kesyn shrugged. "The rock did a good job."

I was thankful and pissed at the same time. I possibly still had my magic; it also couldn't do me or anyone I cared about a damned bit of good right now.

"So I destroy the rock and chances are I get my magic back," I said.

"That would be logical. However, this is the Saghred

we're talking about." Kesyn flashed his broken-fanged grin. "That thing makes its own rules."

Movement out of the corner of my eye drew my attention to the top of the curved staircase.

Tam Nathrach was armed and armored for the end of the world.

His armor was black, but in no way, shape, or form was it plain. Engraved, inlaid, and embossed with silver—this was armor for a battle you intended to win.

Or armor you intended to be buried in.

Tam's long hair was pulled back in an intricate goblin battle braid with the silver circlet resting low on his forehead and set with a single ruby. I'd seen him wear it before. That, and his silver chain of office, now set over his broad, armored shoulders, identified him as a duke of the royal court, chancellor to the prince, and the chief mage of the Mal'Salin family—a family Sarad Nukpana was bent on destroying, along with anything or anyone else he deemed a threat to his new rule.

Everything Tam wore and the way he wore it was meant to be exactly what it looked like—a direct challenge, an affront, and a figurative knee to the nuts. Tam wanted everyone who saw or fought him to have no doubt who he was.

No one said anything. Tam was dressed for Sarad Nukpana's funeral—or his own.

"Sarad's men didn't find my private armory," Tam said. "I usually have Barrett to help me with the back plate buckles. Mychael, would you—"

Mychael had already started up the stairs. "I'd be honored, Tam."

"I keep a second suit. We're of a size, so it should fit you."

Mychael froze and looked up at Tam. "I'd be even more honored, my friend," he said in formal Goblin.

Imala's eyes were glistening with unshed tears.

Kesyn wiped his nose on his sleeve. "Come on, boy," he said to Piaras. "Help me scare up some food to take with us. You could probably gnaw the leg off a table right about now—if we had one. Navinem makes you hungry."

Piaras started to follow without a word.

"Cadet Rivalin," Mychael called down.

Piaras stopped, instinctively at attention. "Sir?"

"Gear up in your Guardian armor."

Piaras's smile was like a sunrise. "It'll be an honor, sir."

Now it was my turn to tear up.

Tam had brought me a present from his bedroom.

I looked at it and then at him. "Tell me you're kidding."

"It's a crossbow pistol," he said flatly.

A really small one. The bolts were no longer than my hand. I made a face. "Again, you're joking, right?"

"I never joke about weapons."

I held up a bolt and studied it. "This itty-bitty thing doesn't look like it could hurt a melon."

"At close range, it'll do just as much damage as what Mother's shot did to Sathrik."

That was worth a whistle. "To be honest, I'd rather not get that close to—"

Tam's lips creased in a crooked smile. "With proper aim, it's lethal to a range of twenty yards."

"Are you insinuating that my aim is less than proper?"

"I'm saying that a little target practice wouldn't hurt before I let you out of here with it."

I examined the bolt mechanism. "Looks like it loads the same as the grown-up version."

"And since the bolts are small, it loads three times faster."

"Then it's better than the grown-up version."

Another advantage to the mini-bolts was that they probably wouldn't leave anything sticking out for a healer to get hold of. It'd hurt like hell to get one carved out of you; that is, if you were still alive enough to make retrieving it worth a healer's while.

I loaded a bolt and kept the point down until I was ready to shoot, then looked around for a target. Since Sarad Nukpana's house-raiding goons hadn't been careful when they ripped things off the walls, I didn't feel bad about adding another couple of holes.

I nodded my head toward the far wall of the next room. "Mind if I . . ."

"Be my guest."

On the far wall was the outline of where a painting had hung. Now it was probably hanging on Sarad Nukpana's wall, but the blank space made a nice target. To make it even nicer, I imagined it was a portrait of everyone's favorite psycho goblin, and aimed the pistol right between his eyes.

I fired.

The little bolt punched through the wall up to the fletching right where the bastard's throat would have been, with an added bonus of hardly any recoil. It wasn't exactly where I'd been aiming, but it still would've killed him. Dead was dead. Or in Nukpana's case, dead again was dead for good. I hoped. Either one worked for me. I was way beyond being picky about how I got the job done.

"Nice," I said. "I like."

"I thought you might." Tam handed me a bandoleer that had to have been loaded with at least fifty bolts.

I took it and draped it across my chest. "You got another one?"

Tam arched a brow. "Ambitious, aren't we?"

"Realistic. That and paranoid. While you're at it, got a backup pistol in case this one jams?"

Tam just looked at me. "It won't jam."

I looked back. "See previous statement regarding paranoid."

Tam handed me another full bandoleer and pistol from the pile of weapons he and Mychael had brought downstairs from his armory. Though if I did manage to take out one Khrynsani per bolt, that'd be a hundred dead Khrynsani courtesy of yours truly. Plus, the loaded bandoleers provided even more steel between me and what any one of those Khrynsani might want to dish out. That is, if they were dishing out steel and not magic. Steel couldn't do a thing to stop a well-slung spell, and neither could I.

I was just as well armored as Tam and Mychael. Some of Imala's agents had left behind enough armor for the two of us to supplement what we came to Regor wearing. Though no one would be seeing anything since we'd be cloaked and hooded, at least until we got into the temple. While Imala and I didn't look as flashy as Tam and Mychael, everything was as protected as it could be, but most important, I could still run. To me, running was just as important as fighting. Running wasn't cowardly; running would let me get to a better place to fight again and actually survive. Though I preferred to think of it as a tactical retreat.

A loud thump rattled the ceiling above our heads. I had a second bolt loaded and almost shot myself in the foot. Another thump came from a different direction, from the far corner of the ceiling. Then another. A low rumbling rolled across the ceiling, almost like thunder. I couldn't see it, but that didn't keep me from smelling it.

Fire.

Normal fire didn't burn this fast or this hot. This was magic, the dark kind, and I knew exactly what was behind it. A firemage, probably more than one. To torch Tam's roof, they would have to be on the roofs of an adjacent house, and the bastards knew what they were doing—if killing everyone inside this house was what they'd been ordered to do.

Without warning, Piaras faced the front doors, and I swear the kid growled. So much for wondering if he still had navinem-addled senses.

A boom shook the massive doors *and* the floor beneath our feet.

"Bastards brought a battering ram," Mychael said.

Glass shattered and wood splintered somewhere at the back of the house.

"To the wine cellar," Tam ordered.

We knew the way and ran for the door leading down to the cellar, the tunnels, and hopefully freedom—or at least temporary escape.

Great. More tunnels.

Tam headed to the front, but Kesyn ran to intercept him. The old goblin might look deceptively ancient, but he could move.

"This one's on me," he told Tam. "Save that fury of yours for when someone worth killing is on the receiving end."

Surprisingly, Tam didn't argue.

If anyone was waiting in the cellar, they'd better have brought a shitload of backup. We were getting out of here and anyone who had the piss-poor luck to have been ordered to block our way wouldn't know what hit them.

The cellar was dark, but Tam, Kesyn, and Imala ran straight through the darkness to where the door to the tunnels was. Mychael, Piaras, and I stumbled along behind in the pale glow of the one miniscule lightglobe Mychael had summoned to try to keep us from falling flat on our faces.

Kesyn had his hand on the latch as Tam and Mychael took up positions on either side of the door. Tam nodded to his teacher, and the old man's hands glowed redder than I'd ever seen Tam's. If anyone was on the other side, this was going to be both their worst day and their last.

Kesyn flung open the door and ran through, closely followed by Tam and Mychael.

The old goblin didn't cut loose, meaning there was no lethal welcoming committee.

When Mychael gave the all clear, the rest of us joined them in the tunnel. Kesyn closed and sealed the door with a spell.

We knew we weren't coming back.

Chapter 13

We surfaced a few blocks away. No one said a word, but every last one of us looked back in the direction of Tam's house. Other houses and buildings kept us from having a direct line of sight, but we didn't need it. It was the middle of the night, and the glow from Tam's burning house lit the sky.

Tam's expression was unreadable. "Let's go."

The six of us moved fast. Tam's front doors wouldn't have held up for long against a battering ram. Though hopefully, setting fire to the house would keep whoever had been sent to flush us out from knowing that we'd escaped through the basement. We opted not to take any chances on the speed of any pursuit, and ran like Death himself was on our collective tail.

To get where we needed to be, we had to get past a place we didn't want to go—at least not again.

Execution Square.

We'd only be skirting the edge of it, but anywhere near it was too close for me. From the looks of things, I wasn't the only one who felt that way. What goblins were out and about near the square were wearing cloaks and hoods. The unofficial uniform of oppressed societies everywhere.

"Looks like our citizens don't want to be recognized by anyone," Imala said to my unspoken question.

Kesyn took a quick swig from his flask. "When you don't know who you can trust, you save yourself the bother of weeding through the chaff and don't trust anyone."

Our destination was to get past Execution Square to a small, rocky beach outside of Regor's harbor. Tam had assured us it wasn't far, but since we were the most wanted people in the city, any distance was too far in my opinion. We weren't going into the square, but now getting past the square might take even more than we'd thought.

A big hand grabbed my bandoleer and hauled me back into a dead-end side street.

Mychael.

"Khrynsani guards," Imala whispered. "They appear to be questioning everyone going into the square." Her dark eyes narrowed dangerously. "I stand corrected. Only one of those men is Khrynsani. The other is one of my agents—or *was*." The glare Imala was giving him promised that not only was his career over, but his life was about to follow in its fading footsteps.

"He was one of Carnades's guards," Tam told her.

Imala nodded once. "And one of my most trusted," she said quietly.

Tam never took his eyes off of the rogue agent. "Would you like to speak with him?"

Imala's smile was chilling. "Yes, thank you. There is nothing I would like more."

"We can't stop for this," Mychael told them.

"Balic's known for putting his nose into everything," Imala said. "He probably knows something we need to."

"Like where Carnades is," I said.

That swayed him. "Okay, but no more than a few minutes."

Imala never took her eyes from her prize. "That's all I'll need."

"Mychael, cover me," Tam said as he stepped forward and vanished behind a veil.

"Wait," Mychael called quietly.

I couldn't tell if Tam waited, but apparently Mychael could. His eyes grew intent on the two men, and I knew his spellsinger magic was soon to follow.

The area around the temple, including the square, was seething with magic. We weren't going to do the magical equivalent of setting off a bomb, but veils and such were quiet and necessary. We needed to move fast, and sneaking wasn't what you'd call speedy; neither was snatching a secret service agent off of a street corner.

Mychael began humming an innocuous tune. The Khrynsani guard's head snapped up as if he'd been slapped. Heck, for all I knew, that was what Mychael had done. The guard told Imala's traitor to stay put and ran across the street and around the corner to investigate whatever Mychael had told him to.

Mychael's hum changed pitch and the agent tilted his head like a dog hearing a whistle. Then he obediently turned and walked right to where Tam and Imala waited in the shadows.

"How very nice of you, Mychael," Imala murmured. "The perfect present."

Mychael flashed a quick smile. "I thought you'd like it."

Tam was still veiled when he grabbed the agent and slammed him against the brick wall. Mychael quickly muttered what I recognized as a spell to ward the entrance to the narrow street. No one could see in, and anyone who passed by would feel an overwhelming urge to keep right on walking.

By the time the goblin agent could see straight again, the first two people his eyes focused on were probably two of the last people he wanted to see. I'd never seen a goblin go so pale, so fast.

"Balic," Imala all but purred. "What an unexpected surprise."

I didn't think he could have gotten any paler, but I was wrong.

He'd just spotted the rest of us.

As one of Imala's agents, he had enough on the ball to know that he wasn't going to be allowed to see us and then leave that alley alive.

"Nukpana forced me to do it," he told his former boss. "He's holding my family prisoner, and—"

Imala silenced him with a hard fist to the gut. Balic gagged and would have doubled over if Tam's armored forearm hadn't had him anchored to the wall.

"Nice try," Imala said. "Your records say your family's in Greypoint and they disowned you years ago. I wish I had done the same."

"I think he meant to say that Nukpana has *my* family prisoner," Tam hissed softly, his face mere inches from the agent's. "And you helped put them there. Where are they?"

"They took everyone to the temple. I don't know anything else; I swear it on my grandmother's grave."

Imala punched him again. "Your grandmother's still alive, too."

"Where's Carnades Silvanus?" I asked. "Spit shining Nukpana's boots?"

Balic's lips slid into a smile.

Oh yeah, he was an oily one, all right.

"That I do know," he said. "The elf wanted us to take him to Sarad Nukpana. He was all eager to share the news that you didn't have your magic anymore. He wanted to go to the temple, so that's where we took him."

"And?" I asked.

"And nothing. We handed him over to the temple guards and left. I imagine he's warming a dungeon cell by now." Balic shot a smug look at Tam. "I've got information about that son of yours."

Tam leaned in closer, his fangs sharp and visible. "Speak."

"Not so fast. I want your word that neither you, nor anyone else here, will kill me." He tried to swallow past Tam's arm against his throat. "If I tell, I walk."

"What if my word is no better than Sarad Nukpana's?" Tam's voice was devoid of any feeling whatsoever.

"Your word's good."

"Give him your word, Tam," Kesyn said. "We don't have time to play."

Tam shot his teacher a withering look. "What?"

The old goblin's dark eyes flickered. "Oh, go on and give it to him."

Tam met Kesyn's look, then pressed his lips together. He slowly turned back to Balic. "Done. You have my word; I won't kill you."

"No one else here will kill me, either."

"Nor anyone else," Kesyn bit the words off. "Now spill it, worm."

"Your son must have a lot of elf in him," Balic said. "That navinem made him go on a rampage. I saw him just after midnight near the city's west wall. He blew up the main bank of latrines the army's using while they build Nukpana's contraption outside the city."

The Gate. That monster Gate. Oh Talon, you devil. If I live through this, you've got a big kiss coming.

"The weekly supply wagons had just arrived," Balic was saying. "The explosion sprayed shit on everything. Heard later that two of Nukpana's pet generals were in the latrine when it went up."

Piaras pumped his fist in the air. "Woooo—"

I elbowed him in the ribs.

Mychael was grinning. "Don't worry; I've warded us for sight *and* sound."

Balic added, "Then the kid dropped his trousers and mooned the lot of them."

Beautiful.

"Of course, they opened up on him: small cannon, crossbow, javelins—anything they had at hand." Balic stopped and looked expectantly at Tam.

"Did he get away?" Tam growled.

"I saw what happened." He smirked. "Let me go and I'll tell you."

Tam drew a dagger and stepped in even closer. I couldn't see where he was holding that dagger, but from Balic's gasp and complete loss of color, I had a good idea.

"I gave my word not to kill you," Tam said calmly. "It'll be only one small cut, perhaps two. It won't be fatal, though you'll wish it had been."

"He got away," Balic squeaked.

Tam stepped back and the dagger vanished back into his sleeve.

"You got anything else to tell us?" Kesyn asked.

"That's all. Now keep your word—"

"I got your word right here," Kesyn said. "Dost ni'kiprat dij'sh."

Balic's eyes rolled back in his head and he went limp in Tam's grasp. Tam let him go and the former secret service agent slid down the wall into a crumpled heap in the street.

"That was more than one word, wasn't it?" the old goblin asked Tam.

Tam was smiling. "Yes, sir, it was. They were well chosen, though."

The rest of us hadn't moved.

Kesyn looked around. "What? I didn't kill him. He's just asleep. Of course, he won't wake up until I tell him to; and if I get killed . . . or forget to come back . . ." The old man shrugged. "My memory's just not what it used to be."

Chapter 14

Kesyn's plan would either get us into the Khrynsani temple, or be an incredibly messy way to get ourselves killed.

Pretty much every ritual the Khrynsani conducted began and ended with some poor sot taking a dagger through the heart. That made for a lot of dead bodies. For the past thousand years, the Saghred hadn't been around to clean up after them, so the Khrynsani had to do their own housekeeping.

Like Magh'Sceadu, sea dragons didn't leave leftovers.

Just south of Regor's harbor was a sheer cliff. I didn't know how high it was because I couldn't see the top from where we stood at the base of the thing. The six of us were on a stretch of rocky beach that was just big enough for us to stand on without getting wet. The height of the cliff didn't matter because our destination was an opening about twenty feet over our heads. There were enough hand- and footholds that we could reach it. At high tide, the sea water could reach it, too. But our concern wasn't that we'd get caught in a flooded tunnel at high tide. We were worried about getting caught by what lived in the cave and lake at the end of those tunnels.

A sea dragon. Definitely one, possibly more; serving the dual purpose of Khrynsani sentinel and undertaker. According to Kesyn, occasionally the Khrynsani would bypass their corpse-consuming sentinel and throw their dead out of the tunnel and into the sea. The tide would come in and take the bodies out. I'd noticed that a lot of the rock and gravel we were standing on was white and shaped suspiciously like bits of ground-up bone. I was making every effort not to notice it again.

I didn't know about Piaras, but I felt like I was just along for the ride. If all spell broke loose, at least he had something to contribute. I felt about as worthless as tits on a bull, and I didn't even have any navinem to fool me into thinking otherwise.

I needed to be worthwhile. I needed to know I was going to do something to help.

Tam, Imala, and Kesyn were climbing up to the cave entrance. Piaras would go next, followed by me and Mychael. I hadn't moved in front of Mychael yet to get ready to climb. He was looking up at Kesyn, marking his progress, waiting until the old goblin was at least halfway up before having Piaras start his climb.

I laid my hand on Mychael's shoulder, and stood on tiptoe, my lips next to his ear. "Mychael, I want to carry the Scythe of Nen into the temple. I need to be the one to use it."

He half turned. "We decided that I—"

"No, you decided that you'd stab the Saghred; I never agreed. For all we know, I might *have* to be the one to stab it. We can't afford to take any chances." I didn't think Piaras could hear me, but I still lowered my voice, my words coming fast. "I'm the one the rock latched onto. I'm the one who's had that thing sharing my head, giving me nightmares while I try to sleep, and taking me over to kill people during the day."

"Raine, for the last time, if you hadn't killed those firemages, none of us would be standing here right now. You saved us and hundreds of others. Killing on a battlefield isn't murder; and make no mistake, that street was a battlefield that day."

"Soldiers don't enjoy the killing. I did."

"Raine, that wasn't—"

I cut him off. "We can argue later. What it boils down to is that the Saghred chose me as its bond slave. Let's call it what it is. I'm not a servant; I'm a slave. It's used me, and because of me, people I love have been in mortal danger." My next words came through clenched teeth. "I've *earned* the right to destroy that rock."

"Raine, you don't have any magic, no shields, no—"

"I could have Justinius Valerian's shields against that rock and it wouldn't do me any good, and you know it. I'll be there with you in a Khrynsani cloak when you're glamoured as Sarad Nukpana." I took a breath and blew it out. "Mychael, please. I *need* to do this. I need to cut my own chains and free myself."

Mychael's eyes were on mine, searching, appraising. Without looking away from me, he reached into a pouch he carried on his belt and took out the Scythe of Nen. He expertly flipped the curved, silver dagger in his hand so that the pommel extended toward me.

I realized that I'd been holding my breath. I reached out and closed my hand around the grip. "Thank you," I said simply.

He closed his big hand over mine. "Remember, we do this together," he whispered. "If you need to be the one to use the Scythe . . ." He paused and squeezed my hand. "I need to be the one to be with you. That's a deal I won't let you talk me out of."

I gave him a little smile, and stood on tiptoe again, kissing him gently. "I wasn't going to try."

We got into the tunnel without incident, and without finding ourselves face-to-face with a sea dragon welcoming committee.

We moved fast and kept quiet. Kesyn was in the lead and Tam brought up the rear. Once we got closer to the dungeons, Tam and Imala would move to the front. Piaras had conjured a lightglobe, but kept it as dim as he could. Sea dragons hunted mainly by sight, but just because hearing wasn't top on their list didn't mean we wanted to trip over something and announce our arrival.

Kesyn stopped, and because of the narrow tunnel, the rest of us had to do the same. Air was moving somewhere up ahead. Piaras directed the lightglobe's glow toward the ceiling. About ten paces ahead was a hole that apparently led to another chamber or tunnel. The source of the air coming down through that hole wasn't fresh: stagnant water and the unmistakable sickly sweetness of decaying flesh. We had to be near the lake Kesyn had told us about. Air wasn't the only thing that was moving. Now that we'd stopped walking, I clearly heard water. Not the endless dripping we'd heard since we came into the tunnel, but waves slamming into rock. Only one thing could push water around with that much violence.

Something that felt like an explosion shook the floor, walls, and ceiling, pelting us with falling rock and dust. Something pounded the wall to our right, and a stench like nothing I'd ever smelled before came through the opening above us.

The stench roared, an enraged roar.

The dragon.

It sounded big. Not just big. Huge.

A voice rang out in challenge, so loud it sounded like it was in the tunnel with us. I shot a look back at Piaras. His eyes were wide and his mouth was shut. Then who was—

The voice called out again. The words were Goblin, the tone imperious, like it expected that dragon to obey.

Oh, freaking hell.

Prince Chigaru Mal'Salin.

I stood there for a few dumbfounded seconds trying to figure out what Chigaru was doing in a cave with a sea dragon. Did he annoy the Khrynsani so much that they chucked him down here?

"You know these caves," Imala snapped at Kesyn. "How do we get out there?"

"*Out* there?" I thought the old goblin's eyes were going to bug out of his head.

"Prince Chigaru's safety is my responsibility," she said through gritted teeth. "I've fought for years to keep him alive, and I'm *not* losing him to an overgrown lizard. I'm saving him."

From himself.

Imala's words came in a cool rush. "Kesyn, if Chigaru dies, we have no one to replace Nukpana. The old-blood families will slaughter each other to get to the throne. It'll be a civil war bloodbath."

Tam jerked his head at the ceiling. "Mychael, boost me up there."

I was incredulous. "You're going to stick your head through a hole into a dragon's lair?"

Mychael made a stirrup with his armored hands and boosted Tam the extra foot he needed to see into the lair. Tam took a look and immediately popped back down.

"Sea dragons," he said. "Adults."

"Plural?" Piaras asked.

"You got it," Tam confirmed. "Two, possibly more. We need to move. From what I saw, Chigaru only has a sword; he isn't going to last long."

"Follow me," Kesyn growled. "One way to die isn't enough for you. No, you have to have *more*."

The roars became louder and even more pissed, if that

was possible. Apparently Prince Chigaru didn't limit his high-bred obnoxiousness to people; he was an equal opportunity offender. I completely understood why the dragons would want to bite his head off.

The tunnels distorted the roar's echo and I had no clue which direction it was coming from. Kesyn seemed to know exactly where he was going, even though he was going there under extreme—and continuous verbal—protest.

"I don't want a king who's too stupid not to pick fights with sea dragons," he snapped.

"If he gets eaten, we'll have a worse problem," Imala shot back.

The roaring stopped. Chigaru's yelling stopped, and so did Kesyn and Imala's bickering.

"Shit!" Imala hissed softly.

The beast obligingly roared again. Now it was Kesyn's turn to swear. His string of good old Goblin profanity was a lot more colorful and descriptive.

"Sounds like The Pools, the deepest part of the tunnels," he said.

We ran toward the roars. If the sea dragons didn't kill Chigaru first, the noise would bring every Khrynsani that the dragons' roar and Chigaru's yelling hadn't already alerted. Mychael stopped and I plowed into him from behind. Only his size kept us both from ending up in a heap on the floor.

I saw what had stopped him. We were at an intersection. Five tunnels radiated out from where we were. Piaras increased the globe's glow. Two of the tunnels went down; the other three sloped upward. That meant nothing. The tunnels were natural, not man-made. Just because they went downhill now didn't mean down was their ultimate direction.

"Which one?" Imala asked urgently.

Kesyn pointed. "It's either that one or that one." He was pointing in opposite directions. "The others go up. Eventually."

Tam went over to the entrance to one of the tunnels Kesyn said led down to The Pools. He took a deep breath, and repeated the same in the opposite tunnel.

He drew an evil-looking wavy blade. "This way."

I got a blade in my own hands. "You're sure?"

"Positive. Old carrion and fresh blood. A goblin nose knows."

The brightened lightglobe danced in front of Tam. He squinted and hissed in pain, his fangs bared. His pupils were enormous. "Dim that thing!"

Piaras looked at Tam like he'd lost his mind. I wasn't sure I disagreed with him.

"All due respect, sir, but I'd like to see the dragons before they take my legs off," Piaras told him.

"The boy's right, Tam," Kesyn said. "Chances are that second one you saw was its mate, and chances are even better that those two big ones have little ones—a lot of little ones. We're down here a couple months on the wrong side of mating season. The little ones grow and eat a lot in the first few weeks."

I couldn't believe what I was hearing. "Why didn't you tell us this before?"

"I can follow the blood," Tam said. "But if I'm going to lead, I need it almost dark, not that thing blinding me." Apparently the light bothered Tam more than the idea of hungry baby sea dragons.

Piaras complied.

The walls were glowing with a pale green luminescence.

"Dragon breath green," Kesyn whispered. "Douse the globe," he told Piaras. "We won't need it."

He did and we didn't. The entire tunnel was speckled with the green light. Farther down the tunnel the glow increased, as did the stench. We were definitely going in the right direction.

Piaras looked around at the sickly glow. "What is it?"

"Some say residue from a dragon's breath," Kesyn said.

"I've also heard it's from scales scraping against rock. I don't think anyone's asked a dragon and found out."

We were moving fast down a nearly dark, wet tunnel, toward a nest of dragons. Hungry little ones, overprotective big ones. All we needed now was someone running ahead of us ringing a dinner bell.

We hadn't heard any roars in the past few minutes—or screams, either.

"We need to go faster," Imala urged Tam.

In response, Tam tripped over something. It was a body. A goblin with eyes wide open and staring. Judging from his clothing and armor, he was Khrynsani. So much for where Chigaru had come by that sword.

"Did a dragon do this?" I asked.

Tam knelt and did a quick inspection. "Chigaru's been putting that sword to good use. This one took a blade through the heart."

Just a few feet farther down the tunnel was another crumpled figure. Also not Chigaru, likewise dead, same cause. It appeared that the sea dragon was only the latest of Chigaru's problems that had just become ours.

Another roar blasted through the air around us—angrier and closer.

It meant Chigaru was still alive. Imala shoved Tam out of her way.

"Imala!" Tam bellowed.

She ignored him and bolted for the end of the tunnel. The green glow was brighter here, and I didn't need a lightglobe to find my way.

The tunnel emptied into a vast chamber. Really vast. I skidded to a halt on something both slimy and crunchy. I didn't look down to find out. The green glow illuminated black water and a soaring ceiling, with the green flecking scattered above us like sickly stars. The air was sea fresh and graveyard fetid at the same time. I couldn't see more than a few feet in front of me, but I could sense the hugeness of the sea cave. I was on the edge of a vast lake. My boots hit something solid. I looked down. I wasn't standing in gravel.

Eggshells. Dragon eggshells.

And the remains of more than a few recent meals.

I was standing in the middle of a freaking sea dragon nest. It was empty, but empty probably just meant that the kids were big enough to be out and about on their own.

Hunting for their own food.

Prince Chigaru was trapped on a narrow shelf of rock, the tip of his sword following the head and sinuous neck of a sea dragon weaving cobra-like within striking distance. Chigaru had nowhere to go and the dragon acted like it had all the time in the world. The sight of us didn't even make it bat an eye, though maybe it didn't have eyelids.

It was a young dragon, about half the size of the one that had flown over Phaelan's ship. This one was old enough to mate, but too young for cunning. Rage had made it clumsy, and the cuts on its throat were evidence that Chigaru had taken advantage. If it'd been any older or craftier, the prince would have been dead.

"Spellsong?" I asked Mychael.

"Only works on things with a certain level of smarts. Sea dragons don't rate that high."

We could use a lightglobe to temporarily blind the dragon, but light would also blind us. The dragons knew these tunnels; we didn't.

The solution grabbed me by the foot.

It was a baby sea dragon, about six feet long. Apparently my boot and the tasty morsel inside were irresistible.

My panic flared—and so did Piaras's magic. In the next instant, the dragon juvenile delinquent was flying through the air, landing with a splash and an enraged squeal in the water on the far side of the cavern. Both parents took off in protective pursuit, the waves they left in their wake soaking us all from the knees down.

Tam's eyes went from the airborne baby dragon to the landlocked goblin prince. "Thanks for the idea, Piaras." He sheathed his blade and extended his arms to Prince Chigaru. "Jump!"

Chigaru looked at his chancellor like he'd lost his mind. *"What?"*

"Jump. I'll catch you and pull you over. Magically, not physically."

"He's good at this," Mychael called to the prince. "Just jump. Your feet won't even get wet."

Chigaru obviously saw several flaws with that plan.

"Dammit, Chigaru! Jump!" Tam roared.

The prince jumped.

Tam's magic caught him in midair. Imala grimaced.

Tam shot a glance at her. "Not you, too."

"I don't doubt your—"

"Yes, you do!"

"Hurry up!" Chigaru shrieked.

We all looked up. When Tam had started talking, Chigaru had stopped moving. Now he was dangling with his boots about five feet from the water's surface. The water was choppy. It was choppy for a reason. Something was moving just beneath the surface. Several somethings, actually. Looked like we'd just found the dragon kiddie pool.

Tam made a jerking motion with his arm, and Chigaru literally flew the rest of the way across. The prince's feet had barely touched the ground, and Tam was pushing him toward the tunnel.

Mom and dad dragon were on the move, and so were we. It's amazing how much noise water can make when it's being pushed out of the way by several tons of enraged sea dragon parents. We ran and we didn't stop running until the tunnels were no longer glowing green. Piaras reignited his light-globe and we stopped to catch our breath.

Chigaru was leaning over, hands on knees, breathing heavily.

"Are you hurt?" Imala asked.

The prince opted for a head shake over words. After a few more breaths, he raised his head. "How did you find me?"

"You made enough noise for us," she said testily.

"That and your breadcrumbs," Tam said.

Chigaru looked puzzled. "What?"

"We found the dead Khrynsani you left in the tunnel back there," Mychael said. "Nice breadcrumbs. Led us right to you."

That triggered a creepy thought. "The bodies weren't there just now." I turned to Tam. "They were definitely dead. Weren't they?"

"Yes."

Kesyn shrugged. "Baby dragons probably got them. That or something else."

I blinked. "Something else?"

The old goblin looked tired. "There's all kinds of creepy-crawlies down here. There's a good reason why these tunnels don't get patrolled."

"Any of those creepy-crawlies between us and the dungeons?"

"Yeah."

"Care to elaborate?"

"The usual. Rats, spiders, salamanders—"

I just looked at him. "Anything *unusually* big and creepy-crawly?"

"They all grow big down here."

Great. From what I had seen, food in the tunnels wasn't exactly in abundance. We were food. There were only six of us, and now Chigaru made seven, but we had to be the most abundant thing to come around in some time.

"What happened, Your Highness?" Imala was asking.

"Make it quick, boy," Kesyn said. "We got business upstairs."

Tam didn't give Chigaru time to have a royal hissy about

being called "boy." "Highness, this is my teacher, Magus Kesyn Badru."

Chigaru regally inclined his head in acknowledgment.

"Yeah, pleasure for me, too," Kesyn said gruffly. "So what the hell you doing down here?"

"I was captive and I escaped," Chigaru said.

Kesyn clapped his hands together. "There you are," he told Imala. "The boy escaped. Can we move our asses now?"

"I was taken into the temple itself, to the high altar," Chigaru continued as if Kesyn wasn't even there. "Sarad Nukpana was there with the Saghred, and he—"

"Wait," Mychael interrupted. "Sarad Nukpana is in the temple? How long ago?"

"An hour, maybe two."

A chill started at the base of my spine and scurried its way up to my neck. We had come into this mission with the assumption that Sarad Nukpana was going to be in the temple when we went after the Saghred. It'd been only a few hours ago, but I'd taken Nukpana's shooting as a sign that Lady Luck had teamed up with Fate, and both had come over to our side. Sarad Nukpana was out of the temple. We were going to make it. We were going to destroy the Saghred, and we were going home alive. Deidre's crossbow bolts had brought death to Sathrik and a world of hurt to Sarad Nukpana. He'd been taken to the palace, and while he was there, we would be coming here while the temple was a blessedly Nukpana-free zone. I knew he was going to recover quickly, but not this fast.

"Sarad was shot two hours ago while on the palace balcony with your brother," Tam was saying.

"So it's true," Chigaru said. "He told me that my brother had been assassinated—by your mother. Is that also true?"

"Sarad dropped the shield around the king," Tam said. "He knew my mother was there, waiting."

"To kill my brother."

"To kill them both."

"When this is over, remind me to make her a duchess." Chigaru paused and frowned. "Sarad may have been wounded then, but he's not now. He was with the Saghred, with both hands on it. He was shirtless with blood on his chest and back, but I didn't see any wounds."

My mouth dropped open and I let it stay that way. Sarad Nukpana was covered in blood and the rock didn't eat him—it healed him. It was like Kesyn said: the rock got a better offer. The Saghred officially considered me expendable, and I was on my way to stab the thing. I didn't know if the rock had actual emotions, but I knew it wouldn't like seeing me again. Then again, maybe it would; it'd get a chance to zap me into a goopy puddle on the floor.

"Sarad said that my brother had named him as his heir," Chigaru said, "so he is the king now." The muscle in his jaw clenched tightly. "He told me that he would wed Princess Mirabai tonight and he wanted me there to witness it as his special guest. Then I would be the first sacrifice of the evening—with Mirabai forced to watch." Chigaru blew his breath out through his nose and I was reminded of a bull right before it charged. "Mirabai was standing in the open doorway, being held back by two guards. She heard everything that monster said. She started screaming. I tried to fight my way to her. I broke free, but one of the guards slammed into me and knocked me against a wall behind the altar. At least I thought it was a wall until it opened and I fell through."

"There's a door directly behind the high altar," Kesyn said. "After a sacrifice has been made, they chuck the body through that door." He took in Chigaru's battered, scraped, and dinted armor. "A chute that goes all the way down here to The Pools."

Chigaru nodded. "It was one hell of a ride."

"I'll bet it was."

"I was fighting to get back up to the temple," the prince said. "To find and free Mirabai."

A prince trying to slay a dragon to save his beloved princess.

Death by cliché.

"Didn't you get a snoot full of that navinem stuff back at Tam's place?" Kesyn asked carefully.

"Yes, I did."

"And you haven't been running around scared shitless?"

"I must not have been exposed to very much of it."

Kesyn looked closely at the prince. "Uh, yeah, that must be it."

I looked at Piaras out of the corner of my eye. He shook his head once. That told me Chigaru did get a good hit of navinem, and he'd proceeded to take on Sarad Nukpana's personal guards, and then attacked a pair of sea dragons to get back upstairs to have at those guards again.

I admit I didn't know Chigaru all that well, because I didn't like him all that well and didn't want to make the effort. But he never struck me as the swashbuckling, save-the-princess type. If he'd gotten a snoot full of navinem and hadn't been curled up in a corner having a good cry or scurrying around the temple with his figurative tail between his legs . . . that could mean only one thing.

Prince Chigaru Mal'Salin wasn't nearly as much goblin as he thought he was, and Chigaru's mom had been a very naughty girl at least once.

"That armor saved your life, Your Highness," Imala said quickly.

Too quickly. I raised a quizzical eyebrow at her. She met my eyes for a brief instant, then looked away. Ditto for Tam. They knew. Chigaru was clueless. Well, that went way beyond interesting.

Chigaru's black eyes were on me. "Carnades Silvanus was there."

I swallowed. "At the altar?"

The prince nodded once, his eyes now glittering with barely contained rage. "He was with Sarad Nukpana."

Chapter 15

"To clarify," I said, *"do you mean 'with' as in Carnades is a pris-*oner chained to the altar, or 'with' as in he's Nukpana's new friend?"

"There were no chains or guards that I could see, but I wasn't there long enough to know his status."

Carnades Silvanus and Sarad Nukpana in the same room together could mean many things, but considering that Nukpana's hatred of the elf mage had been simmering to the boiling point for years, it was probably bad news for Carnades.

But I knew one thing that it did mean—Sarad Nukpana knew that I couldn't use my magic.

"But Carnades hates goblins," Piaras was saying.

"He hates me more, and loves his own miserable hide just as much," I said. "For a chance to get back at me, he'd be willing to breathe Sarad Nukpana's air for a while."

"And Sarad would be willing to let Carnades continue to breathe," Imala said.

"He's trying to make a deal," Mychael said. "Carnades knows that if we make it back to Mid alive and his betrayal becomes known, he's a dead man. But if he's the only survivor, Justinius can't prove that he had anything to do with our deaths."

"Son of a bitch," I muttered.

"Agreed."

"When we bust out those boys and girls upstairs," I said, "you think we could talk them into adding Carnades to their 'to do' list?"

Imala flashed a fierce grin. "I'm certain they'd be delighted."

"I'd love to do it myself, but considering my present circumstances, I don't have a problem with someone else taking out the garbage."

Chigaru's dark eyes were still glittering and his right hand, and the sword it held, were twitching a little too much for my comfort. He'd fought Khrynsani and dragons, and now he was looking for something else to fight. Good old navinem. The prince stood tall, his head up, his shoulders back. At this moment, from this angle, Chigaru looked downright kingly. That gave me an idea. I rolled it around in my head for a moment and deemed it not to be stupid.

"Your Highness, you couldn't have shown up at a better time," I told him. "How would you like to free your people and inspire them in battle?"

Chigaru's eyes lit with a berserker's homicidal glee, and Imala shot me the queen of all dirty looks.

I raised a defensive hand. "I know, I know. Your job is to keep him alive long enough to get his butt on the throne, but if those men and women upstairs are as powerful and influential as you all say, they'll be the ones who can keep him there."

"She's got a good point," Tam said. "They had to have heard by now that Sathrik's dead and Sarad is the king. Most

of those people are in those cells because they favored
Chigaru over Sathrik to begin with. With Sathrik dead, as
far as they're concerned, Chigaru *is* their king—throne or
no throne, crown or no crown. They'll listen to him. Best of
all, they'll follow." Tam turned to his new monarch. "Your
Majesty, your people need your help and your leadership."
He grinned. "We have a plan we'd like to share with you . . ."

Chigaru Mal'Salin was now wearing Tam's spare suit of armor,
and Mychael had on the leather and matte steel armor Chigaru had worn from Mid—and had dinted and torn bounc-
ing down the chute from the temple. Tam's armor was a
little big on Chigaru, but that could be taken care of for the
most part by cinching the straps a little tighter. Mychael
looked like . . . Well, he looked like his armor had shrunk
and he hadn't. So he'd put on the pieces that marginally fit,
and tossed the others aside. Fortunately, both he and Chigaru had kept the padded garments they'd worn underneath
their armor. While I liked seeing Mychael naked, I didn't
want him going into battle that way.

Tam was not happy. "Mychael, I want you to take my
armor. I can—"

"For the last time, no. Now that the prince is here, we
don't need a 'Guardian elf hero' to vouch for our sincerity
with the prisoners. Chigaru needs to look like a king, and
you're his chief mage and chancellor; you need to look the
part. Those people need to know who to follow. I'm just an
elf here to do the dirty work." He flashed a quick, boyish
grin. "Don't worry about me. I'll go shopping when I get
upstairs. The first Khrynsani guard who's my size will have
my undivided attention."

"Your Majesty, I want you to hang back at first when we
attack," Imala said.

Chigaru bristled. "I will not be seen as a coward—"

"It's not cowardly; it's tactical. We need you intact for

the prisoners' sakes. You wouldn't inspire anyone with a bolt or two sticking out of you."

The prince didn't argue. A miracle. Hopefully, it was just the first one we'd get in the next few hours.

"The important prisoners are usually kept on the first level, near the main guard station," Imala continued to Chigaru. "That means warded gates and a lot of guards. Unfortunately, that's not a guarantee—the VIPs being kept on the first level, that is. However, plenty of guards *are* guaranteed. That's why I want you to hang back."

"No one will be masking their magic up there," Tam added. "As long as we don't blow out a wall, anything we do should blend in with the noise."

"And if things get ugly?" Chigaru asked.

"We blow out a wall—and anything else with the poor judgment to get between us and those prisoners."

"Damn right, we do," Piaras said.

Instantly every eye was on him.

The kid glanced around in confusion. "Uh . . . damn right, we *don't*?"

Mychael cleared his throat. "Cadet?"

"Sir?"

"Just stay close." Mychael held up one finger, quickly followed by a second one. "And obey orders. Got it?"

Piaras grinned broadly. "Got it, sir!"

The kid was way too enthusiastic for anyone's safety. Best we could hope for was to point him in the right direction and cut him loose. Mychael caught my eye for the briefest instant. He wasn't smiling anymore. I didn't need any mind-reading bond to tell me what he knew—the navinem could start wearing off soon for Piaras and Chigaru. Considering where we were going and whom we'd be running into, I wanted them to hold on to that navinem-fueled confidence for as long as possible. I didn't want Piaras to be cocky, but I at least wanted him to think he could survive. The power of suggestion was a potent thing.

I caught Piaras's eyes. "Let's get in and get it done, so you can brag to Phaelan about what you did."

The only Khrynsani we encountered had been the dead ones down near the dragon lair. That was the good news. On the downside, it looked like no one had cleaned this tunnel since it'd been made, and the local spider population had been busy for the entire time. The Khrynsani who'd chased Chigaru down here had obviously come in another way. Between the webs and the dust, not sneezing was not an option. Kesyn had assured us that the walls down here were thick, but I was a loud sneezer. Really loud.

I had no clue what this space had been built for. Tam and Mychael's shoulders brushed both sides of the tunnel. We went up a flight of narrow and entirely too steep stairs cut into the stone. Though to say that centuries ago someone intentionally cut these would be an insult to every stonemason who ever lived.

Tam finally stopped and so did we. He spoke in the barest whisper, though we all could hear him just fine. "We're level with the dungeons. Stick to the plan."

"Unless the plan sticks it to us," Chigaru just had to add.

"Then we drop back to Plan B."

I didn't remember that one. "Which is?"

"Kill as many of them as we can."

I'd heard that Plan B more than once. Fortunately, I lived through those times to get to hear it yet again. I also knew the second part of Plan B. Tam thoughtfully neglected to say it, though we all knew what it was.

Don't be taken alive.

Piaras was standing perfectly still, peering intently at something in the shadows. "There's a red toad over there—and two more farther down this side tunnel."

My hand immediately went to my bandoleer. "How big are they?"

"Normal size. They look weird, though."

"Do they have smooth skin?" Kesyn asked.

"Yes, sir. And green eyes, I think."

"Go tell them to 'ka'lit pri'chis talmat.'"

"Uh . . . pardon?"

Kesyn rolled his eyes and said it again.

Piaras repeated the incantation, but flubbed the last word.

"Don't hurt yourself, son. It's 'ka'lit pri'chis talmat.'"

"Ka'lit pri'chis talmat."

"That's it. Now go tell that to the toads."

Piaras took one step, then stopped. "What are they?"

"Khrynsani have been known to use those critters as spies down here. If their eyes had turned red, a Khrynsani guard topside would be seeing what the toads see—namely us." Kesyn shooed his hand at Piaras. "Go on, now. That little spell will take care of everything."

"Yes, sir." Piaras went to do as told.

"Get close enough—and get your aim right," Kesyn called after him.

Tam was laughing as quietly as he could manage. "You didn't tell him those toads are going to explode."

Kesyn gave him an impish little grin. "I thought I'd let that be a surprise."

A startled yelp came from the side tunnel.

Kesyn took a quick bite from his chunk of stinky cheese. "He knows now."

Piaras returned and shot Kesyn a dirty look. The old goblin smiled and raised his cheese in salute.

"Imala and I will take a look first," Tam said. "See what we're walking into. Then we'll take it from there."

According to Tam's memory, the tunnel ended in a storage alcove about twenty paces from the guard station. Imala said she'd heard that the captain of the guard used to scare the hell out of the dungeon guards with surprise inspections. This was no inspection, but I sure hoped it was a surprise.

For them, not us.

Tam and Imala were gone less than five minutes. When they returned, their expressions were neutral, though Imala was fighting a smile.

"Good news?" Mychael asked.

"For once," she said. "There are six guards at the station. Only two are mages. A short stair leads up from the guard station to the temple's main levels. There's a locked and warded gate at the top."

"At least two guards are posted outside the gate," Tam said. "One will be a high-level prison mage and qualified to disable the wards for anyone who wants to see a prisoner. More good news is that they're using the same wards as the palace dungeon, which I'm familiar with. Those wards take thirty seconds to lower, a minute maximum if the guard gets flustered." He turned to Kesyn. "Sir? Would you—"

"Yep, I'll take that one. Flustered guards, coming up."

Tam grinned. "I'd hoped you'd offer."

"Four guards patrol both levels at all times," Imala continued.

"Are there any gates between the levels?" Mychael asked.

"There are, but they're only closed to keep an escaped prisoner from reaching the next level up. Otherwise, they're kept open in case guards on another level need reinforcements."

"Alarms?"

"It looked to me like they're using the same as they always have." Tam looked to Imala for confirmation.

She nodded. "There are two panic alarms at the guard station—one on the desk, the other on the wall behind it. The other level should be equipped the same way."

"Mychael and I will take the guards at the station," Tam said. "Raine, if any of them manage to dodge us, put that dart-spitter of yours to good use. The goal is not to allow an alarm of any kind to be given. No hesitation. No mercy."

Kesyn belched. "No problem."

Tam and Mychael had battlemagic. Imala had her curved sword. Piaras and Chigaru had what the navinem told them they had. And I was armed for ogre with bolt-spitters and two bandoleers of extra ammo. We had a good plan.

I really hoped it stayed that way.

Imala would disable the two main alarms. Tam, Mychael, and I would do the same to the six guards. Kesyn would latch onto the pair of guards standing at attention outside the main dungeon gate with a paralysis spell. To have those two guards hit the ground would attract attention, so Kesyn would just ensure that they stayed at attention. That accomplished, he would throw out a sound-muffling ward. That way when all hell broke loose, no one in the main level of the temple would know a thing. Prince Chigaru's job was to not get himself killed so those mages and military we were about to free would have a living Mal'Salin to take orders from. Piaras's job was to make sure Chigaru did his job.

Tam stepped out of that shadowy alcove like Death himself, his hands glowing with a shade of red found only in Hell's furnace, his expression that of a man who didn't care what he was about to do to any of them. Tam wasn't shielded, at least not that I could see, as if he were daring any and all of them to bring on their best. Try and die.

Khrynsani faces blanched and bodies froze.

Tam's hands came up and a thin shaft of red fire shot from his palm to the nearest black-robed mage's chest, punching a hole through it as clean as a javelin. An instant later, the second mage was slammed up against the guard station wall, an identical hole burned through his throat.

The other four guards hesitated for what would be their last heartbeat. Mychael chose a target, pointed at it, and a fiery needle of blue light shot from the tip of his finger. It was so bright that I had to look away. When I opened my eyes, Mychael's second target was sliding down the wall to the floor, a tiny black hole burned between the Khrynsani guard's eyes.

Imala coolly worked between the flying magic to disable the two alarms. One guard had been on the receiving end of a glancing blow from either Tam or Mychael, and dived for the alarm mounted on the wall. Imala drew, cut, and killed in one smooth and completely silent move.

The last guard was already dead on the floor.

They hadn't left any for me. Not that I had a problem with that.

Kesyn took the stairs three at a time to take care of the prison mage and his Khrynsani partner.

The alarms hadn't gone off and the four guards and two mages had died without a sound. But someone in the dungeon's lower level must have heard something.

They did.

The attack came from below.

A sea of black-clad Khrynsani guards surged up the stairs. The light was dim and I couldn't tell how many there were, but my feet said it was too many and they had a strong opinion on what I should do next.

Kesyn charged up the stairs to the guards stationed on the other side of the temple-level door, snatching the attention of the guards running up from the lower level. In the two seconds that their attention was on the old goblin, I opened fire with satisfactory results.

Imala could handle herself just fine in any kind of fight, but outnumbered was outnumbered. Tam and his battlemagic were taking care of the rest of what came at either one of them.

Tam had said to kill any mages first. I shot whatever came into range first. A pistol crossbow held three bolts. I emptied both pistols in thirty seconds. I had two bandoleers full of bolts, but no time to reload. Whoever made these things assumed six bolts would do what you needed to get done.

I threw the now-worthless pieces of crap aside, drew my swords, and pretended the next guard to reach me was the manufacturer. Though it wasn't the guy who made the weapons' fault; it was mine for wading into more trouble than six bolts (and no time to reload) could handle.

Sometimes it was good when your reputation got somewhere before you did. I was swinging a sword, not magic, but it was apparent that my wanted poster had been seen by more than Regor's general population. However, it was just my luck that enough of the goblins coming at me weren't afraid of being immolated by the wrath of the rock. However, a desperately-fighting-for-her-life elf swinging three feet of steel was at least given a little more respect.

Until I came face-to-face with a Khrynsani mage.

He was armed with a black staff carved with spells. For a goblin prison mage, that was all the weapon they needed.

The cat was probably out of the bag about my magic, but I had no way of knowing if Nukpana had shared that joyous news with his lackeys. But right here, right now, it didn't matter. I'd come too far and was too close to pulverizing that rock to have some jail mage screw this up for me.

I attacked. I couldn't give him time to breathe, let alone point the tip of that staff at me and incant anything. He wasn't shielded; apparently he hadn't thought it was necessary with me. If I had anything to say about it, I was going to show him how wrong he was. No one else was being shy about screaming and yelling, so I joined right in. It felt good. I'd kept too much penned up for too long. Magic had gotten me into this, and now magic, in the form of a Khrynsani jail mage, had the gall to try to take me out. I had news for him; I wasn't going anywhere. And if I was going to die tonight, I wasn't going to be a notch on this guy's staff.

Then he did something I wasn't ready for. He stopped fighting and took a step back. It wasn't a retreat exactly, more like—

A blow across my shoulders drove me to my knees.

He was getting out of someone's way. Someone who was determined to turn me into a notch on his staff. Literally.

The first mage timed it so that when my knees hit the floor, his staff hit the back of my wrist. My hand went completely numb. I saw, but couldn't feel, the sword fall from my useless fingers.

Two Khrynsani prison mages, both armed with staffs, and the spells carved in those staffs were now glowing. I was on the floor and I was unarmed. This was very bad.

I blinked to clear my swirly vision. In that one blink, the jail mage population went from two to one. A fleshy smack against the far wall told me where one of them had landed, and an enraged bellow from the direction he'd been launched from told me I wasn't the only one not using their inside voice. My mystery helper then used the staff he'd yanked from the now unmoving mage to club the remaining mage into unconsciousness.

I turned my head to look, wincing at the pain that lanced through my skull.

Chigaru was the launcher. Piaras was the clubber.

I tried to smile. Damn, even smiling hurt. "Nice," I managed.

As fast as it started, it was over. No one had any obvious injuries that I could see, but Tam's armor was sporting a couple of new dints. Once Piaras helped me to my feet, the two of everything that I'd been seeing lessened to one and a half; and as an added bonus, I could now make something that vaguely resembled a fist. I took both as positive signs.

Mychael rushed over and gently put a hand on either side of my face. He had his healer's frown on as he examined my eyes and felt the base of my skull.

I tried to swat his hands away. "I only see one of you now. I'm fine."

"Paladin," Chigaru called. He'd grabbed a fallen Khrynsani by the back of the neck and had hauled him up for view. The prince grinned. "He looks to be about your size."

"So he does. Are you sure you're all right?" Mychael asked me.

"Yes, now go get dressed before you catch a cold—or a bolt."

Tam had run down the corridor to the first cell door. He stopped about three feet away, hands out, palms facing iron-banded wood. If there were wards in and around those bars, I wouldn't know about it. Tam would, and from the confused look on his face, what he'd expected wasn't there.

No wards.

I'd seen Tam splinter wooden doors or snap cell bars and bend them back like they were hollow. He didn't do that here. He didn't need to.

The door was unlocked.

I looked over Tam's shoulder.

The cell was empty.

Chapter 16

Imala snatched a ring of keys off the desk and threw them to Tam.
Then she shoved a dead guard draped over the desk out of
her way, and started scanning a book lying open there.
Meanwhile Mychael and Tam ran down the corridor, looking in the rest of the cells, which had bars for doors, not
wood. The cells appeared to be lit from inside, but Mychael
and Tam hadn't stopped at any of them. That meant only
one thing.

Empty. All of them were empty.

I looked over Imala's shoulder. She never looked up from
the page, her finger running down the writing there, then
flipped the page. "This says what cells are taken and by who.
Knowing that also tells us what cells are still available."

"I take it there are supposed to be prisoners up here?"
I asked.

Imala furiously flipped the pages. "Yes," she snarled.
"And Tam's father is supposed to be in that first cell. The
Khrynsani keep meticulous records."

Unless they'd been ordered to quickly move the prisoners and not keep meticulous records. I didn't need an announcement complete with trumpets to tell me that we'd stepped in something we should've steered clear of. It was too late now; we were knee-deep in it.

"But Nukpana doesn't start sacrificing until tomorrow night," Piaras said. "There's another level, right? The prisoners must be down there."

I nodded, not taking my eyes from the stairs leading down to that level. The same stairs Khrynsani guards and those two prison mages had come charging up. Stairs that were now empty, leading to a level that was completely silent. With all the hell we'd raised up here, the prisoners should be shouting. If their guards had been in a knock-down, drag-out fight, chances were good that the people they'd fought were here to free them. The prisoners would be calling out to us, letting us know where they were.

No shouts. Silence. Crickets.

I had a really bad feeling about this, bordering on panic. By coming here, we might have doomed the mission—and ourselves. Though we'd all agreed to take the risk. The unspoken question that no one had asked but had to be thinking—what if those prisoners were no longer in the dungeon at all? It was looking like we were the only living people in the dungeon, new prisoners for the taking. This was feeling more like a trap every second.

Kesyn ran halfway down the stairs leading up to the temple. The sleeve of his robe was pushed back to his elbow, his arm extended, fingers spread, palm out toward the door at the top of the stair. The old goblin was out of breath, apparently from holding his spells in place. "Tam, can you track your father? Tell if he's even here?"

"The distortion—"

"Just calm yourself down and do it." Kesyn's firm voice and steady words were those of a veteran teacher of hot-headed young mages-in-training.

Tam's breathing slowed in response, and his eyes grew distant, his magic working feverishly to locate his father.

I didn't know how long it would take, but it was time I could put to good use. I ran back to where I'd thrown my crossbow pistols and quickly reloaded both of them, looking down the stairs leading to the second level what felt like every split second, expecting more guards to come charging up at us swinging swords, spikes, axes, and anything else that'd introduce us to our insides with one slice. Not that I wanted that to happen, but at least it'd be normal, and a hell of a lot less creepy than a dungeon that was quiet as a crypt.

"Mychael," I barely whispered, trying not to disturb Tam's work. "This isn't right. This isn't good."

He was scowling down the stairs, unblinking. "No, it's not."

"Somebody had to have hit the alarm down there. We couldn't have taken out all of them."

Mychael gave me a tight nod, still staring down the stairs into the near darkness.

I'd have preferred if he'd have disagreed with me, but I needed the truth.

I tried for a smile; it came off more like a grimace. "Truth hurts, doesn't it? Though somehow I don't think this truth is going to set us free."

Mychael, bless him, gave me a wink.

I think my heart started beating again. I rotated my bandoleers so I had plenty of bolts within quick reach.

"Got him," Tam whispered, not moving, his eyes staring at an empty place on the wall. "Father's still here," he told Imala.

"Where?"

Tam nodded toward the stairs. "Down there. He's with others."

Down in the silent dark.

Kesyn silently appeared from around the corner. "You're sure of your tracking?"

"Yes, sir." Tam resisted the urge to snap.

"Well, then, go get him," Kesyn said. "We made this trip; let's not waste it. I'll keep the escape route open here."

"Your Majesty, you should stay here," Tam told Chigaru.

"No. These men and women need to see me. I have to prove myself worthy to be their king. I'm going with you."

Tam could have argued with that. He didn't. One, we were way past being out of time. And two, Chigaru was right. Having the Mal'Salin name wasn't enough, not anymore. The name needed to be attached to a man whom these prisoners would see as worthy of it. I was glad no one had to tell Chigaru that; he knew it for himself. At least one thing boded well for the future of the goblin people. That is, if Chigaru and this particular group of goblin people made it out of here alive.

Kesyn had gone back up the stairs to the temple door, and turned his back to us, focusing on guarding that door and maintaining his spell. I'd known Kesyn Badru for only a few hours, but I had no doubt the old goblin could make anyone who thought about keeping us from leaving the dungeon permanently regret that decision.

"If someone gets curious and decides to come down here," Kesyn said over his shoulder, "what I'll do won't be pretty and it sure as hell won't be quiet—so move your asses."

We didn't need to be told twice. In fact, like Chigaru, we didn't need to be told at all; we were already halfway down the stairs to the second level. When we got there, we found something almost as panic inducing as a couple dozen guards running at you.

No guards at all.

My nose told me there were plenty of prisoners down here—at least there had been. Problem was there were no guards or wards down here making sure they stayed.

No one said it. We all knew it.

This had trap written all over it.

Just because armed-to-the-teeth guards weren't there to meet us didn't mean something worse wasn't about to jump us if we so much as twitched. I shot a glance at Mychael. There had to be defenses and they had to be magic ones. It had to be magic, the bad kind. I couldn't sense it, but I knew he'd be able to.

He shook his head once. Slowly.

Crap.

I looked to Tam. His lips were pulled back from his fangs in a snarl. That was answer enough. He knew there was something here, but he couldn't see, sense, or smell it.

No sounds from any potential occupants of the cells. A dozen doors stretched down the corridor on either side of us. No hands were between the bars; no shouting came from inside the cells. It wasn't like any dungeon I'd ever been in. Then again, Sarad Nukpana wasn't just any jailer. Silence meant surprises awaited anyone who came down here with the intent of breaking anyone out.

I'd been in a warded cell recently. It had been blocked with Level Twelve wards, which were the strongest that could be conjured. The soldier who had been standing guard outside didn't dare get closer than arm's length from the red wards that crackled only an inch beyond the bars. Anyone could see Level Twelve wards, mage or mundane. There'd be a lot of fried mundane guards otherwise. If there were wards in front of those dozen cells, I couldn't see them. And if neither Mychael or nor Tam could tell what was out there, then Sarad Nukpana had planned it that way.

The silence was absolute. Whatever kept the prisoners in those cells also kept any sound from getting out.

Imala's voice came from directly behind me. "A plan?"

"You've never seen anything like this?" Mychael asked her.

"Never."

"Tam?"

"No."

About half of the cells were solid iron doors with a barred window at eye level and a slot at the foot of the door for passing food to prisoners. The rest were iron bars. I looked in the one closest to me. Pitch-dark and seemingly empty. While I waited for something to lunge out of that darkness, tear through those bars, and start killing us, my stomach entertained itself by tying itself in knots.

Normally any place where people were regularly held prisoner had odors. None pleasant and all were easily identifiable. I could easily identify them now. There were people down here—a lot of them. A ward that kept prisoners away from the iron bars, smothered sound, but smells made it through. Nasty work.

Torches were mounted in the wall between each cell and the next.

No lightglobes.

The guards had used fire to light the corridor, not magic. Interesting, and not in a good way. Why wouldn't they use lightglobes down here?

Tam strode to the first cell door that was only bars, then quickly went to the next.

And froze.

We didn't know the reason for it, but he did. We ran to Tam and stopped.

It was Cyran Nathrach. He'd been beaten, he was bloody, and he was also holding out both hands, eyes wide with terror, silently screaming, "Stop!" and pointing desperately at the floor. Behind him, the cell was packed with goblin prisoners, men and women. The cell appeared to be huge, and it was full. It looked like all the prisoners had been crammed into one cell. But why?

There was only a pair of torches burning in the cell. When Tam had taken a step closer, the torches had dimmed, and the prisoners had started to panic. Only one thing dimmed fire.

Air. Or, more precisely, a lack of air.

When Tam came close to the cell, the air was somehow taken out of the cell. The torches in the hall didn't flicker one bit, so the hall wasn't booby-trapped, but the cell was. And the prisoners in that cell were emphatic that trap had something to do with the floor.

Tam growled, a full-throated snarl.

"Step back," Mychael told him.

Tam didn't like it, but he did it.

The torches resumed flickering as if they had all the air in the world. Cyran and the other prisoners took relieved gulps of air. Mychael took one step forward, and the torches flickered. Mychael immediately stepped back and they resumed burning normally.

A prisoner from the back of the cell was quickly making his way to the front.

Count Jash Masloc.

Jash held up both hands, telling us to stay where we were. He then pointed to Tam and Mychael, and made a sharp shooing motion. Then he pointed to me and crooked his finger. He wanted Mychael and Tam to back off, and me to come closer.

I knew why.

Suddenly the prisoners in that cell weren't the only ones short of breath, but my breathing problems weren't due to deadly magic, just terror of what only I was apparently able to do. I stepped up to the cell bars despite the panicked look of Cyran Nathrach and the frantic waving of two mages behind him. Jash said a few words to them and they stopped, their expressions stunned.

Cyran and the other prisoners thought I was the Saghred's bond servant with tons of magic. Jash Masloc knew differently. When I stepped up to the door, nothing had happened.

Tam went very still. "Magic-activated trap."

"You got it," I said. "The sensors in the city walls didn't detect me, and the Magh'Sceadu didn't acknowledge my existence. Neither does whatever this trap is." My bound and gagged magic was about to come in handy. "Looks like this one's mine, boys."

Jash calmly pointed down at the floor just outside the cell door. I looked down at the stones beneath my boots, careful not to inadvertently shuffle my feet one inch closer.

Now, if Sarad Nukpana had really wanted to be a son of a bitch, he would have rigged a trap for that cell that only a mundane could approach, but only a mage could disarm. I was hoping our psychotic nemesis had enough on his plate preparing for a combination of wedding and slaughter to waste too much creativity on one cell door. I'd learned a lot about Sarad Nukpana since he'd slithered out from under a rock and into my life, but I didn't know whether he was a stickler for detail.

I was about to find out.

I squatted down to get a closer look at the stones. There it was. It looked like the stone the floor was made of, but a dull gleam betrayed it as something else. I knelt to get an even better look at the thing.

It was a lidded metal box with a small handle set into the top. The handle would either be to lift it out or open it up. I gingerly reached out to touch the handle. No reaction from it, no pained screams from me, and the prisoners were still breathing. Though just because I didn't hear any alarm being given didn't mean that one hadn't been. Without magic, the only way I could tell would be the sound of boot-shod Khrynsani pounding down the stairs.

Whatever was in that box was made to keep any magic users out by killing those inside. If you'd risked life and hide to break someone out of prison, you didn't want your meticulously planned jailbreak to kill the people you'd gone to all the trouble to save.

Jash was gesturing for me to lift the box out of its hole in the floor and to open the lid. I raised my eyebrows to ask if he was sure about that. He nodded once.

This could work, or it could just as easily suffocate the prisoners or fry me.

As far as magic was concerned, I'd never been what you could call a cautious student. It was a wonder that I had all of my parts and pieces in the right places. Some magical risks were fun. Opening a box that could suck the air out of a room and suffocate a dungeon cell full of mages and military officers wasn't one of them. My mind helpfully treated me to a flashback of Sarad Nukpana reaching through that Gate to grab me and the Saghred. The smell of frying flesh wasn't something you got the luxury of forgetting. How come you couldn't remember the fun stuff, but seared meat got top billing?

The goblins locked in that cell obviously knew what we'd just discovered. Sarad Nukpana had probably told them himself just for giggles.

If your rescuer has magic, you all die.

The guards had seen my face on the wanted posters around town. I wondered if the goblins in that cell knew who I was. Judging from the frantic way they'd initially waved me back, they knew full well about me and my pet rock. Those had been the faces of people who knew they had only seconds to live. Now they were confused.

I was confused right along with them. My nose told me there had been Level Twelve wards down here, and they hadn't been disabled for long. I could still smell the burnt sulfur stench left behind when they'd been deactivated. Granted, something that strong tended to linger awhile, but this had to have been in the past hour—after Chigaru had escaped.

And after we had escaped Tam's house.

Suddenly this whole setup smelled like a trap made just for me. A mage couldn't get near it, but I wasn't a mage right now, and thanks to Carnades, Sarad Nukpana knew it. We were here; there was no backing out now. We had to get this cell door open, and I was the only one who could do it. The guards upstairs had fought, but it had been a little too easy. Nukpana wanted me right where I was.

I could almost hear his sadistically silky voice. "Demoralizing, isn't it, Seeker?"

He was probably watching right now with scrying crystals hidden in the wall cracks. And if he was watching, he and about a hundred of his Khrynsani goons might be on their way here right now. In fact, I couldn't imagine Nukpana sitting this one out regardless of who was next on his sacrifice list.

As of now, that could be me. Or maybe he'd want me chained to the side of the altar while he sacrificed life after life to the stone; their souls pulled screaming through me before being dragged into the Saghred. Their life forces being used to take more souls, more lives, more kingdoms, until—

Stop it, Raine! Stop screwing around, get these people out of that cell, and haul your ass out of here.

Time to earn my keep. I lifted the box out and opened it.

It made magic, something only a gifted sentient being should have been able to do, but this was just a box with nothing inside but gears and levers. I had no idea how it could create a ward and sustain or take the air in a stone-walled room. How it did those things didn't matter. How I could stop it did.

The workings of the device reminded me of the locking mechanism on a Caesolian nobleman's vault. Emptying that vault hadn't been my idea; that had been Phaelan. He'd tricked me into coming along because he knew I was better with mechanical gadgets than he was. I hadn't known that a heavily guarded and warded vault was Phaelan's planned after-dinner activity. Note to the wise: if my cousin asked you to dinner, enjoy the meal and get out. Sticking around for cognac and cigars would be a mistake.

It stood to reason that if the gears stopped, the ward and air sucking would stop, too. Or maybe stopping it would simply take the air out of the cell faster. The only way to know was to stop the thing. I was lying flat on the floor, my face inches away from one of Sarad Nukpana's sadistic toys, picklocks out, and tinkering with the insides.

I'd had to do some quick work on that vault in Caesolia, too. The guards that nobleman employed carried what were basically meat hooks on a stick. That the hooks were silver and the pikes inlaid with gold didn't mean that it would feel any fancier sliding through your guts. I was motivated then and I was motivated now.

I couldn't see Sarad Nukpana trusting a prison guard not to screw up his trap and suffocate his valuable sacrifices. There had to be an easy way to do—

A key.

Or at least a slot for one. There was a thin slot, on the outside of the box, concealed among the fancy filigree some royal metalworker covered the box in to try to impress Sarad Nukpana or the late king. Knowing Nukpana, he was the picture of politeness and thanked the man for his artistry right before he had him killed so he couldn't make the same thing for someone else. Probably took the gold right out of his dead hands.

Locks, I could do. I didn't have time to hope that Nukpana's gadget maker had enabled the machine to recognize when someone used picklocks rather than the key. I had to trust that he didn't. There'd be no surer way to get your throat slit than to make a gadget fatal for the man who had paid you to make it.

There was a click.

The gears turned faster.

Oh shit.

I looked into the cell. Torches burning. Prisoners still breathing.

The box's gears clicked and whirled and . . .

. . . and stopped.

A click came from above my head and the cell lock released.

Yes!

I started to pull out the picklock and the gears started whirling again.

In a fumbling panic, I got the picklock back where it was and the whirling stopped. Looked like I'd be holding this thing until everyone was out.

Jash pushed the door and Tam was pulling. It was heavy, but they got it open in short order, and the goblin prisoners quickly got out.

Kesyn came charging down the stairs with shouting and pounding boots entirely too close behind him.

"You got that Plan B ready to go, boy?" he yelled to Tam.

Tam had a string of curses ready. I hoped a brilliant alternate escape plan would come next.

The old goblin stopped next to me. I was crouching on the floor, picklock still in the keyhole.

It was past time to go. I pulled out the picklock.

There was a loud click, the floor opened up, and Kesyn and I fell into darkness.

Chapter 17

I landed hard in something soft—and squirmy.

"Dammit, girl," Kesyn wheezed, "you could kill a man with that bony ass of yours. Ever think about eating?"

I half rolled, but mostly fell off of Kesyn and onto what should have been a floor. However, any floor I'd ever walked, landed, or fell on hadn't been spongy.

I was panting and shaking. I swallowed and panted some more. "What the hell was that?"

Kesyn heaved himself to his feet. "Other than a trapdoor, it's proof Sarad was expecting us."

I scrabbled to stand up, falling twice before I could get my feet steady on the whatever-it-was we'd landed on. It wasn't breathing; at least I didn't think it was. Wherever we were was dark and damp, and from the way our voices bounced off the walls I couldn't see, we were in a room only marginally larger than a closet. Frantically I looked up. No seam of light showed where that trapdoor was, and no sound came from beyond it.

"Can you see anything?" I asked Kesyn.

"Enough to see that no one else is going to be coming down the way we did. I heard the snap after I fell in."

What the hell was he talking about? "Snap?"

"Trapdoor like that has to be reset before it'll open again. I don't know who Sarad was fishing for, but I think the boy will be tickled pink when he sees what he got on the end of his hook."

Us. I didn't want to ponder the image that Sarad Nukpana catching us on a hook conjured. Nor was tickled an emotion I could imagine Sarad Nukpana having. Though if he saw me, he might come close.

I desperately wanted to call out to Mychael, to let him know I was down here.

Raine, he knows exactly where you are—down a hole. If you open your big mouth and yell, you'll let anything down here know you're down here, too. Nukpana could have just as easily rigged his trap to catch food for the nice dragon family downstairs in this godforsaken house of horrors.

"Those prisoners just set foot out of that cell only to get captured again," I muttered.

From the brushing sounds, I assumed that Kesyn was straightening his layers of robes and whatnot. "We don't know that," he said. "All we know for sure is that *we've* been caught. By who is an assumption, but since we're in the Khrynsani temple, and Sarad's in the temple, it's safe to assume that Sarad's on his way here."

Our assumption was all that was safe right now; we sure weren't.

Kesyn just stood there, listening to me panic. "Would you like some light?" he eventually asked.

"That would be helpful."

I waited. No light.

"Well, basilisk balls," Kesyn said mildly.

I tensed. "What is it? Or what *isn't* it?"

"Magic doesn't work. Must be a dampening ward around this cell." He paused. "Nice job, actually."

"Glad you're impressed with their work ethic." My voice was starting to shake right along with the rest of me.

I heard Kesyn fumbling around in his robes.

"If you have to take another whiz, old man, get away from me."

"Nope, saving that for a special occasion." More fumbling. "Let's see if I still have . . . Yes, I always carry spares."

I snorted. "A flask?" Though I wouldn't mind a stiff belt right now.

"That, too."

A spark flared to life in front of me, moving vigorously up and down. It was one of Kesyn's light marbles, activated by shaking, which was what he was doing to it. The light confirmed what my hands had already told me: small cell, high ceiling that was mostly a hole soaring up into darkness, and no apparent door in any of the four walls. There had to be one. Why go to the trouble to bait a trapdoor without any way to extract your prize? That was what the two of us would be. Prizes.

Kesyn moved to the center of the cell and tossed the small green light up into the shaft. A sharp pop and sizzle later, we were dusted with glowing green remains of a destroyed light marble.

Kesyn gave a low whistle. "Nasty ass wards."

I couldn't see the old goblin take a bite out of his never-ending chunk of cheese, but I sure smelled it.

"Well, we won't be climbing out the same way we fell in," he noted. "That's okay; I've got more." He found another light marble in his pocket and shook it up.

Silence. Still no shouts from above. If Mychael and Tam were trying to blast or pound their way through that floor to get to us, I couldn't hear it. Unless they were too busy fighting for their lives against whoever had been wearing those boots running after Kesyn.

"Who was chasing you?" I asked.

"Temple guards."

"And?"

"Some black mages."

"How many are 'some'?"

"More than a few."

Damnation.

Mychael and Tam could fight more than a few, and hopefully the mages among the prisoners they'd just freed would still be able to put up a decent fight after being in that cell for who knew how long.

"Could you tell how strong those Khrynsani mages were?"

"You don't get to be a black mage by being a magical ninety-pound weakling," Kesyn snapped. "I didn't stop and ask for their qualifications."

I blew out the first decent breath I'd managed to get. "Sorry."

Kesyn grunted. I took that as manspeak for "no problem."

"Where do you think we are?" I asked. "Besides up shit creek without a paddle?"

"This is the Khrynsani temple. This whole place is shit creek. Up, down, doesn't matter where. I'd say we're in a cell."

"No kidding."

"Judging from the padded floor, they wanted whoever tripped that trap up there to live, at least for a while."

I did a quick exploration. The cell was as small as our voices made it sound, only five paces in any direction. The walls were rough-hewn rock. I reached as far as I could over my head and didn't feel anything other than air, though we knew only too well that there was a hole big enough for us to have fallen through and not have left bits and pieces of ourselves along the way.

I moved in close to the old guy and tried to ignore the stinky cheese. I kept my voice to a bare whisper and counted on Kesyn's goblin ears to hear me. "If Sarad Nukpana had set the trap, he knew only a null could trip it. We got caught. He knows you pack plenty of magical mojo, but I was the one on the floor, picking at the insides of that gearbox—"

Kesyn was shaking his head while chewing cheese; I was trying to breathe through my mouth. "Sarad couldn't have known we were here until you kids attacked the guard desk on the first level. Cyran Nathrach had to have been moved before that; the same time that trap would have been set."

"Then who was Tam's dad bait for?"

Kesyn gave me a meaningful look. "Who indeed?"

I froze. "Deidre?"

"Or Nath. Or both. Neither have any magic, and both would risk themselves to free Cyran."

"If so, that means they're in the temple," I said. "And from what I could see, they weren't in that cell with Cyran and the others." I didn't exactly feel a spark of hope, more like a damp sputter, but Deidre did strike me as the kind of woman who would finish anything she started. She'd shot one hole in Sarad Nukpana tonight already. Perhaps she and Nath were lurking around here thinking that the second time would be the charm.

I grinned. Oh yeah, that'd be charming as hell. Maybe I could get a better seat for the show this time.

"Regardless of who that hole in the floor was meant for," Kesyn said, "thanks to you, Cyran Nathrach is out of that hellhole and so are some of our best mages and fighters. Better still, those boys and girls didn't look happy. And Mychael, Tam, and that scrawny elf cadet of yours are plenty pissed now that you're down here and they're up there. I wouldn't want to be in the first pack of Khrynsani to run into them." He started running his hands along the walls. "No wards here. They're probably outside wherever the door to this box is."

I hoped Mychael and Tam weren't wasting any time hunting for us. With those prisoners freed, they could get up to the temple altar and get the job done. That was all that mattered. Save yourselves. Destroy the rock.

Then I remembered something.

I frantically patted myself down. When I felt the Scythe of Nen still nestled near my waist, I froze in horror. "I've still got it."

"Got what?"

I scurried over to him and hissed in a whisper, "I have the freaking dagger."

"What freaking dagger?"

"*The* freaking dagger."

"Oh." Kesyn's eyes widened as realization sunk in. "*Oh.* Well, shit."

"Mychael's the only one left free to destroy the Saghred," I said in a strangled whisper. "Now he can't."

And I'd asked him to give it to me, insisted actually. Because I wanted to be useful; I wanted to free myself. Great job I was doing of that. I viciously kicked at whatever the damned floor was made of. I couldn't be any more useless than I was right now. Mychael hadn't just gotten himself captured by Sarad Nukpana—at least I hoped not. I had. Here I stood, caught, caged, and probably about to have my weapons confiscated. The Scythe of Nen wasn't big, but it wasn't small, either. And without it, our mission was history—and so were we.

Kesyn leaned over to whisper in my ear. "Certain ladies in our secret service have often made good use of a hidden pocket in the front of their armor, right about here." He tapped his fingers over his heart and grinned.

I looked down to where that would be on me. Right over my left breast.

I just looked at him. "And you know this how?"

Kesyn winked at me. "Extensive research and exploration in my younger days."

I fumbled around in the inside of the quilted leather doublet where Kesyn had indicated, and sure enough, there it was. Hopefully, no lady agents had ever let Sarad Nukpana go exploring in their chest armor. I tucked the dagger in with even a little room to spare. "Well, *this* lovely turn of events changes our plan," I muttered bitterly.

"Considerably. However, the best plans can be executed many ways."

"Could you use something besides 'executed'? It's not my favorite word right now."

"The point is our goal remains the same; the approach has merely changed. Stay flexible, play it by ear, and when you see a chance, jump on it."

"You mean *if* I see a chance."

"I always say what I mean. *When* you see a chance. If you're looking close like you're supposed to, you'll see it. At least one chance is always there."

I'd rather jump on Sarad Nukpana with a sharp knife, or the Saghred with the Scythe of Nen. Preferably both. Now it didn't look like I'd get a chance to do either.

"Are you armed?" I asked him.

Kesyn took another bite of cheese, his eyes glittering in the dim, green light; an old man with a secret. "Don't worry about me. I'm plenty armed and dangerous. I may have taught Sarad Nukpana a lot of what he knows." Kesyn's smile broadened into a devilish grin. "However, I didn't teach him everything *I* know."

"Your magic doesn't work down here." I almost added "either," but swallowed the word in time.

Kesyn's eyes narrowed. "You're awfully impressed with hocus-pocus, girl."

"Not impressed. I just like having my odds more even."

"No magic is the best magic, Raine." Kesyn's expression turned grim and his words came fast and fierce. "You need to get that through your pretty little head *right now*. You don't have time to worry about what you don't have; concentrate on what you *do* have. What if Sarad was just a man? What would you do?" Kesyn got in my face. "Let's hear it! What would you do?"

"Kick his ass to the Lower Hells," I snarled back. I blinked. I hadn't hesitated. Just a good old-fashioned ass kicking, ending in death, of course. His. "Like that's going to happen."

Kesyn didn't back down. "Why not?"

"Because he—"

"Has more magic than you do?" The old goblin barked a laugh. "From what I hear, until a couple of months ago, damned near *everyone* had more magic than you. You ever let that stop you before?"

I stopped in sudden realization. I hadn't. I'd snuck my way into goblin prisons, freed who I'd come to get, then conned and/or fought my way out. As a seeker, I found people and saved lives. Sure, I'd used my seeking skills and magic to locate them, but after that, more often than not, I'd ended up doing everything else with . . .

No magic.

None. Just me.

Kesyn was smiling. "Have you ever let that stop you before?" he repeated, quietly.

"No. No, I haven't."

"Then don't let it stop you now. Find chances; and when you see them, take them. You need to remember something that I always told Tam—very often a man's greatest strength is also his biggest weakness. Know when to use both to your advantage."

A section of the wall creaked open. A red ward criss-crossed in front of the opening, but I could see through it just fine.

So could all of the Khrynsani mages and guards who were waiting just on the other side. Saying that we were outnumbered would be an absurd understatement. At an unspoken command, the Khrynsani deferentially stepped aside to allow someone to pass through.

Carnades Silvanus.

Wearing Khrynsani black mage robes.

Words completely failed me.

"So it is true," Carnades murmured to me. "Imagine my surprise when I was told that you had dropped into our trap."

"*Our* trap?"

"I might have mentioned to Sarad that you and your friends would be paying him a visit, so he was wise and planned accordingly."

Carnades Silvanus and Sarad Nukpana working together. Hell had officially frozen over, and demons were serving flavored ice.

Kesyn popped the rest of the cheese in his mouth with a flourish. "Remember me?" he asked while chewing.

Carnades looked him up and down with obvious distaste. "Is there a reason why I should?"

The old goblin shrugged. "I guess not. I saw no reason to introduce myself back then. I was on my way out at court during your assignment as Conclave ambassador." He chuckled darkly. "Justinius Valerian probably gave you the job hoping that mouth of yours would earn you a knife in the back." Kesyn reached out and patted Carnades twice on the shoulder in consolation. "I'm sure it wasn't for lack of trying. You must not have been here long enough." He grinned. "You here to give it another go?"

Carnades's blue eyes flashed with murder. "You must be Sarad's *ex*-teacher."

"Yeah, I guess I must be." Kesyn finished chewing the cheese and belched in Carnades's general direction. The elf flinched at the smell.

Khrynsani guards stepped forward and clapped magic-sapping manacles on both of us.

Now it was Carnades's turn to smile. "A mere formality for you, Raine, since you've lost your magic."

"Not lost." I met his smile and raised him a smirk. "I know *exactly* where it is. And now I'll make sure you're the first one to know when I get it back." It was an empty threat, but sowing uncertainty in an enemy was never a bad idea.

Carnades indicated Kesyn. "Search him and be careful about it. Sarad said that his former teacher has many unpleasant surprises hidden in those robes." He turned to me and smiled slowly. "I'll search Raine myself."

Carnades Silvanus searched and he found every single weapon I had.

Including the Scythe of Nen.

Apparently Kesyn wasn't the only one who had had intimate knowledge of secret service armor. I couldn't imagine Imala having an agent who would have willingly let Carnades grope her. Though Carnades did an entirely too thorough job of searching me, and would have found the demonic dagger regardless.

"This was stolen from a collection in my home," Carnades noted. "I always thought you were behind it; you and that pirate cousin of yours."

"The demons that ransacked your house and slaughtered your staff stole that dagger. Me and that pirate cousin of mine followed those demons and saved your miserable life. I've heard you should make sure you don't have any regrets when you die. I regret the hell out of saving your life—that time and all the others." I looked him up and down. "However, it appears Nukpana thinks you're good for something besides Saghred fodder. For now. So what did you have to do to buy yourself more breathing time?"

"Nothing that offended my sensibilities."

"You have those?"

"While we have many fundamental differences, Sarad Nukpana and I have agreed to put them aside for our mutual benefit. The new goblin king recognizes my worth." Carnades's eyes glittered. "Unlike my own government, who are fighting like a pack of mange-ridden curs with the Conclave over who will put me on trial first. With Sarad's help and that of his new goblin government, the changes I have

worked tirelessly for all these years will soon come to pass."
He gripped my upper arm. "Time for your tour of the temple, Raine."

I walked, and my mind was racing. Carnades's idea of change included killing Justinius Valerian, becoming archmagus and undisputed head of all magic users in the seven kingdoms, with the Guardians reduced to his personal enforcers. Carnades hadn't been able to accomplish any of them by himself, but with Sarad Nukpana at his back wielding the Saghred? There wasn't anything he couldn't do, absolutely nothing he couldn't have.

But Sarad Nukpana didn't give anyone anything—especially not an elf—unless he'd been well compensated in return. Letting him know that I didn't have my magic wouldn't have been nearly enough. So what else did Carnades Silvanus have that Sarad Nukpana wanted—or needed? Nukpana might have told him one thing, but the real reason would be something else entirely, something Carnades had no clue about. One thing I did know: whatever Sarad had promised Carnades wasn't what he'd eventually get—betrayal and painful death.

I tried to keep my breathing steady and my words even. "So you're finally going to get the Isle of Mid. Nukpana going to tie a big bow around it for you?"

Carnades laughed, an ugly sound. "Why would I want an empty, barren rock? The students and most of the mages have been evacuated." He gave me a humorless smile. "However, as a member of the Seat of Twelve for many years, I know the Conclave's evacuation routes and destinations."

I couldn't believe what I was hearing, even from Carnades. "You sold out those children."

"They knew when they came to Mid that the profession they chose was dangerous. This is one of those dangers. Sarad is well aware of where your uncle and cousin are taking them. He has a squadron off the coast of Mylora sailing to intercept them as we speak, with orders to take all prisoners alive. Dead mages and magelings are worthless to him."

My upper lip pulled away from my teeth in a snarl. "You've betrayed *children*—and your own people—to that monster."

"The Conclave are not 'my people.' They still are what they have always been—a means to an end."

"Did your new best friend happen to tell you that the elves are the first people he's going to attack using that Gate he's building?"

"I'm well aware of the Gate, and his intentions for it. I told Sarad the locations and strengths of all of the elven defenses. Precision strikes will significantly simplify and expedite the cleansing process."

Cleansing.

I felt sick. I knew what Carnades Silvanus wanted. I knew what he was going to do.

"My allies in the elven military and intelligence service have been imprisoned," he said, "but their incarceration will be brief—as will the rule of our shortsighted government. For far too long we have been passed over while those from polluted bloodlines have risen in positions of power. I won't have to settle for being the power behind the throne. I will be the king of our new and reborn people. My long-suffering allies and I will *be* the elven government—free to reestablish the purity of our ancient race. The elves have become mongrelized by the mixing of races, the tainting and degradation of our noble bloodlines." Carnades looked like it took every ounce of restraint he had not to spit on me.

"You handed Sarad Nukpana our people on a silver platter."

"Not mine. Yours. Elves with certain desirable physical characteristics will be spared."

"And you will be Sarad Nukpana's puppet, to dispose of as he pleases."

Carnades's grip on my arm tightened to the point of pain.

"I will have everything I have ever wanted," he spat. "Everything I deserve. And unlike you—I will be alive."

"To bow and scrape to a goblin. What will your pure-blooded henchmen have to say about that?"

Carnades quickly regained his calm. "A temporary sacrifice of my dignity for the ultimate good of the elven race. History will see me as the savior of my true people."

Then his expression changed. His face became suffused with twisted joy; his pale blue eyes glittered. It was the face of a fanatic. He honestly believed what he was saying. Carnades Silvanus would do whatever he had to do to make his warped and perverted worldview a reality, even if he built it on the corpses of tens of thousands of elves—men, women, and children—who didn't meet his standards of elven purity.

"I've dreamed of this," he said, "but thought I would have to content myself with the changes that I, as only one man, could make. Yes, Sarad Nukpana is using me to get what he wants; but I am using him to get what the elven race needs. The Saghred is evil, but out of evil can come great good. There is nothing that I won't do, no man or woman I won't kill who dares to stand in my way."

"Sarad Nukpana will stand in your way," I snarled. "All you'll be is a king of cattle. The Saghred doesn't care what kind of blood runs in your veins, and Nukpana doesn't give a damn about your *purity*. You'll be raising prime beef for his altar. You may have delayed your slaughter, but you'll never escape."

"Little seeker, are you annoying my new partner?" said a smooth, cool voice.

Sarad Nukpana didn't look like a man who'd taken a crossbow bolt through the shoulder only hours ago, and who had his hands and forearms literally cooked inside armored gauntlets the day before. His unmarked hands were visible from beneath the sleeves of his simple black robe, and he wasn't wearing a sling to take the weight of an arm off of a wounded shoulder.

The Saghred had completely healed him.

He was studying me as well, his dark eyes shining. "You are a constant source of surprises, little seeker. Or since you seem to have lost the use of your magic, that title is no longer appropriate." He cast an amused glance at Kesyn. "And my revered teacher, who endlessly professed that the best magic was no magic. How is that working for you, sir?" Nukpana stepped aside and, with a courtly bow, gestured for me to precede him. "Shall we?"

I was looking for a way out, any way out.

Not that it was easy to see where I was and where I was going while surrounded by a ridiculously large and heavily armed escort. We were going up a lot of stairs, which I took to mean up into the main part of the temple.

"It's not like I can go anywhere," I told Nukpana, indicating the guards.

"You should be flattered, Raine. Not every guest of mine warrants such careful attention."

I raised my manacled hands. "Or this much magic-sapping steel."

All traces of humor vanished. "I have not reached this night by taking chances. You have talents beyond magic. I am merely guarding against any and all of them."

The main level of the temple was full of robed Khrynsani—robed and silent. They moved quickly and with purpose. Their boss had a big night planned.

These Khrynsani were different from any I'd seen before. Each of them—whether mages or guards—wore a long silver chain with a red, glowing gem. Down the long and wide corridor, the black-garbed goblins blended with the shadows. The only way I could tell that some of them were there was that the gems glowed like mutant fireflies. Carnades was sporting one exactly like them.

Nukpana noticed where I was looking. "My brethren all

wear lifestones when inside the temple. Each is calibrated to that individual to ensure their safe passage through the areas they are permitted to enter, and to deny entrance where they are not authorized to go."

"So you don't trust Carnades here enough to give him the run of the place?"

"It is for his own protection," Nukpana replied mildly. "He is unfamiliar with our temple; it is merely a preventative measure to keep him from dangerous areas."

"And if he does go astray, he gets a chastising zap?"

"My other mages would be alerted to his location, and would politely redirect his steps. Magus Silvanus has not and will not abuse my hospitality. He has been a most generous and accommodating guest."

"So I hear." I paused. "So, how does it feel to be on the verge of getting everything you want? Carnades has already told me his feelings."

If Nukpana had been a cat, he'd have been purring. "It's a sensation I most highly recommend. It's a pity you won't be experiencing it."

"I'll just have to live vicariously."

A pair of armed Khrynsani standing guard on either side of an open doorway spotted Sarad Nukpana and instantly snapped to attention as we approached. I casually glanced in just in case it was a way out.

It wasn't.

No. Oh no.

Deidre Nathrach stood just inside the room; Nath was beside her. It was a cell, empty except for a bench bolted to the far wall. Barrett was sitting on the bench. All of them were wearing long, pristinely white robes. Sarad Nukpana was a fastidious psycho; he'd want his sacrifices neat and tidy.

Sacrifices. He was going to kill Tam's mother and brother first, then the elderly butler Tam thought of, and loved, as family.

I stopped breathing, paralyzed with a dread so sharp that it staked me to the stone where I stood.

Nath saw me and ran for the door, stopping short of the opening. There must have been a ward. When he spotted Nukpana, his lips pulled back from his fangs in a feral snarl. I knew Nath, and I still had to force myself not to reach for a weapon.

A weapon I no longer had.

No sound could escape that cell and neither could they.

Sarad Nukpana stood impassively as Nath followed his snarl by screaming a few physically impossible and fatal things he wanted to inflict upon Nukpana's person. I couldn't hear him through the ward, but no sound was needed. It was in Goblin, it was emphatic, and all of it was perfectly clear.

Sarad Nukpana's hand against the small of my back pushed me forward again, but not before Deidre and I locked eyes.

Her large, dark eyes said it all. If I had been captured, then so had Tam, or he would be soon. Her entire family was in the hands of a madman. Her only consolation was that she wouldn't have to watch them die. She would be the first to fall under Sarad Nukpana's sacrificial knife. Deidre Nathrach wasn't chained, just caged, but just as helpless to do anything about it. We were her last hope, and now her hope had failed her.

Nukpana's voice was crisp and formal. "We prefer to give our sacrifices as much freedom as possible in the time remaining to them, hence the lack of restraints and an unobstructed view of open spaces."

A dimly lit corridor, lined in light-sucking black granite, would be their last view, before the altar and Sarad Nukpana's face, as his hand brought the dagger down.

"My first official act as king will be to execute the assassin of my honored predecessor," he continued.

"And the mother of your lifelong nemesis," Kesyn called

from behind us where he was surrounded by his own guards. "Come, now, boy. At least admit the real reason."

"Merely taking the opportunity given to me to settle scores. An opportunity passed is an opportunity wasted. You taught me that, and I learned it well. Uncommonly wise words, sir."

"And you always twisted my words to suit your own purpose."

Nukpana's lips curled in a smirk. "You say that like it's a bad thing."

"You don't want an opportunity," Kesyn spat. "You want an excuse."

"After tonight I'll no longer need either." Nukpana's smile was relaxed and genuinely happy. It was creepy as hell. "You're an old man who is content to live in the past and reject progress. Both are burdens you will not have to bear for much longer." His smile grew. "Guards, prepare him for the altar."

I didn't scream or struggle. Instead I viciously embedded my elbow as far as I could in Sarad Nukpana's gut. I gave it everything I had, and a lot that I didn't. I was a dead woman walking anyway, and I'd be damned if I wasn't going to take as many pieces of Nukpana as I could with me. The Khrynsani guards had been careless enough to chain my hands in front of me and I was only too glad to make their leader pay.

My elbow earned me the reward of a pained gasp from the goblin.

An instant later, I was on the bottom of a pile of Khrynsani. Now I couldn't breathe, either, but knocking some of the hot air out of a baby demigod was worth it.

Nukpana wouldn't kill me. Not yet. He also wouldn't let his goons beat the crap out of me. Hopefully. He wanted me able to stand up next to that altar, or chained to it, and he wanted me fully aware and whole when it happened. *Then* he'd carve my heart out with a spoon. But until then, he wouldn't want a mark on me.

"Raine, no!"

It was Kesyn.

"When you see it—" The old goblin's last word was stopped by a fist. Nukpana wouldn't care if his teacher got roughed up before his turn on the altar.

I knew what he'd tried to say. A chance. When I see it, take it. I hadn't forgotten. I didn't have either the breath or a lack of sense to respond. Kesyn knew I'd heard him. Though Deidre had taken a chance when she saw it, and look what it'd gotten her.

Nukpana straightened up with a ragged hiss. "Take her to my quarters."

One of the guards in the pile decided clubbing me on the head was an appropriate response to that order.

Everything went black.

Chapter 18

I had certain expectations to waking up in Sarad Nukpana's bedroom.

Chained to the wall was one of them. Having a white-robed, wide-eyed goblin lady staring at me like I was one of the dragons downstairs was not.

As my vision cleared from the head clobbering I'd gotten, I realized that she wasn't wearing a white robe. It was a white gown, shimmering with tiny pearls and what appeared to be diamonds.

I did the math: white gown, young, beautiful, bejeweled. I was going to take a big leap here and guess.

"Princess Mirabai?" I said, then winced at the pain in my skull.

She was startled that I knew her, but she didn't jump back. Though I couldn't exactly jump forward since I was attached to an iron ring set in the floor by a three-foot chain linked through my manacles. The area around where I was chained had absolutely nothing within reach, not even a chair to sit on. I felt like an unruly dog that had done something extra naughty. I guess elbowing Sarad Nukpana in the gut in front of his lackeys qualified. And to top it off, I couldn't stand up; the chain was just long enough to let me get to my knees. I didn't even have to wonder if Nukpana had done that on purpose.

"You're Raine Benares." Princess Mirabai's voice was rich and cultured—and surprisingly calm. Her eyes told me she was no longer afraid of me, but was still cautious. Smart lady.

I nodded and immediately regretted that, too. "Right now, I wish I weren't."

"Right now, I would gladly trade places with you." The girl sounded sincere enough; maybe she'd been hit on the noggin, too. "You get to die tonight. I'm to be married and mated to a monster."

"When you put it that way, I do have it better, don't I?" I didn't mention that her monster groom was also technically a reanimated corpse. The poor girl had enough problems.

I took a good look around at what Sarad Nukpana called his quarters. The room was filled with sensual comforts. There was a low bed covered with silken pillows. A plush chaise upholstered with fabric that looked too soft to be real. An elaborately carved and inlaid table with two chairs, set with the remnants of a meal, mostly uneaten. The floor was covered in rugs, mostly of thick, soft fur. Except where I was, of course. I got to sit on cold stone.

It was familiar.

It took me a minute, but I remembered. Soon after I'd arrived on Mid, I'd done something well-intentioned that turned out to be well-intentioned but ill-advised, and had gotten my soul temporarily dragged into the Saghred, where I'd had a nasty encounter with Sarad Nukpana's newly disembodied soul. The goblin had used magic to shape his prison more to his liking. From what I was seeing now, it looked like he had turned the inside of the Saghred into his own personal version of Home Sweet Home.

"Have you seen Prince Chigaru?" Princess Mirabai was asking.

I blinked a few times to refocus my eyes on her. Jeez, even blinking hurt. "Uh, not for a while."

"But you have seen him?"

"Yes."

"He was unharmed?"

"He was the last time I saw him." I didn't mention that the last time I'd seen him was also the same time that Khrynsani black mages were thundering down the stairs at our backs.

Tension visibly drained out of her. "Thank you."

"That doesn't mean he's not being hunted. It's just unlikely he's been caught." I decided to keep "yet" to myself.

"When they brought you, Sarad told me that there would be more new prisoners before sundown—"

"Sundown? It's morning already?"

"It's just after midday."

I blinked. "How long was I out?"

"Nearly an hour."

A knock on the head didn't usually put me out for that long. My body probably took advantage of the fact that I'd stopped moving to fit in a nap. We must have been in those caves and tunnels longer than I thought. As a result, I had less time than I wanted to think of a way out of this mess, and—if I was lucky, blessed, and a miracle magnet—still manage to take out the Saghred as well. Though all three of the above were looking less likely by the second.

"Would you have any way to know if anyone's been caught in the hour I was out?" I asked.

Mirabai shook her head. "This room is soundproof."

Of course it was.

"Sarad told me when they were captured that I wouldn't see them until the ceremony. He wanted it to be a . . .

surprise." The princess bit her bottom lip in a vain attempt to stop the tears welling up in her eyes.

I waved my hands as much as I could while wearing chains. "Oh no. No, no. I don't need that. You don't need that. Besides, you'll ruin your makeup."

Mirabai sniffed and tears ran down both flawless cheeks, cheeks that would probably be just as flawless without makeup.

"I don't care!" she yelled.

Whoa. Big voice from a little girl.

She started to cry, then tried to stop, and ended up hiccupping. "I'm sorry. I'm not angry with you. It's just that everything has gone wrong, and anything I did to stop it hasn't gone right."

"Welcome to my world."

Her words came in a rush. "If I'd stayed hidden, I wouldn't have been caught, and Chigaru wouldn't be . . . be . . ."

Uh-oh, here come the waterworks again.

"He's going to be killed and it's all my fault." Her last words rose to a teary squeak.

I gave her a flat look. "Do you command this pack of black-robed wolves?"

Mirabai sniffed. "No."

"Are you the one with a big psychosis and an even bigger megalomania?"

"No."

"Then none of this is your fault."

"Maybe if I make myself ugly enough, Sarad will not want me." She eyed a knife on the small table.

My hands went from waving to placating. "Hold on, Mirabai. Let's not do anything rash." I stopped and sat up straight. "Is that knife sharp?"

"No," Mirabai huffed and plopped down on her chair, full skirts poofing around her. "It's just a butter knife. Sarad makes certain that I'm not given anything sharp. The servants are Khrynsani guards. They inspect everything that is brought in for me."

"This chain anchoring me to the wall; do you know where the key is?"

"Sarad took it with him."

Of course he did. I knew of another item Nukpana had to be carrying around with him. I paused and almost smiled. That is, he would be carrying it around if Carnades was still being a generous and accommodating guest. "Mirabai, by any chance did he have a small silver dagger with him? It would have been one you haven't seen before."

The princess's eyes went to the wall above my head, her brow creased, concentrating. "Sarad had no daggers in his belt. He was wearing his meditation robe. It's very simple, so I would have noticed if he had been carrying anything."

I didn't want to ask, but I had to. "Meditation?"

"He has been in seclusion since sunrise, meditating, to prepare himself for the Saghred ritual."

Resting up for a long night of slaughtering.

"You're sure he didn't have the dagger?" I asked.

"Positive."

Interesting and potentially useful. It appeared that Carnades hadn't given Nukpana the Scythe of Nen, or even told him that he'd taken it from me. Carnades knew full well what the Scythe was and what it could do. If Carnades had told Nukpana, the goblin would have taken it; therefore, Carnades hadn't told him. Sarad Nukpana couldn't afford to have the one thing that could cut into and empty the Saghred in anyone's hands except his own.

"Mirabai, could you find something I can use to pick this lock with? A thin piece of metal or wood, doesn't need to be sharp—"

"I can't do that."

I froze. Way to go, Raine. Nukpana probably told her they'd have separate bedrooms if she kept me from escaping. Just because the girl doesn't want to marry the guy doesn't mean that she—

Mirabai lifted the hem of her gown off of the floor, showing me her ankles. A shackle was locked around one of them; a shackle attached to a chain, long enough that she could get from the chair to the table—or to the bed—but not long enough to reach me. The shackle glittered. I did a double take and looked closer. The thing was virtually encrusted with diamonds, as was the chain that ran from the princess's ankle to one of the massive bedposts.

Fancy.

And kinky.

"Damn, what a sick bastard," I muttered.

"I am as much a prisoner as you," she said.

The jeweled shackle and chain, the opulent room. Princess Mirabai was a bird in a literal gilded cage.

"My parents betrayed me to Sathrik. I was in hiding, with allies of Chigaru. One of them was a traitor and told my parents where I was. My father sent some of his men for me. Chigaru's friends tried to protect me, but there were too many of my father's men. They killed them all and took me to Sathrik."

"Your *parents* did this?"

Mirabai nodded. "They only care about marrying me to whoever is on the throne. When Chigaru . . ." Her eyes started to well up again. With an angry sniff, she forced them back. "Then Sathrik made a deal with my father. In exchange for me, my father would receive more lands and titles."

I didn't think I could be shocked by much anymore, but this did the trick. "He sold you. Your own father sold you."

"Essentially, yes."

"I take it you didn't want to marry Sathrik, either."

"I love Chigaru." Mirabai held her head high and proud as a single tear flowed down her cheek.

Yeah, he loves you, too. And now Sarad Nukpana was playing a rollicking game of how many lives could he ruin before sundown today—and how many more could he end by daybreak tomorrow.

I gave the princess what I hoped was a reassuring smile. "Well, if I can get a few things to go right in the next couple of hours, my plan is to completely disrupt and utterly ruin your wedding."

Mirabai drew in her breath in a delighted gasp. "Thank you! Is it true that Tamnais Nathrach's mother pulled the trigger that assassinated Sathrik?" The princess's eyes were bright, but not with tears. It was with a ferocity that was at odds with her delicate appearance. At that moment, she reminded me more than a little of a young Imala.

"Yes, she did."

Mirabai nodded with grim satisfaction. "Once Sarad is dead, I will have Chigaru make her a countess."

"Chigaru's already said he'd make her a duchess, but I'm sure Deidre wouldn't object to being both."

At the mere mention of the goblin prince's name, her eyes lit up. The girl had it bad.

"Once Sathrik was out of the way, and Sarad had nothing else between him and the throne, I thought he wouldn't need me, but my father's political ties are still important to him." Mirabai paused. "Sarad told me that he will live forever. Is that true?"

"The Saghred's been known to boost life expectancy, but forever might be a bit ambitious for him to claim. Not to mention, every breathing creature hates him."

"Except for his mother, the witch," Mirabai spat.

"Is that witch description literal or figurative?"

Mirabai flashed her tiny fangs in a fierce smile. "Both. The term 'bitch' also applies. And it's rumored that she bathes in the blood of virgins to keep everything from sagging. Judging from present appearances, virgins must be getting few and far between."

Ouch. I liked this girl.

"And you are an ungrateful brat who does not know her place," said a cool, silky voice, a woman's voice. "Yet."

It came from the doorway; at least I thought it did. From where I was chained, I couldn't see a door anywhere else in the room.

"If you do not learn it soon," the woman's voice continued, "I will be forced to go to great pains to instruct you."

A goblin woman glided into view, her head held high and perfectly still—as if she already wore a crown there. She had a cold, dark beauty that was accentuated by her shimmering silver court gown. Her blue-black hair was elaborately styled, an abundance of hairpins set with sparkling rubies holding it in place. Her makeup had been expertly applied, but it was a little heavy for my taste—or for anyone with taste.

I didn't need an introduction. Sandrina Ghalfari had the whole evil-queen act down pat.

She tossed a disdainful glance at the jewel-encrusted chain linking Mirabai to the bed. "You are a temporary political necessity for us and a plaything for my son— nothing more." Sandrina turned her black eyes on me, glittering with intense satisfaction, and a burning hatred that was just a wee bit on the insane side. Her son definitely had his mother's eyes. "And you have harmed my child for the last time. I only regret that we won't have more time together; I would have enjoyed that."

"Somehow I don't think I would have."

"No, you most definitely would not."

"I hear he's made you his right-hand . . . mom."

Sandrina gave me a brittle smile. It was a wonder her makeup didn't crack. "My son will have more important things to do than rule any single kingdom. I will remain here to protect his interests."

"To make sure he has a cozy home away from Hell to come and rest up for the next round of slaughter?"

"Sarad told me you have an amusing way with words." She gazed down her aristocratic nose at me. It was literally down since I was essentially chained to the floor. "Then again, he is more easily amused than I am."

"And I've been told you have a penchant for poisons."

Sandrina's smile broadened, baring a pair of dazzling white fangs. "Ah, Tamnais has been talking."

"He's been known to do that."

Sandrina looked me up and down. "Among other things. He always had a weakness for elven women. I never understood the appeal of your race. Pale and colorless. Stunted teeth. Hair the color of mud, dirt, and the hay fed to farm animals. As a whole, your race is only marginally above repulsive. Speaking of repulsive, I understand Tamnais's mongrel came to Regor with him."

"I can't help you there. I don't know any mongrels."

"He should be in a kennel, instead of causing difficulties for our soldiers. The creature will be cornered and dealt with accordingly."

Mirabai was right; this one was a real witch with a capital B. Where was a stake, a pile of firewood, and a nice, toasty torch when you needed them?

"If all goes well, by sunrise, the entire Nathrach family will be no more," Sandrina was saying. "Tamnais and that elven paladin won't leave you, and they can't leave the Saghred. So they are here and we will find them."

Which meant it'd been over an hour and they, along with Imala, Piaras, and Chigaru, hadn't been caught. I felt a surge of pride.

"In the meantime, I'm here to see that you're appropriately attired for your role in tonight's festivities." Sandrina held a black-wrapped bundle in her hands that was tied with a thin, red cord. I hadn't noticed it before. I'd been distracted by finally meeting the thing that had hatched Sarad Nukpana. Sandrina untied the cord and pulled aside the wrapping, revealing a silken gown of the purest white.

I looked from the gown to Sandrina's over-painted yet impassive face and back again. "Mine, I take it?"

"Sarad wants even the least of his new vassals in the back of the temple to see your blood spilt. It will show up so much better against the white. Remove your clothes."

"We just met. No offense intended, but you're really not my type."

"The tub in this room will be filled and you *will* bathe yourself. Other than my own tub, Sarad's is the only other one located in a secure area." Her upper lip curled back in revulsion. "He knew that I would never allow a filthy elf in my apartment, let alone in my bathtub, so he was left with no choice but to have you brought here. If you require assistance disrobing, there are a score of temple guards within calling distance. I'm certain it would be their pleasure to help you."

"She means it." Mirabai was blushing furiously.

Holy crap. This woman was way past due for an ass kicking.

I raised my hands, showing the manacles and the length of steel links chaining me to the floor. "If I can't stand, I can't strip."

Sandrina shrugged. "It can do no harm to remove them; you can't escape." She made a small gesture and the manacles simply fell off.

That was way too easy. I cautiously extended my hand about two feet in front of me, and was rewarded with a nasty zap.

Ward. Naturally.

"Pity," Sandrina said. "I was rather hoping that you would do something barbaric and attempt to attack me."

"I'm not sorry to disappoint you."

Sandrina dropped the white gown over a chair. "I will step outside for a few minutes while you disrobe." She tossed me what was probably Mirabai's bathrobe. It passed right through the wards, landing in a silken puddle at my feet. Interesting. Objects could get in, but I couldn't get out.

"What? You don't want to watch?" I asked.

Sandrina raised one over-plucked eyebrow. "You're not my type, either."

"Just how am I supposed to get to the tub with this ward in the way?"

"You will remain precisely where you are until the tub is filled." She gave a little smile. "Then you will be moved across the room."

That didn't sound like something I'd enjoy.

There were times when I didn't want to be right. This turned out to be one of those times.

I quickly undressed and was even faster in putting Mirabai's robe on. Needless to say, I did *not* like getting naked in Sarad Nukpana's bedroom. I had just finished tying the sash when the door opened and a parade of robed and hooded servants quickly came and went from the room, filling the large copper tub with steaming water.

"Would you like some of my bath oil?" Mirabai asked once they'd gone. "It's jasmine."

"I'd love some, thank you. Maybe I can make myself so slick that Nukpana can't get a good grip on me." More likely was that between the gown and the oil, I would have lived fast, died young, and left behind a fine-looking and even better-smelling corpse.

The door opened again and Sandrina swept in, followed by what was quite simply the biggest goblin I had ever seen in my life. He was wearing Khrynsani armor, but it clearly had been extended to its limits and beyond in order to fit him. The thing lumbered into the room, looked around, saw me, and grunted. There had to have been some ogre in his family, like maybe him.

Sandrina gave a negligent wave and the ward around me crackled and vanished, leaving a static charge in the air that made the hairs on the back of my arms stand at attention.

The ogre-goblin came toward me and I swear the stone slabs beneath my feet trembled. I think the floor had the right idea. He extended one massively muscled arm that ended in an even larger hand, wrapped his fingers almost entirely around my waist and simply lifted me off the floor, carried me over to the tub, and set me down next to it. Keeping one hand tight around my waist, he bent, and I felt cold iron around one ankle, followed by the sound of a click of a lock. I looked down. One manacle was around my ankle; the other was around the clawed foot of the big tub. The ogre-goblin looked at the manacles, nodded twice, grunted once, and went back to stand behind Sandrina.

Understand that my mantra was always try to escape. But this time it didn't go very well with one of my other rules: don't be stupid. Putting up a fight against a mountain cleverly disguised as a Khrynsani guard would've taken stupid to a ridiculous level, and possibly gotten me bedecked with even more chains.

I cleared my throat of the lump that'd taken up residence there. "Thanks for the ride, big guy."

Sandrina gathered her skirts and swished her way to the door. "I will see you at the altar this evening." She opened the door and paused, smiling. "I have no doubt that you will give us a memorable performance."

She and the guard left, closing the door behind them.

I dipped my fingers in the bathwater and treated myself to a small smile. I hatched my best plots, plans, and schemes while soaking in a hot bath.

Memorable, indeed.

Chapter 19

A *nice, hot bath gives a girl a better outlook on just about* anything—and helped inspire a possible way to ruin Sarad Nukpana's evening without ending my own life.

The definition of brilliant didn't contain the word complicated. The simpler an idea was, the better the odds for success. Best of all, magic was not involved, just manipulation. And if I still ended up taking a dagger to the heart tonight, I was going to do my damnedest to scuttle an evil master plan or two before I went.

As much as I would have loved to have Mychael and my friends—and all of those enraged mages and soldiers—there with me, there was a very real possibility that this would be my show, no backup, just me and mine. Well, considering that I hadn't exactly been flush with time to figure out a way to free my magic, it'd just be me, with possibly some invaluable assistance from Princess Mirabai. Instead of magic, I would have to make do with my wits. I'd been scared out of them during the past few days—okay, to be honest, the past three months—but I thought I had enough left to get the job done.

But before I could scuttle anyone's plans, Sandrina came in to oversee my dressing. I assumed it was to make sure that the only thing I had under my sacrificial white gown was me, and nothing steely or pointy to use to stab or escape. By the time Sarad Nukpana's goons came for me, I was bathed, perfumed, gowned, and determined to make this a memorable evening for everyone.

Judging from the fanciness of their robes and armor, my escort consisted of six high-level Khrynsani black mages and at least two dozen officers of the temple guard.

Things were looking up.

There was no way all of this attention was for me. My escort wasn't because Nukpana was afraid of me magically cutting loose in his temple, or because he wanted to put on a show for his own people. My mages and guards, as well as those we passed, were moving fast and looking far too nervous for there not to be something happening in the temple that they didn't have control over.

Like several angry, magically and militarily proficient groups hell-bent on destruction.

I couldn't think of any other reason behind my absurdly large escort. If my friends attempted to rescue me, Sarad Nukpana wanted to be certain that it was only that—an attempt.

Imala had told me that there were miles and miles of corridors in the Khrynsani temple. And those were only the ones in use now; there were centuries of passages that ran below and even parallel to those. Corridors and rooms that only the highly initiated knew existed. In their respective positions as chief mage and director of the secret service, Tam and Imala had made it their business to know as much as the highest ranked Khrynsani priest.

Mychael and my friends hadn't been captured, and that had Sarad Nukpana worried.

That was some of the best news I'd gotten since we dived through that mirror.

We turned down a corridor easily twice as wide as the one we'd just been in. Every ten feet or so was a temple guard in ceremonial armor standing at unblinking attention, but that didn't mean they weren't watching. As I passed, black eyes glittered from the depths of their burnished helmets, tracking me as I was led past, reminding me of wolves who'd gone too long between meals. In addition to the usual swords and assortment of daggers, each held a tall pike with a razor-sharp hooked blade at the top. Anyone attempting to come down this corridor uninvited would find themselves impaled and/or slashed to ribbons before they'd managed to get a quarter of the way.

A pair of temple guards opened the rather plain double doors at the end of the corridor. It was a large room, dimly lit with lightglobes, with black-and-white marble floors. A few ornate chairs sat in a semicircle around the first thing I'd seen when they opened the doors. A white marble pillar rose from the floor in the exact center of the room—a pillar with a single iron hook mounted near the top. I didn't need two guesses to know that was where I was going. The two biggest guards grabbed my upper arms and all but carried me to the pillar, where the mage wearing the fanciest robe looped the chain linking my manacles to the hook over my head. Then he murmured a couple of words that sent chills up the back of my neck as the hook glowed red and bent in on itself, embedding its open end into the marble. So much for waiting until they were gone and then jumping up until I unhooked myself.

Then they all left, closing and locking the door behind them, leaving me alone, though I suspected not for long.

But right now I was alone. Don't waste it, Raine. Calm yourself and keep thinking. If you panic, you can't think; and if you can't think, you're dead.

I took a deep breath and let it out. I flexed my shoulders

and tried to relax them as much as possible, considering my hands were chained over my head. Though it could have been all kinds of worse; at least my feet were touching the floor. I breathed in through my nose and out through my mouth. There was no way my fear was going away, but I needed to keep it from turning into mindless terror. Fear wasn't a bad thing; it was all in how I used it, and didn't let it use me. It was amazing how much space fear took up in your head.

Yes, I was chained and likely to remain so. There was a lot I could do in my position. I pulled on the chain linking me to the pillar. Nothing. Well, not in the position I was in *now*, but I wouldn't be hanging here forever. It had to be getting close to sundown, and once the moon rose, Sarad Nukpana would want to start his show. I was sure he had it planned down to the second, and he would stay on schedule or heads would literally roll.

A door opened somewhere to my left. I twisted my head to see, but the hook and pillar did a fine job of keeping me from moving much.

"Patience, Raine," Sarad Nukpana murmured, the click of his boots a slow and steady cadence on the marble floor, getting closer. "I waited decades to get my hands on the Saghred; surely you can wait a few seconds to see me. I promise it will be worth it."

The goblin walked around until he was in front of me then stopped.

I'll admit it; I stared.

"I understand that it's tradition for a groom to look his absolute best for his blushing bride." His dark eyes glittered. "What do you think?"

Sarad Nukpana was wearing formfitting trousers of black suede with matching boots and nothing else. His hair was still wet and glistening from a bath and fell nearly to his waist. Any breathing female with working eyes would think Sarad Nukpana was, quite frankly, perfect.

But what made me stare was that there was no sign that only a few hours before, Nukpana had taken a crossbow bolt in the shoulder. It hadn't been from a dart-spitter like the one Tam had given me; this weapon had been powerful enough to send a bolt completely through Sathrik Mal'Salin and tack the guard behind him to a wall. Sarad Nukpana's shoulder didn't even have a pucker to show where the bolt had entered. It should have shattered his shoulder blade, and it probably had.

I gulped. I couldn't help it. "The Saghred does good work."

The goblin walked toward me until mere inches separated us. "I wanted to show you what the stone can do for someone who is willing to work in partnership with it. What you see is a wedding gift from the Saghred. The stone doesn't bite the hand that feeds it." He held up what should have been horribly burned and scarred hands. They were just as smooth and perfect as his shoulder. "It heals them." His smile was slow and seductive. "Do you like what you see, Raine?"

"You're a corpse. Reanimated, but still a corpse."

"I am beyond life, and Death can never claim me."

"Your new 'allies' are sure to line up and give it a try, and one of them is bound to get lucky eventually. I'd like to see you flipping off Death when you wake up one morning and find your head on the pillow next to you."

He was close enough that I could smell the soap that had just been on his skin.

"If you were my bride," he whispered, "would you be pleased?" He reached out one hand—one flawless and unburned hand—and ran the tips of his fingers down the length of my face and throat. I jumped as if shocked. His smile broadened. "I'll take that as a yes."

I tried to swallow, my mouth suddenly dry. "I'm just a sacrifice, a sideshow to entertain your lackeys and wedding guests, and I can assure you, I couldn't care less how you look."

"Oh, yes, concerning that. There is something you should probably know. I won't be staining that lovely gown of yours quite yet with your blood. However, it will still serve a valuable purpose tonight in ensuring that all of my new subjects see you chained to the Saghred's pedestal next to the altar."

I stood frozen. Chained to the Saghred's pedestal? "You're not sacrificing me tonight?"

"Not for some time. Does that please you, too?"

"You tell me."

"I understand that the Saghred has fed through you once before. Since it was only a few days ago, no doubt you remember the specifics."

I had to force the words out past the rising panic knotting in my chest. "I vaguely recall."

"I imagine there was excruciating pain, the sensation of a violated and murdered soul being pulled inside of you, and then ripped through you into the Saghred." Nukpana wrapped his hand around my throat, stroking, caressing. "I understand that when this happened, you screamed until you could scream no longer. And that was but one soul being pulled through you." He sighed with exaggerated disappointment. "Unfortunately, with the Saghred in its rightful place, the blood from the sacrifices will flow down to the stone's pedestal of honor, eliminating that exquisite communion between you, the sacrifice, and the Saghred." The goblin's fingers lightly slid down to stop just above my breasts— exactly where the Saghred had pulled that elf mage's soul into me. With one finger, Nukpana leisurely traced a tiny circle in that spot. "However, while it healed me last night, the stone shared with me how that communion can be reestablished and even extended to include the agonies of the souls once they're trapped inside."

With dawning horror, I knew what Sarad Nukpana was going to do to me. I stared at him, trying to remember to breathe. It would be worse than death, worse than being sacrificed and being taken inside the Saghred. I would rather die. Literally. After only a few sacrifices, I'd probably be begging for my own death—if I was still capable of speech.

"Other than as a symbol of my power, the Saghred is of no value to me until it is fully fed," Nukpana was saying, though I only half heard him. "What you said is true. There will be more than a few powerful individuals who will plot my death; they want the throne and the Saghred's strength for themselves. So you see my reasoning. I cannot take the risk of being, shall we say . . . distracted, by being the Saghred's bond servant at this time. I need for my sanity to be intact." He smiled. "You're going to be more useful to me than I ever thought possible."

I would be taking the Saghred's sacrifices. Dozens, hundreds of murdered souls pulled into and through me. I would feel every death, every stab and slash of Sarad Nukpana's sacrificial dagger. I pushed down a whimper. It would be as many deaths as it took to bring the Saghred to its full power.

I would feel each and every one of them. During their murders and afterward as they realized they were trapped forever inside of the stone, enduring years of terror and despair that lengthened into centuries, knowing that they would never be free, never truly die, slowly going mad, eventually fading into mindless wraiths.

I would experience and share their suffering, but be powerless to help.

"There's no need for me to be in full possession and control of the stone until it has attained its full strength." His voice became soft, an intimate whisper. "It's no fun to completely control something—or someone—unless you can use it for your enjoyment. To restore the Saghred to its full power will require thousands of souls. Unfortunately, the process of those souls being dragged through you . . . Let's just say that raving insanity won't be very attractive on you."

I expected one of two things to happen to me tonight: I would escape and live, or not escape and die. I was hoping for one, but prepared for the other. I was not prepared to live and linger, feeling death time and time again, but never dying myself, being released from an endless cycle of pain and insanity only when Sarad Nukpana decided that I had suffered enough.

To him, I would never suffer enough.

I could start screaming right now, which was what I really wanted to do, or I could change the topic from me dying a thousand deaths to Nukpana living forever. I wasn't looking to reap a harvest; I just wanted to plant a few seeds of doubt and get the goblin's hands off of me—and get my thoughts away from my impending future.

"The last goblin who shoveled souls into the rock was Rudra Muralin," I said, desperately trying to keep my voice from shaking. "You know how bat-shit crazy he was."

"Rudra was a boy with little training, and less discipline. His mind was easily controlled and consumed by the Saghred. The only source of surprise was that he managed to survive as long as he did."

"And he didn't have his mommy looking out for him. She dropped by your rooms, by the way. Charming woman. I see where you get it. Setting up and killing family and friends must run like a stampede in your family."

Nukpana stood very still. "Mother and I are of one mind."

"You both want to rule the world?"

Something deadly flickered in his eyes. "She knows her limitations."

"And her place?" I met his gaze and forced one corner of my lips to curl into a smile. "She doesn't seem the type to know either one."

"She is content to rule at my side."

I tried a shrug, not easy with my hands chained over my head. "If you say so. You need someone you can trust with you while you're communing with the Saghred. You gave an all-too-accurate description of what it feels like to have souls pulled through you. I scream and eventually pass out, but then I'm just a puny, little mortal elf, and you're on the verge of demigod-dom, so you probably won't have any problems—especially not with Mommy Dearest there to take care of you and watch your back."

Sarad Nukpana smiled and showed me his fangs. "I've always found it best—and more thorough—to deal with one problem at a time. Tonight, I'll begin the lengthy and enjoyable process of dealing with you. I can hardly deny my new vassals the opportunity to see the elf they have heard so much about, brought before them in chains, displayed as the prized catch that you are. They need to see you in torment. It will serve the dual purpose of beginning to take my revenge on you, and showing every last man and woman in the temple that I can and will make them suffer just as much if they make the mistake of defying me. It will save me the trouble and inconvenience of proving myself to them. They will witness your punishment and then go and tell others. Word spreads and my position is more easily secured without the bother of having to put on a vulgar display."

"So you can save your power for the more important—and even more vulgar—things like conquering, enslaving, and slaughtering."

He smiled. "Precisely. One of my most difficult decisions tonight will be who gets the honor of being the Saghred's first public sacrifice."

I froze. "I thought you'd already determined that."

"Sacrificing Deidre Nathrach would make the most effective statement. Killing the killer of my king, and all that. But would it be truly satisfying? Perhaps your paladin lover or your treasured nightingale would be a better choice."

"You haven't caught anyone yet."

One side of his lips curled ever so slightly. "Do you know this for certain? Just because you haven't seen them doesn't mean that one of them isn't chained to the altar at this very moment awaiting our arrival. How do you know I haven't ordered that done so you can see him there as you walk down the aisle?"

"You have me confused with the one marrying you."

"It is my goal to make our unique relationship last much longer than my marriage."

A pair of Khrynsani entered bearing ornate robes draped over their arms.

"Perfect timing, gentlemen," Nukpana said. One of the guards held Sarad Nukpana's shirt for him. As Nukpana buttoned it, he continued to speak to me as if they weren't there. "Since you will play such a critical role in tonight's ceremonies, you should know the schedule of events. If we begin at moonrise, and nothing unforeseen delays the ceremony, I should be able to take care of all of your dear ones before dawn. They will go first to ensure that enough remains of your mind for you to be fully aware of every agony they will endure at my hands before they are allowed to die. Then the Saghred will pick up where I left off, to make certain that you share your loved ones' terror and despair as they realize that their suffering is as eternal as the Saghred. It will be a long night's work, but worth the effort in so many ways."

The next guard held up a purple robe for Nukpana that was embroidered in silver.

"Tamnais's family will go first, including Kesyn Badru," he continued. "Once I have eradicated the stain of the Nathrach bloodline, I will put an appropriate end to Tamnais. Imala Kalis betrayed me and played the late King Sathrik for a fool, which in all honesty wasn't that difficult. Traitors deserve to endure a death as long as their betrayal. Imala betrayed us for years, so she will suffer accordingly."

Nukpana lifted his arms so a scarlet sash could be wrapped around his waist. "As a reward for all of his valuable information, I'm allowing Carnades Silvanus the honor of dispatching one of the sacrifices. He feels that it is fitting—and I agree—that he be allowed to perform a sacrifice himself. It will also show my subjects that even though he is an elf, Magus Silvanus is a valued partner. Carnades selected Paladin Eiliesor, and I've granted his request. He asked for the nightingale as well, but I refused him." He turned to the guards. "Leave us."

Sarad Nukpana approached me again. "I have an intense dislike for leaving what I believe are called loose ends. Without your cunning, Piaras Rivalin would not have escaped death that night in Mermeia; even that magnificent voice of his would not have saved him. Thanks to you, he escaped and has lived to cause me no end of trouble, nearly as much as you yourself." The goblin leaned in to me, his lips soft against my ear. "You will have to tell me what it feels like to have your nightingale's soul pulled through you as the last of his life's blood washes over the Saghred. Not only to watch, but to share in his death, then to feel his soul struggle in vain, imprisoned for eternity in the stone." His voice dropped to caress. "But what I most want you to share with me, through each torment and every death, is what it feels like to know with absolute certainty that there is nothing, *nothing* you can do to save them or yourself."

He left me like that, shaking with terror and rage.

So much for keeping my fear from turning into mindless terror.

Chapter 20

*I wasn't standing outside the temple looking in. No, I wasn't any-*where near that lucky. I think Lady Luck was now sunning herself on the same beach as my magic. I was just inside the front doors, my guards prepared to get me into the temple and to the altar by any means possible: kicking, screaming, carried, or all of the above. I thought I'd just walk. I could see outside, but there was no way in a very hot place my guards were about to let me do anything except look.

Not that out there was much better than in here. The temple's doors looked out over Execution Square. The Blood Moon was rising over the Mal'Salin palace, unless Sarad Nukpana had already ordered it renamed.

The enormity of what the goblin would begin tonight with Deidre Nathrach swept over me, bringing with it a wave of nausea. Innocent people were about to be slaughtered because they chose to fight rather than surrender to the whims of a madman. The men and women now filling the temple, the sheep following Sarad Nukpana, would live but only because he allowed it. For now. When he ran out of those who had the backbone to oppose him, those sheep would find themselves herded to the slaughter. Some of them had to know it; others were in blissful denial, no doubt thinking that agreeing with everything Nukpana said or did or ordered them to do would protect them. By the time they realized otherwise, everyone who could have saved them would already be dead.

At that point, no one anywhere would be safe from Sarad Nukpana once he eventually killed me and took control of the Saghred. His ego let him believe that he would be the one in charge. I'd had the Saghred living in my head for the past three months and knew differently. Nukpana and the scores who came before him were nothing but slaves to provide for the stone's needs while believing the stone was there to serve them. The Saghred would make Nukpana its bond servant only because it knew he would feed and use it. The rock would latch onto him like the soul-sucking parasite it was, though it couldn't steal his sanity. Not because Sarad Nukpana was strong enough to prevent it, but because the rock couldn't take what had never been there to begin with.

No one else was coming up the temple steps from Execution Square. Everyone who was going to be allowed inside was already there. I still held out hope that Mychael, Tam, and company were somewhere among them.

Princess Mirabai was ahead of me and surrounded by eerily silent guards in immaculate formal armor. The bride would make the big entrance; I was just the flower girl. I glanced down at the manacles encircling my wrists—okay, maybe the ring bearer.

At an unspoken signal, the temple guards around me snapped to attention, and an armored hand in the middle of my back gave me a shove to get me moving. I guess Khrynsani never used words when a shove would do. I started forward, my guards spacing themselves so that they could get their hands or weapons on me, but still giving everyone we passed a clear view of their new king's catch of the day.

I had once been inside a cathedral in southern Pengor. The only way I had been able to see the ceiling had been to tilt my head back as far as it would go. Until this moment, it had been the largest indoor space I'd ever been in. The Khrynsani temple was no cathedral; absolutely nothing was sacred about the acts committed here. The lighting was dim enough to be comfortable to goblin eyes, but bright enough that I'd be able to see everything that happened. Sarad Nukpana probably saw to that detail personally.

The floor beneath my feet was dark and polished; I was going to guess black marble, since that seemed to be an all-encompassing decorating theme in this place. Ten gigantic columns, each ringed with huge lightglobes like bands of blue stars, rose from the floor like ancient trees. I could just make out the faint outline of arches reaching like skeletal arms toward the vaulted ceiling.

The temple was completely packed with people. There had to have been thousands of them.

I had no idea Sarad Nukpana had that many friends, or that many people who were desperate that Nukpana think they were his friends. Even if my friends were still free, what could they do against thousands of goblins and probably hundreds of Khrynsani either in the temple itself or within call, all eager to prove how loyal they were to their new king? Our plan had depended on destroying the Saghred before Nukpana began his twisted ceremony, before the place was packed with Saghred-loving goblins. How the hell could we possibly pull this off now?

I didn't realize I had stopped until I got another shove in the back. I growled over my shoulder. The goblins I could see were either in Khrynsani robes or uniforms, goblin army uniforms, or finery that only nobility could afford. No common people were to be seen. It sucked six ways from yesterday when your enemy's support base consisted of a kingdom's most powerful people.

Princess Mirabai's passing had caused a ripple. I caused something just short of a tidal wave. Gasps rolled through the crowd, and the goblins I passed drew back in fear as I walked down the aisle. I was chained and still Sarad Nukpana's allies feared me.

Apparently Nukpana hadn't told his new subjects that I didn't have access to the Saghred's magic. In a way, that made sense; it was even a good call on his part. After all, it wouldn't be impressive to force a chained mundane to come to the altar and endure eternal torture. Nukpana was having me paraded before his subjects to show how he could defeat and control even one with powers as great as mine. That would have these people thinking that if he could do that to someone like me, someone like them would be smart to shake in their handmade boots. Though what was good for the gander might be even better for the goose. If the chance came to make a break for it, I'd much rather have people too terrified to get anywhere near me, let alone try to take me on.

If you've got a reputation, put it to work for you.

I held my head high, met the eyes of anyone who looked at me, and stared them down. I tossed in a contemptuous smile for good measure, a smile that said loud and clear that I was only wearing these chains because it amused me. However, I could become unamused at any moment.

With a phalanx of Khrynsani guards both in front of and behind me, I had no choice but to walk at the pace they set. These guys didn't walk as much as process. Sarad Nukpana wanted to give his new subjects plenty of time to see what he'd caught. For the first and probably the last time, his motivation perfectly matched mine. I was in no hurry to get to where I was going.

Up ahead, Princess Mirabai stopped and turned toward a goblin couple seated in the front row. She carefully raised her veil, which wasn't easy to do with her jeweled manacles and chain. The man stood and smiled, extending his hands to her. With the same care and precision, Mirabai spit in his face.

He must have been the father of the bride.

Mirabai calmly lowered her veil and continued her procession.

I had to admit, the girl had class.

I didn't want to see the Saghred, especially not like this—chained, a prisoner, soon to be tortured with the deaths of those I loved until I lost my mind, my worst nightmares come to life.

The altar rose before me as we ascended the final steps.

It was empty.

My knees went weak with relief. If Mychael or Piaras had been captured, Sarad Nukpana would have had one of them chained there. The bastard had been bluffing. It was all I could do to keep from looking up and all around me for some sign that the cavalry was about to make their entrance. If they were, I didn't want to give them away. If they weren't, my already shaky morale could do without being kicked.

Trumpets sounded a fanfare from a gallery somewhere above our heads.

Two of my guards each put an armored hand on my shoulders, and forced me to my knees on the final step before the dais. I glanced over at Princess Mirabai. She had been permitted to remain standing but, like me, was one step below the dais.

King Sarad Nukpana entered the temple through a door to the side of the altar. I was surprised he didn't come up the aisle to let everyone get a good look at him. I'd gotten an all-too-good look at him two hours ago, but judging from what I could see at knee level, Nukpana had added a few kingly touches to his ensemble. He was still sumptuously attired in purple and black with a scarlet sash, but had added black chest armor intricately embossed with a silver scorpion. Naturally, he now wore a crown, a silvery ring of scorpions with their tails intertwining. I wondered if he had added the armor in case some of his allies weren't feeling as friendly as they professed to be.

Sarad Nukpana was in black; the door he came in through was black; the bloody temple was black marble—it was no wonder he needed those tin horns to let everyone know he'd arrived.

Sandrina Ghalfari followed at a stately pace in her son's wake, similarly gowned and arrayed—and, of course, crowned. Since she was standing behind her son, she'd opted not to wear chest armor in favor of several strands of diamonds that looked like they would be just as effective in stopping an assassin's bolt. Her position relative to her son bore a remarkable resemblance to Nukpana's position in relation to Sathrik before he'd begun his speech. If Sandrina started moving off to the side, I was going to dive for the floor.

Tam had once told me that the scorpion was the Nukpana/Ghalfari heraldic beastie. Scorpions equated nicely with poison, an obvious choice for a family that had Sandrina Ghalfari as its matriarch.

My guards jerked me to my feet and lifted me up onto the dais, half dragging me toward the altar.

The thing was a monstrosity.

I would have thought that a sacrificial altar would be large enough to hold a body. If that was true, the Khrynsani temple altar was at least twice the size it needed to be.

Someone was compensating.

A pair of silver magic-sapping manacles lay at the head and foot of the altar, both attached to the black stone slab by chains that vanished into it. The manacles had been polished until they gleamed, then placed with care at either end. Waiting for the first victim.

The altar itself was scrubbed clean, leaving no trace of blood. Then I saw why there probably had never been much blood spilt on most of the altar to begin with. The Khrynsani weren't wasteful. The Saghred wanted blood, so they had made certain that the victims' blood, like the victims themselves, could not escape. The slab was pitted and grooved, though not from careless stabbing, though no doubt some of the gouges had been created that way. There was a scooped-out section like a small bowl at what would be chest height on the victim chained to the table. One side of the bowl was deeper than the other. Radiating off from the deepest part of the bowl was a pair of grooves carved with care, beginning shallow and growing deeper as they reached the front side of the altar.

I knew what it had to be. A bowl carved into the altar for catching the heart blood, and a pair of grooves for funneling it to the front of the altar to . . .

My eyes followed the groves forward to where they ended—to the place I'd been desperate to avoid seeing.

The Saghred.

An orb the size of a fist, the Saghred was usually black, but I had seen it turn red right before it was about to feed. It was red now, the bright red of the blood it was about to receive, and glowing in what could only be described as eager anticipation.

The grooves went on either side of the Saghred's low, clear pedestal of carved crystal, its center hollow. The path the blood would take was obvious. It would flow around the base of the pedestal and merge, and when the altar grooves had been completely filled, the blood would flow up through the hollow pedestal beneath the Saghred where the stone rested in a shallow crystal bowl. As more blood was released from sacrifices, the pedestal would fill, then the bowl, and the Saghred would all but float in blood. Deidre and Nath's blood would bathe the Saghred and I would be standing next to them, watching—and feeling—them die. If enough people were slaughtered on that altar, the Saghred's bowl would eventually overflow. I looked down at my feet. A metal grate completely encircled the pedestal and altar.

A drain for the excess blood from an endless procession of victims.

Sudden dizziness and nausea made the pedestal and altar waver before my eyes. My guards grabbed my chains and, before I had my feet back underneath me, jerked me to a post in front of the altar. One of the guards roughly seized my wrist. There was a click, then my wrist was held immobile in something even tighter than my manacles had been. Before my vision could clear, Sarad Nukpana was beside me, gripping my manacled hand.

I focused my eyes. My right wrist was chained to an iron post that had been mounted directly behind the Saghred's pedestal, between it and the front of the altar. I was manacled so that I was forced to face the head of the altar. Not only would I feel all of the deaths; I would have to watch them die. My hand and fingers were suspended above the Saghred, held in the goblin's iron grip.

He smiled down at me. "Don't worry, Raine. The Saghred has promised not to take you. I'm not the only one who wants you to suffer."

Sarad Nukpana forced my hand down onto the Saghred and I screamed.

I didn't think I could have stopped that scream tearing its way out of my throat if I'd tried. Nukpana had forced my hand down, but the Saghred had grabbed it, holding it fast against its pulsating surface. My palm and fingers were fused to the stone; even if I hadn't been manacled, I couldn't have pulled away. The Saghred didn't budge from the pedestal; it was as if the rock had become a part of it. Suddenly the stone sent a charge spiking through my body, forcing me to my knees.

I saw the Saghred, truly saw it. The stone filled my vision, then my entire being. The thing I thought I could destroy, what puny and insignificant mortals had pitted themselves against down through the ages and had failed, every last one of them. Even my own father had failed; the best he could do was to keep the rock as far away from himself as possible. It wouldn't have mattered if I'd still had my magic. The vast majority of it had been given, granted, and bestowed by the Saghred. As I had found out the hard way, what had been given could be taken away or denied.

At that moment, the Saghred allowed me to truly see it, to know the breadth of its existence, the extent of its power.

Since the beginning of time, before life walked on this world, it had existed—and it had hungered. Elves, goblins, and humans were born and multiplied, built cities, forged civilizations. As they thrived, so had the Saghred. The stone grew in power and cunning, making itself known to those who desired its power for their own, tricking them into believing such a thing was possible, that mortals could truly possess and control it. The stone granted a select few the strength they desired, gave them the power they craved—in return for their offerings.

And the Saghred had fed and increased in power and influence and worshipers.

I'd never felt so small, so vulnerable, so completely and utterly insignificant.

I thought I could destroy it, to shatter what had existed before time was measured, and would be here long after the last of us were dust. I thought I could destroy that.

I came back to myself only to discover that not only was I on my knees before the Saghred's pedestal, but my head was bowed, my forehead resting reverently against the cool crystal of its base—and standing beside the pedestal was a smiling Sarad Nukpana.

Oh. Hell. No.

With a snarl, I staggered to my feet. It took nearly everything I had, but I would not bow my head or bend my knee to either rock or goblin.

"Bravo, Raine," Nukpana murmured. "You can see the festivities so much better if you're standing." He then turned and swept to the center of the dais.

Out of the shadows at the foot of the altar came a figure in white, flanked by a pair of Khrynsani black mages, and followed by temple guards.

Kesyn Badru grinned and gave me as much of a wave as he could with chained hands. One of the mages pushed him to the altar.

"You look like hell, girl."

I drew a ragged breath. "Feel like hell, sir."

The old mage saw my hand locked to the Saghred, and his eyes narrowed to black pinpoints of rage. "Death is too good for him."

"Tell me about it."

Kesyn looked from the Khrynsani mages to the altar and back again, gave a derisive bark of a laugh, and sat right down on the floor. "You want me on that butcher's slab, do it yourself." Kesyn's words carried to the last goblin ears on the last row. Ever the showman, he leisurely crossed his legs and with a contented sigh, leaned back against the altar. "I hope you bust a gut."

A couple of snorts and a few chuckles came up from the goblins assembled in the darkness. I smiled; I couldn't help it. Kesyn saw and gave me a roguish wink. If I had to share what was happening to the souls trapped inside the Saghred, at least I could count on Kesyn's spirit to be there with me to make jokes about it.

If you're going to die, first make sure the man who'll be wielding the knife looks ridiculous. Mirabai had class, but the old man had style.

Sarad Nukpana's imperious gaze swept over both of us. He'd heard Kesyn and he was going to ignore him. But I had a feeling that while the old man might die from a single dagger to the heart, his corpse was going to be on the receiving end of multiple stab wounds.

And I'd feel every last one of them.

It took six Khrynsani, but they managed to heave Kesyn onto the altar and chain him to make sure he stayed there. Once they moved away, Kesyn started squirming, not like he was trying to escape, but like he was trying to work the lumps out of a really bad mattress.

"Sarad said he needs the first sacrifice to be a mage of power," he told me. "I guess you don't qualify right now. Sorry about that. Though I suppose I shouldn't complain, at least I finally get to lie down."

I wasn't believing this. I thought I'd be the first one to lose my mind. "Old man, you've lost it."

"Some have said so," he mused thoughtfully. "But here, at this moment, I can assure you I am in full command of my faculties."

That did it. He was nuts.

The temple guards who had brought Kesyn in had left the dais and returned with Deidre and Nath Nathrach, and Tam's elderly butler, Barrett. Deidre and Barrett were the personification of elegance and poise. Nath looked like he'd had several accidents involving falling on half a dozen temple guards' fists. Tam's little brother had fought back. Hard. Good for him. The guards chained them to posts spaced at equal distances from the foot of the altar. Deidre gave me an encouraging nod.

Sarad Nukpana faced his new subjects. It was speech time or, in Nukpana's case, gloat time. The lighting on the dais dimmed slightly, leaving Nukpana in a pool of light, while casting the rest of us into shadow, ensuring that all eyes would be on the new goblin king. I had a feeling this wasn't going to be a short speech. Since none of his guests of honor had been captured yet, the goblin would want to stall for time. Either way, it'd give me a chance to catch my breath. In the next few minutes, I was going to need it.

There were now several Khrynsani black mages standing to the right of the altar who hadn't been there before I'd been manacled to the rock. Judging from the ornateness of their robes, these must have been Sarad Nukpana's heavy hitters. I caught a scent of spices and smoke. I took a big sniff. It was coming from the black mages. Imala was right; you *could* smell them.

Carnades Silvanus was with them, standing less than ten feet away. I let out a little relieved burst of air. For the first and last time, I was actually glad to see him. Sarad Nukpana had promised him Mychael, but with Mychael still free, there'd been the possibility that Carnades wouldn't be on the dais. I needed him to be here.

The elf mage was far enough from the altar that the goblins in the temple wouldn't mistake him for a sacrifice, but close enough so that he'd be able to enjoy the killings. Mychael's not having been captured had to be a big disappointment to him; he'd only get to watch, not participate.

Carnades went with a solemn expression, but considering how many goblins were in the audience, and especially the large number of old-blood aristocrats in the front rows, Carnades had to have been shaking in his borrowed Khrynsani robes. The elf mage never got into a fight unless he knew he could win either fairly or by cheating. I could tell he was having serious doubts now about what he'd gotten himself into. If there was anything old-blood goblins hated worse than an old-blood elf, it was an old-blood elf traitor.

No one was about to confuse Carnades with a Khrynsani, unless one had taken a dip recently in a vat of bleach. Wearing black robes and standing next to those goblin mages, Carnades virtually glowed with his white-blond hair and skin so pale he was damned near translucent. The only thing keeping one or more of those goblin nobles from plugging Carnades with a crossbow pistol was Sarad Nukpana's protection.

Protection I was about to remove.

I caught his eye. Carnades's facial expression didn't change, but his pale eyes glittered in utter triumph. No doubt he'd heard me scream and seen me fall to my knees. It was all he could do not to come over to me and do some gloating of his own. I would like nothing more. He'd ask Sarad Nukpana for a few minutes with me before the sacrifices began. I knew he would, and Nukpana would grant it, if only to make me suffer more. Carnades couldn't bear not being able to whisper sadistic nothings in my ear before Nukpana and the Saghred got hold of me.

My right hand was locked against the Saghred, but my left was still free, at least for now. I wasn't as nimble with my left hand, but with literally everything at stake, I'd make do. Part of my concern had been being able to get close to the Saghred. I looked at the rock and blew out a shaky breath. Well, I couldn't get any closer than I was right now.

Whether I died tonight, managed by some miracle to escape, or began a never-ending torture session, I'd at least go to my death or go insane secure in the knowledge that I'd done everything I could to prevent Carnades's genocide of the elven people. If this worked, I might still die, but I'd take the Saghred with me. If it didn't work, I'd get to feel Carnades die and hear his soul screaming from inside the Saghred. Though, while initially enjoyable, it could become tedious after a while. But if Carnades Silvanus's soul was dragged through me tonight, I fully planned to laugh the entire time. It'd probably be crazy-lady maniacal laughter, but to end Carnades's miserable life would make it all worthwhile.

Suddenly Sarad Nukpana paused in his speech, looked directly at Carnades, and graciously gestured toward me. I just stood there stupefied. I couldn't believe this. Nukpana was giving Carnades his royal blessing and personal permission to come over to me to gloat right now—or he had something else up his embroidered sleeve.

Either way, Lady Luck had just tossed me a bone, and I wasn't about to turn my nose up at it.

"I have never beheld such a vision of loveliness," Carnades purred just above a whisper once he was next to me. "I'm sure His Majesty would agree with me. You on your knees before him and the Saghred . . . Jealousy nearly overcame me."

"Don't stand next to me; I'm not going to protect you," I purred right back, keeping my voice for Carnades's ears only and barely moving my lips. "Every goblin in this place would love to see you chained to that altar. You're not just an elf; you're a traitor."

"It's merely a word."

"Everyone hates a traitor. It doesn't matter that you're betraying your own people for goblins. If spit would fly that far—and if Sarad Nukpana wouldn't strike them dead for trying it—you'd be taking a shower right now. You're up here because Nukpana wants you to know that the only thing keeping you from being torn limb from limb is his royal goodwill."

Sarad Nukpana was stepping carefully now. He was explaining to his subjects why an elf was wearing the sacred robes of a Khrynsani. Nukpana told his people exactly what Carnades had done: revealed to him the Conclave's evacuation routes, as well as all of the elven defenses and their locations. As a result of Carnades's strategic and magnanimous generosity, the elves would be the first to be attacked when the Saghred reached full power and the Gate was activated.

"Hated traitor," I said in a singsong voice out of the corner of my mouth.

"And as his reward," Sarad Nukpana was saying. "Magus Silvanus will be the representative of our new government in the elven capital until such time as I can appoint a regency there."

Carnades kept the smile on his face, but sucked in his breath through his clenched teeth.

I bit my bottom lip against a smile. You know, it was downright enjoyable when Sarad Nukpana did his sadistic bit with someone I hated. "He didn't mention anything about you being king, did he? You think that's just an oversight?"

Out of the corner of my eye, I could see that two Khrynsani black mages were closely watching Carnades. They had been standing on either side of the elf mage before Nukpana gestured him over to me.

"Those two are sticking close enough to you to qualify as a second skin. They must be a recent acquisition. I don't believe they were with you when you confiscated the Scythe of Nen from me, were they? You can't risk hiding it anywhere in the temple, so you've got it on you."

Carnades's left eyelid twitched once.

"I'll take that as a yes. You shared the evacuation routes and elven defenses with Nukpana, but you didn't share your shiny, new dagger. Best friends should share everything."

Carnades's upper lip was beading with nervous sweat. "You wouldn't dare."

"Oh, you bet your baby blues I would. Give me that dagger, put it in my hand, or I'll share *you* with Nukpana."

"You're bluffing. If you tell him I have the dagger, he'll take it and you will still have nothing."

"Wrong. I'll be taking you down with me. Either way I win."

"What's to stop me from giving it to you and then telling Sarad that you have it?"

"I'll say you gave it to me to destroy the Saghred, *traitor.* You wanted to be king of the elves. Nukpana just screwed you over in front of everyone, so you're trying to use me to take your revenge."

Carnades turned smug. "He'll never believe you."

"Think not? I'm naked under this gown; I'm not even wearing shoes. Nukpana's mom personally oversaw my undressing and dressing to make sure I didn't pick up any sharp trinkets. You're the one who searched me when we were caught, and I know the guards with you recall you finding and pocketing a certain silver dagger."

"Filthy bitch."

"I'll have you know I just had a bath." I put my free hand at my side and beside Carnades's robes. "I either get to destroy the Saghred, or I will destroy you. I win either way." I gave his robe a sharp tug. "I know you've got it where you can get to it. Put that dagger in my hand now, and both of us might just make it out of here alive."

Carnades's breath came in a hiss, but two seconds later, he slipped the Scythe of Nen into my waiting hand.

Yes.

I closed my hand around the small scabbard, my fingers quickly working to free the blade. Suddenly, the temple went completely silent.

Sarad Nukpana had stopped talking and was looking at us.

Carnades's voice rang out. "Raine Benares has the Scythe of Nen!"

Asshole.

An unseen hand snatched the dagger free of the scabbard, slicing my fingers as it was pulled away from me.

The Scythe of Nen now glittered in Sarad Nukpana's upraised hand.

My hand was bleeding, and the Saghred blazed red.

Oh, crap.

Chapter 21

I dropped the scabbard and pressed my bleeding fingers as hard as I could against my thigh, desperate to get the bleeding stopped. That blazing red glow told me the rock was getting impatient. It must not like long speeches.

Sarad Nukpana tucked the Scythe in his sash and leisurely walked toward us, his own personal spotlight keeping perfect pace with him. This was a game to him, entertainment for his guests, and Carnades and I were the game pieces the goblin was playing with at the moment.

"Raine, do not concern yourself with the Saghred's intentions," Nukpana said. "It assured me it would not take you until such time as I give it leave to do so." His black eyes glittered as he shifted his attention to Carnades. "The *Saghred's* loyalty is unquestioned."

Ouch.

"From her injured hand, it is quite obvious that Mistress Benares was in possession of the Scythe—however briefly,"

Nukpana continued smoothly. "But that begs the question of how she came by it. She has been closely watched."

"Told you so," I muttered to Carnades.

"She's a thief who picked my pocket and stole it before I could present it to you," the elf mage replied.

I had to hand it to him; Carnades was doing a fine impersonation of righteous indignation.

"Nice recovery, but no dice," I told him.

Carnades bristled.

Nukpana's voice was amused. "Magus Silvanus, nothing happens in this temple that I do not know—or am made aware of."

The elf mage drew himself up. "Are you questioning my loyalty?"

I snorted. "He's already said the rock's more loyal than you."

Carnades turned on me and hissed, "Shut up!"

Fear makes a man *so* much easier to goad. I smiled. "Wrong move. I won."

The elf mage froze as if the Scythe of Nen had already been plunged into his back. He could feel Sarad Nukpana's presence looming behind him like Death himself. The goblin was holding out his arm and hand, stopping his personal guard from coming any closer. This was still a game and Nukpana wasn't finished playing yet.

"Magus Silvanus, I permitted your conversation with Mistress Benares because I wanted confirmation that you had the Scythe in your possession, instead of being forced to be so crass as to have my new partner searched. As a host, I owe that courtesy to my guests. You have abused my hospitality."

Carnades's face twisted into something ugly. "You promised that I would be king of the elves."

"I promised nothing aside from what I have just told my people," Nukpana replied mildly.

Unlike Carnades, the goblin had himself under complete

control. Then again, he wasn't the one staring Death in the face.

"Any conclusions you arrived at were driven by your own grandiose imagination," Nukpana added. Then he smiled. "I possess a unique gift of simultaneously speaking and listening from a distance. It is a talent I have cultivated over many years in the goblin court. As Mistress Benares so eloquently stated, everyone hates a traitor. By keeping the Scythe of Nen from me, you have unequivocally proven that you cannot be trusted by anyone. Therefore you have no worth to me." He lowered his arm, the only thing that was keeping his guards at bay.

Game over.

"Strip him of that robe and then burn it," Nukpana told his guards. "It's been tainted. Then prepare him for the altar."

Carnades Silvanus was in the top 5 percent of the most powerful mages in the seven kingdoms. Did he cut loose with everything he had? Try to take out as many Khrynsani as he could before they brought him down?

No and no.

Carnades knew this was a fight he was going to lose. Badly. So what did he do? The chickenshit coward used me as a shield. I was shackled to the Saghred and couldn't move, so I didn't know what he hoped to accomplish.

Sarad Nukpana's voice dripped with contempt. "Once again, *Magus* Silvanus, you lay hands on what is mine."

Faster than thought, Nukpana shoved me aside, grabbed Carnades's shoulder, and plunged the Scythe of Nen to the hilt in the elf's chest. The goblin gripped Carnades's shoulder, holding the elf upright until the last signs of life had faded from his ice blue eyes. Then and only then did Nukpana release him, and Carnades Silvanus's dead body slid off of the blade and crumpled at my feet.

"Dispose of that," Nukpana told the guards.

I watched as Carnades's body was dragged away, his final expression one of utter disbelief.

One of the Khrynsani had retrieved the Scythe's scabbard from the floor and presented it to his leader. Without another word, Nukpana sheathed the Scythe, tucked it into his sash, and descended the steps to where Princess Mirabai stood flanked by her needlessly big guards. I'd almost forgotten about the wedding. He had to marry Mirabai first to secure the alliance of her family. Then he'd come back to me and celebrate with a night of sacrificing.

Business before pleasure.

Nukpana glanced up at me and smiled. I wouldn't have been surprised to hear a little sigh of contentment. If my hands had been free I would have given that smile the response it deserved. I had to settle for an aloof glare. He'd finally gotten everything he wanted; he was one happy psycho. A beautiful, stolen bride at his side to secure his political power, the family of his lifelong enemy at his mercy, and me chained to the Saghred's pedestal, my torture the icing on his wedding cake.

Sarad Nukpana turned to Princess Mirabai and lifted her veil. With an involuntary whimper, the girl stepped back— trapped against the crossed pikes of the guards behind her. Sarad smiled and reached out to touch her face.

"Take your filthy hands off of her!"

The roar came from everywhere at once, echoing off of the ceiling vaults and filling the temple with his rage.

I knew that voice.

I wasn't the only one. Mirabai's head came up, her face the very picture of hope.

Her prince had come to save her. Either that or die a really slow and gruesome death.

The people began murmuring and looking around trying to locate where the voice was coming from.

You'd expect one of the most wanted men in the city to stay hidden, or if he was going to taunt Sarad Nukpana directly to do it from afar—way afar. In the time that I'd known him, Prince Chigaru Mal'Salin had never done the expected. The crazy and suicidal, yes. The expected, no. I just hoped he'd had the sense not to be this crazy without backup.

Not only had Chigaru made himself heard; he'd ensured that he could be seen. There he was on a gallery right above the door that Kesyn and the Nathrachs had been brought through, dressed like a king about to go into battle in Tam's spare suit of armor. Chigaru looked appropriately regal and, if Mirabai's expression was any indicator, sexy as hell.

The people's mutterings turned to shouts and gasps of surprise and shock.

While I didn't doubt that the prince could bellow when he put his gut to it, Chigaru's volume went way beyond that of a prince being trained to project. There was master spellsinger magic at work. Now it was my turn to grin like a smitten schoolgirl.

Mychael was here and he was close.

Sarad Nukpana suddenly had a public relations problem on his hands.

Yes, Sathrik had named Nukpana as his heir, and had been conveniently assassinated immediately afterward, but Chigaru was the legitimate successor. The goblins in the temple had supported Sathrik Mal'Salin, and had transferred that support to Sarad Nukpana because of his power over them, not due to any dynastic loyalty. They may not have agreed with Prince Chigaru's politics or even liked him, but he was the only sibling of their late king, and, most important, his last name was Mal'Salin, the family that had been their ruling dynasty for the past two thousand years.

Goblins were big on intrigue, but even bigger on tradition. It didn't get more intriguing than what was happening right now.

To the goblins in the temple, it appeared that Sarad Nukpana had merely taken the position that was his by right, along with possession of his late king's bride. However, with only his presence and the demand that Nukpana unhand his woman, Prince Chigaru Mal'Salin told everyone within sound of his voice that the only thing Sarad Nukpana had the right to was his choice of method of execution.

Nukpana could have quickly eliminated the problem by eliminating Chigaru, but he'd risk scuttling his plans. If he killed the prince now, he might be doing the same to a lot of his political alliances. Until I was dead and the Saghred's power his, Sarad Nukpana wasn't a demigod yet. I stood perfectly still, and tried not to breathe or otherwise draw attention to myself. Hopefully Nukpana was too focused on Chigaru to use the Scythe of Nen or any other handy, sharp object on me to correct his oversight.

I needn't have worried; Sarad Nukpana had come too far to let a little thing like the appearance of the legitimate successor ruin his night.

Nukpana stared at the prince impassively for a moment, his eyes steady. Then without melodrama, he said, "Kill him."

In an instant, two temple guards raised their crossbows and fired. The bolts shattered on impact with some kind of shield. I didn't recognize the pattern of the bright green lattice that flared when the bolt hit, but I did know it as goblin mage work.

Looked like the newly freed mages had joined our side.

Only a couple of them would have been needed to keep Chigaru shielded. Which left the question: what mischief were the rest of them up to? I couldn't wait to find out. I normally didn't like surprises, but I'd gladly make an exception for this one and anything else they'd like to pull out of their collective bag of tricks.

The crossbowmen continued to fire, Khrynsani mages started lobbing fireballs, the shield continued to protect, and Prince Chigaru's voice rang clear and compelling against the vaults of the temple's ceiling.

"This treasonous usurper was responsible for the murder of my brother and your king. He has kidnapped with intent to defile my fiancée and your future queen, and he has betrayed the goblin people—your brothers and sisters whose only crime was loyalty to our people, defending our right to live in peace, and holding high the ideals we prize above all."

Those were the kinds of words that ended up in history books, read by children of future generations—that is, if Chigaru didn't take a steel bolt or fireball through the throat first. Though that possibility decreased with each word the prince spoke; the Khrynsani firing on him were lowering their weapons and hands, their eyes on Chigaru, their expressions vaguely dazed.

Spellsingers could do a lot with their voices, and Mychael was doing one of the most difficult using Chigaru's voice, not his own. That took skill that only a very few spellsingers ever attained. It was one of the reasons why spellsingers were so dangerous, and so prized by rulers and the politically powerful. A spellsinger's influence running beneath the words of a speech couldn't change minds, but they could make an audience believe that the words being said sounded reasonable and rang true.

The magnifying magic was Mychael's, but the words and their passion were all Chigaru.

It was one hell of a potent combination.

"You remain free—for now," Chigaru continued. "Until this creature that stands before you takes your life and the lives and blood of your loved ones to preserve his own foulness, a *thing* bent on the destruction of the goblin people to feed his own demented appetites. He cares not for you. He loves not our people. He will feed on you until the goblins are no more and he is but a monster bloated from feasting on your souls. Will you allow that to happen?" The prince's question rang with challenge. He turned to face Sarad Nukpana and his voice dropped to a growl seething with barely contained rage. "I. Will. *Not.*"

Running under the prince's words was the message he and Mychael wanted the people to not only hear, but believe: Chigaru would fight to his last breath to prevent even one of his people—any and all of his people—from being sacrificed.

Chigaru Mal'Salin looked like a king, but even more important, he was acting like one. He was a warrior focused on the target he had chosen, the one who had stolen his woman, his throne, and his people. Mirabai was thrilled. I had to admit I was enjoying the sight myself. I enjoyed the other thing I saw even more. Mychael in the rafters. I looked away, but not so fast as to draw attention. Though I think I could have jumped up and down and waved my one free arm at him and no one would have turned from the drama unfolding right in front of them.

I couldn't help but notice that Chigaru didn't mention the Saghred. Not once. It was an impressive display of political acumen. The goblin people had missed their legendary stone of power, but it'd been over a thousand years since their ancestors lived and died under the rock's influence and insatiable hunger. If he survived this, Chigaru would have to remind them that the Saghred hadn't been finicky about whose souls it took—and many of their rulers had used the stone to rid themselves of people who had become personally or politically inconvenient. For now the prince had his attention squarely where it needed to be—bringing down the true monster.

"The boy's got potential," Kesyn murmured in approval.

Sarad Nukpana was in danger of losing them before he officially had them—and he knew it. His hand shot out toward Chigaru, what looked like blue lightning crackling at the tips of his fingers. No shield could stand against that, especially one that had been under constant assault and had to have been weakened.

It happened too fast. The prince didn't stand a chance.

A pair of armored hands snatched the prince back and off of the balcony at the instant Sarad Nukpana released that spell. Armored hands that were attached to Tam Nathrach. Now it was Deidre, Nath, and Barrett's turn to be happy.

No one's happy lasted for long. The lightning that had shot from Nukpana's fingers closed like a massive fist around the gallery, instantly reducing the wood to charred remains. A temple guard had the supreme misfortune to be standing directly beneath the gallery. The lightning engulfed him as well—but it didn't engulf his screams or block the sight of him being roasted alive inside the blue crackling sphere. The lightning vanished, revealing a charred corpse that crumpled to the ground in a pile of blackened bone and ash.

Utter silence filled the temple. You could have heard a charred tooth drop.

I couldn't imagine anyone wanting to stay after seeing a man burned alive, but these were goblin nobles and military—and the goblin who'd dealt the death was Sarad Nukpana. There were a few screams here and there, but they were quickly cut off by either the screamer themselves or muffled by their neighbor. No one wanted to be *openly* horrified. Self-preservation could justify almost anything. To scream would be to disapprove, and disapproval could earn you a one-way trip to the Saghred's altar.

Right there was a really big difference between goblins and elves—at least my kind of elves. The first cooked corpse we saw and we'd be the hell out of there.

"Find them," Sarad Nukpana snarled, "and bring them to me."

The surviving temple guards on the dais rushed to obey, or to get out of Nukpana's range.

Nukpana stalked over to Princess Mirabai, seized her by the wrist, and jerked her in the direction of the Khrynsani high priest. "A momentary interruption, my love," he said, voice tight. "Let us be married."

Mirabai got her feet solidly under her, and attacked Sarad Nukpana.

It was apparent that at some point Mirabai had been taught to fight, or at least to defend herself. Emboldened by Chigaru's gallant speech, the little princess began screaming and punching Nukpana with admirable gusto, showing everyone that she felt she didn't have anything left to lose and had decided to go out in a way that would at least let her keep her self-respect intact, even if she was going to be reduced to a pile of charred ashes.

That was what she wanted them to think.

I knew differently.

Sarad Nukpana pulled the girl close, one arm locked around her waist, the other hand tightly griping her throat. "Patience, Your Highness. We will play soon enough."

Mirabai stopped struggling, her chained hands clenched together at her waist.

I took a deep breath and held it, and kept my eyes on her hands.

At that moment, a dead Khrynsani guard dropped out of thin air, landing wetly on the goblin nobles in the fifth row, immediately followed by another falling into the section occupied by Mirabai's parents.

Now, *that* got the screams started and kept them going. Still others decided that dead bodies falling on them gave them the best excuse they'd had all night to be both openly horrified *and* get the hell out.

Kesyn was chuckling from the altar. "Disrupt, disgust, and disperse—excellent tactics. Clears out the people you don't really want to kill to make room to do a better job of killing the ones you really need dead. Our boys and girls are professionals."

I squinted into the dark beyond the lights, trying to see without really wanting to. Though from what I could see, I had to admit the Resistance's mages were doing a fine job inciting a panicked stampede. As gruesome as it was, corpses raining down from above did the trick for court goblins who had probably seen it all and done most of it themselves. Falling dead bodies definitely made them want to leave. I didn't dwell on how our mages had gotten the Khrynsani bodies up in the air in the first place.

I snapped my attention back to Mirabai. The princess was still clutched in Sarad Nukpana's arms.

Sarad Nukpana looked pleased, and it had nothing to do with his bride-to-be. His black eyes scanned the temple floor, assessing the situation. I didn't need to look to know; I'd already seen it. All of Nukpana's enemies gathered in one place, and his allies fleeing for safety. I felt the goblin gathering his will. The son of a bitch was giving his bootlickers a little more time to get clear of the temple before he opened up on the Resistance.

Sarad Nukpana viciously flung Mirabai aside. The princess hit the stone floor hard, rolled twice, and lay unmoving.

Dammit!

Nukpana encased himself in the same ball of blue lightning that had incinerated the guard. Unfortunately, it didn't torch him; the thing protected him. Both hands blazed with blue flame, which he launched into the darkness toward the left side of the temple. Men and women were illuminated and engulfed in the lightning, burning them alive, their screams turning to shrieks that should have been impossible for a throat to make. They weren't in Khrynsani uniforms or court dress.

Resistance fighters.

Destroyed in half a minute of the worst agony imaginable.

I screamed in rage and pulled against the Saghred, damned near ripping the skin from my hand. Now I screamed in white-hot pain. I panted to catch my breath. *Think, Raine! Think!*

Nukpana had left me barefooted. This was going to hurt, but perpetual torture would hurt a hell of a lot worse and for as long as Nukpana could keep me alive. At that point, a broken foot would be the least of my problems. A broken foot would heal. My sanity wouldn't.

I pounded the base of the Saghred's pedestal with my heel, and ignored the pain that shot up my leg. Once. Again. And again.

Nothing.

I roared in rage at the pedestal and the smug-ass rock it held.

A deep rumbling shook the marble slab floor beneath my feet, and it wasn't from me kicking a pedestal.

It wasn't coming from Sarad Nukpana, but I had a sinking feeling he had everything to do with it. It wasn't magic. I didn't feel it in the way that magic could be felt. I felt it in my bones, shaking me from my feet on up. Now would be a hell of a time to find out that the bastard could summon an earthquake on command.

Kesyn went pale. "Oh, hell."

"What is it?"

"Something we don't want up here with us."

"That doesn't tell me—" I froze.

A crack appeared in the center of the temple floor, quickly spreading in both directions at once, toward the doors and toward the dais—and us.

"Oh, hell" was right.

A monstrous scaled claw reached up through the crack, grasping a chunk of marble the size of the altar Kesyn was chained to, flinging it aside like a chair in a barroom brawl. A pair of familiar scaled heads broke through with roars that made my knees go weak. The fleeing goblin allies screamed in terror as if from a single ragged throat.

The sea dragons liked that.

Sarad Nukpana shouted over the screams and roars, making himself heard—by the dragons. Their heads turned and faced him, like dogs waiting for a command.

He could control them.

This was worse than earthquakes on command.

If those things managed to claw their way into the temple, they'd bring the walls down on us all, and Sarad Nukpana wouldn't have to lift a finger to do anything else. The Saghred would survive. I was certain Sarad Nukpana would find a way to survive, but no one else would.

I saw a movement of white on the edge of my vision. Mirabai was slowly getting to her feet, bleeding from a cut on her forehead. She raised one hand to her head; the other held something glittering of silver.

Oh, good girl!

The Scythe of Nen. The fruit of her labor for attacking Sarad Nukpana.

The only thing that could have made me happier was the Saghred letting my hand go. But if everything went according to Plan B, that would happen soon enough.

Never come up with only one plan when you'll probably need two. I'd hoped I could get Carnades to give me the Scythe, then immediately stab the Saghred and screw the consequences. I'd rather have had Reapers to suck up the escaping souls, but Kesyn was chained with magic-sapping manacles, so I'd just have to work with what I had. If that plan had failed (it had), and Sarad Nukpana had taken the Scythe (he did), Princess Mirabai was my Plan B—get that dagger by any means possible. She went with a straightforward, and probably intensely satisfying, attack.

That girl had my vote for goblin queen.

The dragon-ripped chasm in the floor had extended up the stairs to the dais. Between that and the firepower being flung around, Mirabai couldn't get to me. But we'd planned for this, practicing with that butter knife in Sarad Nukpana's bedroom. It had been about the same size and weight as the Scythe, and Mirabai had proven herself to have an impressively accurate throwing arm. Now the princess took the time she needed with the aim, then gave it an underhanded toss—just as the female dragon punched through another piece of the floor and began pulling her sinuous body through. The chunk of marble slid along the floor and crashed into one of the pillars, threatening to bring it down.

The impact sent the Scythe of Nen skittering along the dais.

Stopping less than three feet out of my reach.

It was all I could do not to scream in frustration.

Sarad Nukpana's attention was on directing his new pets in death and destruction, and for the moment, I needed him to keep his eyes, ears, and full attention exactly where they were.

Lightning cackled and killed, the floor shook, and mundane bolts and blades flew and clashed around me.

I ignored it all. Yes, my hand was attached to the Saghred, but I had really long legs. Best of all, I was barefooted. I dropped to my knees, which had the dual benefit of getting me closer to the floor, and out of a lot of people's line of sight and fire. I twisted my forearm in the manacle as far as I could, pushing the pain aside. A broken arm would heal, too. I stretched out the leg closest to the Scythe as far as I could, reaching out with my bare feet, and wishing I had longer toes. I stretched and squirmed and swore. I blew all of my breath out in the vain hope that maybe it'd make me a fraction taller.

My big toe touched cool silver.

Yes!

I'd never been so glad to be barefooted in my life. It was amazing what your toes could do when you were motivated enough, and right now my motivation knew no bounds.

But touching wasn't having, and having wasn't stabbing the Saghred. Kesyn was still chained with magic-sapping manacles and still couldn't summon any Reapers.

One problem at a time, Raine.

Sarad Nukpana didn't see me do any of this.

But his mother did.

There I was, stretched out like the perfect—and perfectly stupid—sacrifice.

Sandrina Ghalfari's eyes lit with homicidal glee as she drew a pair of stilettos from her jeweled belt. The blades glistened wetly with what had to be poison.

Crap in a bucket.

Chapter 22

I was stretched out like the catch of the day just waiting to be fil-leted.

Sandrina Ghalfari's dark, glittering eyes told me that I wasn't the only one having that image, but unlike me, she was enjoying it. At least if she decided to indulge herself, I wouldn't be around for it, at least not for long; a single nick from one of those poisoned blades and I'd be gone. Though with Sandrina's sadistic history, more than likely the poison would paralyze me first, giving Sarad Nukpana's mom plenty of time to relish my agonizing death.

Nothing like impending torment to give you a positive outlook.

My feet and legs were free, so I could have the satisfaction of at least kicking the bitch first, but they were also bare.

See above concerning one nick equaling painful death or paralysis.

Sandrina glanced at the Scythe of Nen and kicked it

down the stairs and into the carnage-filled chaos the temple floor had become. I didn't have a Plan C, but if I did, it would have involved my unfettered fists and Sandrina's face.

"My only regret is that I won't have the time to inflict the agonies on you that you inflicted on my son." Her eyes narrowed and her lips curled into a vulpine smile. "Sarad has forbidden you to be killed, so to repay you for all that you've done, I will go to great pains to ensure that your loved ones linger for as long as possible." Her voice dropped to a purr. "Rest easy and know that I will take *very* good care of them."

A banshee shriek shook the air as a broken pike came down on Sandrina's head, dropping Nukpana's mom like a rock.

Princess Mirabai stood over Sandrina's crumpled form, clutching a blood-spattered pike from one of her guards. Guards that were now nowhere in sight, though the floor where they'd been standing was nowhere in sight, either. The hooked blade had been broken off; the wood was split and splintered on one end, making a half-respectable spear. Mirabai held it with a practiced grip; her feet spread shoulder-width apart in a solid stance. It looked like a certain princess had had quarterstaff training.

"Plan B is back on the table!" I crowed.

If only we could find the damned dagger.

As I scrambled to my feet, a shadow fell over us and Mirabai gasped.

It was Mychael. And he was armed with a huge battle-ax that would have been the envy of Vegard and homicidal berserkers everywhere. Now, that was what I called sexy.

"I want you now," I told him.

Mychael gathered me to him with his free arm, and for the next few moments, I was out of breath for all the right reasons.

"He's on our side," I told Mirabai once Mychael's lips let me speak.

The little princess had lowered her pike. "I assumed as much. Your fiancé?"

"Not exactly."

Mychael's eyes gleamed. "At least not yet."

I jerked my head toward the temple floor. "The Scythe is down there, somewhere around the foot of the steps."

Mychael looked where I'd indicated, noted the location, then ignored it, whipping out a picklock to open the manacle binding me to the Saghred's pedestal.

There was blood on his hand.

"No!" I screamed.

"What is—"

"Your hand's bloody!"

"It's not my blood."

"It doesn't care!"

Mychael saw my hand fused to the rock and his expression darkened to the blackest murder. If Tam wanted to take out Sarad Nukpana, he'd better hurry up and do it, because Mychael was about to cut in line.

"Yeah, I feel the same way," I said, taking the picklock. "Free the others, then go find that dagger."

"Put your chains flat on the floor," Mychael told Mirabai, "and close your eyes."

Without a trace of fear, Mirabai quickly knelt on the floor, bowed her head so her face was protectively tucked against her knees, and put her chained wrists out as far from her body as she could. Mychael brought the ax down, the blade biting through the chains with a single stroke, then went to do the same for Kesyn and the Nathrachs.

I got to work on my manacle. If I got it open, my hand would still be fused to the rock, but at least I'd be able to straighten my arm. Small improvement, but I'd take it. The manacle opened with a sharp click, revealing my cut and bloody wrist.

Oh no.

Before I could stop it, a single drop of blood fell from

my wrist to sizzle on the Saghred's fiery surface. I froze and held my breath.

Nothing.

The stone simply absorbed the blood and didn't do the same to me. Nukpana had said the rock had agreed not to eat me; it wanted me to suffer as much it had. I tried to flex my fingers and the Saghred vibrated, almost like a growl.

"Okay, okay. You're the boss." I clenched my teeth. "For now."

"Give me the ax; I'll take care of these," came Tam's voice from behind me. "Go find the Scythe." I tried to turn to see, but the Saghred would let me move only so far.

Mychael emerged from the back of the dais with a curved goblin sword, and ran down what was left of the stairs to the temple floor.

"Save yourself the trouble," Deidre was telling Tam. "See that weasel of a guard cowering over there?"

"I see more than one."

"The one trying to push himself into the corner. He has the keys on his belt."

I couldn't see Tam, but I could see that Khrynsani guard just fine. He went wide-eyed with panic, presumably at having the complete and undivided attention of the chief mage for the House of Mal'Salin holding a big ax. The guard did what most people in his predicament would—he ran; at least he tried to. There was a loop of keys on his belt one moment, then the keys went flying through the air back toward Tam, and the guard was jerked forward to smack face-first into the marble floor. Magic could be both useful and fun.

Seconds later, Mirabai ran back to Sandrina's still unconscious form and cuffed her hands behind her back with what I assumed were Deidre's manacles.

"Tam, stop playing and go help Mychael find that dagger," Kesyn ordered.

The temple had gone insane, scenes from a hundred nightmares playing out in horrific reality. The goblins of the

Resistance were fighting with a desperation that came from struggling not only for their lives, but for the future of their entire race. The sea dragons had broken through the floor only a minute or two ago. The female had clawed her way free of the shattered marble and with tail, claws, and teeth was tearing into any goblin flesh she could reach. Her only slightly smaller mate soon joined her in the carnage.

Jash Masloc snatched a pair of Resistance mages out of range just as one of the dragon's claws slashed through the air where they had stood. The goblin mage then punched the air before the dragon's face and a blazing white shield blocked an incoming snap of teeth the length of his forearm.

Piaras's voice was ringing with a battlefield sleepsong aimed at two large groups of Khrynsani guards. They were locked in combat with what appeared to be goblin army officers led by Imala Kalis. The Khrynsani struck by Piaras's song were dropping to the ground where they stood. They were dropping and the dragons were eating, for the most part without pausing to chew, merely tossing back their huge heads to swallow entire sections of bodies whole. It was gruesome as hell, but Piaras was doing what had to be done. It was us or them, and while the dragons were busy eating Khrynsani they couldn't do the same to the Resistance fighters. He was buying time for all of us.

A flash of bright light came from just beyond the temple doors instantly followed by two deafening explosions, one right after the other. An orange glow filled the doorway. What the hell? Execution Square had been completely empty when I'd been brought in, and there hadn't been anything combustible or flammable already there. Even the dragons were startled enough to stop feeding for all of two seconds. Sarad Nukpana's allies, who had been stampeding out of the temple, screamed and ran back in—until they saw the dragons again. They'd come here to see a wedding and enjoy a nice evening of sacrifices. Now they had to choose which way to die: dragon or whatever hell had broken loose outside in the square. Most of them wisely decided to take their chances outside.

"Raine, we have a situation," Kesyn said.

Mirabai looked at the floor around the altar and jumped back, stifling a scream.

A numbing coldness lapped against my legs. A churning black mist was up past my knees and climbing fast. Admittedly, I'd been a little preoccupied, but I should have noticed *that*. I was fused to the Saghred and couldn't escape, but Kesyn could.

"Kesyn, run!" I screamed.

The old goblin mage had seen it before I had, and not only did he not run; he stayed right where he was. I grabbed his arm and, with my free hand, tried with everything I had to drag him off of the altar.

"I'm not leaving you," Kesyn told me. "I can help."

"By getting yourself killed?"

In the next two seconds, the wall of mist was almost up to my waist. Parts of it broke off from the rest and rapidly spiraled upward even farther to form bars. I reached out with one finger and barely touched a single bar of mist. My hand instantly went numb to the wrist.

Kesyn was actually grinning. "Don't worry. Getting killed is not going to happen."

No. *This* was not happening. I didn't nearly get the Scythe only to lose the Scythe, only to almost get the Scythe again, to be imprisoned in freaking mist bars, with a lunatic old goblin sitting behind me who wasn't going to do a damned thing about any of it.

"It's a Level Thirteen ward," Kesyn continued, seemingly unconcerned. "We can't get out and no one else can get in."

The crazy coot. "Wards only go to twelve," I snarled.

Kesyn shrugged. "These pricks are real go-getters. This level of work is beyond what I've ever seen."

Not only was he crazy; he was hallucinating. "What pricks?"

"Remember those five black mages who were standing over there with Carnades?" Kesyn asked mildly. "Well, apparently they never left. I could kick myself for not noticing until now. Must be getting feebleminded in my old age. Though they do have the best damned veils I've ever seen."

I looked into the shadows behind the altar. There had been several Khrynsani black mages standing with Carnades. They weren't there now. I hadn't seen them go anywhere, and with their fancy robes, I would have noticed that.

I stopped and sniffed. Spices and incense. Dammit, I could still smell them. With all the blood and smoke and dragon breath flying around here, I hadn't noticed that the spicy smell hadn't gone away, even though there was no incense burning. The bastards were still here, and obviously they weren't just standing around anymore. They were veiled and working hard. If I hadn't already been hurt enough, I would have smacked myself in the head for being so stupid. Sarad Nukpana would have been prepared for anything. He wasn't depending on mere guards to keep the Saghred safe. The Khrynsani had been trying to get the Saghred back for nearly a thousand years. They would never leave it unguarded.

And it wasn't unguarded now.

Why did Nukpana's best black mages wait until now to encase the altar and Saghred in a ward? Maybe it had taken them that long to get the ward started. Carnades had said that he couldn't activate a mirror in less than fifteen minutes; maybe this was similar. I didn't know and it didn't matter. That Kesyn and I were stuck in a ward with five of Nukpana's biggest and baddest did. Even if Mychael or Tam found the Scythe, it wouldn't do us a damned bit of good if they couldn't get it to me.

The black mages hadn't dropped their veils, but the mist flowed around them, outlining their shapes. One of the bastards was standing less than three feet away and I'd been completely clueless. The ward spinning and solidifying around us looked like black mist swirling with motes of bright red light like thousands of demonic eyes.

Kesyn shook his head in disgust. "These are Sarad's top spellslingers; and the grandstanding sons of bitches can't resist showing off." He snorted. "Spells with sparklies. Why didn't they just tie a bow around it?"

"Do something!" I hissed to Kesyn.

"I can't use magic in here," he said. "We'd fry. They wouldn't."

"There's nothing you can do? Because there sure as hell isn't anything I can do."

"I didn't say that. It's taking all the strength and concentration this bunch has to hold the ward together. They can't even risk letting their concentration waver to lower their veils, and I doubt they can even spare the thought to listen to us. They've positioned themselves between two layers of wards, so they're shielded from the outside and inside against magic, weapons, and sound. So spellsongs won't work, either." The old goblin leaned back and twisted from side to side, cracking his back. "So we're waiting on your lover boy to get back with that dagger. Though I do wish he'd hurry. I wouldn't want this happening prematurely."

I was tempted to smack Kesyn upside the head. "He won't be able to *get in*!"

The old goblin gave me a sly wink. "I've got a key."

Sarad Nukpana was directing his dragons to slaughter the Resistance; he wasn't defending the Saghred, because he knew it was being taken care of. He knew that I wasn't going anywhere and neither was the Saghred. To keep the two of us right where he wanted us until he dealt with the Resistance, Nukpana had tasked his top black mages with wrapping us in a lethal Level Thirteen blanket.

Suddenly the air in the temple crackled with static like right before a lightning strike, quivering, eager, and alive . . . and wrong.

At its epicenter stood Sarad Nukpana.

He began gathering his power like one of the dragons drawing in a massive breath. In an instant, all of the chaos and death fell into the background as a sound like a distant thunder built until it vibrated the very air around us with its intensity. It shook the ground beneath our feet with a rumbling throb. Once. Twice. Three times.

Everyone felt it. Most of the combatants down on the temple floor retreated to the far walls, thinking another dragon was coming up through what was left of the floor.

I couldn't drag my eyes away from Sarad Nukpana. "I have a feeling this is worse than dragons."

Kesyn was off of the altar and standing beside me, his face grim, all signs of humor gone. "It'll make them look like puppies. Sarad hasn't even broken a sweat yet, but he's about to. I hear he picked up a major power boost a few weeks ago."

I nodded and continued staring. Sarad Nukpana had more power to draw on now, more magic at his command than anyone or anything except the Saghred itself. Nukpana had recently eaten the souls and consumed the life forces and magic of history's strongest and most evil sorcerers. Men who had been conquerors and killers, who had cut swaths of death and destruction through entire kingdoms. They had been prisoners inside the Saghred along with Sarad Nukpana. And along with Nukpana, they had escaped. The goblin had methodically hunted them down and consumed every last one of them.

Sarad Nukpana had all of that knowledge, all of that killing power at his disposal, and he had yet to truly unleash it.

Until now.

Time slowed to a stop.

It hadn't really, but my mind made it seem that everyone was moving in slow motion. This had happened to me before when I was in the middle of something that had a high probability of getting me killed. It was my mind's way of giving me a chance to figure out how to undo my stupid.

This wasn't my doing, not this time.

Sarad Nukpana stood as a statue, his beautiful face drawn into a rictus of rage, releasing his power, giving his magic flesh.

It took form, born from what Nukpana had become, created out of his own poisoned mind, the manifestation of his twisted soul. The air wavered before the goblin's upraised hands, wavered and came together as a living thing that only vaguely held a human shape. It was easily three times Mychael's height, its pallid skin stretched and rippling, not from muscle, but from things moving inside. Huge, distorted faces with mouths stretched in silent screams, fangs pressed against the skin, stretching it to the point of splitting open, eager and desperate to feed. Monstrous hands, grasping and pushing, arms and legs writhing inside determined to escape the skinform Sarad Nukpana had created.

Prince Chigaru and a handful of army officers were closest to the thing when it manifested. The prince led the attack. The creature bent and, with a mere swat of its fingers, sent Chigaru flying toward the opening in the floor. The prince stopped just short of falling in. Princess Mirabai ran to his side, armed with nothing except her broken pike. The officers rushed to protect their prince.

The remaining people still in the temple who had stood with Sarad Nukpana for whatever reason—terror, intimidation or like-minded sick souls, twisted by an all-consuming desire for power—they all ran. Loyalty held by fear or intimidation was quickly abandoned when something even scarier showed up.

I spotted Mychael using Tam's curved blade, carving his way back toward us.

"Does he have it?" Kesyn snapped.

If Mychael had found the Scythe, I couldn't see it. "Your eyes are better in this murk than mine," I shot back.

The old mage stared intently. "I think he's got it in his other hand. Come on, elf; get your ass up here."

Mychael saw Nukpana's living nightmare come to unholy life at the same time as everyone else. He glanced sharply between where Kesyn and I were sealed in the Khrynsani's ward to the gigantic, patchwork monster that Nukpana had created and was about to unleash on the Resistance. Even with the dragons against them, they had been winning, but Nukpana's creature was about to change that. Mychael's frustration and rage were clear. He could take on one, not both.

Tam made the choice for all of us.

Only one thing could keep Sarad Nukpana occupied long enough to at least give us a chance to destroy the Saghred. Only one thing had the strength and cunning to bring down a monster.

A major-class demon summoned by black magic.

Mychael had found the Scythe of Nen.

Now Tam was going to sell his soul to buy us time to use it.

"We won't let you down, boy," Kesyn whispered.

Tam stepped out onto one of the few sections of the temple floor that hadn't been cracked or broken, his back toward the mysterious blaze just outside the temple in Execution Square, the flames' reflection licking hungrily at his gleaming black armor.

Tam didn't say a word. There were no incantations, no raised arms, no shouts of challenge. In testament to his skill, he simply stepped aside as the shadows to his left parted like a curtain.

The demon was shorter than Sarad Nukpana's creature, but height was the only thing it lacked. It was part man, part bull, and all demon—from his cloven hooves to his massive, horned head.

The monster and Tam's demon took measure of each other, then began slowly circling, drawing closer to their intended kill with every step.

The time to stop Tam was long gone. The demon had

been summoned and released, the damage done. Tam was one of the most powerful mages I'd ever met, but Sarad Nukpana had the knowledge, cunning, and power of six of history's magical heavyweights.

Without the Saghred's power, what I wanted to do and what I could do were worlds away from each other. Right now I was less useful against both demon and monster than Mirabai and her broken stick.

Mychael raced up the stairs to the altar, and Kesyn didn't give him time to start trying to blast his way through. The old goblin quickly held out both hands telling him to stop and then a single finger asking him to wait. Mychael gave a tight nod, and stood ready just outside the ward, facing the Khrynsani black mages with his magic flaring, bright and white-hot. He held it in check, letting it swirl and quickly grow around him like a contained cyclone, ready for release.

"We don't have to break their spell, just their concentration." Kesyn told me with grim satisfaction. "I've been arming myself for the past day in case something like this happened. It's one of the many advantages to being old. There's one thing that can get through any ward. Air. These bastards can't concentrate if they can't breathe—or don't want to." The old mage grinned. "Take a breath and hold it."

"What? I don't unde—"

"You don't have to understand, just do it. Do you think I've been eating that cheese because I liked the taste? Take one old man and add stinky cheese. Do the math, girl—or in this case, the chemistry."

One second those black mages were sealed in a Level Thirteen ward; the next they were gasping for fresh air that no longer existed.

Their concentration broke when Kesyn broke wind.

The mighty mage Kesyn Badru released a spell that laid low the collective strength of the Khrynsani's most evil archsorcerers.

That'd sound better in the history books than one fart made the old man a hero.

When the Khrynsani lost their concentration, the spell controlling the ward buckled and broke, releasing a backlash that left only two of the mages standing, though staggering would be a more accurate description.

Mychael and his magic were waiting for them. When the crackling light dimmed, the mages weren't dead at his feet. They were simply gone. A wisp of smoke floating in the air and the fading scent of incense were the only clues to what had happened to them.

Then there was no ward, no black mages. It was just us with the Scythe of Nen and the Saghred.

Mychael removed the Scythe from its scabbard.

Carnades's blood still coated the blade, blood that had to be present before the Scythe could cut into the Saghred. For possibly the first and definitely the last time, Carnades Silvanus was about to do something noble.

Mychael started to give me the Scythe, then hesitated, his eyes on mine.

"You promised," I said quietly. "I have to do this, not you." I had to swallow to get the rest of the words out. "If this . . . goes bad, I'm not going to die knowing you're living with that guilt."

Mychael's hand tightened around the Scythe of Nen until his knuckles showed white against his tanned skin.

Then he put it in my outstretched hand, and stepped back to give me and Kesyn room to work. I knew he'd stay close. He couldn't protect me from the Saghred, but he would keep anything and everything else from harming me.

The Saghred was on its pedestal, no shields protecting it now. I didn't kid myself for one instant; the Saghred didn't need any help. It'd kept itself intact and feeding for thousands of years, maybe longer.

Somehow the stone knew what I was about to do. It hadn't resisted when the demon queen had thrust the Scythe into it to free her husband and king. I was only one elf with no magic, and the rock knew it because we were bonded and it'd taken my magic itself. It knew my fears and my weaknesses; and believe me, there were a lot of both right now, especially fears. But Tam had killed the demon queen with good old stealth and cunning. I had both of those. However, Tam had also had surprise on his side. He'd snuck up on the demon queen and lobbed her head off. There wasn't going to be any sneaking up on the Saghred.

Kesyn had been standing a little off to the side to give Mychael and me some semblance of privacy. He stepped up to stand by my side. "Let me get some Reapers down here first," he said quietly.

An instant later, I felt the old goblin mage's call, literally felt it, his thoughts brushing like butterfly wings against my mind. I resisted the urge to shiver. The Reapers appeared almost instantly.

Kesyn and I looked up. A vortex had opened that went through and beyond the temple ceiling. We couldn't see the end of it, or out into the temple. The swirling wasn't some kind of gray mist; it was Reapers. Thousands of them.

Instantly the Saghred was in my mind, whispering to me without words, a sibilant hiss that pushed the vision of the Reapers aside and replaced them with what was happening right now to the people I loved. Tam clenched in one hand of Nukpana's creature, while it fought the demon with the other hand for possession of Tam. Piaras snapped up by a dragon and dragged screaming into the bowels of the temple. Sarad Nukpana had turned his attention from his monster to Mychael. Mychael was now on his knees, magic fading, strength almost gone, struggling under Nukpana's unrelenting attack. Khrynsani black mages surrounded him, sacrificial daggers at the ready.

"*No!*" I screamed the word out loud and in my mind.

None of it was true. The Saghred knew me; it knew what scared me.

It was the Saghred that was afraid. Sarad Nukpana had somehow bound it; it couldn't take me until the goblin gave his permission. But that didn't mean that the thousands of souls about to be ripped from the stone through me wouldn't kill me or drive me irrevocably insane. Like me, the Saghred was vulnerable, possibly for the first time in its existence. An existence I was going to end, even if I ended my own life.

I was afraid, too. Hell, I was terrified. But my fears weren't for me, not anymore. Some things were worth dying for. Tam knew that. He had made that decision for himself, determined that an eternity of torment was worth destroying the Saghred to save those he loved, and his people, *all* of his people.

The Saghred wasn't giving up. It weighed down my mind, sending my thoughts into a tailspin of torturous images.

My fear will not control me. My fear will not *control me. The Saghred will not control me.*

I had a power that the Saghred didn't have and would never have. In its own way it was magic, magic that the Saghred could never bury or bind or take away from me.

Love.

Tam was risking his soul for it. Mychael had fought for me all these months and was now by my side protecting me. Chigaru's love for Mirabai and his people inspired him to challenge the evil of Sarad Nukpana.

One rock wasn't going to take that away from any of us.

I got a death grip on the Scythe.

For an instant, I could see through the Reapers. The dark energy swirling around Sarad Nukpana shifted as he saw me poised with the Scythe. All of his attention, the entire focus of his vast power, was caught up in controlling his monstrous creation.

Nukpana's mad eyes widened in desperation as he screamed to the Saghred, "Take her!"

I drove the Scythe of Nen into the Saghred up to the hilt.

Shrieks, screams, agonized wailing, whether from me or the Saghred or its captive souls, I didn't know and was beyond caring. It was as if I'd plunged the Scythe into my own guts. My breath froze, my heart fluttering in shock and panic, fluttering, then slowing, stopping. My fingers weakened on the Scythe's grip, the cold metal sliding away. Suddenly another hand covered mine, warm and strong, keeping my fingers tight around the dagger, sharing his strength, his determination.

"Hang on, girl. We're almost there."

Kesyn Badru.

I managed to raise my head. I could no longer see through the spirits swirling around me and Kesyn. I looked up. The Saghred's souls were escaping, the Reapers guiding them up into the vortex and on to whatever came after.

When the souls finally stopped coming out of the stone, I glanced down. The Saghred was smooth and as opaque as fine alabaster. I could see the blade of the Scythe of Nen inside, its grip protruding from between my trembling fingers. There were no more souls inside. My breath came in ragged gasps. The stone wasn't the only one that had been drained. I pulled the blade out, immediately reversing the grip and bringing both the pommel and my free fist down on the Saghred, shattering it into glittering dust.

Sarad Nukpana's scream turned to a howl of rage and disbelief, of ambitions dashed, plans in ruins. He'd seen the Saghred destroyed. He staggered back and nearly fell, maybe from witnessing the obliteration of his future, but his focus on his monster had wavered and broken; the backlash from the botched link drove him to his knees. The creature began folding in on itself as if deflating, emitting a keening cry as the magic that made it vanished.

Tam's demon ignored the monster completely, his gleaming red eyes hungrily locked on Sarad Nukpana. The goblin recovered quickly, but the demon was faster. With a bellow of triumph, he charged toward the steps and Nukpana, his hooves striking sparks from the floor, each strike like a clap of thunder. The goblin shielded himself and defiantly stood his ground, snarling a guttural spell that rocked the stone beneath our feet, throwing us to the floor.

The demon kept coming; his gleaming black horns gored Sarad Nukpana's shields and contemptuously tossed them aside like a bullfighter's cloak. The demon grabbed Nukpana, and still the goblin fought, his magic flaying the demon in uncontrolled rage and dawning terror. The seared streaks in the demon's flesh healed instantly, and a sound escaped his throat that sounded almost like laughter.

The demon turned and inclined his massive head to Tam. Tam bowed in return.

The darkness next to the dais rippled and opened revealing a dim oval of reddish light. The stench of sulfur-scented hot air flowed out of the passage that the demon had opened.

The demon charged toward the Hellgate with his prize, as our ears rang with Sarad Nukpana's screams.

Chapter 23

All of the magic Sarad Nukpana had murdered to have for his own, the power he had hoarded for his moment of triumph, had been his undoing, twisted into his ultimate weakness.

Kesyn Badru had been right.

But right now, standing outside the Khrynsani temple, Tam had some explaining to do to his old teacher and a livid Imala Kalis. Yes, Tam had summoned a demon, but before he'd released it, there'd been some fast talking and even faster deal making on Tam's part. With his obscene level of power, Sarad Nukpana had turned himself into a veritable demonic feast. Tam told the demon that he'd release him, but only if he gave his word that he'd only take Sarad Nukpana. Tam's soul wasn't part of the deal or even on the table.

Demons were, well . . . demons, but if you managed to get one to give you its word, it was good. However, you had to be careful not to give them a loophole in that verbal contract to pick up a couple of extra treats while they were here.

Tam gave the demon a look at the buffet, then made him promise not to get greedy.

It had worked.

Being the right-hand mage and counselor of the goblin queen for five years had taught Tam how to close loopholes like little nooses.

Tam had gambled on the strength and appeal of Sarad Nukpana's power, betting that the demon would want Nukpana worse than the demon would want him. I wondered if the demon felt cheated. Probably. If he did, Tam would have to watch his back from now on. That thing would want payback of the eternal kind. Then again, didn't we all have to watch our backs against someone—or something? The more power you had just meant there were bigger and meaner things stalking you.

Tam was explaining all this to Kesyn and Imala. Or trying to. It wasn't that Imala didn't understand it; she understood only too well. She was infuriated that Tam had dangled himself like an hors d'oeuvre to lure a demon to a Sarad Nukpana feast.

"Because if I had told you," Tam was saying, "the demon would have known, and I'd have been a greasy spot on the floor. Calling a demon, then putting conditions on their release, really pisses them off."

Imala's dark eyes glared daggers at Tam. "And you risked yourself on the *chance* that thing would want Sarad more than you."

"I only have one soul in me," Tam said. "Sarad had six ancient sorcerers, Rudra Muralin, *and* some Saghred mojo. Me? Just one soul, and in comparison, miniscule power. Scrawny power versus fat and juicy with evil. It was no contest."

Imala was quivering with fury. "What would have stopped him from taking both of you?"

Tam was confused and well on his way to annoyed. "We. Had. A deal." This was the third time he'd had to repeat that particular fact, and couldn't understand why Imala wasn't getting it.

"And if he'd failed to catch Sarad?" Imala asked.

Tam shrugged. "Then I probably would have ended up as the consolation prize."

Imala flung her hands up in exasperation. "Precisely!"

"But it worked. I'm still here."

Imala's fists were clenched, she was virtually shaking with rage, and her restraint was about to take off for hell in a handbasket. Should she use her fists to beat some sense into Tam, or should she—

Imala unclenched her fists, grabbed Tam's head in both hands, pulled him down, and kissed him. Hard.

Tam hadn't expected that, but he recovered quickly and Imala found herself lifted off her feet. I don't think she noticed.

Tam's parents were having a similarly passionate reunion; but unlike Imala, Deidre hadn't needed to fight the urge to punch Cyran before kissing him.

We were out of the temple and in Execution Square near the palace, surrounded by those Resistance fighters who weren't presently occupied hunting down any and every Khrynsani they could find. The Mal'Salin palace also had dungeons, and that had been where Sarad Nukpana had imprisoned the goblin nobles who'd refused to bow down to him.

Apparently the explosions and resulting blaze had been a result of a massive wagon full of armaments with just enough Nebian black powder inside to make for one heck of a pyrotechnics display, and to blast a sizeable crater at the foot of the Khrynsani temple stairs. Witnesses said the wagon had been driven into the square and parked in front of the temple by a lone goblin, who released the wagon's team of horses, hurled a torch on top of the wagon, and then ran like hell.

Damage to the inside of the temple had been even more

extensive. The sea dragons had been big enough to break through the temple floor, but fortunately weren't small enough to get through the front doors. Once Sarad Nukpana was gone, so was his control over the dragons, and the pair had gone back where they'd come from; that is, once all of their food had run screaming outside and out of their reach. The Resistance mages had a couple of weather wizards among their number, and they were presently exhausting themselves trying to put out the still burning crater.

Prince Chigaru and Princess Mirabai were being celebrated by their nobles as their new goblin king and queen. Chigaru was the last Mal'Salin heir standing, so that was enough for the nobles to begin sucking up. More than a few of them were wearing the same fancy clothes that marked them as having been in the temple just an hour before. However, most were the nobles who had been newly released from the palace dungeons. Their sincerity didn't sound forced, unlike their well-dressed counterparts'. I hoped Imala had some trusted agents in the crowd noting who was dressed up and who looked like they'd been languishing in a dungeon. That knowledge would come in handy for culling the wheat from the chaff later. For now, the army officers and some newly handpicked loyal soldiers had established a heavily armed perimeter around their new monarchs and were allowing the nobles to get only marginally close and only one at a time. From time to time, as a particularly well-dressed noble was allowed to approach and bow, Mirabai would whisper in her soon-to-be husband's ear. In response, Chigaru would scowl at the now-shaking supplicant.

Oh yeah, those two were going to clean house.

Goblin politics was a fluid thing, and goblin courtiers were, shall we say, flexible in their loyalties. Loyalty seemed to pass easily from Sathrik to Sarad Nukpana to Chigaru. I didn't think they could help themselves. If a goblin aristocrat was breathing, they were plotting. And if they were plotting, they were happy.

They weren't the only ones—who were happy, that is.

I had my arms around the waist of a certain Guardian paladin, and he had one arm tightly around me. The hand of his other arm still had a tight grip on that curved goblin sword, his sharp blue eyes taking in every threat within fifty feet in every direction. Seeing that we were surrounded by scheming goblin courtiers, regardless of how well behaved, I wholeheartedly approved of how Mychael was dividing his attentions.

Words couldn't describe how wonderful it was not to have a target on my forehead or anywhere else. The Saghred was dust, and Sarad Nukpana was in whatever circle of the Lower Hells had been prepared especially for him.

No one would gain anything by killing me anymore.

At least for now.

Mychael was warm, he was holding me, and both of us were alive and breathing. Life was good. I nuzzled Mychael's neck, then stood on tiptoe and nibbled his earlobe.

The sword promptly lost Mychael's attention. Take that, piece of metal.

"Mmm," Mychael murmured. Then I was on the receiving end of some nuzzles and nibbles of my own.

I suddenly sensed a pair of entirely too watchful eyes. I tried to turn and see who it was, but that wasn't easy with Mychael still holding on. Kesyn Badru was standing a few feet away.

"You were listening," I accused.

"Yep." The old mage smiled, exposing his chipped fang. "And watching. When you get to be my age, you take your thrills anywhere and way you can find 'em." He nodded with approval and his dark eyes gleamed. "You did good; I'm proud of you."

"And thank *you* for being a stinky old man."

Kesyn laughed. "Never try to be anything you're not." He lowered his voice. "Any sign of your magic?"

"Not yet." I concentrated for a moment, probing around a little in my head. "At least I don't think so."

"Give it some time; it'll come back."

I nodded, surprised at the sudden realization that I really wouldn't mind all that much if it didn't come back. I'd done pretty well over the past few days without it.

"Sir," Piaras called to Tam. He pointed at a figure on the palace's garden wall.

The figure whooped.

I squinted through the smoke still coming from the now-extinguished crater. Hmm, a crater made by an exploding wagon—much like a certain exploding goblin army latrine. That explosion had been followed by a mooning from a certain goblin teenager running amuck.

We weren't being mooned—we were getting the full frontal treatment. Well, navinem did lower your inhibitions. Too bad Talon didn't have any of those to begin with.

Piaras got a good look at his friend and cracked up.

Talon was whooping up a storm, swinging what looked to be his trousers in victory circles over his head. I said they were probably his trousers because he wasn't wearing any—or anything else, for that matter.

Lord Talon Nathrach, son of the chancellor to the king, heir and scion of the noble House of Nathrach, was standing above Execution Square, in front of hundreds of goblin aristocrats, buck naked, and loving it. From what I could tell, the kid had nothing to be ashamed of, and many of the ladies of the court shared my opinion.

"That your boy?" Kesyn asked.

Tam sighed. "I'm afraid so, sir."

The old mage grinned. "Well, I think that takes care of his introduction to the court."

Tam desperately wanted to be somewhere else as Talon leapt down from the wall and took a victory lap around the square.

"He's all yours," Tam told his teacher.

"Oh joy."

The old mage's words said one thing; the gleam in his eyes told anyone watching him something else.

Kesyn Badru lived for a challenge.

Talon was taking the last half of his victory lap. Kesyn for a teacher. I almost felt sorry for Talon. I grinned slowly. Almost.

Since there was no longer a father of the bride, Kesyn stood in. And I was thrilled and honored when Princess Mirabai asked if I would stand in for the mother of the bride.

The new goblin queen had to be the happiest-looking new orphan I'd ever seen.

It was a beautiful wedding. The throne room was lit by what had to be hundreds of candles with not a blue light-globe in sight, filling the room with a warm, golden glow. The room was far from being full. The only courtiers in attendance were those whom the new king trusted not to put a knife in his back. Though I bet the kitchen staff loved it; less people to feed at the reception.

At the end of the ceremony, when the priest had told the king that he could kiss his bride, he probably didn't think he'd have to ask him to stop.

The marriage of the new goblin king and queen was off to a good start.

Though one person in attendance was a little on edge. King Chigaru had named Tam as his heir until such time as he and Queen Mirabai had a child.

Tam was standing off to the side, wearing full court robes, having what I'd counted as his third glass of wine. I noticed that Tam's simple circlet had been replaced by an only slightly less ornate version of the crown Chigaru was wearing.

"Fancy headgear," I noted, determined to keep a straight face. "Nice."

Tam grunted. It wasn't a particularly enthusiastic one. "I've never wanted anyone to survive this badly."

"Maybe your new king thinks that after what you pulled off in the temple, no assassin would be suicidal enough to come after him with you around."

Without changing expression, Tam brushed the tip of his nose with his finger. "That and one more level for an assassin to go through."

"Gee, wasn't that nice of him?"

"For once, His Majesty is right. However, one shrewd move deserves another." Tam inclined his head toward where a black-garbed mage stood guard over the royal couple. I spotted more, strategically placed throughout the reception room watching king, queen, and guests. These guys looked familiar.

I smiled. "Your dark mage hit squad buddies from Mid?"

Tam grinned with satisfaction and no small level of relief. "That's them."

"So you don't want to be king?"

"You've seen the job. Would you want it?"

"Can't say that I would."

I glanced over to where Talon was essentially holding court and basking in the grateful glow of a bevy of beautiful young noblewomen. I wondered how many of those noble ladies had seen the kid naked? Heck, probably all of them. And if any of them hadn't seen, they'd heard.

"I see what you mean," I said. "You as king would make Talon a prince. That's an ego boost the kid doesn't need."

Chigaru had maneuvered Mirabai to a cozy corner where they were engaged in some serious smooching.

"You shouldn't have to wait long for that heir," I noted. "Though I have to say that baby goblins must make for some painful nursing."

Tam smiled, leaning down close to my ear, and whispered, "Our fangs don't come in until after we're weaned."

"Oh." I felt a flush creep up my neck into my face as I

had a visual of Tam and breast-feeding. That image would be staying with me for a while and making repeat appearances at inconvenient times.

Imala swept over to where Tam and I were standing, looking drop-dead gorgeous in a formfitting silver velvet gown. For her service to the crown, Chigaru had made her a duchess and given her lands to go with it.

In addition to the deemed-to-be-trustworthy palace guard and Tam's buddies turned bodyguards, Mychael had arranged for some Guardian backup troops to supplement Chigaru's forces in the city until the transition was complete—which meant once all the traitors had been rounded up and dealt with according to their level of treason. I hoped Mychael's men liked goblin food; they were going to be here awhile. This place had been a bubbling vat of treason.

"How's the roundup going?" I asked her.

"Fast enough for progress and too damned slow for me. Separating the merely manipulative from the hardened opportunist is proving difficult."

"In other words, all of them are back-stabbing hypocrites."

"If there weren't any hypocrites, we'd have no royal court," Imala said. "And we're questioning all of them." She sighed.

I whistled. "All of them are a lot."

The chief of the secret service and, for now, palace security raised her glass, then drained it. Imala had some catching up to do if she wanted to keep up with Tam.

"Job security at its finest," she said.

"Anyone who's willing to oversee this . . . Imala, don't take this the wrong way, but you've inherited a nut farm."

She grinned. "They are my people."

"They're nuts."

"That doesn't make them any less my people."

Mychael was talking with Cyran and Deidre Nathrach.

Nath had wandered over to Talon to see if his nephew needed any help with his flock of admiring beauties.

Chigaru and Mirabai had given the Nathrach family all of the Nukpana and Ghalfari lands and titles, making them among the wealthiest goblins in the kingdom.

"We thought we'd stay here in the capital and bask in the glow of our reunited family," Deidre was telling Mychael.

Cyran slid an arm around his wife and pulled her closer. "Then we're going to go off together for a long romantic holiday." He and Deidre exchanged a glance, their dark eyes sparkling. "And do a little hunting."

Mychael looked from one to the other. "I take it you won't be hunting boar."

"Correct," Cyran said. "I'm married to the best mortekal in the kingdom. It would be a shame not to exercise her talents."

"You're going after Sandrina," I said.

"I said that I had business to settle with her," Deidre said. "And I never leave loose ends."

Sandrina remained unaccounted for after Sarad Nukpana had been taken by the demon. Since Deidre wasn't a magic user, the Khrynsani hadn't used magic-sapping manacles on her. So when Mirabai had cuffed Sandrina with them, those manacles had only contained her, not her magic. It wouldn't have taken much for a mage of Sandrina's skill to free herself. She'd probably been free and running for the hills by the time that demon had dragged her son to his just reward. The city had been turned inside out looking for her. No luck. Cyran and Deidre were going to make their own luck.

Cryan spoke. "We have reason to believe that Sandrina is running to her family stronghold near the Great Rift, believing that they will protect her."

"Will they?" I asked.

Deidre shrugged. "They might if they were still free to do so, though I doubt it. Regardless, it doesn't matter. The

Ghalfari family has been taken into custody. So Sandrina is in the wilds of the Northern Reach all alone."

Cyran smiled. "And she's never been much of an outdoor type."

"And the two of you are going hunting."

"We can't spend all of our time in bed," Deidre said.

Cyran's wicked grin was a mirror image of Tam's. "We could try."

Mychael, Piaras, and I were due to go home after the reception. Kesyn knew an expert mirror mage who was standing by to take us back to Mid. Once we'd secured a way home, Mychael had immediately contacted Justinius and Vegard to let them know and fill them in on events. Our mission had been a success and Justinius was thrilled. He reported that the goblin invasion had stopped soon after it had begun. The ships with the students were being recalled. Phaelan and Uncle Ryn had easily spotted the ambush that Sarad Nukpana had set up. The students had been all too glad to lend their magical assistance. The result? Nukpana's ships had been completely and creatively defeated.

"Tam wants to keep Talon with him for a while," Mychael told me.

"And have Kesyn teach him," I chimed in.

"A place will be held for him if he wants to return to Mid." Mychael took stock of Talon's admirers and gave a low laugh. "Though that's looking less likely by the moment."

Imala had loaned me a breathtaking midnight blue gown with a silver belt, set with moonstones. Wedding finery had likewise been found for Mychael and Piaras.

Piaras was on the receiving end of his own share of come-hither looks.

"I'll be knighting him within the year, you know," Mychael said.

Mychael was getting his share of admiring glances, too. I growled. They stopped.

Mychael's blue eyes sparkled. "Jealous?"

"Just defending my territory."

I stepped in close and took his face in my hands. The stubble was nice, sexy nice. The paladin would have shaved for the wedding; Mychael had opted not to. He was relaxed, but most of all he was happy.

"We'll be returning to Mid tonight," Mychael said. "Justinius and Vegard will be waiting for us."

"I'll give both of them a kiss smack-dab on the lips. I cannot *wait* to get home."

"Do you mean Mid—or Mermeia?" he asked quietly.

I knew what he was asking, and I was going to be honest with him and myself. Over the past few days my magic had come back. Not the catastrophic, taking-over-the-world power. Just mine, plus a little extra. Not impressive as most mages went, but I liked it. I would have eventually gotten used to not having magic, but it was a big part of me; and to be honest, words couldn't describe how glad I was to have it back.

Mychael was waiting for an answer.

"I don't know," I said frankly. "It depends."

"On what?" His eyes searched my face, uncertain.

"I had a life in Mermeia, with people there who love me and need me."

"You have someone who loves you right here," Mychael said softly. "And needs you."

I laid a hand on his chest. "I know; and I love you, too."

"There's a 'but' in there. What is it?"

"What would I do on Mid?"

Mychael's hands went to my shoulders, and he gazed down at me. "You could marry me."

There was a difference between eventually expecting to be asked a particular question and actually hearing it. I kind of stopped breathing there for a minute. "Marry?"

Mychael bent his head and his smiling lips brushed mine. "Me."

I actually took a breath and then managed to exhale, too. I was on a roll. "Marry you?"

Mychael kept his lips close to mine. "That was the question."

"And if I agreed to become the wife of the paladin, what would I do?"

"Do?"

I pulled back from him. "Yes, do. I'm not going to sit around the citadel all day waiting to shine your armor. I don't do armor."

Mychael looked so honestly horrified that I had to laugh.

"I have squires who do that," he said.

"Sharpen swords?" I asked.

"An armorer."

"Feed Kalinpar?"

"Junior knights."

"Warm your bed?"

"Now, that position is open." His voice was a husky whisper.

One corner of my lips curled in a tiny smile. "As nice as I know that job is, I need more."

"I know."

I knew I could set up shop in Mid or offer my seeking skills to the city watch as a consultant, and I'd be good at either one. But it wasn't enough, not anymore. "I can't go back to what I was before," I said.

Mychael gave a low laugh. "So now that you've help save the world, you want more? Raine Benares, Danger Addict."

"I wouldn't go that far."

His eyes shone. "How far would you go?"

I ignored the double entendre. "I want to help people. *Really* help people. I want to make a difference." I winced. "That sounded hokey as hell, didn't it?"

"I've heard the words before."

"From who?"

"Almost every Guardian candidate." He gave me a long,

appreciative look. Imala's gown did look amazing. "You'd make our uniform look good."

"You run an all-boys club, remember? Though Justinius's granddaughter is working to change that, and I think she's right. Besides, me and taking orders don't go together."

"I'm only too aware that you and orders are like oil and water. As to missing the people in Mermeia who love you, by the time Justinius is through cleaning house of Carnades's Conclave allies, there are going to be quite a few high-level teaching positions vacant, some in the Guardians. I believe Justinius and Piaras's grandmother, Tarsilia Rivalin, know each other."

I cleared my throat. "Intimately."

Mychael raised a brow. "Really?"

"And then some."

"I would also like to see if I can't talk your godfather into coming out of retirement. We're going to have a large influx of cadets who will need specialized instruction. Tarsilia and Garadin's talents and knowledge would be a much-needed addition to our curriculum."

"Influx of cadets?"

"I think you know by now that Justinius likes shaking things up," Mychael said.

I was instantly on guard. "Uh . . . yes, I noticed that."

"Katelyn's arguments haven't been falling on deaf ears with the old man. He wants to begin admitting women into the Guardians—and he'd like for you to be the first."

There were times when someone said something so completely unexpected that all you could do was stand there with your mouth open.

Eventually I managed to get out words. "And break a millennium of tradition?"

Mychael nodded. "Katelyn forced him to consider it, but it was you that influenced his final decision."

"Me?" I was down to one word. Next I'd be speechless.

"Justinius said that if any Conclave mage questioned your

or any woman's qualifications for the job, that he'd point you in their direction, stand back, and enjoy the show."

"The old man knows I can't magically punch holes in walls—or mages—anymore, doesn't he? And quite frankly, I'm glad I can't."

"He knows that. He also knows that five hundred Guardians aren't enough anymore, and I agree. These past three months with the Saghred proved that."

"The Saghred is gone. Nothing that big will happen again."

Silence from Mychael.

Suddenly the crab puffs I'd plucked off a passing tray and eaten weren't sitting so well. "You're supposed to say, 'No, that'll never happen again.'"

"I can't do that."

"And why not?"

Mychael actually started ticking off items on his fingers. "Well, there's this cursed ring that was last seen in the mountains of Mylora. I believe there were nine others forged around the same time."

"Nine?"

"Plus the original one which makes ten. Then there's a scepter in Nebia that one of the desert chieftains sold to a Caesolian crime cartel, which bears a striking resemblance to the legendary Scepter of Haz'Ghul."

I just scowled at him. "Which does what?"

Mychael had to work to keep the smile off of his face, but he couldn't keep it from his eyes. "It depends on the power of the person who has it during the full moon. And then there's the mythical Treasure of Relmbek said to contain several magical objects that could be cataclysmic if they ended up in the wrong hands. Even worse, this treasure may not be mythical."

"Lovely. Just lovely."

"Its rumored location can only be reached by a nimble ship with a lunatic captain, and an even crazier crew." One side of Mychael's mouth curled in a crooked grin. "Would you happen to know a treasure-loving, seafaring madman?"

"I'm not even going to dignify that with a response. I take it you want my help with all of these?"

"And a few other similar items, like the occasional rogue black mage. I don't want you in danger, but I know you won't be happy unless you're neck deep in it." Mychael put his big hands around my waist and pulled me closer. "And I want you to be happy more than anything. This way you can do what you do best and know that you're making a difference. Plus, you will be a shining example and inspiration to the first generation of female Guardians."

"And just how do your men feel about this?"

"Surprisingly agreeable and open to the idea."

I glanced over at Talon and grinned. "I think girl Guardians could even lure Talon back to Mid."

"Chigaru has expressed interest in sending young goblins for training."

"Including girls?"

"Oh, yes. And of course of those presently in the Conclave college, Justinius's granddaughter will be one of our first recruits."

Katelyn Valerian, spellsinger extraordinaire, also known as Piaras's girlfriend. "Piaras would like that."

"I like to keep my men happy." Mychael ran his hands slowly down my back. "And if you're in the Guardians, I can keep an eye on you."

"And give me orders. Now we come to the *real* reason. You know I'm not the order-taking kind—"

"How about strongly worded suggestions?"

I snorted. "You've been doing that for the past three months. How's it been going for you?"

"I'm a man who knows my limitations," Mychael replied with mock gravity. "So, do you want to go out into the world to fight evil and rescue the downtrodden?"

I gave a little shrug. "Eh, it has its appeal."

"You'd have a team with you. Occasionally that team would only be the two of us."

I snuggled in closer. "That definitely has appeal."

"Raine, I think we make a great team—that is, if you'll have me."

Mychael wasn't only talking about a fulfilling career in fighting the forces of evil. I knew it and so did he.

I stood on tiptoe and gave him a lingering kiss. "Sign me up, Paladin Eiliesor," I whispered. "It sounds like the adventure of a lifetime."

About the Author

Lisa is the editor and quality control manager at an advertising agency. She has been a magazine editor and writer of corporate marketing materials of every description. She lives in North Carolina with her very patient and understanding husband, two retired racing greyhounds, and a Jack Russell terrier who rules them all.

For more information about Lisa and her books, visit her at www.lisashearin.com.